The Last Days Conclude

By Chris Ayala

For my best friend Kristina.
Thank you for telling me my writing was good, even when it wasn't.

CHAPTER ONE

Blue. Purple. Yellow. And then some color that Adam couldn't describe; there wasn't a name for that shade. Mars wasn't red, but more like a maroon. Uranus looked similar to purple, not blue. Adam had to remember, when it was time to awake from this beautiful dream, to find his fifth grade Science teacher and explain the universe didn't look anyway like he taught. It glimmered, but didn't twinkle. Planets don't twinkle; Brent taught him that. The clouds didn't do much to hide that bright sky. But it wasn't a brightness that would cause someone to turn away, instead it drew Adam in like a vacuum.

"Grandpa?" a tiny voice said. "Grandpa? Are you listening?"

His head turned. But Adam didn't turn it himself. Anxiety couldn't grasp his breath since he couldn't breathe where he was. Adam was in the future. A precognition of the future. With no senses, control of his movements, or the ability to close his eyes, Adam was at the mercy of this vision. Unlike his previous visits, he didn't feel afraid. This version of him wasn't in a dangerous situation.

"I'm listening, Yvette. Tell me all about what you learned today in Alchemy." His voice said, sounding deep and constricted. "I'm going to stare at the sky some more."

"The sky is boring." The girl in pigtails said as she combed her doll's hair with her hand.

"That's because you are too young to remember what it used to be like."

Adam's head turned back to the window. The landscape flew by; they must've been on a train. The grass was pure green and the trees reached up for the sun. An expensive landscape company couldn't get results like that. And what about that sky? Stars and planets aren't that visible.

As if Adam could accept anymore surprises, another one materialized. Adam's reflection wasn't his own. It was someone else. Or was it? Wrinkles lined up his cheeks, skin bobbled off his chin, gray hair poked out of his eyebrows...but it was definitely him. A much older incarnation. Even more bizarre, a crystal clear device hovered over his eyes and ears. The device created a prism of light when he slightly moved.

"Grandpa, did you hear me?"

Neither past or present Adams were paying attention. But he lied genuinely, "Yes, honey."

"How long do you have to wear that funny thing?"

"Until I've uploaded the memories I need to send."

"What memories? Like happy memories?"

"No. Like bad ones."

The little girl named Yvette swung her legs back and forth on the train's seat. "Why?"

"So my past self can fix them. Make my bad memories into happy ones."

It was the time machine. Well, sort of. More like a time machine *link* between two time frames. Adam wanted to see it again and maybe take some notes on how to build it. But, of course, somehow he would build it because *somehow* this future would happen.

"I don't get it."

Adam took the doll in the girl's hand. "Imagine if...what's her name again...Dolly?"

"No," Yvette said as if Adam was supposed to know already, "Francesca."

"Okay, well, let's say Francesca...what a weird name for a doll...anyways, let's say Francesca found a way to communicate with her younger self. That way her younger self could change the future. Make things easier. Better."

"But would that mean she wouldn't be my friend anymore?"

"No, sweetie. You can only change the paths but not the outcomes."

"It sounds complicated," the youngster said pronouncing the *p* like a *b*.

Adam smirked. The train began to slow. He looked down at his arm for the time. Regardless of the shiny watch on the wrist, the past-Adam asleep in this dream was mesmerized by the arm itself. Tattoos blanketed his arms. Tattoos? Adam hated tattoos and certainly hated pain. Why did this future version have them? And what were they? They looked like names. "Almost there. Did you bring something for the nice man?"

"I drew him a picture of the day he saved us."

From her pink backpack, she excitedly yanked out a piece of cardboard paper. On it, drawn in various colors of crayon, was a man standing above a castle. The girl had dragged black lines coming from the sky, the ground, and all the stick figure people outside the castle. All the black lines led the man on top of the castle. Elder Adam whispered, "Very well done. It's exactly the way I remember it. You're so talented. I'll make sure to give it to him."

Her big grin faded, "But I want to see the nice man."

"He's not well. We will see if it's okay with the doctors, okay?"

The train stopped. Whoever this "nice man" was, Yvette seemed excited to have a chance to see him. She swept up her backpack. Unfortunately, older Adam's movements weren't as rapid. Growing old was something Adam promised himself never to do; his future grunts and wheezes were louder than the train's noises. Around them, people were different. Not a negative way, such as in past precognitions. But in positive ways. Citizens radiated with flawless skin and fits of laughter amongst each other. Adam saw a woman breast-feeding her child with no angry mob ready to escort her out the train. A guitar strummed from a bearded man with crooked teeth and messy hair. As he played, he did something Adam hadn't seen in a while. The bearded man began to glow. A light inside him, coming from his mind, lit up his blood. This phenomenon should've made people run for the door, but no one paid any mind. Adam had seen this trick before; a magic performed by the People of Bliss.

Train doors slid open with a loud hiss. Him and Yvette were escorted off onto a platform by a lovely woman in uniform. The uniform with its green stripes became instantly familiar. Adam recognized it from his own timeframe. A uniform worn only by the diabolical Union Keepers. But this woman didn't bully them, yet aided them with a genuine smile. "Thank you," Adam replied.

He turned to see the train depart. It floated on a rail that glowed the most vibrant white Adam had ever seen. It gave a new meaning to the term "light rail".

The two turned and exited the train station. Adam could see an enormous structure, more wide than tall, marked "New Haven Hospital". Besides an occasional polite nod from a Union Keeper or a polite wave from a person in white hospital gown, Adam and his granddaughter were mostly left alone as they traveled toward the building.

"What's that?" the child said breaking the silence.

Adam looked to see a vast garden filled with various types of fruits and vegetables. If Adam could control his lips, he would've smacked them together. With such lively colors, the fruits looked like they belonged in a museum rather than his stomach. "Those are for the patients here. Remember, *only* for the patients. If you take one, its considered stealing."

"What's 'stealing', grandpa?"

How can a child not be familiar with stealing? Yvette's voice didn't sound naive or idiotic, so Adam had to assume this place really was the definition of a Utopia. "It's something we used to do a long time ago."

The hospital doors opened and they entered without the fuss of checking in to the front desk. Adam sat his grandchild on a chair outside the door. "Now, I'm just going to check with the nice man and see if he's okay before you can come in. I want you to stay here. You understand, Yvette?"

She nodded then handed him the drawing. "Can you give it to him? I hope he likes it."

"He'll love it."

Adam stepped inside the hospital room and closed the door behind him. A patient laid in bed, with IVs feeding him fluids. An EKG gave a subtle beep.

"Well," Adam mumbled, "I guess you look...*better*."

"That's because I can't look *worse.*"

Immediately recognizing the voice, there was no doubt who the patient could be. Of all the surprises in this precognition, this seemed to top them all. It was Marcel Celest.

The politician that had created a pact for a unionized government, sat idle as countries attacked each other, gained supernatural abilities to attack innocent people, used fear to become the world's leader, and murdered Adam's best friend...was being called a "nice man"?

The future Adam handed the drawing to Marcel. His hands were more wrinkled than Adam's. Wishing he could reach over and strangle the last of this evil man's breath out of him, Adam just had to sit and watch this vision unfold.

"It's incredible," Marcel whimpered.

"It's incredible what you agreed to after our pact."

His shaky hands placed Yvette's drawings upright against many bouquets of flowers. "It's been forty years. Forty years since I submerged all the darkness into me. And the cancer grew instead of weakening." Marcel took a deep breath and glanced at Adam with tired eyes for a long minute. "What on earth is on your head, friend?"

Friend? None of this made sense.

"Well, we were able to harness the Light and create a device that creates a wormhole to when I was an embryo and change time..." Adam stopped speaking at the sight of Marcel's confused face, "...you know what? It's...complicated. What are the doctors saying about you?"

Brushing the white sheets over his stomach, Marcel answered. "Doctors say it's...complicated." After a brief pause, he continued, "They did some tests last week. First, it was I had *years*. Then, *months*. Then, *weeks*. Now," Marcel shrugged. "*days*."

Nodding, Adam said, "I think it's better Yvette not see you like this."

Marcel agreed, giving a slight nod and sigh. His gray mustache quivered. "I wish time was on my side."

"Well," Adam thumped the device on his head, "it technically is."

His face lit up. Marcel sat up, cringing his teeth. "You mean...we could change all this?"

"Why would we want to?"

"Because," Marcel broke out into a fitted cough then continued, "The darkness. That's why."

"The *darkness*? But you absorbed it -"

"And it strengthened the monster in me. It was a mistake." Marcel coughed into his hand, then looked at it. With one tired swoop, he grabbed a napkin and wiped away a bloody glob of mucus. "When I die, the monster won't die with me."

"What monster?"

Another dry cough made the politician lean his head on the pillow. What hair he had left on his head bobbled to the side. He looked like his father Nelson at that moment.

Adam patted him on the back. "Let me get a nurse. You don't sound too good."

In between spurts of coughing, Marcel gave out half sentences. "Kill me..."

"Don't be silly."

"In the past. Kill me. Before the treaty with the People of Bliss. Kill me."

"But, Marcel, you were too strong for any of us to even -" Adam shivered heavily. Suddenly the room seemed like the inside of a freezer. "How did it get so cold in here?"

"Adam, you have to stop me. When I'm young. The only way to do it -" Another spastic cough. The EKG machine began to blink a yellow tint. "There's only one person who can stop me." Marcel whispered, "Tell my sister *we all were supposed to die that day. We all were supposed to die with Mom.* I altered our fate and it changed everything. I'm unique, I have no fate…I can alter fates."

"You're not making any sense. I need to find someone to -"

Grasping his collar, Marcel looked into the device's vision. Right into the eyeballs of the present day Adam. "It's all about the darkness."

The words gave Adam the creeps. "I don't understand." And neither did the present day Adam. Marcel's breaths began to slow. The EKG calmed. And Adam shivered again. He could see his breath. "What's happening?"

"Oh God," Marcel stuttered. "It's happening. Death is yanking me away." With the last of his strength, Marcel grasped Adam's collar. "Run."

"What?"

"It's coming. It will kill all of you. Run. It's too late. The darkness is too strong now. Change the past to save the future. Kill me, kill the darkness."

"Marcel. How?"

"The only way you can kill the Darkness is…" Marcel took his last breath. "…with the Light."

The EKG machine stopped. The politician's hand loosened and fell to the side of the bed. Then the room grew dark. Shadows seemed to grow more black. Adam took a few steps back as nurses rushed to the door. Everyone stopped and stared at what was happening in front of them. Black specks rose out of Marcel's skin, gathering together into a goo. The goo meshed into a solid mass. A nurse screamed at the top of her throat. From the goo, a creature climbed out of it. Wings swung out of its sides. Horns broke out of its skull. Teeth gnashed into a large grin. The creature filled up a quarter of the room. It laughed. Laughed so loud that its voice echoed in every direction of the air.

Adam dashed out of the room. The nurse behind him tried to run, but her leg was grasped by the monster. Its fingernails scrapped along the tile floor, but the sound was deafened by the nurse's cry for help.

Without looking back, Adam went into the hallway. His granddaughter was nowhere to be found. "Yvette? Yvette!" Being overheard through all these panicked yells wouldn't be enough. From hallway to hallway, Adam frantically searched for the little girl. "Yvette?" He could see his own cold breath like a smoke out of his mouth. What caused it to get so cold all the sudden?

In the lobby, people crowded to the front door and pushed each other to get out. The darkness grew to cloud every source of light. Whatever that creature was, it had a thurst for havoc. It slammed its fist against a group of doctors. Adam turned the other way and ran for a side door. With his shoulder, he shoved open the door.

Outside, the sparkles of stars were gone. Dark clouds began to loom. Adam's body shivered as he wrapped his arms around himself. "Yvette?" he screamed.

Then in the distance, the little girl could be seen wandering in that beautiful garden of fruits and vegetables. Just moments ago, it was colorful and vibrant. Now, the leaves were beginning to welt right before Adam's eyes. He ran, as fast as an old man can, toward her. Before he reached her, she turned slowly. Yvette's mouth was cherry red from munching on berries.

"Yvette," Adam scolded, "I said not to eat from here. It's stealing."

"I don't care!" the girl grumbled with a tone of spite. "Leave me alone!" She continued eating from the fruit tree.

"What has gotten into you? I -" Before Adam had continued, the air made him shiver even more. His teeth chattered. Yvette's breaths began to hasten and smoke the air. She glanced at something behind him. Adam, slowly looked behind him. From atop a tree, a snake longer and thicker than any snake Adam had seen before, wiggled its way down. Its skin was so black that no texture could be seen. A gray tongue whipped out of its mouth.

The snake's red fiery eyes peered into Adam's. It whispered, "Hello."

"Holy shit! Snnnnaaaaakkkeeeee!" Adam screamed, pushed back into his reality away from the precognition. He was on a train, but not one floating on a mystical light. This rickety train wobbled along the rail with dozens of passengers who all turned to him. His outburst caused their eyes to widen.

"Did someone say snake?"

"There's a snake in here?"

"Oh, God."

"I hates snakes!"

"Is it poisonous?"

Before Adam could explain it's an unfortunate reflect of awakening from a vision of the future, panic ensued in the train.

"I got to get out of here!"

"Run!"

"Snake!"

"Where is it?"

Hysteria caused people to climb over each other, rushing for the door. Next to Adam's seat, his companion Royal gave an angry whisper. "You idiot! What are you doing?"

Covered in sweat, Adam could barely mutter a word. On his left side, a bald man with burn scars across his face stood on his seat. "I'll burn it!"

"No, Victor, sit down," Royal commanded in that hushed upset whisper.

Victor didn't listen. "Burn! Fire! We need fire! Fire will kill snake! Fire!"

While the pyromanic hurried through the overhead compartments for tools, Adam tried to speak. "I'm sorry, guys. I just had a bad dream. There's no snake. No reason to panic."

Just as the hysteria began to calm, somehow with a mix of chemicals and a lighter Victor created a fire. "Burn!" The fire lit up the overhead compartments.

Adam wondered where things went wrong. Not with the blazing train catastrophe before him that took four fire trucks to extinguish, that *might've* been his fault. But with the future. Marcel Celest was alive. And worse, he was an ally. How? The politician that let global catastrophes happen, the politician that could magically sway the elements to his favor, the politician that began a new world order and put their lives in danger…*that* man was a friend?

He sketched what he could remember onto the back of a train schedule pamphlet using an ink pen.

"Really? You're doodling right now? Our train ride home is up in flames." Royal's nagging voice continued.

"Flames." Victor hummed next to her, like it was a song in his head. "Big flames."

A beefy fellow, a real life version of the lumberjack on the paper towels, plopped down on the curb next to them. "Bruno find nothing to eat. Bruno hungry." He whined, grasping his stomach in those clothes that were somehow too big to fit him.

"Oh, for heaven's sake. So far I've seen you eat just about everything, even my can of Altoids." Royal griped.

Bruno's stomach rumbled. He mumbled in his thick German accent. "It tasted like Sweet Tarts. Anymore left?"

Adam couldn't think with these grown children complaining and the sound of fire trucks. He stood and found a quiet corner by the train station that smelled like piss and vomit. As soon as the pen touched the paper, Royal appeared. "What are you doing? We got to make a new plan."

"I'm trying to work. God, I wish Janice wasn't recovering from surgery or I would've brought her."

"Well, you're stuck with me, ain't ya?" Royal folded her arms together. "We only gotta find Pierre and we're done with the list. Our train is now going to be very late. That leaves us only nine hours, 43 minutes to find him, in the middle of Paris might I add. Then we gotta get seven hours of sleep, catch a taxi in the morning to the airport which takes 32 minutes, and get the plane back to La Guardia which takes 10 hours and 57 minutes."

Rubbing his temples didn't seem to shut Royal up. "I know that…can I just…I need a minute. This is important. If I don't draw out the dream, then it'll disappear."

Suddenly, Royal's lenient side surfaced which was much more easier to handle than her stringent side. "Oh, you had one of them…vision things? Premonition?"

"Precognition," Adam corrected her as he shaded in a picture of the gooey monster rising from Marcel's future avatar. "Premonition is a feeling something is going to happen. Precognition is when you actually see it."

"Oh," Royal said, even though Adam already knew she probably didn't understand a word he just said and would probably ask again someday. "Well? What did you…precog or whatever?" She sat down on the dirty ground next to him.

Being so hard to put into words, Adam closed his eyes and concentrated for a moment. "It was the future. Like, the *really really* future. Forty years from now. The world was just so…I dunno…different." Adam looked to the sky for some kind of explanation of his dream. The sun could barely be seen through the black haze left behind from 98 nuclear strikes. If the closest star in the galaxy couldn't be seen, then how could a flurry of stars be seen in his vision? Those clouds hadn't changed that shade of gray in almost eight months. "And Marcel Celest was there."

"Say what? Marcel Celest was there?" Royal whispered, "You mean, like, on *our* side? How?"

Bruno six-and-a-half foot tall stature cast a shadow as it walked by. He looked at the vending machine next to the restroom area. After inserting some change, nothing happened. He lifted it up the entire vending machine; his biceps barely bulged through his muscle shirt. Various candies and potato chips fell to the compartment below before Bruno slammed back to the ground. "Damn. Bruno wanted Snickers." He grabbed the dozen other candies and walked away.

Royal gave a long sigh.

Before her complaining started about the two difficult passengers on their trip for resistance fighters, Adam corrected her assumption. "No, my visions can be changed. I altered one before."

"You did?"

With all the stress of carrying for a newborn baby, leading a rebellion of three thousand people, and mourning the death of a best friend - it never occurred to Adam he never told Royal of her fate in his previous precognition. The young blonde with her hair in the same ponytail poking through a baseball cap had died in his vision. Adam stopped it before it could happen, which made him wonder how this original moment in time would've been. Would he be mourning not only Brent's murder but Royal's too? Would he have even made this trip to find men with supernatural abilities to join the rebellion? If he couldn't fathom such a possibility, maybe Royal couldn't either. Especially since it was her life that should've ended that day. He decided to lie with a subtle shrug, "Nothing spectacular."

Something else occurred to him. In his precognition, Marcel Celest knew his words could change the past and his future. For him to suggest what he had…it made the scoundrel seem almost heroic. Adam continued drawing and distracting his head before he began to have respect for Marcel Celest. The murdering politician deserved no respect from anyone, especially Adam.

"That's weird," Royal said looking over his shoulder. "It looks like…" She looked at Adam's drawing from several angles. "…a demon? You saw that in your dream?"

There was no use in hiding anything from Royal; she'd bother him enough to just say it anyway. Adam said, "It's the darkness. During our battle, Marcel Celest will magically absorb all the…evil…in this world. And he'll harbor it. But when he dies…it turns into that. It'll come alive and slaughter us all."

Royal's chest heaved up and down. "Well ain't that a little *unsettling*. So then, what we do?"

"Easy," Adam said it as if it was actually *easy.* "We have to stop Marcel Celest before he saves the world."

"How?"

Slowly and unintentionally sadistic, Adam answered, "By killing him."

CHAPTER TWO

"Scientists are optimistic in this new discovery that perhaps we can return to normal weather. The cloud seeds, that originally were intended to control the escalation of global warming, can manually be extracted from the clouds. The problem? Time. And of course...manpower. Planes would need to be flown through the clouds with a device scientists say acts sort of like a vacuum. Some clouds are so blackened that planes have no choice but to fly blind. What's been cleared out, so far, is quite alarming. Not only sulfur, but several other dangerous pollutants were found such as asbestos, glass, metals, and even...human remains. Sissy Perkins, FOX News."

Those cloud seeds kept this world dark. Marcel liked the darkness. It didn't burn skin, produce sweat, or make it difficult to breath. As the Supreme Leader of the Union, he had to show concern to the masses. He used phrases like *unfortunate consequence of Doomsday* and *constant reminder of the billions dead.* Deep down he knew, the world was better without all the sunlight. This was Lucifer's plan. And so far, the Supreme Leader of the Darkness hadn't steered him wrong.

He clicked the television through more channels. Television had been so boring lately. Most studios and news-stations didn't rebuild after Doomsday. Either for cost or out of respect for the lives lost. Static crowded most of the air waves. Maybe less television was a positive aspect in this new world, but in times when Marcel only wanted to relax…it became a negative aspect.

Finally, CNN was back on the air.

"Shortly after confirmation that CNN's own Sirius Dawson was the voice behind the 'People of Bliss' movement, she has been reported missing. Some members of this rebellion of the Union have said Sirius Dawson was captured and murdered."

Marcel wouldn't call it "murdered". It certainly hadn't been anyone's attention for her torture to cause cardiac arrest. But it had been his attention to use her as bait for his brother Brent. Instead of a tragic end for Marcel like he craved, that night had turned into a tragic end for the lives of Brent Celest and Sirius Dawson. And him, all alone, with only a demon of dark matter to be his friend. Perhaps it had been a tragic end for him too.

Still grasping the remote control, Marcel rubbed his forefinger along the scar down his wrist. So many years since it bled and still the scar wouldn't heal. All the other scars he had endured disappeared, but this memory held onto his wrist. What would the world be like now if Marcel had succeeded that day after his mother's funeral? What would the world be like without its leader, Marcel Celest? Nuclear weapons may not have fallen. The Union proposal would've certainly perished a slower death than Brent had. Maybe the world would've been better off without Marcel Celest?

He tossed the thought aside immediately. To endure meant to succeed. One day, the world would peace. Then that day – maybe, just maybe, Marcel might try to run another blade along that scar on his wrist.

The television shook him awake from his lost ravine in thought. *"As the one year anniversary of Doomsday closes in, violence continues to erupt worldwide. The Union's new Helix program is making many upset. Some say the Helix chip doesn't only share your personal information, but also your location. Though very convenient, the Helix has been questioned for its security. The mainframe server is located in a secret location, but how long will it remain secret? And what would happen if it got into the wrong hands?"* The screen changed from the lovely red head at her desk to a group of protestors covered in their bright red blood. This was disturbing, and definitely not part of Marcel's plan. Why didn't citizens just trust him? Trust the Union? There was nothing but good intent for their well-being. The Helix could revolutionize this planet, make it simple and organized. *"Morocco saw the bloodiest protest today as they stormed the Union embassy, demanding food and supplies without the need for the Helix chip implant."* The chip hadn't even been mandated, not yet anyway, so there was no need for violence. If his sister Janice was here, and not raging with abomination for Marcel after seeing him accidentally stab their brother Brent through the stomach, she would describe this situation as *unwarranted*. People still had ways to purchase goods without the chip. It was inconvenient; not convenient like the Helix. Protests weren't necessary, neither was the blood shed.

Maybe he had an idea of how to force this ideology. Marcel picked up the landline phone by his sofa and dialed for his secretary. "I need you to setup a press conference at the Union Keepers training center. Make sure there's plenty of Press….I have a major announcement to make…Let's just call it the next step in worldwide peace."

Marcel stuck another piece of nicotine gum in his mouth and chewed vigorously. It was his fourth one in the last hour. Doing speeches wasn't his thing. When he was young, he imagined being a film director and the thought of being an actor made him pale. The limelight wasn't for everyone but the light was, his mother once told Marcel. Her words always had a way of making him think outside the lockbox inside his brain.

"Three minutes, Supreme Leader." His secretary said from down the empty hallway.

Marcel nodded. He rubbed his hands together, reciting his speech aloud. When he looked down to his palms – blood smeared across the skin.

Before he could question it, he dashed for the restroom. Inside, he turned on the hot faucet and lifted his hands out – the blood was gone. Marcel rubbed the palm with his forefinger. It couldn't have been his imagination. Or could it have been? But blood had clearly been there just a moment ago. He checked the sleeves of his suit and pockets. No blood anywhere.

Had it been Brent's blood? His brother reminding him from beyond the grave of his brutal sin? Murder. To kill an enemy was one thing, to kill a family enemy was another. Marcel relived the moment in his mind. The blade in his grasp, the rage in his heart, thrusting the sharp edge into Brent's stomach, feeling the satisfaction of –

"What's up?" a voice said, making Marcel nearly jump out of his skin. It was Gerard. "Jesus, you pick now to get the runs? My officers are waiting."

"No," Marcel muttered. "Just…straightening my tie. That's all."

"Jesus, you really *do* look like a politician, Marcel."

His brother-in-law was right. The mirror reflected the perfect black hair, trimmed eyebrows, powdered cheeks, and stinging blue eyes. Marcel stared at his reflection and wondered if he'd actually grown more pale since he's bond with the darkness. His allergy to light gave him the nickname Casper in Middle School. What was he now? Something between life and death, but definitely not a friendly ghost.

"Gum? Really? Spit it. It would look more professional if you went on stage smoking a cigarette."

Marcel spat the gum into the sink. "I want to be healthy."

"What world leader was ever healthy? That's the point. You're supposed to look like one us unhealthy third-class citizens. That is how you get support. Being one of us."

Though a good point, Marcel wouldn't call Gerard either unhealthy or third-class. His brother-in-law had sparkling white teeth, muscles practically ripping through his uniform; he kept his nails trimmed and his hair trimmed even closer. If Marcel had ever become a film directer, he would've surely cast Gerard as his leading action hero.

"Any news?"

Gerard sighed. "You going to ask me that everyday?"

"Yes," Marcel nodded.

"No news. Your dad hasn't been spotted for weeks. And Janice…well, I think I know my wife…she won't be found unless she wants to be found."

They hated him. His own family. The thought never crossed his mind that the only family member to be by his side in this new world order would be his brother-in-law. "I have to convince them, somehow, it was an accident. Maybe we should just do the Press thing. Admit that my brother was in custody and it escalated –"

"No one will believe it."

The tie was complete, maybe a little too tight but it did seem more professional. Marcel turned to Gerard. "You *believe* me, don't you? It was an accident. You know how Brent used to get. He got violent, I had to…" He might as well ended the sentence with the words *dot, dot, dot.*

Gerard stared for maybe too long and said. "Yeah, of course. I know. Let's get going. Everybody's excited to see you speak."

As he followed him out the door, Marcel couldn't help but feel that Gerard didn't seem convinced. Maybe he wasn't such a good actor.

Applause made him tone deaf. His father was right; the clapping can change the beat of your heart. These hundreds of people crowding a gymnasium-style training center for Union Keepers were different than the usual crowds Marcel spoke to. Those crowds were bitter, disgusted, and upset; his job was to make them enthusiastic, proud, and relieved with the prospects of the Union. But this crowd didn't need convincing. They loved him to the ends of this earth.

Union Keepers were his first line of defense. An army built to protect the last government and ensure the welfare of its leader. Hand-picked by Gerard, these soldiers would gladly die if it meant Marcel would live.

Marcel clasped his hands together on the podium. He took a brief moment to look down. There was no blood on his hands. After a low sigh of relief, he adjusted the microphone to his tall stature. "Hello."

The crowd roared again in applause. Marcel laughed. He could wonder if even his father, the President of the United States, would've gotten such an ovation from the simple word *Hello.*

Unfortunately, the last audience Marcel spoke to ended in a horrific scene. He lost his temper. The weather grew angry with his power from the Darkness. People were attacked by bolts of lightning, bursts of wind, flying debris – he pushed the memory aside. Fortunately, without cameras, the scene just became rumors and scare tactics by the opposing movement.

Once the cheers receded, the officers took a seat. Most of them wore the signature Union Keeper uniform, all black with blue trim that seemed to glow in both light and darkness. Trainees wore a plain uniform, black A-shirt with straight legged black pants. If the auditorium's generator died and the lights went out, surely most of these men wouldn't be seen.

From his front pocket, Marcel unfolded a piece of paper. "I...uh...sat and wrote this entire speech during breakfast this morning. I –"

"What did you eat?" someone screamed from the crowd.

Being used to hearing outbursts like *Are you the Anti-Christ?, You're going to Hell!*, or *Only a madman could believe one government is all you need around the world!*, Marcel felt himself caught off-guard. After a brief snort, he spoke into the microphone, "Frosted Flakes."

The crowd clapped again. Marcel felt himself blushing. "I shouldn't read a speech to you guys, because you all are almost like friends to me." Immediately after saying the word *friends*, Marcel regretted it. It sounded desperate. He cleared his throat. "No. Maybe more like family. A family with the same goal. All we want is...serenity. Worldwide. Everyone needs to just take a deep breath and be content with what's around us. There's so much negativity in this world lately, that I've found myself nearly drowning in it. I feel there is only one way to end all this violence around the planet..." Marcel paused for dramatic appeal, something his father did in his inauguration speech several times, "...with violence."

Marcel had to look around to make sure the people in the auditorium were still breathing. Voices could echo easily off these walls, but he didn't hear a single objection. He emphasized, "Violence must be met with violence. It's the only way to destroy it."

Placing his elbows on the podium, he pictured his advising team smacking their heads saying that poll numbers disagree with a politician leaning against a podium. He continued, "When I was in Middle School, we used to have this group called we used to call the Daryl Dixons. You know…from that television show with the zombies?" Nods and smirks from the onlookers answered his question. Marcel said, "They were the *rough 'n tough* types. Born in the lower class neighborhoods. Carried a knife around with them. Needless to say, if the entire faculty turned into zombies – we'd still be more scared of the Daryl Dixons. We got bullied everyday. They were bigger than us, stronger than us, and had more numbers."

Marcel took his hands off the podium and placed them in his pockets. Poll numbers hated hands in the pockets too. "One day, they didn't know I was there, but I overheard them talking about us. From the point-of-view of these jerks, we were the bad guys. Rich mommies and daddies. Privileged. Smart. Goals for our future. *We* were the bad guys. Silly, right? I'd go home for lunch because they stole my money or I'd go home with bruises for trying to fight back. But *we* were the bad guys?" Everyone in the room nearly scoffed at the same time. "Well, anyway, we got sick of it. Us 'nerd terds', as we were called, decided to ban together to come up with a plan. After school, the brutes chased us. But we were ready. We got them cornered into an alley way, then when they least expected it – we pulled out the bats."

The crowd roared so loud that Marcel didn't have to finish the story. If fists weren't up in the air, then their hands were slamming together. The men and women loved the story. He smiled. When the noise died down, he said, "I'm looking around this room and I'm seeing those same faces. The same bullied faces." More nods and smirks reaffirmed his assumption. "There's nothing wrong with trying to be better. But we get picked on for it?"

Marcel placed his hands behind his back and straightened his back, "So, starting immediately, I'm giving Union Keepers the authority to use whatever means necessary to take down these bullies. No miranda rights, no forms to fill out, and no permission needed. We share the same goals. Let's shut down this movement. By…whatever…means necessary."

The auditorium was filled with screams of agreement, claps of encouragement, and chants of excitement. Marcel didn't need to say anything further. These deadly protests were soon going to be over. The Union Keepers were sure to put an end to the People of Bliss.

CHAPTER THREE

HEY WILLIE,

IT'S ADAM. THIS SEEMS SO STRANGE WRITING A LETTER. MY CURSIVE ~~WAS~~ IS SO BAD THAT I RESORTED TO PRINTING. AND EVEN THEN THE SMALL LETTERS ~~WERE ARE~~ WERE SO HARD TO READ THAT I GOT TO WRITE IN ALL CAPITAL LETTERS. I SURE HOPE, I'M PUTTING THE COMMAS IN THE RIGHT PLACES? FUCK IT I'M SO SICK OF REWRITING THIS ~~LATTER~~ LETTER AND I'M RUNNING OUT OF PAPER. ISN'T THIS CRAZY - THIS IS LIFE NOW? WE DEPENDING ON EMAILS, TEXTS, I MEAN WHATEVER - TO COMMUNICATE THAT WE'VE FORGOTTEN HOW TO LIVE LIFE WITHOUT TECHNOLOGY. I'M USE TO MY COMPUTER AUTO-CORRECTING ME THAT I CAN'T DO SIMPLE GRAMMER. OR IS IT GRAMMAR WITH AN "A"? I DON'T EVEN HAVE GOOGLE TO ANSWER THAT QUESTION! I DON'T TELL ANYONE, EVEN JANICE, BUT I STILL HAVE MY DEAD SMARTPHONE. I SLEEP WITH IT UNDER MY BED. I PRETEND LIKE IT WORKS

SOMETIMES. KINDA WEIRD, ~~WRITE~~ RIGHT? AS THE NEW LEADER OF THE REBELLION, I THINK NIGHTS ABOUT WHO IS THE TRUE ENEMY? IS IT GENERAL VANDERBILT, THE DOUCHEBAG THAT DEFINITELY KILLED SIRIUS? IS IT MARCEL CELEST? IS IT THE UNION? I'VE COME TO THE ~~CONCLESION CONKLUSION~~ DECISION IT IS TECHNOLOGY. THINK ABOUT IT. IT RUINED EVERYTHING. WERE SO USE TO IT, THAT WE CAN'T FUNCTION WITHOUT IT. THE COMRORITY BETWEEN THE PEOPLE OF BLISS IS ASTOUNDING. IVE MADE MORE FRIENDS HERE THAN FACEBBOK. AND MORE MEANINGFUL ONES THAN SHARING CAT PICS.

*SO I GOT A MISSION FOR YOU. I WOULD ASK YOU IN PERSON - BUT IT'S A SECRET MISSION AND I WANT **NO ONE** TO KNOW. BOLDING WORDS IS NOT THAT EFFECTIVE IN PENCIL, HUH? ANYWAY -*

*UNFORTUNATELY, THE UNION HAS MADE IT DIFFICULT TO GET OUR HANDS ON ANYTHING WITHOUT THIS NEW PALM CHIP. AND IN A MONTH, FOOD IS GOING TO RUN OUT IN THE SILO. AGAIN I WANT **NO ONE** TO KNOW ABOUT IT. THAT LAST THING I NEED IS A PANIC.*

IN THIS ENVELOPE IS A SYRINGE WITH A DECOY CHIP I CREATED. WELL, I DIDN'T TECHNICALLY CREATE IT BY HAND - I'M SMART BUT NOT THAT SMART. I FOUND A BOX OF OLD NANO PROCESSING CHIPS WHEN I WAS IN THE CITY. THE TECH COMPANY'S BUILDING WAS BLASTED PRETTY BAD BUT THEY HAD STOCK PILES OF THESE THINGS IN THE RUINS. I MEAN LIKE THOUSANDS OF THEM. ANYWAYS, I WANT TO SEE IF THEY CAN BYPASS THE UNION'S SYSTEM AND GET US THE NECESSITIES WE NEED.

THIS MISSION (SHOULD YOU CHOOSE TO ACCEPT IT) IS TO INFILTRATE THE UNION INSTITUTE AND ATTEMPT TO USE THE CHIP. I CAN'T BELIEVE I JUST QUOTED MISSION: IMPOSSIBLE. PLEASE DON'T TELL ANYONE THAT EITHER.

FIRST, YOU ARE GOING TO HAVE TO INJECT IT INTO YOUR PALM MUSCLE. I DREW A DIAGRAM. DON'T HIT A NERVE OR YOU'LL CAUSE PARALYSIS. NO PRESSURE HUH? LOL.

IF IT WORKS - REPORT BACK TO US IMMEDIATELY. IF IT DON'T WORK - RUN AS FAST AS YOU CAN.

I'M OUT OF PAPER. GOOD LUCK!

YOURE PAL, ADAM.

There are several things William Cooper had to live with the rest of his life. Like, when he decided to slide to third base instead of staying on second. Three legs surgeries later, Willie would never play baseball again. Another regret, never coming out of the closet to his mother before she died. "When you going to find the right woman, Papi?" she would ask. He'd answer, "Soon, Mama...soon." Even in a time when sexuality didn't define a person much, it still seemed shameful to admit it. Admit it to his teammates. Admit it to his family. Admit it to himself. But above all these things, the most nagging regret he had to live with was Sirius Dawson. The People of Bliss adored her as much as he did. She was like a sister. And Willie always promised to protect his family. But yet again, he let a family member down. And Sirius Dawson lost her life.

So how could he react to Adam's letter? Was "no" even an option? The decoy chip in his palm itched sometimes, but otherwise painless. Not even a scar when he injected it.

Willie wrapped his arms under each other. It couldn't be his imagination; the temperatures have been dropping lately.

Considering the month of August should be warm, wearing a thick wool coat and beanie cap felt unsettling.

"This shit's taking forever," the scruffy thin man in front of Willie mumbled. He'd been in line for six hours behind this guy and this was the first they'd spoke.

Willie nodded.

The man rubbed his fingerless gloves together. "What choice we got, right? Leader's dead."

Leader's dead. Those exact words made Willie want to leave the missile silo in the first place. Now this stranger was saying the same thing. Sirius Dawson, the leader of the rebellion was dead and hope died with her. At least that's what the rebellion told him in a condescending tone. Willie had enough of the tones. This was his redemption. He scratched the chip in his palm.

"I'm Joseph," he said with a hand extended. It had been so long since simple male camaraderie had been offered to Willie that he just stood there; the last man Willie saw fought him for a leftover Subway sandwich in the trashcan. He extended his hand to a sturdy handshake. "This is my brother Joey."

"Joseph and…Joey? Sounds like your parents weren't very original, huh? Know what I'm saying?"

Joseph and his little brother that looked like a shier version of him just stared at Willie. Maybe that joke had gotten old to them. Joey whispered, "Nice to meet you, Sir."

The handshake hurt his palm. Maybe that shot did hit a nerve in his hand.

A woman, dressed in a white suit that must've been soaked in Clorox the night before, stepped out of the building. The line of people leaning against the wall finally stood with back grunts and impatient groans. She spoke, perhaps too chipper. "Hello, everyone! We are so thrilled to have you all here. Remember…you must have a Helix chip before you can qualify for benefits! Please follow me inside…in a single file line…and we'll get started!"

Joseph whispered, "Just like the Margarethen police station."

"The what?" Willie asked, scratching his palm.

"Margarethen police station. When the Jews were released from Germany, they all lined up…just like this…to get exit visas. Funny, ain't it? They had that same feeling we do."

"And what feeling is that?"

"Cautious optimism."

Hours had past. Willie's left butt cheek went numb from the stiff, metal chair and now his right cheek was tingling. Whatever order they were calling people into the room, it didn't seem alphabetical because over half the waiting area had been seen already.

He read the letter from Adam again. What did he mean by technology was the enemy? It sure saved lives, didn't it? It even brought billions of people together. How could that be bad?

The television set attached to the corner of the waiting area played that movie again. A propaganda film bent on explaining the positive side of the Union. It showed smiling children playing in a backyard pool, Dad frying steaks on the grill, and Mom serving iced tea. The captions stated: JOIN THE UNION INSTITUTE AND YOUR LIFE WILL BE LIKE THIS. Willie never owned a grill or swam in anything besides a public pool. He had to admit – his curiosity got the better of him. The caption even used the word *will* not *maybe* or *could be*. Your life *will* be like this.

Joey twiddled his fingers for over an hour sitting next to him. Willie tried several conversation starters like: *Where you from?*, *What's it like living in Virginia?,* and *Did you know anyone who died on Doomsday?* All he got were one word answers: *Roanoke, Fine,* and *No.*

Various footage played on the television from Doomsday. Nuclear missiles striking the center of major cities. Locusts attacking reporters. The plague leaving disgusting bodies on the streets. Cloud seeds blackening the skies. The captions read: WE WILL NEVER FORGET.

Technology sure didn't save lives that day.

Joey's macho brother Joseph walked out of the room. "Let's go."

Jumping to his feet, Joey handed his sibling his coat. "Joseph, they gave me a mason job. I've always wanted —"

"I *said* let's….go…" Without even a good-bye, the brothers left.

"William Cooper," the administrator dressed in an ungodly white uniform said.

He stood up too fast, reminding himself to be calm. "How's it going?"

"I'm great. Come inside and have a seat. Don't be nervous."

Sure, no reason to be nervous. If the decoy chip didn't work, maybe the Union Keepers would just beat him to a pulp instead of killing him. Willie sat across from the strawberry blonde.

After minutes of typing, he couldn't stand it. Not only was the clicking of fingernails to keyboard keys annoying, but the fear of the decoy chip failing kept him on edge. "What do you use…to you know…scan me?"

"Oh! Sorry, William, you were already scanned when you walked in the door."

His gulp sounded like something out of Looney Tunes cartoon. "Did it all…come out okay?"

"Yes, of course! There's a few blank fields, but otherwise okay. Did you receive your watch yet?"

Not until that moment did Willie realize how much he had been sweating. He wiped his forehead with his sleeve. The fake Helix chip had worked. Adam would be thrilled. This meant the Union's computer system could be hacked.

"Sir?"

"Yeah?"

"Your watch? Did you get one?"

Since Willie had no idea what she meant, he just sat there. He muttered, "What watch?"

She smirked and dug in her desk. "The smartwatch syncs up to your Helix chip and keeps all your information in one place. You can also place free phone calls using the bluetooth ear microphone."

When the Apple iPhone was first released, Willie waited in a longer line than the one outside this building. He loved fancy new devices and the watch immediately drew his eye. It looked more like a wristband than a typical watch. Underneath it, she showcased how the tiny bluetooth earpiece detached. There was no face just an entire band streamed the user interface using color e-ink tech. With a few clicks of her mouse, she synced up the device and handed it to him.

Willie felt the material. Soft, yet firm. It wasn't metal or plastic. He secured it to his wrist. No discomfort what-so-ever. "It makes phone calls how? I mean, we ain't got many towers up, you know what I'm saying?"

"Well, not all cellular towers are operational yet but some are. There's a locator app on the watch that will show you areas to make phone calls. No more cellphones because the watch and chip do it all. Let me tell you, since…you know what happened…making phone calls has been *so* easy. Like, I had to fix a problem on my credit card – and someone *actually* picked up the phone. No annoying computer voice or annoying hold music, an *actual* person."

Three billion people had died globally. Sure, a lower
population meant a higher care for those still alive. But
Willie feel like this woman shouldn't boast about it. "Swell,"
he said placing the tiny bluetooth headset into his ear.

"And I called my dentist. No waiting period, I had an
appointment that same day. So nice, isn't it?"

"Swell," Willie repeated. He decided to change the
subject. "So what else can I do with this thing?"

"Everything," she said as though he was supposed to know
that. "It does some of the typical things smart watches do,
like track your exercise and calories to keep you in shape.
But it also senses your blood pulse and stores health records.
Even notifies a local hospital in the event you show physical
signs of a stroke, heart attack, or any other emergency."

Not a bad idea, so Willie couldn't object to that. Certainly
if his watch could've called an ambulance, Willie's father
wouldn't have passed from a heart attack.

She continued, more enthusiastic with each word. "And
you will have access to a free account with the Union bank.
All your bills will be displayed through the bank's app. No
more mail correspondence. And interest rates are gone, so no
more credit cards getting out of control. Limits are given by
how income you receive and you won't be able to spend
more than what's out of your budget. Utilities are covered by
the Union. Groceries are shipped to your new home, minus
all the unhealthy foods and allergies, of course. You will be
much better off nowadays."

All this sounded overwhelming. No more stress of a credit
card balance that never seemed to shrink? Bills won't be
piling up inside his mailbox? And he didn't have to educate
himself on what's unhealthy and healthy to eat? The Union
would do it all for him. Willie couldn't help but be happy.
"Did you mention a new home?"

"Yes. Since you are registered single, the Union will give you a single a condominium - free, of course. We evaluate everyone a year after employment, if you improve at your job then you will receive better living quarters. Pay will stay the same, but your lifestyle wouldn't. Our top residence for singles even get a boat and home on the river."

It didn't seem like such a bad idea. Wasn't that what was the point of getting raises? To live a better life? It didn't matter what the paycheck was. Certainly, this was the drive he needed to perform better at his job. "What job would I be doing?"

"Let's find out." She said, scrambling inside her desk again. From the bottom drawer, she pulled out a pair of surgical gloves and small needle. "Finger please."

Willie held out his index finger. Before he could ask what was about to happen, she wiped his finger with an alcohol swab and pricked it with the tiny needle. As though it was her thousandth time (it probably was), she inserted the needle into a device connected to the computer. "What did you need my blood for?"

"Because, William, we need to know your ancestry. So much can told about a person from their genetics." Her eyes scanned the computer screen back and forth. "Like, for instance, did you know you are 1/18 Cherokee Indian?"

"Explains my craving for gambling then, huh?" Willie smirked. Since she didn't laugh, he reminded himself to calm the stupid statements. "So, you're saying that my genes show what job is good for me?"

"Right. You have been selected by the system for Shipping and Receiving Manager. You would be in charge of trucks coming in and out of the Union's buildings. Make sure merchandise is organized. Pallets need to be stored appropriately. You are in command of the forklift drivers."

The position sounded like everything Willie had ever wanted. Job after job, he'd given his all to get a management position. Instead he received a low wage and more work. Now, Willie would be in charge. And he always enjoyed the warehouse lifestyle. Just enough hustle to keep someone on their toes, but not enough to make someone exhausted. How could a computer figure out the perfect fit for him from a drop of blood? "Sounds dope," he said, sounding more surprised than he intended.

"Great! So I uploaded your new home address to the GPS app on your watch. I've also uploaded the work address along with your schedule. If you're ever unhappy, come back and I'll find you a better position."

Doubting he'd ever be *unhappy* with the position, he politely shook her hand and walked out the door.

Back outside in the chilly night air, he played with his new watch device. It slid open to reveal a bigger interface and was so simple to use. The bank app kept his finances nice and organized. The food app showed recipes and order status. The home app displayed temperature, utility use, and he could turn on the lights from his watch. The work app showed his schedule. And the GPS app mapped out the area around him; lucky for him since he knew little about the Allentown area and his dirty, thin map was shredding to pieces.

They selected a home for him in Brookhaven outside of Philadelphia, his birth city and where he spent most of his life. The Union did their research when selecting homes because Willie felt overwhelming excited to see his hometown.

Staring at the GPS app made him wonder if he had the energy to the walk back to the missile silo. It took three days of chilly nights in his sleeping bag, insect bites, and eating food from cans to get to the center of Pennsylvania. It could be easier to just see his new home, maybe enjoy a fresh healthy meal, and try out the new job for a few days. He could make some money. Having access to the internet again brought joy back to his soul. Going back to the missile silo and seeing those disappointed faces on the People of Bliss took that joy away. Adam's letter didn't say they were running out of food immediately, so there shouldn't be any harm in enjoying the Union lifestyle for a bit.

He clicked the GPS app, chose his new home address outside of Philadelphia, and selected *Free Taxi.*

CHAPTER FOUR

Royal Declan grew up in the town of Union Grove, right in the center of Marshall County. Alabama taught her a thing or two about country-style living. Neighbors helped each other, the local bar knew everything about each other, and the townsfolk said hello to each other. Men acted like gentlemen to the ladies. It was moments like this, Royal missed home.

She had been smushed into the back of the taxi cab. One side of her face was inches from Bruno's enormous elbow and the other side of her face against the taxi's dirty window. He smelled like he bathed in Peroxide and Witch Hazel. On the other side of the giant, Victor drew flames on the condensation inside the window. All this, while Adam sat comfortably in the passenger seat of the cab. Why did he get to sit in the front? Shouldn't a lady be treated more fairly than this?

Bruno crossed his arms and rested them on his plumb stomach. In this long trip to Paris, she'd heard his insides grumble at every hour on the dime.

Adam continued his gingerly chat with the cab driver, while Royal wondered if her back would be permanently shaped into this smushed form. "So the Union forbid all cars?"

"All of them," the taxi driver said ecstatically, "and we couldn't be more grateful. The money is fantastic, my friend. Only public transit is allowed. And the traffic in big cities are gone."

Adam turned to the window and mumbled, "Yeah, because most of them are dead."

The driver's name was Anton. He was the only cab sitting outside the train station and had graciously given them rides around town, for free. A true gentleman. His English was flawless, thank God, even though it made Royal disappointed not to use the Russian-to-English book for translation, then she could be sitting in the front seat.

A button popped off Bruno's tight shirt. Royal grabbed it, without thinking, and flicked it. The button bounced off the stick shaft, ricocheted off the rear view mirror, rolled on the side handle, and hit Adam square in the center of his forehead. "Ow!" He cried, rubbing the red spot forming. "Why did you do that?" It was more like why *didn't* she do that earlier? About time he suffered a little too.

"That's incredible aim," the driver smirked, winking at her in the rear view mirror. That look made her heart feel like it was bouncing on cotton candy.

"It's not about the aim, it's about the timing." She replied.

And right on time, Bruno's stomach grumbled. He moaned. From his right pocket, the gargantuan German pulled out a piece of red Lego block. Without hesitating, he crunched down on it and began to chew like the toy was made of taffy not plastic.

"Don't that hurt your teeth?" Royal asked.

"No."

"Weird," she whispered.

Bruno's face drooped and shoulders slumped. "Bruno no weird."

Guilt splashed like a bucket of water on Royal's head. She'd been treating these two men like they were weird freaks. When she was young, her timing ability should've made her the most popular girl in the school. Instead she overhead the High School quarterback call her *weird* behind her back once, just because she excelled at archery, softball, tennis, basketball, and soccer. Excellence lead to jealousy and scorn. Nobody liked her. If only they had got to know her first before making assumptions. And yet, Royal was doing the same thing here.

"Sorry, I didn't mean it like *that*." She cleared her throat. Leaning over, Royal looked at the bald-headed and burnt face of Victor. He must've been called worse names than *weird*. "So, um, Victor. How you doin'?"

He hesitated then answered, "Nice."

Now that she opened the mental doors to a conversation, she had no idea what to ask next. "Um. So what do you for fun?"

"Burn things."`

Royal sighed, she should've expected that answer. "Well, I mean…you must like other things. How about some music? You like to listen to music? I like good old country tunes. Mostly from the 70s. Patsy Cline's my favorite. How about you? What's your favorite artist?"

"The Prodigy," he said.

"Hmm. I don't know that one. What song do they sing?"

"Firestarter."

Obviously, Victor wasn't much for a conversation. Silence filled the back seat again. Bruno munched on another Lego block. "Sorry," he said, "Bruno hungry when nervous."

"Why you nervous, sugar?"

"Scared of fight. Bruno no like fighting. Rebels want to fight."

Royal nodded slowly, noticing for the first time a soft soul hid inside this six foot behemoth with massive arms and twenty inch neck. She whispered, enough so the front seat couldn't hear. "I'm scared too."

Adam dug through his backpack and extracted a photograph he showed the taxi cab driver. The driver glanced then answered, "No, I do not recognize him. Pierre Durand? A famous blind acrobat? How does he see what he's doing?"

"Not sure. He's some kind of parkour expert too. Has a lot of followers. He joined Cirque de Solllle…whatever that circus thing is called, about two years ago. Hope to find him there."

Her compadre seemed desperate for information. The last target on the Servo Clementia's list had little intel. So far, luck been good to them on their journey to find the list. To find Victor, all they had to do was travel to the local police station in Tunari, Romania and ask for any arsonists. He'd been the only one. Bruno had been just as simple to locate, since he belonged to a traveling circus team near Munich, Germany. Both men didn't hesitate to join the rebellion. But what about Pierre Durand? Would it be more difficult to find him or convince him to join the People of Bliss in their efforts to end the Union?

After about an hour of winding roads and thick forests, they began to approach the bright lights of Paris. Royal stared out the window at the Eiffel Tower. It seemed so much bigger on television. Streets that should've been filled with tourists and lights were blandly empty. France's apocalypse didn't fair well either on Doomsday. At least America's demise came brutally and striking, France had a slow chaotic death as a government-created Flu rapidly spread.

They drove by a park, unkept gardens and trees littered the view. "Luxembourg Gardens," their driver said. The world famous park looked like the set of a horror movie, and the darkness of the clouds just made it more eerie. "It pains me to see Mother Nature like this." After a long sigh, Anton said, "*Be not a cancer on the earth -- leave room for nature.*"

Royal glanced at the rear view mirror and caught Anton staring. She asked, "Is that from a song or something."

Before Anton could answer, Adam rudely interrupted. "It's the last step in the Georgia Guidestones, duh."

Sensing from Adam's abruptness, he was either jealous or being grumpy. Neither of which Royal was having. She crossed her arms, "Well, how was I supposed to know that, dummy."

"I bet you don't even know what the Georgia Guidestones are, do you?"

"I do too!" She didn't. But no sense in letting Adam know that.

Thankfully, Bruno asked. "Bruno not know."

Adam turned his body around, bothering to wear a seatbelt like there were any cars to crash into. "In 1980, stones were erected in the center of the State of Georgia. Not the country Georgia, the state. Anyways, they were created by a religious group of nut jobs. In eight different languages, these crazy big stones, give specific instructions on how to survive an apocalypse and rebuild society."

Interesting.

The massive theater took Royal's breath away. She never been to a show, except when her High School did a revival of Grease. They didn't have enough men that could hold a note so Danny was played by a female. Somehow she doubted any subpar performances could fill that many seats. There must've been thousands of seats and just as many on the balcony. Large wheels that looked like something a hamster the size of an envelope would exercise in occupied both sides of the stage. In the center, a turntable with a glimmering purple curtain surrounded it. The whole set must've been based on a jungle theme with those vibrant red, yellow, and orange. Set pieces of tall green grass and flowery art pieces crowded the empty corners. Two trapeze dangled from the ceiling by ropes fashioned with vines.

Only her and Adam had decided to enter the establishment, the others agreed to wait behind in the cab with the cute Russian driver. Being just the two of them hadn't felt as odd as when they begun their travels to Europe for recruitments; actually, it felt reliving and Royal couldn't quite put a finger on why. Maybe it was all the babysitting they finally got a relief from.

"Looks empty," Adam said, scouring the seats with his eyes. "Power is on though." Both of those statements were obvious, but Royal decided to keep her lips shut. Neither of them moved, afraid or mesmerized by the stage. Lights popped off as they had started their descent between the aisles. Adam paused in the darkness. "What in the –"

Lights slowly faded up. Gentle operatic music played from the dozens of speakers around the auditorium. Then the purple curtain lowered. On a sort of round metal reel that looked like something you'd wrap your garden hose around, was a man balancing himself. Assuming this was Pierre, she found herself impressed already. His skin tight red spandex costume left little to the imagination, glitter accented his stellar physique. Adam crossed his arms.

"That him?" Royal whispered.

"Yep," Adam grumbled, a little too quickly. Was he jealous?

Laser lights danced around the stage and Pierre spun that reel with his feet, motioning around the monstrous wheels in a figure eight formation. The music and lights enchanted Royal. Pierre waved his arms and body to the score, in sync like the breeze on a grassy hill.

"I thought," Royal whispered again, "you said he was blind."

"He is." Adam shrugged.

They watched as Pierre leapt from onto the stage left wheel and it begun to spin. Flipping and dangling in a routine that even with Royal's power of timing couldn't master. "Sure don't look blind to me."

Pierre leapt into thin air and grasped the trapeze, nearly falling to his death. Royal's hand wrapped around Adam's arm as she gasped. She quickly removed it, questioning why she did that. Adam never even budged, he stared in amazement. "It's the lasers. Gotta be."

"What do you mean?"

"He only sees high-end spectral density. A light source is calculated by the spectrum of the electromagnetic wave's electric field. Understand?"

Royal sighed, "I ain't got no idea what you talking about."

"It's sort of like," Adam thought for a moment, "Like, turning off the lights in your room and only seeing the glow-in-the-dark stars on the walls. Pierre can only see very blinding lights. Nothing else."

The music intensified and so did Pierre's routine. He bounced from the trapezes to the wheels, back and forth, up and down, until even Royal experienced nausea. Spinning and cartwheeling, Pierre landed on his feet in the center of the stage as the music ended. This would be the time for applause as a spotlight formed on him.

Except no one was here.

Even through the white powder, excessive eye lashes, and bright red makeup, Royal could see the disappointment in his face. His chest heaved up and down. He obviously knew no one could be here, so why perform to an empty audience? Many years ago she used to go to the marketplace every Sunday morning for fresh fruits and vegetables back home. And every morning, she'd see the same elderly homeless man outside playing the drums with a cup full of pity change. Once, she asked his name. He didn't answer. After repeating the question, his eyes gazed on her mouth. He had a pad in his hand and wrote with a pen that was deaf. She asked why play then? To this day, she never forgot the words he wrote down. *Because it's what I do.*

Pierre was no different. His passion didn't end the same day the population of France did. It just weakened. Royal stepped forward and applauded loudly.

The sound of her clapping made Pierre jump and step back, alarmed. "Bonjour? Qui est la?" He called out, with a high pitched and thrilled voice. With the lights dimming down,

"Americans," she answered, approaching the stage. Expecting to hear Adam objecting, she was pleased to see him join the applause.

"That was magnifique," Adam said, failing at mimicking a French accent with possibly the only word he knew in the language.

"Oh!" Pierre said, taking in a deep breath of satisfaction before bowing. "Americans! I love Americans! Come! Come! Into the spotlight." They approached the light, so that the Frenchman could presumably see them. He focused on them both for a while before smiling. "I can see sparkles in everyone, but you two shine like stars. Light has touched you both. Glorious light. Like the rainbows above us, blinded by the darkness. Who are you, gorgeous?"

Judging by his feminine movements and staring in the direction of Adam, Royal assumed she wasn't the one he called *gorgeous*. Adam blushed, the way straight men did with gay men. Royal replied, "I'm Royal, this is Adam. We've come to find you, actually."

"Me? Pourquoi? I'm just some mere man who sleeps in a theater every night, hoping to awaken and the nightmare fades away like the evening sun. That the cast, my friends, return to dazzle yet another bewildered audience."

This was the part she left up to Adam. The part to explain why they had travelled so far, for one person. He cleared his throat. "What if I told you, we have a way of…foreseeing the future?"

Victor snorted and Bruno laughed when Adam used that first line on them, but Pierre didn't react negatively. He smiled, "I've seen the miracles light can do. Lloyd and Nina gathered many of us followers here, in Paris. This cosmic intuition seems not so far out of reach."

"Well," Adam looked to Royal then back to Pierre, "I can. And some very bad people studied me as a child. My first vision was a list, sent to me by a future version of myself. A list he titled: Those that can alter the future. Unfortunately these bad people, Servo Clementia, decided to chase down and execute most of the people on that list. But since my vision of an apocalyptic future didn't change, and still came into fruition, I came the conclusion –"

Royal interrupted, "Excuse me."

Adam corrected himself and continued, "I mean, *we* came to the conclusion whoever is still alive on the list must be recruited not murdered."

"Ah, those damn terrorists again, the Servo Clementia." Pierre said, stretching his neck back and studying the ceiling. At this view she could see the blue tint in his eyes. She wondered what his eye color was before he lost vision. "And you want me to join your war." He flipped and tumbled over flawlessly over the stage, then stood in front of Adam. "But I hate wars. Fighting for the right to fight more."

"Then you're the perfect candidate," Royal said, "Because this is the war to end all wars."

Still not seemingly convinced, Pierre grasped onto Adam's arm. "Would you mind walking me to my dressing room, stud? Let's talk some more on the way." Adam didn't seem uncomfortable and walked up the aisle, with Pierre firmly holding him even though she suspected there were enough bright bulbs for Pierre to find his own way. "Your name again? Adam? Right? Have you ever heard of ant mill?"

"You mean, worker ants?"

"Right. I love a smart man. Anyway. Worker ants are significantly blind. They follow each other through a trail of pheromones," he stressed the word *pheromones* in a metaphoric way, "But when one ant gets off track, it circles around and around. Eventually, other ants, just as confused, circle around that one. Eventually, you have dozens of ants circling and circling, going nowhere. Going nowhere, until they die of exhaustion." They stopped at the doorway of the auditorium, inside the lobby. "Do you understand, Monsieur? War after war, movement after movement, and protest after protest…it won't end."

Seriously stern, Adam replied. "This time it will."

A stranger's voice interrupted from inside the lobby. "No, it won't." The taxi driver Anton, for some reason, was inside the lobby facing the three of them. Tall enough to play basketball, but probably too muscular to be fast at it, this was the best view Royal had gotten of Anton outside of his seat. His neck had to be thicker than her thigh. At 5'4, everyone seemed big to her but this guy seemed monstrous. "I've finally found you, Pierre."

Before Royal could ask how they knew each other, the cab driver lifted a gun from his inner pocket and pointed it. Adam's hands went up, "Woah, what's this about?"

The Frenchman looked even more concerned. "This bastard has been after me for years. I hid in the spotlight, where people like him couldn't murder me and get away with it. Still trying to impress Mommy?"

Anton sniffed. "Shut it. You all are coming with me. I'll fire at the first one who tries to run. And I'm an excellent aim."

Royal had never had a gun pointed at her, so she did the same as the other two captives and lifted her hands.

Adam asked, "Who are you? Illuminati?"

"No." Anton grumbled.

Eyes narrowing, Adam said, "That sounds like something the Illuminati would say."

"God," Royal shouted, "Don't be stupid. He's got a gun. Ain't it obvious who he is." She eyed the member of the most powerful worldwide covert organization. "He's Servo Clementia."

Anton smiled and had every reason to, because now he had captured those left on their kill list.

We need to be needed, because feeling unwanted means feeling no purpose.

-Victoria Celest
First Lady of the United States
2033-2038

CHAPTER FIVE

Normal never fit in Gerard's vocabulary. He enjoyed spontaneous behavior, even mischievous behavior. But being common was just so…common. Normal sucked.

"Are you listening?" The CEO barked.

"Yep," Gerard lied.

"They are starting to break the glass down there! What if they get in? My employees could be in danger! The Supreme Leader promised me your protection!" The rattled CEO stared out the window, his gray toupee beginning to wobble.

Slowly getting off the leather couch, Gerard stretched his arms out before moving towards the windows. The couch had made a perfect indent of his butt and back. That couch probably cost more than his car, but also had been more comfortable. The flight here to Seattle had been hectic. Not only was the seat stiff, the ride had been bumpy and lengthy as the plane couldn't fly directly the tainted clouds. Flying below the clouds had been eerie and hours longer.

Gerard yawned and moved next to the CEO staring intently out the window. There was still four more hours of security detail before his shift ended. Might as well calm the snob down before his toupee fell on the floor. Marcel owed Gerard big for this one. He didn't become the Union Security Czar to be babysitting.

Out the double plated windows, hundreds of protestors threw rocks, Molotov cocktails, and even toilet paper rolls. The action gave him a sense of excitement even from 49 stories above. But the CEO didn't share his enthusiasm. "Do you see this? They are ruining my building!"

Twisting the wedding ring on his left hand, her heartbeat engraved in the silver band, he thought about Janice. Could his wife be down there in that crazed mob of protestors? Did her devotion to the rebellion turn her into one of these ants in the Union's path, waiting to get stepped on? Then he thought of his child. Would he be raised with these heathens?

"Are you listening?" the CEO snapped.

"Yep," Gerard lied again.

The capitalist loosened up his tie. "Why do they bother? I mean, it's so stupid. The Union doesn't want to release a government bailout, so what are we supposed to do? Huh? We *have* to withhold cash withdrawals or our business bankrupts." He tossed his hundred dollar tie onto the thousand dollar coffee table like a dirty handkerchief. "Jesus, it's stuffy in here. We can't even afford to run the generator. No air conditioning, no electricity, and all those dumb people outside…the Supreme Leader owes us big." He unbuttoned the top three snaps of his shirt and a bushel of gray hair popped out. "Think about it…what's the point of protesting? Does it honestly change anything? I mean, how many people occupied Wall Street, marched against police brutality, stormed the White House for black rights…did any of it make a difference? It's stupid!" After a moment of huffed breaths, he asked, "Are you listening?"

"Yep," Gerard lied again.

His eyes tried to focus on the crowd, like he had any chance of seeing familiar faces. But instead of facades, he caught a glimpse of something strange. Over his shoulder, the CEO stared down at what caught Gerard's attention. "Did you order drones?"

"No," Gerard whispered in confusion. He squinted to make sure he was seeing the same thing. Sure enough, dozens of armored drones flew ten feet above the protesters. Each was equipped with two automatic side arms and thick aluminum plating. Protesters threw whatever in their disposal at the drones. Shoes, rocks, fruits, none of it could persuade the drones to leave. Automated voices spoke to crowd. They sounded like mumbles from here. Gerard pressed his ear against the glass. "What are the machines saying?"

A robotic voice from behind them entered the room. "They are saying…*You have fifteen more minutes to disperse before being fired on.*"

Gerard turned, knowing only one person who could have an artificial voice coming from a device around his neck. The Union General Vanderbilt closed the door behind him and sat in Gerard's perfectly shaped butt print on the couch. In charge of the Union's army, the general constantly walked and talked like he was in charge of much more. "I knew it! You are a robot!" Gerard mocked him.

Securing the device necklace around his neck, Vanderbilt tried to smile when he wanted to frown. "I'm slightly hurt you didn't have time to visit me in the hospital."

"I heard Brent Celest broke that vocal chord of yours. You're lucky to survive in the grips of a terrorist. I was going to visit, but…you know…Security Czar work is tough, watching dipshits all day." The CEO was too busy filing down his recently manicured nails to notice Gerard's insult to him. "Did it hurt? Replacing your throat with an electronic voice box. I'm so sorry, Vandi-boo. I would've visited, but my watch was off," Gerard said sounding like a parent apologizing to a child. He stared at the bald-headed war veteran with broad shoulders. If only one of these funny nicknames would anger Vanderbilt enough that the general would try to attack Gerard. Then he would snap that device in his thick neck and finish the job Brent started. It would be a joy to watch the general's face turn from pale to blue as he gasped for air.

"But," Vanderbilt said partaking in a bowl of peanuts on the coffee table, "rumor has it that *you* were seen at Brent Celest's grave." He paused waiting for a shocked reaction from Gerard, but after a moment of unaltered stares he continued, "My colleagues question your loyalty to the Union."

Ready as always with a witty response, Gerard said sarcastically, "I was there hoping to see some of the People of Bliss. You are still looking to capture them, correct?"

"No, actually. We've captured plenty of them." the general dropped the bowl of peanuts on the glass table, maybe too loud because it caught the attention of the CEO. "But as you can see, I've eaten a dozen of these peanuts and the bowl still looks full, doesn't it? It's a waste of resources to imprison them. The Union is taking a different stance on the rebellion, remember?"

Marcel's speech suddenly sparked in Gerard's mind. With any means necessary, the opposition had to stop. Martial Law had been subtly commanded. How would a nut-bag like Vanderbilt interpret those instructions? As if there wasn't enough dead bodies on the streets; anyone who defied a Union Keeper would receive a bullet to the head now. "Wait a minute. Those drones…that's just a scare tactic, right? You don't plan on shooting down a bunch of innocent protesters."

Vanderbilt watched him with wide eyes like an owl. He scoffed, "*Innocent?*"

For someone so confident in his own words, even Gerard found himself caught off guard. *Innocent* wasn't the right word to use. The general's suspicious eyes gazed into his and left Gerard with no choice but to act rigid.

After a moment of chewing some leftover peanut in his teeth, Vanderbilt swallowed hard and then spoke, "I wonder how the Supreme Leader would feel about his best friend showing sympathy to those savages outside?"

This time, Gerard swallowed hard.

Vanderbilt looked at his watch, "Seven more minutes. I sure hope those protesters listen."

"It's in English, what if they don't -"

"If," Vanderbilt interrupted, "you read your memos, you'd know English is now the official language worldwide. The smart watches can interrupt for those still learning. Too bad these rebels didn't visit the Union Institute to receive the tech. As well as a new job and home, so they wouldn't be wasting their breath outside a banking company."

"You mean, it's not just a ploy? They are going to be shot?" The CEO said, turning to watch out the window, hands wrapped together like it was Christmas and he had to chose which present to open first. Gerard didn't look out the window. Instead he chose to watch Vanderbilt and lock eyes. What did it look like to stare into a madman? A madman that murdered Sirius Dawson, the previous leader of the People of Bliss. He literally damaged her mind so much, that she perished. What did he do to her?

"So English is the main language now? Good," the CEO said gleefully. "Finally I can talk to these damn Mexicans and tell them to keep the windows clean. It's all smudgy."

"That's right," Vanderbilt smirked, "The Union makes sense and will finally give us peace. And I'm sure the

Supreme Leader was absolutely clear when he said to protect the Union's interests by *any* means necessary." He glanced down at his watch. "Five minutes." The CEO stood as stiff as a lightpole while Gerard and Vanderbilt continued their terminal stare.

Five minutes was plenty of time for Gerard to think. Could he somehow save those people down there? Maybe get Marcel on the phone and –

Gunfire ignited the air outside. Screams were louder than the bullets. The CEO gasped, "My God!" Gerard kept his eyes secured to Vanderbilt. The general gave no sign of regret. He had lied. Drones with high-ammunition artillery plowed the protesters down as though their lives didn't matter. As though murder was as easy as changing the sheets in a hotel room. Marcel wouldn't have approved of this…would he?

As quickly as the sound of mayhem began…it ended. Vanderbilt smirked and said sarcastically, "Oops…my watch was off." He got up and zipped up his coat. Without another word, the general exited the room.

Clenching his fist was all Gerard could do to keep from exploding in rage. Fury had been Brent's outlet; composure was Gerard's. Being patient got him further than being impatient. One day, Vanderbilt would pay. There were children down there. Women. Grandfathers. People crying out to be heard were crying out in slow death.

"My God," the CEO said again. "I mean, who's supposed to clean up that mess of dead bodies?"

CHAPTER SIX

History repeats itself. For whatever reason. Nelson couldn't explain it, but knew it to be true. His adopted daughter Janice gave a convoluted explanation about how history followed a spiral. A spiral that would eventually collapse upon itself.

The smell of eggs, bacon, sausage, and oatmeal filled his nostrils as he made his way down to the cafeteria. Holding an empty coffee cup in his hand, he couldn't help but notice the staircase down formed a spiral. A spiral of rebels and their families lined up. Nelson wondered how it would be, in this moment, if his family had made it here. His wife Victoria would've had everyone's food order prepared *(Let's make it easy on the hardworking cafeteria staff)*. The older of two brothers, Marcel, would've been iffy about what was in the oatmeal *(Why do they add so much? Oatmeal is fine on its own.)* The young of two brothers, Brent, would've complained about the line *(What's taking so long?)*. And his sweetheart daughter Janice, persuaded by Victoria to adopt, would've questioned the necessity of eating breakfast

(Earlier human civilizations survived on several small meals, so what's the necessity of three large meals?)

Once downstairs, Nelson immediately filled up his cup with black coffee and made his way to the buffet with a paper plate and plastic fork. When was the last time he shared breakfast with his son? Not including their scavenging through abandoned supermarkets and opening canned goods with their teeth. No. An actual breakfast. He thought about this as he waited in line at the cafeteria. One by one, each person would get a glop of oatmeal dropped into the bowl on their trays. Not exactly an actual breakfast, but Brent loved oatmeal and would've enjoyed this.

This morning, he hadn't bothered to dress and wore just a robe. Almost the exact same robe he used to wear around the Oval Office in his final days as President. If only Fox News had seen him slumming like a hippie on the last days of Woodstock.

"Nelson? Hello? You there?"

So used to being called Mr. President, Mr. Celest, or Dad ⌐ he didn't even react to his first name. "Huh?"

"Bring your plate up, Nelson." The man behind the food counter beckoned. It was like being in the Air Force Mess Hall again. Everyone so impatient.

He couldn't help but feel a little offended by the food server's lack of respect. Nelson slid his tray over, his sandals clicking against the back of his feet. When his wife had died, Nelson wore sandals for nearly three days in the Oval Office. After Brent's death, it's been three months. Half his family was gone. All that remained was his alcoholic daughter Janice and his autocrat son Marcel. The attempt of giving up everything to save the family had failed.

A glob of raw and barely scrambled eggs hit his plate. Startled, like he just been woken up, Nelson looked up from his plate that he'd been dreamily staring into. An Hispanic man, older than Nelson in years and by the look of those eyes…by experience too, gawked at him behind the counter. "I voted for you," the man said spitefully. "Not the first time, but the second time. You know why?"

"Papa, please," a younger light skin girl next to him sighed.

Who Nelson could only assume was the father ignored the girl's subtle anguish and continued. "Because you promised change. That's all you people, you fancy rich people, always say. That same word. Change. What change? This?" the man said waving his spoon around the silo's cafeteria. "The country mourned when the First Lady died. I get it. But you let the country fall apart. You're supposed to be stronger than us, that's why we voted for you."

Nelson looked around, but no one seemed to be stepping forward to defend his presidency. Even his throat tightened up not allowing a single syllable escape. Frankly, he deserved this verbal attack.

The man pointed his spoon viciously. "You attacked their religions and *they* attacked us for it."

Partly true, but true nonetheless. Nelson could feel the insides of him cave where his heart barely beat. This devastating moment would forever be impeded in his mind, because everyone stared with those similar disappointed eyes. He stepped out of line slowly. Behind him, whispers grew. Such words as *useless, liar,* and *typical* could be heard. Other words he dared not focus on. Standing next to the trash can, he suddenly didn't feel hungry anymore and tossed the practically raw eggs into the receptacle.

History had once again repeated itself. Instead of stepping forward and protecting the goodwill of Americans, he stepped back and wallowed in self pity. The last time his melancholy actions cost the country its lives, economy, and more than the ridiculous religions he politically attacked.

Was he doomed to lead this country down an even deeper crater of destruction because of his apathy?

An idea formulated in his head. The only way to regain trust was to show the people why they voted for his leadership in the first place…because he had been willing to sacrifice everything.

In her decade and a half of schooling, not including the dull years before college and trying to fit in, Janice Celest had extensive knowledge. She solved the Sellmejer Equation easily, understood (the only one in her class to) Gauss's Law for Magnetism, and breezed through Newton's Laws of Motion. All these accomplishments and Janice found herself confused at the notion of wrapping a cloth diaper around her newborn.

Yet here she sat, knees up to her head, butt on the cold cement ground, hands wrapped around herself, and completely dumbfounded. Being forced to use cloth diapers and the even worse task of cleaning them had been daunting. Shopping for typical baby diapers would even be more daunting, considering the strict guidelines from most grocery stores nowadays asking for digital chips to make purchases. So Janice had no choice but to get the hang of tying and wrapping these difficult cloths.

Baby Colin seemed constantly agitated with her. She never promised him she'd be good at the mothering thing. It wasn't like she had Google to ask questions to. Instead of the internet, Janice had to rely on two things: instinct and the experience of others. His cries turned to wails. He hated laying on the bumpy mattress as much as she did. There would be these longs periods were Baby Colin would lie still and not make a sound, almost like he was planning something like Gerard. Or maybe admiring her like Marcel. Or maybe trying to find something to make Janice laugh, like Adam. Whoever the father was, she found herself analyzing every movement and noise out of the infant.

A knock on the door. She already knew who it was. Adam would've just barged in; her father Nelson never stepped out of his room so it wasn't him. "Come in, Matley."

Matley entered, her dreadlocks so decorated with colored rubberbands and ties that she looked ready for Christmas. "Hello, deary, sorry I'm late."

"Don't apologize. I appreciate taking…" Janice trailed off, trying to think of a better phrase to use than *taking my shift*. "…Giving me some time off."

"Oh, I'm more than happy to," Matley said already playing with the baby's feet. Her thick Creole accent sounded creepy in this dark room. "I remember needing my own time alone when I first became a mother."

Slightly older than Janice, but more experienced in several ways, made her feel inadequate. She watched Matley wrap the diaper with ease and calm Colin in seconds. No college degree could accomplish what she did. Perhaps being a mother took more work than Janice imagined.

Standing up, Janice felt that odd sensation again. A pain tightened just in the pit of her stomach. Often this aliment would come and go, but at this moment it lingered. Matley must've noticed her wince. "Something wrong, child?"

Known as the silo's botanist and medicine doctor (some even called her a shaman) Matley might be helpful. Janice asked, "Anything in that…garden…of yours that could help abdominal pain?"

"The plants will always provide. I could concoct a mixture. I make a paste of Asafetida, add two drops of the clove oil —"

"I mean something stronger," Janice interrupted. "Like opiates?"

She immediately saw the awkwardness in Matley's shoulders. "I hear you have a past, child. Perhaps a past that shouldn't be –"

Janice knew her own past well, the nights of drunken stupor and cloudy highs, but didn't need a lecture. She plead, "Please? Something has been wrong with me. Ever since the baby was born. Something…wrong."

Matley nodded. "Okay, I see what I can come with."

Remembering that she was no longer the President's daughter and in the position to order people around, Janice added. "Thank you. I appreciate it."

"I be happy to help."

Noticing a band-aid covering a vital vein in Matley's forearm, Janice commented, "Are you diabetic?"

"Oh, no, child. I was teaching some of the boys how to draw blood in the hospital wing. We got together some of them chemicals and found out our blood types. Quite fun."

Instead of playing video games, children were playing with needles in a hospital. Times had definitely change. But this activity peaked Janice's interest. "Wait a minute. You can figure out blood type? Can you -" She paused trying to search for a way to ask the question. Blood types are a definitive way of narrowing down possibilities of who Baby Colin's dad was.

"You mean…get the baby's blood type? I could. But why? I thought your man Adam be the boy's father."

Janice decided not to answer. Moments like this, she felt dirty. Why had she gone on such a mean streak of drinking, partying, and playing with men she barely knew? That was maybe what defined "evil"…how it felt afterwards. Matley nodded and gently said, "I found out for you soon."

"Thank you. I appreciate it."

With that, Janice left the room for her motherhood break.

What could be causing this pain? Surely, the pain of giving birth should have subsided by now. It had been ten weeks since little Colin was born. Janice chose not to recall the anguish *that* caused her. But wounds are supposed to heal in time. In theory anyways. Still reeling from the wounds of an adopted mother killed in a horrific car crash, a failed marriage to Gerard, her biological parents' death at a time when she finally found them, and the murder of her own brother…it all seemed that the scars were worse than the cuts.

Not in the mood to chat, Janice walked the darker corridors towards the silo's library hoping to avoid passersby. The library had been such a marvel. Built as a gift to the newborn Colin by the People of Bliss, the thought almost brought another tear to her eye. Gatherers had gone through great lengths to find hardcover books, almost nonexistence since ebooks surfaced, to stock those shelves.

As she entered the library, the librarian, an older gentleman with reading glasses that clung to the edge of that stout nose, gave a polite wave to her. Since chosen to organize the library, the librarian had seemed to be so alive with a constant smile and adorable old man dimples. Beforehand, all he had done was gripe about his life as an author and the terrible decision by his publishing company to stop printing copies of his books. Now all his stories were lost in the digital desert that only the Union had managed to salvage.

Just like any library, rows were categorized by subject. Janice found the health section almost immediately. About five books could be found in the Anatomy section, but she only needed one. Inside the drastically heavy paperback were illustrations of the human body. Janice tried to zero in on where the pain in her gut could be coming from. And of course…why. Maybe she was pregnant again? That couldn't be possible since Adam barely touched her, yet alone sexually. Ever since Brent's murder he had been more distracted than she had been.

Placing the book back on the shelf, she felt frustrated. If only WebMD.com or MayoClinic.com existed in this room. What she would give for a patch of the illegal substance Lust. It brought her away from the physical, and mental pain, that life constantly plagued her with. But playing in illegal drugs was about as ridiculous as playing with Silly String. Sure it could be fun while it lasted, but left you in a total mess.

After walking a few aisles, Janice saw a face she thought would never step foot in a library. Nelson, her adopted father, had his nose stuck in a book at a table. Next to him was a pile of maybe a dozen books. "Hey, Daddy," she said.

Looking up, Nelson gave a genuine grin. It was the third grin she'd seen today, but couldn't muster up one of her own. "Pumpkin. How you feeling?"

"Great," she lied and sat down across the table. Janice grabbed one of the books. "What are you reading? Aviation?" Maybe this was the root of Nelson's visible merriment. Before she joined the Celest family, he'd flown over a decade in the US Navy. The first time they took a ride in Air Force One, he couldn't stop talking about the technology behind the plane that had been flying presidents since 1953.

"Yes. Look at this plane, sweetie. It's called the Raptor F-43, created by joint efforts of Northrop and Lockhead Martin." He turned the book he read around to face her. She slid in closer, but none of it made sense. Not to a woman who barely knew anything about jets. The illustration might've been mistaken for something in a science fiction novel. Colored black except for a gray trim, the jet seemed extraterrestrial. "You see that coating? It's not actually paint, but a cloth coating. It absorbs light to make it nearly invisible. The gray lighting helps the navigator see. Oh! And it runs on zero emissions and no electricity. All of its power is drawn from the air. Get this…electrodes around the plane ionize the air; it harnesses the negative electrons and converts it to plasma energy."

Many questions crowded Janice's mouth, but she decided on just one. "Why are you researching this jet?"

He held up a finger and dug through his pile of books before settling on the thickest one. Nelson flipped through a few pages and showed Janice. It was a photograph of a Navy vessel called the USS Mitchell. "It's there," Nelson explained. "The jet. I did some research. The aircraft is one of three worldwide. According to the prison records we have here, the pilot had been arrested under treason accusations and the plane decommissioned on the USS Mitchell. Right now, the ship is docked at Port Authority near Long Island. Do you understand?" Not at all and her expression must've said it for her because he continued. "Look. Do you remember Adam's vision of the future?"

Only recently she had learned of her boyfriend (or whatever she referred to him as) and his ability to foresee the coming future. Just months ago, she had witnessed People of Bliss go into such a deep concentration that they glowed internally with a white light, so the notion that Adam had a supernatural ability seemed not all that far-fetched. "You mean his premonition of the final war?"

"Yes! In it, he saw me. He saw me flying…" he pointed to the jet's illustration, "…this aircraft. Don't you understand? I just found my purpose."

Janice wondered what that must feel like. Lately, even being a new mother didn't fill that void in everyone's mind. That empty void of purpose. "So you're suggesting traveling nearly 40 miles in hopes of going onto a heavily guarded

United States warship and taking one of their planes? That's more preposterous than some of the fictionalized books in this room."

"This morning, at breakfast, I was ridiculed by the People of Bliss again. And you know what? I deserved it. My entire presidency, I got nothing accomplished. This is my opportunity to accomplish *something*."

Janice sighed, "What is this sudden rush to fight? We finally banded the family together. Why can't we just raise the baby and be a Celest family again?"

"This is war," he said firmly. She noticed Nelson's tone, a reflection of Brent. It was filled with anger not directed at a certain person but a certain idealism.

Brushing her hair aside, Janice demanded, "But why does it have to be?"

Nelson closed the book and placed his elbows on the table, "Last week, Marcel gave Union Keepers the power to be execute innocent people. Hundreds have died already. That's the start of a war. Period. Marcel isn't my enemy. But the Union is."

"He *is* the Union. What are you going to do if it all comes down to the decision to end him? Are you really going to kill your own son?"

Immediately realizing how delicate that question seemed, Janice decided to retract. Not only did she not want to hear the answer, Nelson probably didn't want to give it. Janice's side stung again. Trying not to show the pain, she gently sat back. Talking sense into her father, a stubborn Republican Senator and eventually the President of the United States, wouldn't be an easy task. But she'd have to talk sense into him before his life ended too. "Daddy, can you contemplate what you are saying? You could get recognized by any fascist during that journey, Union Keeper, or just anyone wanting to collect on some sort of bounty for you. You could die. We just lost Brent and now you want to risk your life too? After all we did to come together?"

"I have to," Nelson shrugged.

"Before you…" She was about to say *left office* but that wouldn't be accurate since Doomsday annihilated his job and government before his term ended. "…right after your last State of the Union address, your Gallop poll approval rating plummeted to below 10%. Sure that had mostly to do because of your attack on religious rights, but even prior to that – let's face it, Daddy, people just didn't appreciate you. Vanity named you 'President Celest the Pest'. Wall Street Journal said the electoral system must be rigged to vote in such a 'incompetent leader'. NewsWeek called you 'a worse choice than Donald Trump'. And now, you want to sacrifice your life for them?"

He sat back and slumped into his chair. Combing his hair back with one hand, Nelson took a deep breath. "When your mother was pregnant with Marcel, many moons ago, she had this insane appetite." He smiled at the memory, "Like clockwork, four in the morning she'd nudge me to go pickup whatever 'the baby craved'. Sometimes pickles and ice cream or peanut butter and whip cream. To be fair to me, she'd ride along. Dead tired, I still enjoyed those moments with her. We lived twenty-some miles from the closest grocery stores. Arkansas got icy cold during the winters. I made sure to always drive below the speed limit. But some had no fear of black ice." His smile faded and he spoke so softly Janice had to struggle to hear over the generator next door roaring. "One night, a pickup truck slid. You're supposed to veer toward the skid, but no one remembers all those driver safety videos in the middle of crisis like that. That night the highway turned into a carnival game of bumper cars. It happened in matter of seconds. Four cars got hit, one car got turned over, and another car slammed into the guardrail." Nelson squeezed his eyes closed then relaxed them. Whatever he saw that day, Janice rest assured it was horrific enough for his attempt at erasing the memory. "I pulled aside immediately without even a bit of hesitation. Your mother, eight months pregnant, was out of the car faster than I was. She wobbled to help people out of their vehicles while I rushed to stop the traffic before the situation became worse. I'd say in maybe less than thirty seconds, more and more people rushed to the rescue. Three onlookers were on the phone with 911, five of us were pulling people out of the wreckage...Hell, one of the cars was on fire and two guys rushed to yank the driver out. By the time the police arrived, everyone had been pulled out to safety." He took another deep breath. "I learned something valuable that day. Something so valuable that I decided to run for office. That below all these nasty layers of bad attitudes, conflicted opinions, and unwarranted rages...there is actually *good* in people." He teared up with the word *good*. "Something so powerful, an energy that we create and connect to, existed that day. And everyday since. We just don't harness it. Don't even realize its existence. And it's worth sacrificing everything."

She recognized this power he spoke of; it existed in her baby's eyes. It existed in everyone, at same point. But in times like these, that power was often overlooked or pushed aside. "You believe there's good in Marcel too?"

Nelson answered with a brief, "He's dangerous." After closing the books, he announced, "I'm going to my room to pack up supplies. I'll be leaving first thing in the morning. Alone. I can make it to the ship by Friday. Once I'm there, I'll have to steal the jet. Not sure how, but...it's worth it."

Already set on his path, Janice knew he wouldn't change his mind. That stubbornness was a reflection of Marcel. Perhaps Nelson could be right in implying that he was dangerous. Especially after murdering their brother Brent, Marcel Celest could be capable of anything. But after all she had done to bring this family together, the Celests were separating again and Janice felt helpless. As though somehow Nelson had the power to see the future like Adam, she asked, "Will we see each other again?"

He ended the conversation with a simple sigh and kiss on her cheek, "Yes, pumpkin. Promise."

CHAPTER SEVEN

On Doomsday, January 7th, citizens did all they could to scramble away from the Kremlin where several chemical weapons exploded. Millions died. And yet, Royal found herself in a situation where she was heading directly in the center of the Kremlin. Gas masks did little to protect the rest of her body. The bright green gas that lingered in the air stung any skin not covered by clothing.

Anton, the friendly taxi driver that turned into a terrorist villain, lingered behind. Every once in a while, he poked one of them with that gun to remind the group who was in charge. The duck tape around her wrists stayed intact the entire trip here. She tried to questioned Anton of where they were going; he answered by turning up the music in his headphones. Not much else had been said

"I thought you were *trained,* dagnabit? You know, by them *Servo Clementia* people?" she asked Adam in the cab, during their drive through the ghettos of Moscow.

"Actually," Adam had answered, sarcastically as he could under his breath, "Brent trained me."

"So," Royal had whispered even more sarcastically, "These are very bad people. Get us out of here."

After a long pause, Adam shook his head. "If he wanted us dead, he would've done it already. It's because he's not in charge. I wanna meet who is."

Whoever was in charge, he chose a peculiar spot to have his evil lair. Royal imagined this person as an old silver haired man with goons surrounding him. He would be muscular and tall, like all the Russian men around here. Maybe a cigar would dangle out of his mouth and he would talk with a hoarse manly voice.

Normally, the Kremlin would be engulfed with armed guards. If they were any, Royal couldn't see them through the green haze. She wondered if Anton had gotten them lost a few times, because she past that same trash can twice already. Besides their little group of hostages, no one else seemed to be around. The last news she heard was everyone in the city had perished on Doomsday.

"There!" Anton screamed and pointed, trying to sound demanding but sounding thrilled to finally find it.

Before them, a door had been marked in Russian. If her hands were tied behind her back, this would've been the joyous moment Royal yanked out her language books to translate. After he opened the door and waved them with the chamber of gun, no translation was needed. The kitchen area seemed the typical silver appliances, silver pots, silver utensils, and silver cabinets. Everything had a layer of dust that would've made her panicked mother scrub the entire kitchen down with good old-fashioned baking soda.

"Line up against wall," Anton barked. With that gas mask on, it was like taking instructions from an angry elephant. Everyone listened, except Victor who always seemed drugged or confused. Maybe both. Adam shoved him against the wall.

From a cabinet, Anton pulled out a hand-sized yellow box with scribbly letters handwritten on it. Before she could be nosy and ask what it was, he popped open the box and poured the contents on himself. He coated himself in the white powder, covering his mask, neck, torso and arms. By the time he coated his legs, more of the powder ended up on the floor than his body. He inspected every part of his body, squinting through the coated gas mask. A slight nod and his jittery demeanor began to calm.

"Everyone turn. I'm cutting your restraints. Run out of here and you'll die in the green fog trying to find your way out," he said.

The group listened and turned. Royal felt Anton slice the duck tape and her hands finally free. She rubbed her wrists; through her mask she could see the red markings around them. Her nails were a pale green color. Had the outside chemical penetrated her skin? As though he could read her mind, she heard Anton say, "It's only deadly when inhaled."

They all turned back around when finally free.

Stepping over the mess of powder on the floor, Anton took out five more of the yellow boxes and put them on the counter. "Make sure, you cover every bit. All it takes is a small vial to start the bloody coughs." Without a warning, he tossed one box toward each of the prisoners; Royal had been the only one to catch it. Adam picked his up off the floor and popped it open. He poured the white powder on himself.

"Okay," Royal said, "I guess I'll be the one to ask…what in sam hill is this?"

"Cornstarch. It sticks to the green chemical and makes it a solid – so can't be inhaled."

While everyone caked themselves in cornstarch, Anton sprayed something out of an aerosol can. "This is hairspray. Very sticky."

After a few minutes of waiting, Anton slowly pulled off his mask and took a deep breath. Seeing that he didn't fall over in a coughing death, the others figured it was safe to do the same. Royal waited until after Adam pulled his mask off before doing the same. Besides the stench of cornstarch and hairspray, nothing else smelled peculiar.

"Let's go. Time to meet leader." Anton said, opening a side door. His head almost hit the top of the door.

Through a long hallway, they were led to a large dining room. Candles lit up the room causing sparkles from the enormous chandelier. At first, Royal thought the subtle whirring sound was a circulating fan, but no fan could be found. It must've taken the others a moment for their eyes to adjust to the darkness too, because everyone stood at the doorway for almost a minute. The noise began to shift from curiosity to creepiness. It almost sounded like a monster snoring in the corner of the room.

A candle wobbled as a shadow past by it. Royal grasped Adam's arm, only to feel humiliated when the shadow began to take shape. It was a cat. The blackest cat she'd ever seen. Licking its paw, the animal purred.

That was the noise! But it wasn't just the pleasant purr of the cat…it came from several of them. Royal quickly let of Adam's arm. Pierre whispered, "There's gotta be twenty of them."

"Sixteen. Where did you learn to count?" a voice grumbled.

Sitting at the head of the table, a frail woman pet an even more frail cat. She had silver hair pulled back into a bun. Wrinkles aligned every inch of her face and neck. Her bony fingers had unpainted fingernails that were gray and filthy. Was this the evil leader Royal imagined? Instead of being surrounded by goons, cats surrounded the mistress. Instead of being muscular and tall, she was skinny and short. Instead of a hoarse manly voice, she spoke every word bitterly like a nun with disobedient students.

"Why are you people here? Where's my food?"

Anton stepped out from behind them. Was he more scared than them? "These are the targets of Servo Clementia. We –"

"Would you all just sit down! It hurts my neck to look up at all of you."

Royal said, "But, Ma'am, we're covered in corn –"

"Shush! Sit down!"

If the group had been on edge this entire kidnapping, they physically hadn't seemed this frightened until now. Adam pulled out a chair and sat, covering it with cornstarch powder. Seeing that the flaky old woman hadn't stabbed him with a fork yet, the others followed suit and sat. Anton stood, as though he knew he hadn't been invited to a seat.

"I asked you to bring me Rassolnik and you brought me five homeless people?"

"Actually, Madame," Pierre whispered, "He kidnapped us. Quiet vigorously, might I add."

"Kidnapped?" the old woman said as though she didn't understand what the word meant. "With what? That stupid air gun? You idiots fell for that?" she yanked the gun from Anton's belt loop and tapped it on the table. Instead of solid metal clanks, it made the sound of hollow plastic. "My son can't even fire a gun. He's…what is that English word…Vegan. So that means I have to eat like a fucking deer!" She turned to Anton. "Get out and find me some Rassolnik! And don't forget to salt it. Now!" She barked something in Russian and Anton rushed out of the dining room.

Having no idea what to say next, Royal let Adam do the talking. She nudged him as a reminder that he deemed himself the leader of the rebellion.

"Um," Adam spoke, "Who are you?"

"Anna Zharkova. What the hell is an American doing in the Kremlin? If I was still Prime Minister, I'd have you all hanged for looking goddamn stupid! My son listens to all your rap music and it's your fault."

Under her breath, Royal said, "Please don't use the Lord's name in vain."

Zharkova slammed her fist on the table, her wig wobbled and almost departed her head. "I've fought in six wars with bullets grazing near my ear, if you want to be heard…speak up!"

"I said," Royal spoke a little louder, "*Please* don't use the Lord's name in vain."

After the lady stared at her for several seconds, Royal wondered if she needed to repeat what she said. When she opened her mouth, Zharkova screamed, "Goddamnit! Shush! You come into my land and disrespect me? You are all the same. Oh, *poor* Americans with their nuclear blasts. Oh, *poor* French and British with their flu virus. Oh, *poor* Africans with their lethal locusts. What about Russians? Nothing. Chemical bombs have slaughtered 82 percent of our population and media forgets about us. No one ever bats an eye for *goddamn* Mother Russia."

Grasping Royal's arm, Adam tried to assure her that he'd handle this. "Your son said you're with Servo Clementia." He paused maybe expecting Zharkova to clasp her hands together and then grasp in a tight bear hug, but since no reaction crossed her face – he continued. "So am I. I'm 'the Source'."

Squinting her eyes, Zharkova stared at Adam. "Oh. I see now," she said softly, straightening her wig. "I recall this scheme clearly. The plan to stop the apocalypse by using a human from the future to foresee the mistakes. And then fix the mistakes. Is this why my boy thinks I'd be happy to see you bunch of weirdos? Because now I could just execute you all and change the future? You bring in a pyromaniac, a homosexual, a giant, and a clairvoyant? This sounds like the beginning of a stupid bar joke."

Straightening his back, Pierre reiterated, "Actually, Madam, I'm a pansexual."

Zharkova's eyes shot to him like lasers, "And you'll receive a *pan* to the side of your head the next time you interrupt!"

Bruno spoke up. "Bruno don't want to die on empty stomach."

Adam put his finger up, "We've come up with a better plan. All the ones on the Servo Clementia's kill list can be recruited to –"

"I don't care!" Zharkova shouted, throwing the cat that had been comfortably on her lap the whole time. "I don't care if you all live or die. It was a stupid plan! Charles Declan's plan! A stupid plan by a stupid man!"

Before she could take her next breath, Royal had picked up the steak knife, stood up, held it an inch from Zharkova's neck, and screamed, "Don't talk about my daddy that way!"

The Russian woman stared with wide eyes that made the wrinkles in her face droop. Royal's hand trembled as she held the knife near Zharkova's jugular vein. What just happened? An instinct? She'd never held a knife to anyone's throat before. No. Instinct, as her father would say, was something routine. So, holding an unsteady knife to someone's throat definitely didn't fit that description. Royal settled on the word *impulse*. But couldn't understand why. Why did she want nothing more than to slit open Zharkova's throat onto this perfectly white dining table cloth? An even more peculiar question in her head…why couldn't she?

Zharkova stared into her eyes as though she just discovered a blood diamond in her backyard. "I know you.

Secretary Charles Declan's little secret. A bastard child. Royal, is it? You have his eyes. Those menacing eyes that turn a dark shade of brown when you aren't getting your way and action must replace hope. But why haven't you cut my throat open? I'm sure no one here would mind. Hell, even my son would clean up the mess and enjoy a hot bowl of Rassolnik right here, where his own mother perished. Just get it over with."

Royal's hand closed in, but stopped a centimeter from the vein in the witch's throat.

Zharkova asked, "Have you ever even killed anyone before? That's not what I heard about your 'daddy'. He went into a government building and shot over a hundred of the world leaders. Point blank with a shotgun, from what I hear. Heh, more blood than floor wax on the ground. Then he detonated a nuclear device. I bet his fingers didn't quiver like yours now. He did what was necessary. Though, even you have to admit, it was stupid. Because he didn't end the life of the world leader that actually matters…Mr. Marcel Celest. Now, because of your father, the world has a dictator."

A gentle hand touched Royal's. She flinched before realizing it was Adam. His hand reached up and grasped hers. For the first time, they shared a moment of sadness. Royal's father was a mentor to Adam. So, in a way, he lost someone too. He bit his lip and then shook his head. "We need her. She might be able to help us fix this."

Royal understood what Adam meant. She couldn't make a decision on impulse. That's what her father did, which led them to this predicament.

Zharkova scoffed, "My son is too weak to shoot just like you are too weak to slice my throat. Sit, before your leg goes numb from standing there."

Royal slowly put down the steak knife and sat down in a puff of cornstarch, sensing a tone of disappointment in Zharkova's voice.

"So, Miss Zharkova," Adam said, putting his elbows on the table, "what exactly was Servo Clementia's plan then?"

"I spent fifteen years as this country's prime minister before joining the organization. Back then, the goal was simple: stop the impending apocalypse. Of course, eventually there would be just one world leader. An 'anti-christ' some would call, which is silly considering the fight isn't against religion. The fight is against freedom. All government leaders want to strip away rights. The less rights, the less worries.

"Sensing that silly country accent of yours, *Royal*, I'll give you a relatable metaphor. Imagine, if you will, being left in charge of a farm. This farm is nothing but an open field. Ducks can roam free and fuck other ducks, maybe even fuck the pigs. There's no roofs, so the dumb chickens keep looking up when it rains and die drowning. Since there's no gates either, sheep keep escaping. And the cattle just keep attacking anything that gets in the way. So what do you do? You let this farm of yours collapse on itself? No, of course not. You build walls to separate the animals, install roofs, make houses, feed them to make them happy, and build gates so none of them escape. You make a…perfect…society."

Pierre said, "Sounds nice to me."

"It does, doesn't it?" Zharkova smiled. "Because perfection takes control. But does it ever cross your mind that it took only *one* person to accomplish it? So, in a way…*you* are the animals' very own 'anti-christ'."

She still hated her, but Royal could only admit to herself that Zharkova had a point. She asked, "But what if the animals wanted to accomplish that on their own?"

"Exactly!" Zharkova yelled, holding up a finger. "That's where Servo Clementia was born. Oh, we tried and tried, to dismantle governments from the inside. The attempts were as worthless as that damn boy of mine. While Charles Declan came up with his naive plan, we came up with a better one."

It felt less insulting to use the word *naive* rather than *stupid* to describe her father and his plans, but Royal still had the urge to cut this woman's throat.

"And what would that be?" Adam asked.

A wide grin revealed Zharkova's yellow teeth. "Gather as many sheep as possible to take the leader down."

Like so many, Royal couldn't comprehend if Servo Clementia were the good guys or the bad ones. Several terrorist attacks had been pinpointed to the group bent on ending a worldwide government before it began. Hundreds had died because of their missions. If they were the good guys, her ravenous father and this bitter woman didn't do well to justify that reputation. For now, Royal felt to completely trust their intensions would be *naive*.

Adam sat up. "That's my vision. A war. Right to the castle's doors. With the help of our friends."

Zharkova laughed. "What friends? You mean the ones sitting here?" She pointed at Victor, "This pyromaniac that hasn't listened to a word we've said because he's been staring at that same candle all this time?"

Victor whispered to the candle's flame, "Fire."

"And how about this brute who's stomach won't stop growling and he's been staring at my dinnerware like he wants to eat it?"

Bruno's eyes lit up. "May I?"

Ignoring him, she turned to Pierre. "And what? A blind man will help you in a war?"

"I can see high intensity lights," the Frenchman said defensively.

Zharkova's lip curled as she looked at Royal. "And this one. She's supposed to have incredible aim. Yet, she couldn't even slice my throat."

"It's not about the aim, it's about the timing," Royal said, sounding routinely.

Adam interjected, "We have more. I even have William Cooper."

Zharkova rolled her eyes. "Oh God, Charles Declan always whined about how they could never track him down. William Cooper, the human conduit that controls electricity. Is that all you got?"

"No," Adam said, crossing his arms, "we still have a couple thousand inhabitants in the silo. They –"

Zharkova interrupted to finish the sentence in a way Royal assumed Adam didn't intend to finish it. "– *Maybe* willing to fight? You have no idea how to recruit followers. Not the way Lloyd and Nina did." For the first time this evening, Royal saw a twinkle on Zharkova's face that might prove she wasn't complete evil. It was at the mention of "Lloyd and Nina." The couple did everything they could to try and defeat Marcel Celest, but failed. Even though they had incredible powers that only those with an open-mind could believe. Royal saw firsthand when Nina made a white pulse glow from her bare hand to heal an open wound. That was just one of the many miracles they were capable of, including creating thousands of followers. "It's all just a waste. I cannot help fight a war that has ended before it began."

"Well," Royal hinted, "the followers are still around, right? I mean, there got to be like thousands."

Rolling her eyes again, Zharkova stood up using a walking cane. Her muu muu dress hung just above her socks revealing scabby knee caps. Probably in her early 70s Royal guessed from the slouch in her back. Not that folks at that age looked practically healthy in times like this, the elderly lady seemed worse off. Something about her made Royal wonder if she was dying. Maybe cancer, heart disease, or hundreds of other possibilities. She walked to a window and looked out. Anton could be seen, using a flashlight to find his way, "He takes too damn long, that boy."

"Miss Zharkova," Adam said, "we can do this. 6 billion, 287 million, 312 thousand, and 284. That's the last update of how many have died since Doomsday. Three billion, with a *b*. The governments of this world are responsible. This isn't just about securing our future...it's about avenging our past." After Sirius Dawson died, the rebellion elected a new leader. Adam had such big shoes to fill, like jumping on a rollercoaster while it was still moving. Moments like this, Royal could see the defeat in his eyes.

Without turning around, she asked, "And how exactly do you plan on organizing a movement in the hundred thousand number range? When do we attack? How do we attack? They've got big guns, we don't. They've got jets, we don't. They've got a man with the power to control elements..." she sighed, "...and we don't."

The room fell silent besides the contempt purr of the cats.

From the kitchen, Anton stepped out, coated in fresh cornstarch with a paper bag.

"Warm it up! It's probably cold!" Zharkova demanded.

Anton ran back into the kitchen.

The Russian Prime Minister turned to the group and said in her least bitter tone, "And what exactly do you plan to do with Marcel Celest? Kill me? Enslave him? Let the people decide? So many questions and yet so little answers."

Feeling defeated, Adam leaned back in his chair and bit his nails.

Zharkova continued, "Stay for the night but leave in the morning. Now, go. He only brought enough soup for me. There's a diner up the street."

"Bruno hungry," Bruno whined.

Adam gave out a long sigh. "Come on, guys, let's find a place to eat."

Losing a best friend meant as much as losing a family member. Royal sometimes gave herself a mental slap for thinking of Sirius' death more than her own father's death. Maybe it was the way they went. While Sirius Dawson lost her life in a defiant torture with the Union; Charles Declan lost his life by murdering innocent people in the Capitol Building. One peaceful and the other angry, but both lost in the end. What kind of fighter was Royal going to be?

The bathroom mirror gave no answer. It just showed a young woman with the same "tomboy" ponytail since she was fifteen and "girly" cute chin. Royal put her baseball cap back on and finished washing her hands.

When she stepped out of the bathroom, the diner was still empty of patrons besides her table of oddball friends. Adam blotted a napkin on the bloody chin. He had that same sad look on his face. When Adam thought of Brent, his lips would tighten and eyes would stare forward. If Royal thought of Sirius, her lips would quiver and eyes water.

Royal sat down next to Victor. "You okay, Adam?"

As usual, he snapped out of his mourning aggressively, "Yeah. Fine. What took you so long? We already ordered. Get something to eat." He held up his hand to the waitress without asking if Royal was even hungry. Which she wasn't, but he had a point.

After Royal rolled her eyes, she took a look around. Russia had some interesting diners. They had a thing for the color red. Their table cloths were checkered with red and white. The chairs were red. The bartender wore a red shirt. Even the waitress had a red lipstick. She approached with a digital tablet speaking in Russian.

"Um, hello." Royal swallowed and looked at the menu. All of it was in Russian and she immediately hated Adam for putting her in this predicament. "I don't really know you people's food...do you guys have hamburgers?"

The waitress nodded slowly, making Royal feel dumb for basically asking if there are cows in this country. "I'll take that please."

Without another word, the waitress grabbed the menus off the table and left.

Pierre straightened his sunglasses. Feeling his way around with the tips of his fingers, he found the creamer and poured it slowly into his coffee. "I recommend the both of you attempt to not be so...American."

Since the notion seemed directed at her, Royal asked defensively, "Why?"

"In case of you haven't noticed, Mademoiselle...you Americans are not exactly welcome in Europe."

Adam shrugged. "What did we do?"

"Have you seen the sky lately? Your nuclear war's ash clung to the clouds and put us all in darkness."

Holding his finger up, Adam corrected him. "Actually, ash clung onto the cloud seeds that were supposed to save our world from global warming."

"Irregardless, Americans are loathed here. Try an accent for the rest of your stay here."

Both Adam and Royal stared at each other with this blank stare like it was the final round of Family Feud. Royal said, "Well, I watched a lot of Downtown Abbey. Maybe I can do a British accent."

"Are you mad? That's even worse. The brits are responsible for the flu outbreak."

Adam held up a finger. "I know! I can do Australian."

The waitress walked up and placed everyone's dinner down. Bruno's plate had a stack of a dozen pancakes which he licked his lips at the sight of. Victor ordered a bowl of steaming hot soup. Adam's strawberry crepe looked so much more satisfying than Royal's boring hamburger and bun.

"Enjoy," the waitress said politely.

"Good day, mate!" Adam said.

Even though the diner was empty, Adam's outburst made the diner seem even more quiet. Royal sighed and covered her face. The waitress left the most awkward table she'd probably ever served.

Pierre sipped his coffee then broke the silence. "A pyromaniac, a brute man with strong teeth and even stronger stomach, and a gorgeous blonde with a knack for timing."

Royal felt her cheeks warm. Adam grunted.

Pierre continued, "But it's you I'm still unsure of, Adam. What is this 'Source' you named yourself?"

Adam thought for a moment before answering. "The Source is the outcome of a project to create time travel." Everyone stopped eating, except Royal. She heard the story a dozen times. He continued, "Essentially, I was born with memories from a future version of myself. Therefore, the source of Servo Clementia's outlook of the apocalypse is…me."

She enjoyed this intellectual side of him. This *confident* side of him. Adam spoke like this around Janice. Women noticed these things.

"Interesting," Pierre said buttering his toast with a knife. Royal didn't like the idea of a blind man using a sharp object, but he did it with ease. "So this group is the last of the list? Sitting at this table?"

"Not exactly. There's two people not here." Adam explained. "One of them is William Cooper, who I sent on assignment."

Since he'd never mentioned this to her, Royal felt a slight betrayal. Sure it wasn't his duty to disclose information on the revolution's plans, but Adam could've mentioned the fact Willie had been on a secret job.

"Marcel Celest is last on this list." Royal interjected before Adam could speak.

Sensing a bit of power struggle, Pierre paused to take a sip of his coffee. "Marcel Celest? How intriguing. So the stories of his weather controlling are true. Far exceeds *our* special abilities."

Adam answered with his mouth full. "Yes and no. Marcel Celest wasn't born with that…magic. It was something he gained from his coma, Brent and I assumed. The ability that placed him on the Servo Clementia list was rapid healing. Very rapid. He's had a history of short visits to hospitals, leaving doctors scratching their heads."

"A politician that can't be killed and can control the elements, so the idea was to…go to war with him?" Pierre smirked. Royal expected at this moment for the frenchman to wipe his mouth with a napkin and walk out of the restaurant. Instead he smiled again. "Sounds fun."

Pleased, Adam smiled too. "Thought you might see our side of the game now. Thank you. Welcome to the People of Bliss."

"Better to have a purpose, than none at all." Pierre said, then changed the subject, "So, handsome, what is the future like?"

He may never been asked this because Adam paused for a long time before answering. "Before the war…horrific. After the war…amazing. You know all those colors on the spectrum you can see? There's more, in my vision of after the war. Truly incredible."

"So what's Bruno's future?" Bruno said, licking the plate. Royal hadn't even finished her first bite.

Adam's head hung low in thought. "I'm not sure. The only one I can recall is Victor."

Stopping his spoon, mid-sip, Victor stared. Adam grinned and looked into the madman's eyes. He told the story like they were sitting next to a campfire roasting marshmallows and telling ghost stories. "Victor, in your future, *we* are in a stampede toward the Union Castle. Thousands of us! All ready to kill and maim. There's Union Keepers, blocking our way and ready to fire on us. Then *you* come up to the front of our ravenous mob. You're wearing a mechanical suit with these two large tanks of propane and a hose in each hand." While Adam continued his story, Victor's hand began to quiver and the soup dribbled onto the table. "Then you ignite a flame in each of these tubes. The propane spurts out and creates this massive plume of fire. You burn the Union Keepers, blow up their vans, cause explosions everywhere…"

Victor made a low vocal squeal that sounded like a mixture of an orgasm, an inhale after a deep swim, and a stroke. He dropped the spoon without moving at all. Royal down and saw a wet spot form on Victor's crotch. She sighed, "Oh dear God, he just peed his pants."

The pyromanic whispered, "Me?…Burn?…Everything?"

Adam again gave that devilish smile. "Yes. All of you are a part of this revolution."

After a full minute, Victor still hadn't moved. Perhaps he had a stroke. Royal could see not only the desire in Pierre and Victor, but also Bruno after he happily ordered another stack of pancakes. However this team would accomplished it, they were all ready to fight. The only question remained…was she?

A little sunlight came into her window that next morning. At least the star in the center of the solar system still existed, even though its warmth had been masked by the ugliest of clouds.

The group had stayed in a room that must've been intended for the Kremlin's housecleaning staff. Couches would've been more comfortable than these bunk beds. Royal had slept below Adam's bed, hearing him give a slight snore. It brought her peace listening to her friend snore rather than complain about the brick wall they've reached with the rebellion. At nearly three o'clock in the morning, Adam woke her up to tell her their movement was as disorganized as the Million Man March in Washington DC; a good cause without a clear purpose.

A bang on the door woke up the team. Anton's voice came from behind the closed door, "Everyone come!" He exclaimed in a strange sense of excitement. "I made waffles!" A man with the stature of a quarterback but the heart of a chef was every girl's fantasy. While Royal sat up thrilled, the others woke with annoyed groans.

Faces brightened up at breakfast. Anton had no problems serving endless waffles to the black hole in Bruno's stomach. Royal found herself not having much of an appetite, as Miss Zharkova sat across the dining table from her. For whatever reason, the old woman kept staring uncomfortably at Royal and not saying much of anything.

Adam tried his best to sound like a leader, at times, but failed miserably. "So, I just wanna say that…like…we appreciate food and…um…shelter and stuff. But there's a plane taking us out of her and back home. Better get a cab and…um…you know, fly away and stuff. Thanks."

Zharkova spoke so loud that Adam's words just sounded like mumbles. "I've given thought to this war. Leave Anton an email address for correspondence. When you have a solid plan to storm the Union castle and get past their securities, contact me." Looking directly at Royal, she added, "I could gather enough forces here, if I had help."

The last words didn't seem to mean anything to anyone as they gathered their bags and headed for the kitchen area. But Royal felt bothered. Why did Zharkova look directly at her when she mentioned the need for help? Barely making eye contact at all since the night before, she was surprised the Russian woman even remembered Royal existed.

Anton prepared their chemical suits, that had been washed free of the cornstarch. In the kitchen, the others got dressed while not saying a word to her. Though she was sure it wasn't their faults, Royal felt disregarded. Charles Declan ignored his daughter all her life. She had been tolerant of it, but not okay with it. Being the illegitimate child of a politician could mean doom for his campaign. Especially a poor child in a poor town in a poor state. She thought about what it meant to have a "say". Her father never gave her a chance to give have a say on their situation. Perhaps if he had, matters would've been different. Maybe Charles Declan might have enjoyed Royal's company. The last time she saw her dad alive was six years ago. Secret Service drove him out in five vehicles, which not only was the most amount of cars to visit her farm but also seemed redundant. He didn't have much to talk about. The usual questions like *how's school* or *what do you want to be when you grow up* were pointless for a woman nearly thirty years old. After a home-cooked dinner of catfish chowder, honey fried chicken, buttered corn on the cob, and black bean chopped salad, Secretary Declan made an excuse to leave. As the vehicles sped away in a trail of dust, Royal wished she had given her say. *Daddy, why don't you come visit more often? Daddy, why are you ashamed of me? Daddy, I need help with the farm Mom left us.*

Finally someone noticed Royal just standing at the door of the kitchen and not suiting up. Adam scowled, "Royal. Hurry up. Let's go."

"Would you stop bossing me around! I've had it!" she snapped. There it was again. That impulse. Adam didn't expect and neither did she.

Men always reacted with the same avoidance when a women snapped, Bruno, Pierre, and Victor huddled in a corner of the room to evade the irritated female dragon. But Adam, trying to be brave, approached her. Near the door where they had a bit of privacy, he mumbled something that sounded like *sorry.*

Royal brushed hair out of her face and found a tear trickling down the right side of her cheek. "Look, I get it. You trying to handle this the way Brent would, all tough and brutal. So maybe I gots to handle this the way Sirius would, calm and organized. She'd find followers."

Adam checked his watch, which seemed weird since that always seemed to be Royal's job. "We got to get going, we're going to miss the flight."

"Why am I supposed to be just a 'tag-a-long' to everyone? When do I get a say?" Royal wiped the tear away. "How about someone stay and work with Miss Zharkova? She gonna need help." Hoping she'd never regret these words, she said, "How about *I* stay?"

Adam put his hands in his pockets and strained, like opening a can of peas. For someone that treated her so harshly the last few weeks, he seemed very concerned to part ways. After biting his lip, he whispered, "I want a weekly update…no, I want a *daily* update. Email only. Secured. Got it?"

"Yeah," Royal said feeling the panic in the back of her throat. Was she really about to do this? Be an aide to that demon in a muumuu?

Adam asked, "What's the date we decided last night to strike?"

"August fourteenth. I got it, Adam. We'll be ready. What about you?"

He bit his lip and decided not to answer, because there was still the problem of weaponry. The castle and the Union Keepers would surely be armed better than a bunch of homeless men and women. He admitted, "Goddamnit, why am I so scared?" After a deep breath, Adam exhaled slowly.

"Don't use the lord's name in vain," Royal whispered.

Since they had never said goodbye before, she didn't know what to do next. Adam reached for a hug at the same time she reached out to shake hands. When Royal went in for a hug, Adam put out his hand to shake. They agreed on the handshake, firm and confident. "Bye, Adam."

"Bye, Royal."

As he walked away to put on his suit, Bruno stepped walked up to her. Typical men, saying women were nosy when they had been listening the whole time. "Bruno going to miss Royal. Can Bruno get hug goodbye?"

After a small smirk, she hugged his belly since her hands couldn't completely get around him. He gave her a warm embrace. Someone patted her shoulder. Pierre was there to say, "Good luck, Mademoiselle."

The last of the group, Victor, sat in a seat doodling on a notepad. Before she could ask what he was doing, Pierre answered. "He's been trying to draw schematics for the suit Adam spoke about last night."

"Oh," Royal nodded.

She watched as the team got dressed and walked out the door. Even through the green scum covering the window, she watched as they walked toward the cab and placed their bags into the truck. She watched as the cab eventually drove away. And just like that…Royal was on her own.

CHAPTER EIGHT

Cab drivers didn't usually talk so much, but this one had plenty to say. Admittedly, Willie felt pleasure in speaking to another Philly native. After the hour long drive, he had caught up on all the recent sports news since being locked away in the missile silo with the People of Bliss. To his disappointment and expectancy, both the NFL and the MBA skipped this season to mourn the overwhelming global catastrophes while soccer continued its season around the world to empty stadiums. Though never a fan of the brutal antics of hockey, the cab driver seemed opposite. NHL prepped for a new season of what they called "the apocalypse in the rink". Using the billions of deaths worldwide to backpack an advertising slogan left a bad taste in Willie's mouth. For whatever reason, the tag lines worked and NHL filled the stadiums.

The sun attempted again to puncture through the opaque clouds. Instead of an array of beautiful colors at sunset, Willie was left with just a boring, barely visible dot disappearing behind a hill then the sky grew from a pallet of dull grays to pure black. Will the sun ever shine again?

Since nuclear weapons blasted all major cities making them dangerous habitats, the cab driver took the long way around Philadelphia to Willie's new home in Brookhaven. They past familiar exits. He tried his best to peer at what remained of the first capital in the United States...Philadelphia. The airport had four upside-down planes in the runway and at least a dozen with charred remains. What must've the airport been like on Doomsday? Panicked screams or quick deaths, as the nukes threw airplanes around as frisbees. Initial estimates of the wind blast from the nuclear weapons had been in the 350 mph range, but scientists said numbers far exceeded that in windy areas.

The drive took less than an hour, which had been practically unheard of before Doomsday.Traffic meant hours of standstill on the I-476. Cars had been left abandoned with news of nuclear strikes happening around the country. Sadly, most people didn't make it out of the 98 cities struck that day. No matter how fast they ran. Besides, where was there to run? Especially when no one had any idea what city was next. It all made 9/11 seem second nature. If only Willie had gotten the call of a possible nuclear strike, maybe his family would still be with him.

Almost twenty miles outside of the strike zone, Brookhaven didn't seem much better. Most of it he didn't recognize because the town had been practically flattened. Driving through demolished houses and crumbled businesses of his hometown gave Willie little hope this condo from the Union would be ideal. He just prayed for a fresh meal and bed. Since his plan had been to deceive the Union, it felt someone distracting that he was taking a free cab to his free home. Sort of like enjoying your stay in the White House, when you're intention is to the assassinate the President.

At the end of the 2016, Willie spent about a year in prison. Whatever this home from the Union was going to be, it couldn't be worse than a cell. He had accidentally, still understanding his control over electricity, murdered a home owner. Being an electrician seemed the perfect way to hone in on his skills, but his simple wiring project turned into a nightmare and the house caught fire. The home owner never made it out. Willie got sentenced three years for manslaughter and was out in thirteen months. A grueling thirteen months. That cell had a permanent stench of what smelled like rotted feces and cheese, brown water to brush your teeth, and paper-thin blankets to cover yourself in the cold. He just prayed his assigned home had hot water.

They entered a white gate that opened automatically. The cab driver kept talking. Unsure of where the conversation had gone, Willie just continued to nod. Once inside the community, he felt a guilty sense of comfort. Trees with gold colored mulch were on both ends of the cobble-stoned street. Nicely trimmed green bushes meant the landscaping team cared about their jobs, much like the cab driver cared about his and how Willie already felt about his new position at the warehouse. They drove for only a quarter of mile before the condominium could be seen. Lit up like a tree on Christmas morning, Willie smiled at the thought of adequate electricity in his new home. The missile silo had a generator that died on a weekly basis.

He was dropped off at the cul-de-sac in front of the condos. Five buildings surrounded the enormous circle drive. His complex, letter A, had been painted a gentle brown color with aluminum siding and glassed balconies. After staring for too long, Willie said farewell to the driver and finally grabbed his heavy backpack. He walked through a steel gate to look for condo number 184. Lucky for him, it was the first door on the left. He'd never been good with directions; his husband did all the navigating.

Coming from a boy who had an iPhone at eight years old, a tablet at eleven, and laptop at thirteen - Willie Cooper would call himself a "tech geek". But standing before the door to his condo, he couldn't figure out how to open this electronic contraption. There was no keypad or even a door knob. Besides the metal plate with the condo number, nothing else could be seen.

He turned to see the driver, outside of the gate, hanging out the car window and making large waving movements with his arm. They had already said goodbye, so why was he waving? A little awkward. Willie gave a slight wave back.

"Wave!" The driver exclaimed.

More awkward. Willie gave a bigger wave.

"No, silly!" He shouted. "Wave to the door!"

Extremely awkward. Wave to a door? Willie turned and faced the door. Using the hand implanted with the chip, he waved at the inanimate door.

"Hello, Mr. Cooper," a polite mechanical female voice said from a speaker above the hinge. The door unlocked. Willie pushed and the door opened. "Sick!" He giggled; quickly realizing he hadn't smiled in weeks. It felt good.

This time he turned and gave a genuine wave to the cab driver who drove off. Willie entered his new home and closed the door behind him. Lights came on automatically and an ice cool breeze hit his face from the vent above. With no air conditioning in the missile silo, the smell of freon gave him relief.

He looked around and dropped his bag, not because he'd been lugging it all day and it had gotten too heavy…but because of his surprise. Expecting a puny worn-out condo from the Union, Willie had been overwhelmingly surprised. If this was the low end of the Union's residence chain, what was the high end? Already furnished, the living room had a two-piece sectional made from soft microfiber and a plush ottoman. "This is fucking nuts," Willie said to himself, grabbing his shabby hair on both sides. He dashed, then leapt onto the couch. It bounced back like landing on a plush mattress. Willie smiled again as he body melted into the sofa. As much as he wanted to see the inside of his eyelids, he wanted to see the rest of the place even more.

The kitchen had a washer and dryer, which at first seemed very odd. Both machines were a single appliance; he'd seen something like that on the DIY Network. But when he thought about it, the kitchen had been built efficiently. Scarce electricity meant the Union needed to conserve all utilities. China must've had some influence, since their tight, yet roomy living styles could be pointed out everywhere around him. Connected to the washer/dryer combo was the dishwasher, to save on water flow. The refrigerator had been filled with fruits, vegetables, and frozen foods. All the food looked more delicious than the pots of beef stew made at the missile silo's cafeteria practically daily. Willie shoveled down a bowl of chicken and rice before the microwave even finished heating it, not feeling full but satisfied.

Being so blindsided by this incredible home, he didn't notice there wasn't a bedroom. Instead, in the living room, a wall-mounted bed retracted with the push of a button. Willie watched the murphy bed recline. Unlike the couch, he took his time and didn't leap on this furniture. Carefully, he sat and let his body soak into the mattress; the nights of back pain from the cot at the missile silo melted like the cushion. Using the remote control, he turned on the television. Very few channels actually worked. The dark days of the apocalypse certainly didn't leave a lot to watch. He settled on a comic book movie, remembering the nights he would settle in with his husband and adopted boy. They loved the Marvel films, but Willie was more a DC fan. Tobey Maguire swung in his Spiderman suit through the buildings in Manhattan. Buildings that were no longer there. Why did they keep rebooting this movie? Tobey Maguire had been a great superhero actor. He watched the scenes of beautiful Manhattan. Or what it used to look like. Brightly lit billboards no longer cornered Time Square, instead the leftover nuclear missile sat impeded in the center. Wouldn't it be nice if they could reboot the city?

He must've fallen asleep, because he opened his eyes and the room was dimmer. The movie changed. Dorothy had her eyes closed and repeated, "There's no place like home." Her bright ruby slippers clicked together. She was right, there was no place like home. And the Union just gave Willie a superb one. But it still felt empty. His home, before Doomsday began, had a loving partner and an energetic nine-year old boy. This home had neither.

On the other side of the living room, an office table connected snugly into the corner. Willie got up and sat in the computer chair. The laptop on the desk was nothing to get excited about, a plastic casing and thirteen inch screen housed a probably weak processor and storage. But it get on the internet.

The internet.

Willie hadn't surfed the worldwide web in over a year. He opened the laptop and after a few clicks, his browser opened a new window. Unlike the typical Google, Bing, or Yahoo homepage, this browser opened a page called The Union Search Engine. Anytime he'd type a different homepage like Google or Bing, he'd be met with the same message flashing: Internet Searches have been Merged into One Convenient Website. Boring, more like it. The Union Search Engine, or USE as they cleverly named it, compiled lists into simple text. Searches had been drastically reduced into one page. Willie typed Facebook into the search bar. Another friendly worked message informed him all social media websites had been consolidated into one. Ever since joining the Union, Willie noticed how much the word "one" was used.

Lucky for him, the Union's worldwide social media website did a nice job of restoring all his old posts. Of course, he hadn't tweeted in a very long time. *Front row seats and sunny day, go Eagles! #thisislife.* His last post seemed like it was from a different person.

His photo album still stored digital pictures, all five thousand of them. As fathers, both of them were so thrilled at their new lives that the camera's storage would run out of room on a weekly basis. So many pictures, that if printed, he could probably make it a flip book. Pictures of the wedding day. Pictures of the adoption agency. Pictures of the a baby boy in a hospital. Pictures of Willie holding him. A drop smacked his hand on the keyboard. It was a tear that had travelled off his nose, one of many lining up on his nose. He wiped his face harshly, wishing it could wipe the memories away too. Because memories hurt.

Trying to take his mind off the past, he focused on the future. In the search bar, he typed in "People of Bliss". Expecting slews of degrading stories or hateful posts, Willie found himself in a state of shock. The search came up with no results. Maybe he lost internet connection? He tried it again. And again, no results. On Google, even the phrase "eating pumpkins on a stick" turned up millions of results, he knew because his son tried. He typed in "Sirius Dawson". She'd worked as a journalist two decades before leading the opposition, surely there would be some results.

Nothing. The existence of an rebellion against the Union had been erased. Leaning back, Willie couldn't decide how he felt about this. It all reminded him of prison, where the computers were so restricted that even Words With Friends had been banned because of the chat feature. Could this be worse than a prison cell? At least prisoners tried to escape their cells. Here, prisoners of the Union tried to stay.

CHAPTER NINE

Everything was at his command. Elements obeyed his whispers. Colleagues would look into his eyes, opening a tunnel into their soul, allowing him to tweak the darkness deep within. Even his body would heal expediently from any wound. Marcel wondered at times, if that ability, made him immortal. If so, then he was a step above humanity. Immortality, magic, and leadership meant he had the makings of a god. Marcel smiled at the thought. A god that had nothing to be afraid of.

With all this, why did emptiness still haunt him? An emptiness that only his family could fill. The Celests. If only his mother Victoria could see them now. What would she think of his brutal murder of Brent? He rubbed his palms together, imagining the night he stabbed his own brother and Brent's blood stained his palm.

"Everything okay, Supreme Leader?" someone said.

Sometimes he would do this, stare off into nothingness like an online video stuck buffering. He looked up. Wind blew and parted his hair. It was chilly here, more than anywhere in the world.

Behind him, the Union castle was nearing completion. Scaffolding covered every parameter, but the moonlight struck the breathtaking structure like light gleaming through a crystal. At every angle, it dazzled the eyes. Perfect for glamorizing his ideals.

Being that this was his first televised speech, he couldn't help but feel slightly nervous. His father Nelson had a knack for putting on the appearance of stern professionalism even in the most dreadful of moods. Marcel had to do the same. "Yes, I'm fine. When will the uplink be ready?"

The cameraman, who seemed to be the only one who knew the answer to the question, spat out, "Should be any moment now, Supreme Leader." His hand trembled as he typed into the laptop on a stool next to him. Either it was impatient or nerves, Marcel couldn't tell. Not until the seven people around him quieted so much that their breathing could barely be heard did Marcel realize the truth. He made these people very tense. Tense to the point of fear.

Before he became this godlike figure, he never experience tension from his employees. Saying the word *boo* might make them jump out of their shoes. He brushed his hair with his hand. "Is my hair okay?"

"Fabulous!"

"Great!"

"Tremendous!"

The wind laughed into his ear. He could always here the elements and feel their emotions. For some reason, the air element enjoyed these moments where Marcel questioned his loyalty. "So, I have enough powder? How's my makeup?"

"Perfect."

"Spectacular!"

"Fantastic!"

Before this filming group ran out of positive words in the thesaurus, Marcel asked a yes or no question. Something that might garner a smile from them. "Is there anything in my teeth?"

"No, Sir."

"Nope!"

"I see nothing."

Not even a coy smile. Marcel gave up and looked at his speech notes.

A car drove up the steep hill toward them. The trail of dust clung in the air as the vehicle stopped, then settled calmly. From the driver's seat, his brother-in-law Gerard stepped out casually as though he wasn't an hour late. Marcel didn't bother to look at his watch to show his discontent. They've known each other since high school and neither of them had changed...or ever would.

"Okay, uplink is ready," the cameraman said a little too excitedly.

Gerard walked up and said, "Wait." He straightened the tie around Marcel's neck. "Jesus, you've never been able to get this right."

For the moment, Gerard was his only loyal family left. And he found himself giving a genuine smile. "Remember when Dad lost a percentage point in the polls before his re-election because people thought his green tie clashed with his blue suit?"

"Well," his brother-in-law smirked, "not like you have that to worry about. Doubt any polls are going to change your leadership position."

As it stood, Marcel had a comfort that most politicians would sell a right arm for...he couldn't be voted out of his office. Because he was a god. And gods had nothing to fear. Especially not from the lesser beings.

"We got to start rolling soon," someone on the film crew said.

Gerard looked into Marcel's eyes. He rarely met his eye. Maybe he suspected Marcel's ability to peer into the soul via the entrance in the eyes. "Hey," he snorted, "you've got something in your teeth."

His shoulders sank. The film crew glanced in different directions as Marcel stared angrily. After sucking between his teeth with the tongue, he looked for a visual confirmation. Gerard nodded and gave a thumbs up. He quickly exited the camera's path.

"Okay, we're on," the cameraman whispered.

Marcel stared into the camera, a trick his father told him to do. People enjoyed eye contact. Even through the television screen. "Good evening. I'm Marcel Celest, Supreme Leader of the Union. Today, it's been eight months, since tragedies struck around the globe. Countless lives were lost and countless lives became lost. Lost in hope. Lost in sadness." Marcel stepped aside so the camera could a larger shot of the building behind him. "Not that long ago, this castle was a barren wasteland. Vines had shadowed much of its landscape. The environment had eroded much of its construction. Rain had flooded and destroyed most of the ground levels. But just like this glorious landmark, we too can be rebuilt. We as a nation. We as one world. And with the help of the Union. Already jobs and infrastructure are being returned. Imported goods are hitting shelves again. Humanity had been pushed into a hole on Doomsday, but we will ascent out with the hand of the Union." Marcel paused for a moment, just like his Dad would say. "And you can help by joining our cause. As agreed by world leaders before their demise at the actions of a cowardly terrorist, the Union will be led by three leaders. Being the only one to survive recent events, I've had to endure this burden alone. But that will change. And we need your help."

Something changed. Marcel's vision went from the subtle darker palette of colors to a grayscale. His pause went for too long because Gerard gave a subtle cough.

Marcel blink several times but his vision didn't return. He continued at a more uncomfortable voice that he wanted, "Democracy is about the power of the vote. And you shall vote for two other supreme leaders to join the Union's government. To avoid voter fraud as we transition a new licensing procedure, all votes must be cast using the palm chip. In 160 days, you will have the chance to take charge of our –"

The air turned cold. Much colder than it had ever been. So frigid that Marcel felt his chest heave in. What was happening?

Someone else appeared. Someone he hadn't seen in ages. Not alive anyways. Even visits from the master of darkness never left him this frightened. Standing behind Gerard's car stood the image of a man. A man that he'd known his entire life. Ever since they fought over the remote control for which cartoon to watch on Saturday morning.

Brent.

His dead brother gave no expression. No anger that Marcel had murdered him. No sadness that the family missed him everyday. No bitterness that few showed up to his funeral. His diamond eyes cut into Marcel's soul. He whispered, "Brent?"

The film crew turned around but shrugged to each other. Nothing was there.

Brent mouthed something. Words that Marcel couldn't understand.

Gerard shouted, "Goddamnit, stop rolling."

"It's a live feed," the cameraman said sarcastically.

"Then cut it!"

Marcel couldn't keep his eyes off the shade of his brother. Even in the grayness, he could almost see those blue frightening eyes. Brent repeated his unheard words. Marcel found his knees weaken and he nearly tripped backwards.

Those words again. Haunting words. He could now read the lips of his pale sibling. *Join us.*

"Brent?" Marcel said again.

Join us.

"Brent? I'm sorry. I'm sorry!"

Join us.

"Turn the camera off!" Gerard ran and kicked over the camera. It shattered into pieces.

Marcel looked down, then glanced back up. Brent was gone. Colors began to return to his vision. The bitter cold returned to the regular chill. Wind cackled again.

Worrying about the embarrassment later, Marcel stumbled toward to the car. "Brent! Come back! What did you mean?"

Gerard chased after him. "Marcel, calm down. Breath."

"I saw him! My brother."

Join us.

Marcel circled the car. No one was here. Maybe inside the car? He opened the door. "Brent?" Nothing.

"Sit down. Relax," Gerard commanded.

He obeyed and sat. His knees were shaking. "I saw him, Gerard. I swear."

With an eyebrow raised, his brother-in-law stared at him for a while then said, "Catch your breath. I'll be back." He closed the door leaving Marcel in the silence of the car.

Hands shaking, breathing rapid, face trembling…he realized that perhaps gods can be scared of something.

For nearly fifteen years, Gerard had protected Marcel Celest. First, as a paid bodyguard from bullies (he loved being a Senior beating up Freshman bullies). Second, as a paid Secret Serviceman. Now, as a paid Czar for the Union Security division. A lot of money had been made, but also a lot of stress. That meant for nearly a quarter of life, he'd been by Marcel's side. But he'd *never* seen him act this way. Never seen him so scared.

Gerard walked away from the car and towards the film crew. Before he could make it up the hill, the cameraman already began the bitching. "Did you have to crash my camera? Know how much that camera cost?"

"Where's the footage?" Gerard asked, keeping Marcel's image in mind. The Supreme Leader, after all, couldn't made a mockery of.

"It was *live*," the woman who he'd suspected was the producer said snidely, "it's already on the website."

Reporters, at this very moment, were probably contemplating the headlines: *Supreme Leader loses mind! Marcel Celest sees dead brother? Not fit for his position?*

Gerard said calmly, with his hand moving up and down like petting an invisible dog. "This is what we do. I realize you people work for the Press Czar, but something like this could cause the uprising to get worse. Let's just stick with story that Marcel is under a lot of pressure and hasn't had much rest."

"Looks fine to me," someone whispered.

"That's the story," Gerard stressed, "Understand?"

A few hesitant nods, but it was enough to give him solace. For now, anyways. He walked away, back down the hill, towards the car. Better chat with the Supreme Leader. Marcel was the most troubled of the Celest family, constantly on edge of mental breakdown since their mother's death. Gerard's wife Janice always knew what to say; he tried to put himself in her shoes. But it only reminded him of how much he missed her. He wondered who slept by her side each night, instead of him. He wondered if she thought about him. He wondered if they would ever weld this broken marriage back together.

At the car now, he decided against knocking and just simply walked in. He sat across from the still shaken Marcel Celest. Was it his imagination or had he'd grown more pale? His black hair had a few gray hairs growing. Those blue eyes that could catch any girl's attention now seemed terrifying rather than alluring.

"You think I'm crazy, don't you?" Marcel stuttered. "That I saw Brent."

"Brent's dead." Gerard was never good at consoling and realized immediately that stating the obvious didn't seem sympathetic enough. He added, "Accident on the rooftop, remember?"

Hesitating longer than usual, Marcel opened his mouth then closed it then opened it again. "My earliest memory of me and my brother was back in the days when we lived in Arkansas. God, must've been about…twenty-something years ago. Before Janice was adopted into the family. Back then, it was just me and Brent. We enjoyed hanging out by the Mississippi River. Fishing was something Dad got us into. But one day, we decided to give catching catfish a shot. Ever tried it?"

Gerard shook his head no. He grew up Washington DC where the only catfish in town had a long reservation list and came served fried on a fancy dinner plate.

"Well, anyway," Marcel continued, "the best way to catch them is with your hand. You could use chicken hearts or livers, but Brent wanted live bait. He caught a bluegill. I let him do all the work because I didn't like the idea of using live bait. It seemed…inhumane. The bait didn't ask for its sacrifice.

Anyway, after what felt like hours of fishing, we caught nothing. He had tied the bluegill and kept it alive. The poor little thing kept trying to swim away, but Brent wouldn't let it escape."

"Did you eventually catch one?" Gerard asked.

"Yes," he swallowed back hard, "Yes. But not the way you'd think. The catfish swam around the bluegill but didn't go for the bait. It's like it didn't fall for the trick. For what, as far as I could recall, was Brent's first fit of anger…he ran into the water and caught the catfish with his hand. It wiggled around trying to free itself, but he held it by the gills. He cursed a few times; words that Mom would've never allowed around the house. Eventually he lifted the catfish above a rock and smashed it's head into it several times." Marcel made swooshing motions, somewhat too dramatically. "It didn't take long before it was dead. Brent stared at. I don't think he'd ever killed anything before. I'll never know for sure, but I swear he enjoyed it."

Considering Marcel's brother grew up to be an assassin for the terrorist group Servo Clementia, Gerard didn't doubt the slight psychopath might've enjoyed it.

After a few minutes, he waited for Marcel to say something. Obviously there had to be a point to this story.

Finally, the Union's Supreme Leader spoke. "That night…I played the role of the bluegill. The role of the live bait."

"What night?"

"*That* night." Marcel stressed. "The night Brent died."

Gerard found himself holding his breath. "You said it was an accident right?"

His brother-in-law shook his head. "I knew he'd come for me when we arrested his girlfriend Sirius. Brent's wanted to kill me since joining that terrorist organization. I'm one of their targets, remember?"

The insane Christian radicals had it in their manuals that Marcel, as well as a dozen others, were going to bring about an apocalypse. Gerard had done his research because protecting this politician was his job. But maybe the Servo Clementia had been so...radical. He asked, "So what happened on that rooftop, Marcel?"

"He didn't...even...fight...me. Just like that catfish. It just swirled and swirled. I can understand the frustration of my little brother then. A murder was supposed to happen and it didn't. Me. I wanted to die. But Brent didn't fall for it. So I...had a fit of anger."

Marcel didn't have to finish, Gerard knew enough. The stab wound in Brent's body was intentional. And here he sat, in a car, with the murderer. Marcel buried his face into his hands and wept. Every time Gerard would watch a movie and the woman cried, he didn't react, but to see a grown man cry made him weak at the knees. Especially if it someone as close as Marcel. "Have you admitted this to anyone else?"

"No. And now his ghost is haunting me." Marcel sniffled. He looked up. "Am I the bad one? The bad guy? I mean, Brent smashed an innocent animal to death. He was the monster."

Gerard sat and leaned his back to the wall. He thought about how to answer for seconds, but it seemed like hours. "I don't think you're the bad guy or the good guy. It's too early in the game to decide."

"What do you mean?"

"Secretary Charles Declan protected this country from several international attacks. He won a Medal of Honor in the early century. Several coalitions praised his actions in fighting terrorism. Yet, when he walked into a federal building with pockets full of ammo and assault weapons then murdered over a hundred innocent people...he was branded 'the bad guy'. Forever. But was he? Everyone will have that moment that defines them in the end. And it's up to the individual to decide."

Marcel nodded, his tears stopped flowing and wiped the leftovers on his sleeve.

"Do you..." Gerard unsure of how to ask this paused and decided to be blunt. "Do you still want to die?" Suicide had been on Marcel's agenda once before, shortly after Victoria Celest died.

After a moment of hesitation, Marcel answered, "No. The Union needs me."

Mixed with the mucus from Marcel's nose, a red liquid began to exit. Gerard squinted his eyes. "Is that...that blood coming from your nose?"

Immediately wiping his nose with the side of his hand and looking, Marcel stared at red smear. It was definitely blood. "That's new."

CHAPTER TEN

Aurora

The setting was surreal. Royal had been offered one of the finest rooms beneath the Russian Prime Minister's mansion. Coming from sleeping on cold hard floors or stiff cots in the silo, she felt overwhelmed to almost the point of tears. The bed had four posts around it, a thick pillow top layer for comfort, warm blankets, and pillows with goose feathers. Royal slid her fingers across it. Next to the bed was a dresser; her entire backpack of clothes and essentials fit in the top drawer. She only wished she had more stuff to fill the drawers up. On top of the dresser was a bowl of candy. She took one bite of the chewy morsel and almost died from the delicious sweet taste.

There was a television, but she was afraid to turn it on. No doubt every station only reported about the Union, the chaos of Doomsday, or the worldwide death tolls still on the rise in the eight months since the world ended. None of it sounded appealing.

Royal plopped herself on the bed, not even taking a moment to remove her clothes and shoes. Suddenly her body felt heavy; her eyelids even heavier. She started to snore with her eyes open. So unladylike. Maybe skipping the shower tonight wouldn't be so bad.

What seemed like only a blink of her eyes was actually a passage in time. Because sitting on a bed bench in the room was Zharkova's assistant Anton. He wore headphones and moved his head to the best of his music. She could hear the booming rap tunes from even across the room.

Royal sat up. "Holy Toledo! Did I just fall asleep?"

Anton took his headphones off. "You have twenty-two minutes to get ready before the Prime Minister arrives."

Royal wiped dry saliva from the side of her face. So much for trying to impress the sexy Russian hunk. "I'm. Why are you in my room?"

"I am told to observe." He pronounced the *O* like a *U*.

"I am just so dog tired, I don't even care how creepy that sounds. How long was I out for?"

"Almost two hours."

Just two hours? It felt like two minutes. "Gimme just a few more minutes of sleep." Royal laid her head back down on the cool, plump pillow.

"I wouldn't upset the Prime Minister."

Royal waved him off and felt her eyelids become heavy again. "Wait. We are leaving? Where we going?" She looked to see Anton had placed his headphone back on and beat his hands to an invisible drum set.

Sleep stole her time again. And unfortunately it wasn't a gentle awakening.

Slap!

The sound hit her before the pain did. Royal awoke to a stinging pain along her leg. Before she could react, another smack hit her back along the spine.

Zharkova's voice shouted out. "All you Americans have such nerve! I tell you wake up early and you go back to sleep! Do you think you are some fairy tale princess? Yes, that's it. You believe you are Aurora, the Sleeping Beauty."

Royal would never compare herself to a Disney character. Maybe Cinderella before she put on that glass slipper. But definitely not a princess.

Slap!

This time Zharkova's cane hit Royal's arm hard. Half dazed and startled, she sat up quickly. The cane left a red welt on her forearm. "That one was quite a doozy! Please don't hit me. I'm tired. I need more sleep."

"Sleep?" Zharkova shouted as she struck again. Royal covered her face. "You Americans - all you want to do is sleep."

Snap!

"You slept during a civil war in Rwanda."

Snap!

"You slept while Somalians slaughtered children."

Snap!

"You slept while a madman formulated Al-Qaeda."

Snap!

"You slept while an Islamic terrorist group threw innocent people off of roofs."

Snap!

"You slept while an Iranian President planned an attack with nuclear weapons! You slept while Russian radicals got their hands on chemical weapons! You slept while Africa manufactured lethal locusts! You slept while those French assholes made an airborne flu virus to wipe out millions!"

Snap!
Snap!
Snap!

By the time Zharkova's tantrum was over, Royal shook in terror underneath her blanket. Blood began to soak the white, comfortable sheet. She pulled the blanket away to see the Russian Prime Minister grasping her cane with those bony fingers like she was about peel husks off a corn cob.

With teary eyes, Royal met the icy gaze of Zharkova. The Prime Minister muttered, "That's right, Princess Aurora. You bleed and you cry. And then you go back to sleep."

Not another word was said as the world leader turned around and walked out the door. Royal took a series a timid breaths before the situation settled into her mind. The words struck her harder than that cane had. Though it wasn't easy to admit, the crazy woman made a valid point. Could Royal just turn back around and fall back asleep in this pillow of feathers? Let the world crumble around her while she dreamt of a better one? Or could she stand up, grab her backpack, and follow the wench to their unknown destination?

After a deep breath, Royal stood and snatched her backpack. Then headed out the door.

Inscriptions of the Georgia Guidestones

1. Maintain humanity under 500,000,000 in perpetual balance with nature.
2. Guide reproduction wisely -- improving fitness and diversity.
3. Unite humanity with a living new language.
4. Rule passion -- faith -- tradition -- and all things with tempered reason.
5. Protect people and nations with fair laws and just courts.
6. Let all nations rule internally resolving external disputes in a world court.
7. Avoid petty laws and useless officials.
8. Balance personal rights with social duties.
9. Prize truth -- beauty -- love -- seeking harmony with the infinite.
10. Be not a cancer on the earth -- leave room for nature.

CHAPTER ELEVEN

Pause.

The frame froze on Marcel, standing on the podium poised and confident. That timid kid in High School that Gerard used to stand up for, now stood up for himself. Students would whisper behind his back. *He's too quiet. His dad's a Senator. He'll never be anything.* Gerard restarted the video on his computer screen. The crowd's cheer could've knocked the planet out of orbit. What changed? But when he paused the video at one minute and fifty-five seconds, the answer was seen.

His eyes.

Marcel's eyes were black as coal. Even blacker…if that was even possible. Gerard minimized the video window and opened the file explorer on his PC. If the Union Tech Czar, Lester, ever found out Gerard had hacked his private server there would be hell to pay. Lester happened to be an online gamer and online gamers became obsessed with their mystical worlds. "Azeroth" had been the most obvious of passwords, named after the fantasy land in World of Warcraft. Lester couldn't have made it more obvious. So in a way, Gerard was teaching them a lesson about internet security.

Thousands of videos from YouTube had been stored on the Union's servers, until Lester and his team decided what could be released to the public. Censorship at its finest. But who was going to stop them?

Gerard found more videos of Marcel, pausing at exact moments when the Supreme Leader's eyes went black. What did it mean? It all changed after that coma. Changed him in even deeper ways then simply discovering his brother Brent placed him in that state. Gerard deduced from several videos that the black eyes always happened during speeches, when Marcel wanted something. Something normal people would object to. Or at least one person would object to. But no one ever walked away from his speeches without doubt. Union Keepers walked away like zombies when he ordered them use their own judgments and bypass any laws. Even in Nazi Germany, someone would surely feel doubt about Hitler's actions. So how was Marcel performing a stronger feat than that of the Master Speaker? And better yet, how was Marcel capable of controlling the weather? Did both phenomenon's have a link?

Persuasion.

He sank back in his office chair and crossed his arms. Not sure why, but certain of how, Gerard took a deep breath. Marcel had harnessed something beyond simple mind control. This power could turn the elements to his will.

The office door swung open. Gerard quickly closed the file explorer on the PC with one swift click.

General Vanderbilt, robotic voicebox and all, walked into the office as though he owned it. "What the hell?" Gerard objected. "Don't you knock?"

"What were you doing?"

"Watching porn before Tech Czar takes that away too." Gerard offered to swing the monitor around. "Want to watch how far this woman can split?"

Just as expected, Vanderbilt shook his head and took a seat. "Since you keep ignoring my emails to watch...disgusting pornography...I figured I'd stop by."

Launching his email application, Gerard could see the folder he set for the general's emails named "Robot Douchebag". He opened it and glanced through the most recent one. Double clicking opened up a series of JPEG picture files. A perfect female, with a perfect bod and perfect teeth, modeled a futuristic suit behind an all-white background. Without the white background, the clothing would've disappeared. Gerard recognized this type of fabric; it had the ability to make the wearer practically invisible in dark settings by absorbing light around it. In fact, Brent Celest wore it the night he attacked Marcel. "What is this?"

"Schematics for a new suit for Union Keepers. Since the Supreme Leader doesn't believe in separating our armed forces from your..." Vanderbilt trailed on, looking for a word. "...security guards? We have to come to agreements between our departments."

Gerard scoffed. Calling his group of well-trained personnel "security guards" was like calling female wrestlers just simple Girl Scouts. He scanned the pictures and diagrams for the new suit. Attached to various parts of the body were black mechanical devices. It took him a moment to see the knives protruding them. "Retractable blades in the arms? In the wrists? Even in the feet? Jesus, is it a new uniform for Union Keepers or the kitchen staff?"

"Don't make fun. We've spent hundreds of hours coming up with this plan. Our military isn't safe. The uprising has taken a turn for the worse."

Vanderbilt reminded Gerard of one of those conspiracy freaks with a tin foil hat to avoid government mind control. He leaned back in his chair and crossed his arms. "What are you talking about, Vandy? There hasn't been any protests since you mowed down that group outside the bank headquarters." The memory of peoples' screams had been the alarm clock in his head every morning.

Smug and confident, Vanderbilt smirked. "You have no idea." He stood and walked around Gerard's tiny office with his hands cupped behind him. Gerard had so little things on the wall. Since his home had been crushed by a Baltimore nuke, he couldn't salvage much. A few pictures of his wife Janice, their wedding day, and a picture of the White House he bought on sale at Sam's Club. Vanderbilt, like others who came into his office, stared at the photo for a while. Currently, the Presidential Mansion looked nothing like the picture with bright green grass and pure white paint; instead it looked like a building abandoned by its country. Which in a way…it was. The Union was the future. With his back still to him, Vanderbilt said, "Vicious acts, like those of our military, should've angered more of the rebels. Not less. They're hiding. Recruiting. Building up. And our actions aren't bringing them out."

The phone rang. Gerard took this opportunity to get rid of the general. "Alright, well. I'm busy. So you need an answer? No. The uniform sucks; no matter how sexy the model is. It's prone to bullets, which our opponents still have, remember?"

Vanderbilt nodded, "That's right. They are still somewhat armed. But maybe not forever." With that vague hint of a more restricted future for citizens, Vanderbilt left the office.

Alone now, Gerard picked up the phone. It still bothered him. What did the general mean by the citizens wouldn't be armed much longer? "Yeah?" Gerard answered.

A polite professional male voice spoke. "Mr. Security Czar, we have instructions to contact you immediately before allowing Adam Durham back into the country."

Gerard sat up immediately, knocking the keyboard off his desk. He frantically picked it up. "You have Mr. Durham in custody?"

"Not exactly. He's awaiting your approval at the airport –"

"Let him in."

After a short silence on the line, the airport security officer asked, "Are you certain, Sir? There's quite a record on this individual. Adam Durham is linked to both Servo Clementia and protest efforts –"

Again, Gerard interrupted anxiously. "I said, let him in." No one was more planned and ready. He expected Adam's return and this phone call. He also knew that Adam would head next to the underground colony known as the People of Bliss.

"Yes, Sir," the airport officer said then hung up.

Gerard needed this good news. Adam had returned from his trek and he was essential to the next part of his plan.

It was time for a face-to-face meeting with the fugitive Adam Durham.

Somehow Adam had managed to remain calm on the outside, while the others physically showed their angst. Victor was on his third attempt at fidgeting the knob to see if the door would finally open; lucky for them, there was no combustible products around for him to create a fire. Pierre paced the floor like he had nowhere to sit, when there were plenty of seats in the confinement room. Bruno used the sleeve of his sweater to wipe sweat from his forehead. Airport Security had kept them in this room for six hours now. The conference room with a mahogany round table didn't seem like much of a jail, but sure felt like one. Bruno had already eaten the fruit in the glass bowl at the center of the table. Adam watched with bewilderment and amusement as the six and a half foot man began to munch on the glass bowl. No blood poured from his mouth; something that would happen to practically anyone else that chewed glass. It was like his teeth were made of diamonds.

"Doesn't that hurt?" Adam asked.

Bruno shrugged. "Bruno is freak. That's what children call Bruno."

Adam couldn't argue the downfall of being different. Deep in his head, he often wondered why life chose him to be this way. The precognition he had a few days ago still lingered in his head like that failed calculus test. He should've been more prepared, but his panic seized him up again. Only bits and pieces of the future had been noted. He struggled, even at this dire moment of being held against their will at an international airport, to remember the entire precognition. Marcel had been there. A monster came out from his skin. A black monster. *The only way to destroy darkness is with light.* What did that mean? Why, if all the important glimpses of the future, did he recall this one? What significance would this be for the upcoming war? Were they supposed to storm the hill with flashlights in their hands? And that monster climbing out of Marcel. What was it?

He stayed calm, because that's what Brent Celest would've done. His idol, confidant, and best friend. Even though Marcel had brutally murdered Brent, he couldn't help but sense sympathy for the "Supreme Leader" in the precognition. Whatever Marcel Celest did, to keep all that darkness in himself, it would eventually kill him.

"I still don't understand. If our passports are *utterly* fool-proof, why are we here?" Pierre asked no one in particular. "It's...how you say?...*suspicious*."

That it was. Without any Customs issues, just weeks prior,Adam expected the same returning to the United States. But Airport Security felt differently. *Random Screening.* That's what they called it. But four men in a room with a locked door seemed beyond simple screening.

What would Brent do?

A decade of hardcore training taught Brent Celest how to snap three necks and disarm two men in less than eight seconds. On the other hand, Adam's lack of discipline in fight training meant the same could be done in eight minutes. Eight minutes that could quadruple the size of armed Airport Security. Adam's shoulders sank as he slumped backwards into the admittedly comfy chair. Opposites attracted. That old saying. Adam and Brent were opposites and that's why their friendship worked. For every angry rant Brent gave, Adam would instill realism into the situation. While for every pitiful idea Adam would have, Brent would remind him to tough it up. But violence couldn't remove them from this situation, only faith.

The door opened.

Instead of five men with semi-automatic weapons ready to fire, a nerdy suited man stood at the door with a clipboard. As if holding people against their will was routine, the man said, "You have been cleared to enter the United States. Please remember not to leave any baggage and exit out the left door." And like that, he left.

An applause or cheer should've been apt for this situation, but instead the group just sat there. Like Adam, the others might've been worried what awaited them outside that door. Courageous, like Brent, he decided to be the first to walk out the door. No guns awaited them. No cautious eyes. No sneers. Nobody cared. After clearing his throat, Adam said, "See. Told you guys I'd get you out of this."

"But, you didn't do anything," Pierre retorted.

"Let's go." Adam commanded.

In College, Adam had this old clunker of a car. Certainly after a nuclear weapon with the capability of untold amounts of wind probably carried that car from the University of Baltimore to somewhere in the next state. But what Adam would do to have that Nissan Altima right at this moment. His legs burned from walking. Taxi drivers asked too many questions and this group of odd men didn't seem appeasing to those willing to pickup hitchhikers. The group kept quiet for most of the trek, stopping when Adam said it was time to rest and waking up when it was time to beat the afternoon showers. Victor loved the night stops and opportunity to build a campfire. Food had been scarce, since Adam hadn't anticipated feeding three more mouths including Bruno's endless appetite; his canned food supply could only last so long. They relied on hunting squirrels for the last days of their walk; without Royal's impeccable aim…hunting had been difficult.

As they munched on bowls of squirrel stew around a campfire, Adam reflected on today. Today was his birthday. Twenty-eight didn't physically feel much different than twenty-seven. But mentally…much had changed. Planning a government ambush with thousands of people could make anyone "grow up". Mr. Declan used to say Adam barely had the guts to be a follower, much less a leader. If only he could see his adopted boy now. Adam became a major leader. An unconfident leader, but a leader nonetheless. But the words of Zharkova reminded him of the truth. The truth that the rebellion needed a more solid plan. A plan rooted in the ground that couldn't be ripped out or fall apart. Ideas could only go so far. Adam needed to organize opposition from around the world with limited communication and extreme caution.

Before bedtime, Adam drank a large amount of water from the stream. The bladder alarm clock, like always, woke him up six hours later. Hidden behind blackened clouds, the sunrise often didn't wake anyone. But Adam's bladder kindly reminded him in the morning to get up and urinate. After a long bathroom break, he awoke the others and their final day of travel began.

Pierre barely spoke. Either he wasn't confident in his English or he didn't have much to say…or both. Using his walking stick, he moved through the forest with more ease than Adam and the others. Blindness gave him heightened skills that the others couldn't possibly understand. Dangerous animals had started making their ways back into the wilderness. Thanks to Pierre, the group had avoided desperate black bears and starved mountain lions.

The People of Bliss had invented an ingenious way of finding the compound. Fallen trees had been placed symmetrically on the ground around a single rock axis, forming a clock. The closer the tree structure was to midnight, the closer they were to the silo. Since the stars, moon, and sun hid behind black clouds, relying on a compass had to be the only reliable navigation. Journeying through these woods for the good part of a year, Adam became more familiar with the surroundings. His home was close.

Sideways cars and upside-down helicopters were the norm, but the occasional skittish deer or scavenging raccoon were not. Adam felt pleased to see wildlife return to their native lands. Yet, he wished he felt just as enthusiastic to return to his dwellings. Certainly, he'd be bombarded with questions about the next course of action now that this part of the plan had been complete. Even though funding the trip overseas was met with criticism from the People of Bliss, he promised finding Victor, Bruno, and Pierre would help their ambush of the Union. The next course of action wouldn't be so easy.

The forest had become somewhat of a junkyard for the nuclear weapon that spat out debris in this direction. The gang had their own catastrophic events on Doomsday and only heard of the United States on the news. Pierre, who usually stayed ahead of the gang, was suddenly found sitting on the ground in the distance. Hearing Royal's voice in his head about staying on time, Adam opened his mouth to object to Pierre's sudden break. Until he saw what made the Frenchman to sit down. Laying on the ground next to him was the familiar stench and stiff shape of a dead body.

When Adam walked closer, he noticed flowers had been placed in the wound of the corpse's stomach. Pierre understood the world differently, so what must've death been like to him? Could he feel their souls? Smell them? See them? As much as Adam had seen the dead, it still never settled that bubbly feeling in his gut. Billions had perished around the world because of the Union. Because of Marcel Celest and his vision. Nothing was said. Nothing could be said. The group stood over the body for several minutes before silently gathering their backpacks to leave.

Several more hours passed until the cold became more bitter and the clouds became slightly darker. What Adam would give to see the sunset one more time. Normally, this would be the time to find a place to camp, but they carried on more north. Just one more mile.

Thirty minutes later, he stopped.

"We're here." Adam exhaled. He walked up to several shrubs and pushed them aside. Hidden underneath the mess of foliage was a rusted metal door in the ground, slightly larger than a sewer manhole.

"There's a rebellion here?" Victor asked, sounding more like a grievance than a bafflement.

Adam paid no mind as he unlocked the door with a slight twist. He tossed his rucksack down before climbing inside. The first room was big enough to fit a chair, desk, and a watchman. A watchman that never seemed to stay awake. Adam sighed at the snoring old man that somehow slept with his head straight up.

"Some security," he griped as he kicked the watchman's chair. He barely woke up the elder. Adam reached down and grabbed the keys.

Being so late at night, the team didn't have the opportunity to meet many of the People of Bliss. After showers and a warm meal at the cafeteria, Adam found a few empty rooms for them to sleep in. Finding a bed big enough for Bruno seemed impossible, so he settled on the couch in one of the break rooms. Victor and Pierre shared a room; Victor practically fell asleep the moment he hit the cot. Pierre gave a kind smile and hug to Adam. "Thank you."

It took him almost an hour before Adam made the way to his own room. Janice would, no doubt, be awake. Why didn't he feel pleased to be back home to his girlfriend and her baby? *Their* baby. Well, *possibly* their baby. Truth was, Janice had no clue. And it wasn't like they could order a DNA test.

Without knocking on the steel door, Adam entered room 113. Like all the rooms in the missile silo, it seemed like what it was…an office. No matter how much decor was added to it, it didn't have the comfort of an actual bedroom. He wanted more for the People of Bliss. Actual homes. But how? How when everyone was in constant hiding from the Union? What would Brent do? How would he free these people from the slums?

Janice's eyes looked tired. Old. She showed her age in the shadows of a single candle lighting the room. When they first met, Adam couldn't see how this woman could be 42. Now he could clearly see it; reminding him of their nearly two decades of age difference.

"Hey," she whispered.

"Hey," he answered with his mind elsewhere. Zharkova could gather enough forces to storm the Union castle. But how would she get them here? Doubtful that American Airlines would give "rebellion" discount flights.

"You seem distant."

"Hmm? No. I'm good. Just a lot of work to do." He said, preparing a cup of tea. Being the stereotypical coffee addict in college, Adam didn't care for the bitter taste of tea. But Janice loved it; which meant he had to enjoy it. "I had another precog."

Always the disbeliever in the supernatural, Janice blinked several times before uttering, "About what?"

"Your brother."

She sat up slightly from the dent in the mattress and placed her back to the concrete wall. Adam could see her mind juggling rapid thoughts, but what about he had no clue. "When...in the future?"

"Long time from now. Really long time. He was super old. We were...friends." Adam said *friends* nastily because saying it tasted worse than the tea. "He was dying. From some cancer or something. He said he made a mistake. Something about...he absorbed all the darkness in the world to save us."

Janice's twisted her lip. "Sounds like something he would do," she said sympathetically.

Adam had enough of drinking this disgusting tea and being told what he should believe. He spat out, "You're defending him? Seriously?"

Caught of guard, she whispered so the baby wouldn't wake. "I didn't insinuate that –"

He didn't let her finish. "Brent's dead. By his hand, remember? His bloody fucking hands." Adam slammed the cup down and the baby stirred in his crib. "Billions are dead. He could've saved us from Doomsday. I know it. *You* know it." He walked toward her, his shadow growing next to the candlelight. "In my vision, he dies. And from his corpse, an enormous black…monster grew. Like nothing I've ever seen. It had skeletal wings, dark red eyes, sharp teeth…That's what Marcel Celest has created. Not *peace* and *tranquility*, but a demon. A demon so full of rage that it attacks us all. Devours and kills everyone! We have to kill him first. We have to murder Marcel Celest!"

The baby bursts out into tears. It stops Adam's blinding wrath. Janice had swayed back into the corner of the room, eyes wide. His head spun. "I'm sorry," he said.

His child, his *supposed* child, kicked his legs in the air and wriggled his fists. Adam stared over the edge of the crib. "What do…I do? How do I…"

"Hold him, he probably had a nightmare." Janice asked.

He stared, watching the boy eyes water. What it must be like to enter this world. Strange noises. Strange emotions. Strange sights. Adam mumbled, "I can't do this. It's too much."

Without another word, he grabbed a pillow and blanket then left the room.

Oatmeal tasted God-awful with water. Especially cold since the damn hot water wasn't working again. Adam munched loudly because he could. No one else was here. He sat at a table in the kitchen where frogs had just been cut up for tomorrow's dinner. The blood-stained knife still sat on the cutting board unwashed.

In one hand, he used a bent spoon to scoop up another bite of oatmeal. With his other hand, he wrote more notes. *Need encryption for correspondence.* Just another task on the growing list of a rebellion. Four question marks were drawn next to the first item on the list: *Contact followers.* How in the Hell could they hide against the "all-seeing eye" of the Union? Cameras were everywhere with undoubtedly a staff of enforcers watching. And it wasn't like Adam could simply put out a Facebook group or garner Twitter fans.

Something creaked behind him. Adam spun around and saw nothing. The kitchen was vast. During breakfast times, it could fit a kitchen workforce of twenty. But at four in the morning, no one should be here. "Hello?" He said to the darkness, immediately regretting that he had only brought one candle downstairs.

Being thousands of feet underground in a silo brought some of the strangest noises. Adam wanted to dismiss it as just that, but something didn't feel right. He remembered a year ago, when him and Brent had planned a sneak attack to maim Marcel Celest. This must've been how the politician felt. A feeling of being watched by eyes that couldn't be seen. Adam stood up slowly.

"I've gotta a gun," he said to the empty air.

From the shadows, someone snorted and whispered. "You don't have a gun."

Startled, Adam fell backwards and nearly knocked over the table. He reached for the candle. He needed light.

The person in the kitchen with him flicked a match. Adam was stunned. This man didn't belong here. With the ignited match, the intruder lit a lantern on the other side of the room. "Must be tough living without electricity for most of the day. My home's got endless amounts of power. And I don't even have to pay for it."

The last moment these two met was months ago. When Adam had been discovered as a member of Servo Clementia, locked away, and this very man before him had laughed.

"What are you doing here, Gerard?"

That same suppressed giggle came from his throat. "If I remembered right, *you* should be dead. I arrested you. The last I heard was that prison got destroyed during Doomsday. Then, lucky me, I found your record on the Union's database."

The pieces of the puzzle came together in Adam's head. "You're the reason they stopped us at the border. How'd you find our hideout?" Truthfully, Adam didn't care but needed to buy time to figure out what to do. One of the top leaders in the Union entered their establishment; most likely to kill him. Adam could only think of all the regret he had for angering Janice.

"I've known about it for months," Gerard shrugged as he circled the room. Adam backed away in the opposite direction. "By the way, every facility has a sewage exit. It wasn't a pretty climb in here, but an easy one."

What would Brent do? Adam's head scattered in a tornado of actions. He could scream for help. He could run. Or...he could fight. His fist clenched.

Gerard looked down and noticed Adam's aggressive stance. "From my investigation, Brent trained you. But from your arrest, he didn't train you well." With a smile, he whispered, "You'll lose."

Brent would fight.

Adam dashed at Gerard. He leapt over the kitchen counter. Gerard grabbed his leg and twisted. Everything became a blur as Adam's body flung across the room. He crashed into a pile of pots and pans. Without thinking, he began tossing them. Gerard swatted them away as he charged at him, like a storm approaching that seemed more lethal at closer range. Quickly, Adam ran. The knife! On the counter. In one swoop, he sprinted and picked up the still bloody knife. He turned, then started swinging the blade blindly. Gerard, ever cunning and in perfect shape, dodged every swing. Before Adam knew it, he'd been disarmed and thrown to the ground. The brute held him down with his weight.

"Where's my wife? Where's my boy?" Gerard shouted.

"Is that why you came here?"

Gerard held Adam down and looked to the door. He stared for too long. Maybe this was an opportunity for Adam to get the upper hand and run, but he saw sympathy in that aged face. As quickly as the emotion came to his face, it disappeared. "No," he spat out. "No. No. Not yet." He gazed into Adam's eyes. "I'm here for *you*."

"Me? Why?"

"Because," he panted, "I need a digital registry. A registry of every known deflector of the Union. Every damn person that we know is on the side of the rebellion. Every...single...one."

Improbable, but not impossible. Adam could collect such a list. But for what purpose? Whatever his plan was, Gerard couldn't be trusted with such information. "I'll never do that."

With a sly smile, Gerard whispered.

"Oh...yes...you...will."

CHAPTER TWELVE

It started to snow. Being that frigid temperatures blanketed the entire world, it wasn't a surprising phenomenon. But the discolor of the snow was. Nelson grasped a chunk of it from the ground with his thick gloves. He wiggled his fingers through the ball until it crumbled. Black, almost gray, the snow looked more like coffee grinds. After a quick sniff, Nelson immediately regretted. Nuclear fallout and charred cities sure stained the clouds thoroughly. It stunk like a dead raccoon left on the driveway for a weekend. The thought made his stomach grumble, either from disgust or hunger.

Walking these forests now for a week, with nothing but secondhand clothes and navigation equipment, made Nelson regret his decision of leaving behind a vehicle at the silo. The People of Bliss had only a handful of transportation, taking just one of them seemed selfish. Especially since this mission was anything but selfish. He stopped once again to yank the map out of his back pocket. The snow dirtied up his goggles and smearing the snow just made it worse. He removed them briefly, squinting at the compass in his hand.

According to his calculations, it should be close. It should be visibly easy to see, even as the snow fluttered and blocked his eyesight.

After he climbed a hill, propping himself with a thick branch he found miles back, he saw *it*.

Planted in the center of the city of Newport, Rhode Island, was a circular structure that towered above the ruins of tumbled buildings. From afar, the nuclear missile almost looked like a skyscraper, that it somehow belonged to the city skyline. But it didn't. The missile buried itself so deep into the ground, that it would take a city effort to remove it. Like a confederate statue, the missile, as well as the other dozens across the nation, were left standing to remind everyone the horrors of history.

Nelson caught his breath, observing the destruction for perhaps the first time. As President, he never experienced the calamity of war. Not like this anyways. His visits were secured by Secret Service and tidied up with no chance of a dead body or threatening presence to be around. But at this moment, Nelson didn't have that luxury. For whatever reason, that made him feel alive.

He walked down the hill, hurried past the empty freeway like a car could actually come at any minute, and entered the city grounds. It didn't take long before he nearly tripped over a dead corpse. A mother grasping a child. Nelson hadn't intended it, but his foot tapped their burnt bodies just enough to make them crumble. Their bone hands seemed to be reaching out, asking for help. He fell backwards and landed on the side of an upside-down car.

When he was President-Elect Celest, the prior President gave him advice that stuck to him even today. *It gets easier. Everything gets easier with time.* As much as Nelson had traveled through ruined towns, it *never* got easier. He got up, wiping the snow off his coat, and lifted his neck up to view the missile. He'd visited the Freedom Tower many times, but never lifted his head that back. Snow had coated most of the missile's surface, including the mechanical vents that extracted air and shot it out at 300-500 miles per hour, but the American flag symbol could still be seen. Someone had spray painted *Fuck America* on the smooth metal surface.

After a few hours, and not a single survivor passing by in this town, Nelson found his way to the port. He used a set of wire cutters from his backpack to snip open the chain fence. It wouldn't be hard to find the ship, since it was the only one docked.

Staring at the vast naval boat, with the stenciled letters U.S.S. JOHN F KENNEDY printed on the side, Nelson found something peculiar. Snow had *not* collected over it. This was unfortunate, because that meant it was manned when he hoped it had been abandoned. Wherever the fleet had been recently didn't have a bit of ice, because the deck looked clean. Why on Earth would there still be a crew on this vessel? Were the crew members replaced by Union Keepers? Does the Union even use ships anymore? Questions like these would have to wait. With no food left and water even scarcer, Nelson needed a place to camp. Even more than that...he needed the jet. It was his whole purpose here and his only ride home, a walk back would be futile.

Using a pair of binoculars, he tried to survey the boat. He could see no movement through the port holes or on the surface. But after several minutes of searching, he got a clear view of the jet. His heart fluttered. It was just like he imagined, and how Adam had described in his precognition. Black, slick, gray outlines, sharp wings, pointed nose, six external armaments, and four engine inlets made the vehicle look like it was constructed on a different, more advanced planet.

But how was he going to get it? The military side of him begged for a uniformed plan, in case the occupants of the boat wanted to protect the only aircraft available to them. The frustrated, tired, bitter side of him begged to just run in and steal it quickly. He'd never been a thief, so he wasn't certain if planned executions worked less times than impetuous ones. On the other hand, if anyone was on this boat, surely there weren't many. Nelson was positive he could nab the plane before anyone noticed.

He dropped his backpack behind a pair of bushes, figuring clunky baggage with pots and supplies wouldn't be very incognito. After removing his shoes, exposing his holed socks, he hustled up the plank connected to the boat, careful not to rush too much or slide down the icy surface into the frigid sea. Feeling his old age, Nelson's back was too sore to be sneaking about in a huddled position. He used his ears to listen, perched next to a stack of crates next. If there were people onboard, they must've been in the quarters, expecting no visitors in the wasteland of a city.

He snuck through past more crates, filled with arsenal and food, until the jet came into view. Gawking at now, Nelson felt angst that he wouldn't know how to fly the thing. Very little was explained in the books he managed to find about it. Staring at it, he couldn't even figure out how to open the hatch. He walked slowly to it, rubbing his hand against the surface. It had been washed recently; the waxy exterior reflected his tired old face and beard. After climbing the ladder, he found himself still questioning how to even open the hatch door and climb in. He removed his glove and felt for buttons, since he could find none he tried tapping on certain sections like it was an iPad. The jet, according to his research, used no electronic equipment, but instead charged up with solar cells and used fusion technology to operate.

This was becoming more overwhelming than the stack of paperwork in the Oval Office on his first day.

Something moved in the glass reflection. Before Nelson could even turn, someone grabbed his ankle and yanked him. Falling six feet face down broke his nose immediately. Navy standard Bates brand boots with steel toes began kicking him. There was more than one attacker, he tried to get up but was battered back to the ground. His only choice now was to plead. "Please! Don't! I didn't mean it!"

All the kicks stopped simultaneously.

"No way. I know that voice," one of the attackers said, kicking Nelson backwards so they could see his face, bleeding and beaten. "Well, I'll be a monkey's uncle."

With one swollen eye already, Nelson could only focus slowly. Four men, in naval uniforms, stood above him cackling. Another man didn't laugh. He seemed more skeptical, crossing his arms and staring at Nelson. "Naw, guys, I don't think it's him."

"That's him, all right," another voice said, joining the group. Wearing a very different uniform, white with a shoulder covered in strips and awards, the captain approached. "You don't recognize that pretty face since it ain't dolled up with powder and clean, slick back hair. That, my friends, is the god-dang President of the United States."

The captain bent down, chewing on a toothpick manically. He was older, probably older than Nelson, with a pointed nose and permanent sour look on his face, like he kept losing at slots no matter how much he pulled the handle. From his back pocket, he pulls out a dirty handkerchief and licks it, then smears the wet cloth over Nelson's face. This was the first moment he wished he brought a weapon, even a knife could've had a chance of escape. "He look like shit don't he? Stinks too. When's the last time you took a shower, Mr. *President*?"

The men laughed, even though it wasn't much of a jab to be laughing about.

Nelson muttered, "Please. I made a mistake. I –"

The captain interrupted, "Maybe if he done a better job he wouldn't be in this little predicament huh? *We* wouldn't be in this little predicament. You know...the whole missile apocalypse thing." He wipe his own nose with the handkerchief and put it away. "When I turned 18, I voted for Barack Obama to be President. Now, I know what you all are thinking. Me? Vote for a nigger?" His crew snickered. "But I had to do it. My high school sweetheart was one of them stupid ass liberals. Oh, you know, all about rights for faggots and Muslims and shit. I said okay, I'll do it. Man, did that chump disappoint me. Ever since then, every damn president has disappointed me. You know what you all lack?" The captain grasped Nelson's testicles, making him screech. "Balls, my friend. Where's the President I voted for? This is it? Some wussy in that comfy little Oval Office while the rest of us fought and died for our country." He released the testicles, leaving Nelson to grasp them praying the pain would go away.

"He was trying to steal the jet," one of the men stated.

"Well, no shit, Sherlock." The captain answered, removing his cap to pat off the dirty snow. His bleach white uniform was already becoming stained outside. "Let's get inside."

Two of the men grasped each side of Nelson. One of them said, "We report it to the Supreme Leader?"

At first, Nelson didn't understand until he remembered the radio referring to Marcel as the Supreme Leader. His son...the leader of the world? Still didn't settle right in his head.

"Of course we do, dipshit. We wanna get on the Supreme Leader's good side, don't we?"

This day had turned into a whirlwind of unexpected events. First, the ship was manned. Second, the jet would be more complicated to operate than expect. Third, he'd been captured by lunatic naval personnel. And worse of all, Marcel was going to be notified.

"What's he got on him?"

The crew searched his pockets. Not until one of the men grabbed the map from his back pocket did Nelson realize his fatal mistake. "No," he shouted, "that's mine!"

Snatching it from the crew member, the captain opened up the map. He read it for a moment, then smiled. He bent down to Nelson's level, his breath smelled like bacon. "Well, what do you know. You drew a route here. But I wonder..." the captain turned the map around. A big red X, Nelson had drawn, indicated the location of where he started. The missile silo. He tapped his finger on it. "...Now, I'd bet my right hand this is that secret location for the People of Bliss."

All sorts of lies came to Nelson's head. He could say it was a watering hole, where his vehicle broke down, or even his personal camping area. But that was the power of the captain's intimidation, the wide eyeballs and deep breath. Lying wouldn't work, the captain could see through it. Nelson chose to say nothing, feeling his hands shaking.

The captain spat out his toothpick and it hit Nelson's cheek. "Yeah, you're one of them. I can tell. You all are a bunch of pussies or else you would've won this war by now. Now, I ain't got nothing against a rebellion. I love war, to be frank. I'm gonna hold onto this for a while. Call it my 'collateral'. And I love collateral. Gives you a sense of power, know what I'm saying?" He stood up, pulling out another toothpick from his pocket and biting on it. "But, it'll take a while before word gets the Union's leader that we found his father. Until then, he's a prisoner. And you all know what we do with prisoners, right? We are going to have some fun."

CHAPTER THIRTEEN

If you want to build a ship, don't drum up the men to gather wood, divide the work and give orders. Instead, teach them to yearn for the vast and endless seas. - Antoine de Saint-Exupery.

Marcel based that quote on how he wanted operations to be conducted at the castle job site. Hundreds of men and some women had done extensive work rebuilding the castle's foundation and structure. In exchange, the food and lodging the crew surpassed their expectations.

He made an effort, once a week, to join the construction. Being a leader was more respectful than being a conqueror. Marcel knew little about tools, but learned every chance he got. According to the contractors, another couple months and the project would be complete. Besides furnishings and the scaffolding alongside the castle, not much could set it apart from a construction site.

Outside the vast courtyard, he took a moment to observe the land while hammers clanked together the wall surrounding the perimeter, something he objected to, but Gerard insisted on. As much as Marcel couldn't accept it, their were opposers that would be willing to climb that wall to strangle his throat. Standing over twenty feet, the metal wall would be impenetrable. It was like adding WI-FI to a Buddhist temple, sure it was necessary but it also stole the soul of the structure away. The magnificent castle overshadowed in comparison to the White House. In fact, eighteen White Houses could fit inside the land, he actually had done the calculations. Maybe its alluring landscape could be enough to persuade his family to return. Just maybe.

He wished he didn't have to fear opposition; that he could just chat with commoners. Truth be told, besides what the News channels said of him, praise as always, he didn't know what common folk thought of his endeavors. Were they afraid of the rumors spread, but not confirmed, that he can control weather and minds? Were they appreciative of what the Union offered them? Were they satisfied that Union Keepers upheld martial law?

Lost in his thoughts again, imagining the night that a helicopter with his father and sister hovered over him atop the castle - a bloodied knife in his hand next to the corpse of his brother, he never noticed the rain pouring down until a Union Keeper covered him with a coat. "It's coming down hard. Should we go inside?"

Nodding, he followed the guard towards the limousine. Water, still bitter at times, liked to remind him on clear days that the element could only be persuaded not commanded. An umbrella over his head and guards to lead him away, Marcel looked at his outfit. Those Corthay leather shoes, suit from Neiman Marcus, and Brunello Cucinelli coat combined cost more than this limousine. He felt like some New York City successful entrepreneur, not the leader of a poverty-stricken country. If he wanted to become one of them, he had to be one of them.

Stopping in front of the limousine, he scanned the courtyard as he listened to the rain pelt the umbrella like the element was throwing rocks. Nestled in front of the castle's left side entrance was a cottage, brick-layered walls and two stories tall. Out the windows of the structure, he could see a face staring out the weather with a candle. "Isn't that the crew break area?"

"Yes. But most of the crew is gone for the day."

Judging by the candlelights of the German-styled cottage, most of the crew wasn't gone. "I'd like to go there." Unlike the weather elements, he didn't have to reason with his guards, they did his bidding. Marcel travelled back up the hill, over the steps, and towards the cottage. Puddles swallowed his shoes and the dark rain smelled like sulfur. By the time he made it to the door of the cottage, the umbrella only kept his hair from getting wet.

Wiping his shoes on the mat marked THE NEIGHBORS HAVE BETTER STUFF, he entered the warm cottage. Solar energy did little to run the heaters, since the sun barely made an appearance so a fireplace kept the space comfy. Expecting a dozen men and women, griping about their job and smoking cigarettes, Marcel was pleasantly surprised to see only two men in the room. Well, one more a boy than a man. He looked old enough to drive, but not old enough to be any good at it. "Wow, the Supreme Leader. Welcome, Mr. Celest! Want me to find you a towel?" The young man said, annunciating the last word of each sentence too enthusiastically.

Stopping himself from bossing the crew around, Marcel politely asked, "I can grab it.". Heading for the bathroom, he was already hit by the stench of urine. At the back of the den area, the restroom was smaller than his closet. After using a white washcloth to wipe his face, he looked at the towel to see it had turned gray. Gray as the cosmos he visited on his mystical trek with Lucifer. The rainwater was spoiled and he remained unsure how to fix an environment plagued by the destructive apocalypse. He threw the towel in the mop pail that was being used as a trash can, making a mental note to see the building planners about a more apt crew area.

Awaiting outside his door, the youngster Joey held a cup of a steaming liquid in his hand. He held it out. "Do you like hot cocoa, Mr. Celest? I made it the way Mom did. Marshmallows, peppermints, and crushed chocolate chips. And whisk the milk first, she used to say."

Marcel took a sip and it was the best hit chocolate he'd ever tasted, sweet and tangy and subtle. "It's great," he said softly, feeling the warmth in his lungs and wishing it could cure the cancer in them. "Where is she now?"

Joey looked to the other man in the room. Hands still covered in dust and his white shirt plastered with mortar powder mix, the man eyed Joey. Besides the premature loss of hair, he looked about the same age as Marcel. He didn't say anything, settled in his chair by the fire with a board game on a small table in front of him. Finally, Joey turned back to Marcel. "Our house was in the middle of Detroit."

Detroit was one of the first dozen cities hit by simultaneous nuclear missiles. "Oh," was all Marcel could say. A day didn't pass, when he was being bogged by work, that he wondered if he should've just made the call, stop the world leaders from their childish war games, and save billions. But the choice given to him by Lucifer was clear, a world without the Union or a world with it. "You guys weren't with her?"

"We were working on a house, outside of Detroit. I still remember, driving back, the radio talking about some city blasts. We didn't need the radio to see Detroit had been flattened."

Marcel shook his head. "I wasn't aware radio stations had broadcast an emergency. It all happened so quickly."

"Better than the warning the government gave us," the brother said, speaking for the first time and never looking up from his board game.

"Again," Marcel defended himself, even though he didn't need to, "it all happened so quickly."

Joey bobbed his head to some invisible music, "Okay! Well, want something to eat? I'm gonna make myself some cereal, if you want some."

Knowing now that the boy lost his family, except for his seemingly bitter sibling, made Marcel sympathize. He remembered what it was like, a mother dying then suddenly feeling the need please everyone except himself. "I'm good."

Joey scurried off, leaving Marcel to move closer to the fire and get warmth. "I'm Joseph, by the way." The brother said, holding his hand out to shake. The polite gesture of a handshake made the room less awkward. Marcel shook hands, skipping the tradition of introducing himself. He was, perhaps, the most well-known man in the world. "You play?" Joseph pointed to the board game.

Scrabble was his favorite game. "Me and my brother spent many nights fighting over this game," Marcel said, smiling.

"Good. Because my little brother learned all his vocabulary from Twitter. I need a challenge."

Marcel pulled up a chair and sat across from the scruffy man. Joseph shuffled the chips in the bag, while Marcel attempted to break the ice. "So. Joey and Joseph?"

"Yeah, parents weren't very original, huh?"

"That's okay, my parents named me and my brother after some players in a tennis match." Marcel said, rearranging the tiles on his rack searching for a word. He laid the tile letters on the board to spell S-A-P-I-D.

Squinting out of one eye, Joseph said, "That a word?"

"Brent used to say the same thing." Marcel laughed, realizing it was the first time that week he'd found anything amusing.

Flipping through the pages of a tiny dictionary in the box of the board game, Joseph stopped and read. "*Pleasant or interesting. As in a conversation.* Hmph. Well, I'll be goddamn." After writing the score down, he thought for a minute, moving around his letters.

"Well, I'm gonna head to bed," Joey interrupted, an empty cereal bowl in his hand.

"Bed?" Marcel asked, "You guys sleep here?"

"We aren't registered yet," Joey said from the bathroom where he washed his bowl in the sink, "It ain't so bad. There's a TV in the break room, I fall asleep to old episodes of South Park. Love that show. Beats sleeping in the truck. Anyways. Good night, Mr. Marcel!" He said, exiting a door, leaving Marcel feeling more guilt that the two brothers were essentially homeless.

Alone now with Joseph, Marcel realized he was never good at this. His family was his only friends. Making new ones always seemed like a complicated task. In sixth grade, he tried to get a group of friends to come over to the house and play his new XBox One he'd gotten for Christmas. He stumbled and toppled over his words that most of the kids had no idea what he was asking. Eventually, that night, he played the system alone. Seeing his anguish and embarrassment, the next day his mother invited neighborhood children over to play. He loved her so much that day.

Joseph added some letters to the table. H-A-M-M-E-R. Then added up his score. "You got some catching up to do."

"I see," Marcel smirked, flipping tiles around. And indeed, he had met his match. Fifteen minutes later, Joseph had used words like *mag*, *grip*, and then *magazine*. Marcel's weak words were no match, *door*, *often*, and *people*. He stared at the host of choices on the board and on his rack. After flipping around some letters, Marcel accidentally stumbled on the word M-U-R-D-E-R. He swallowed hard, envisioning his brother's hot blood sticking to his hands. "I got nothing," he stated quickly, "I'll swap." His shaky hand placed tiles down and grabbed more from the bag. After a moment, he said, "You're turn." But Joseph didn't move. Marcel glanced up to see the man staring at the far right wall. There was nothing there but tacky wallpaper and a clock. This must've been how ridiculous Marcel looked, peering at the ghost of his brother when others saw could only see the wall. "You okay, Joseph?"

He blinked several times before looking down at the board. "I get that sometimes."

"Get what?"

Joseph curled his fingers together as he rested his elbows on his knees. "You know, sometimes when you mix mortar, you can shovel it around and around for several minutes…and it just never seems right. It can be too clumpy. And you can keep working at it, but it still won't end up…smooth." He paused, as his eyes began to water. "I get lost in thoughts of Mom." With his calloused hand, he wiped his wet face. "What do I do? I can't…concentrate."

Guilt ravaged Marcel's soul. He'd seen, first hand, the destruction of cities but never seen the destruction of souls. He said, "What if I told you, everyone has a fate? That there's only a select few that have no fate and can alter the future?"

Sniffling, Joseph questioned, "Who told you that?"

Answering that Lucifer told him this in the darkness of his coma and bargained to change the future for mankind didn't seem like an appropriate response. He was here to make friends, not enemies. So Marcel settled on a less dramatic response. "I read it somewhere in a magazine."

"You saying it was her fate to die?"

He shook his head, "No. But. It was your fate to live."

Nodding, Joseph took a deep breath and exhaled slowly. "Thanks. You're a good guy."

"Thanks. You too." Marcel smiled. "You guys should stay in the main castle. We have plenty of better beds to sleep in. Kitchen staff has got warm food."

Grinning widely, Joseph said, "We'd appreciate that. *After* I win this game."

"You're on." Marcel said, returning to the board. "You know something? I have a feeling we're going to be good friends, Joseph."

"Me too, bud."

CHAPTER FOURTEEN

Nelson's face smacked against the cold concrete floor. It smelled like piss and flaked like dry blood. He spat out what must've been a tooth. On the bright side, that tooth had gone rotten since leaving the lavish lifestyle of a politician. He questioned his decisions to this point as he used both hands to hoist himself up slowly, bones popping like firecrackers. Something more than three billion people died on Doomsday. Money, status, and respect perished that day too.

The Navy personnel stood at the doorway, three brute men with bloody knuckles. After three days of imaginable torture, Nelson accepted he wasn't getting beat for fun but for justice.

Behind them, the captain crossed his arms. "He can't even get up. When's the last time you took a beating like that, Mr. *President*? I mean, that wasn't in the polls?" It wasn't a good joke, but didn't keep his guards from cackling. "And what you going tell the Supreme Leader about what happened here?"

If the word *torture* was even muttered to Marcel, surely the entire crew would be hung for this. But the captain was smart for someone that lost most of his hair and still did a combover. That map was the captain's guarantee Nelson would keep his mouth shut about the beatings. Hellfire would surely be sprayed at the People of Bliss and their home. "I tell my son that I was robbed by survivors in the city. And the captain saved me."

"That's right. Good old captain save ya."

With the only one eye not bruised shut, Nelson scanned his surroundings. His closet at the White House was bigger. There wasn't even a toilet or a sink. In the corner of the cell, flies buzzed around a pile of old feces from whoever the team had wrongly imprisoned. It was true that he couldn't rise, only on all fours like the dog he was. For no reason, no particular reason he could decide on anyways, they had beaten and tortured him two days straight. Sleep was something he needed more than pain pills.

"Did you hear the story about this guy? When he was in the military?" The captain chimed in, looking down from this height made him look gigantic. "They called him a war hero and I gave him a checkmark on the ballot. Then, the truth comes out. Ooh wee, was that a duzzy. Get this. During his campaign, it was all about his military background. It won him the election. Ain't going to lie, pretty damn smart, if you ask me." Nelson tried to crawl toward the wall, maybe use it to him climb to his feet, while the captain taunted him further. "Took like a year before the papers found out the dirt on him. Get this, he joins the Navy, *barely* passes even a damn swim test, then they this give this guy a Hornet. You kidding me? A Hornet? Don't ask me whose dick he sucked to get his hands on that. During training, this idiot gets lost with his trainer, maneuvers too close to the mountain, gets all freaked out, panics, and takes out the wing."

In just one sentence, the captain explained a situation that was hours in Nelson's younger years. Hours that he tried not to think of. He stands up against the wall, leaning on it for support. His breath nearly out from just that short endeavor.

The captain mimicked an explosion with his hands, puffing out his cheeks to make the sound. He continues, "They eject. Trainer and him were found six days later. But two different stories. I believe the one where he's a pussy. Trainer reportedly said his hand shakes on the controls. He said he pissed *and* shit his pants in the air. Said he ran from a black bear. A black bear, fellas. Practically can sneeze at a black bear and scare it away. If it wasn't for the trainer, neither of them would've survived. Paid him a lot of money to keep him quiet. But money don't last forever now, do it? Truth always resurfaces."

Since his battered body could barely stand, the thought of Nelson punching the disrespectful captain in the face didn't seem plausible. So he had to take the internal beating, just like he took the external one.

The captain shook his head, then whispered, "So disappointed. That's not the President I voted for." He motioned for the guards to lock up. Nelson watched helplessly as the door slid closed and clanked shut. He wiped his watered eyes. Watery from either the broken nose or broken mind.

"Is it true?" A voice said from somewhere.

Nelson looked around, searching from the male voice.

"Right here," it said.

Through a hole, not even big enough to fit a hand into, he could see some motions. Someone in the next cell said again, "Is it true?"

If he was going to spend an untold amount of time in this cell, at least he better make friends. "Which part? That I'm the President or that I wasn't a war hero?" Both felt good to say. He was the President of the United States and he wasn't a hero.

"Either." The man's voice said. "Or both?"

Nelson continued to peek through the hole. It wasn't the best of views, but he could get a good look at his new neighbor. In a dirty naval uniform, a young black cadet sat in the corner. His brown wide eyes stared back. He must've been in his twenties, with broad shoulders and a thick stature for a starved prisoner. Nelson slid down the side of the wall and rested some more. "Both are true, kid."

Expecting to hear another rant about how awful a President he turned out to be, Nelson was pleasantly surprised to be answered with silence. Maybe his neighbor didn't have much to say.

The vessel surged and moved suddenly. This was all a familiar feeling, but Nelson still asked, "We're moving?"

"Going mid-Atlantic for a while."

Any hope of being found or rescued drifted away like this boat. He could hear the engine whir, they must've been only two stories above it. Without a window, he couldn't enjoy the breathtaking view of the ocean waves and passing land, something he found joy in. In better circumstance anyways. What now? His daughter was right. He should've stayed at the silo. One poor decision after another had Nelson no closer to his true destiny. Or even understanding what his destiny was at all.

"Why you in here?" The cadet asked.

"Funny. I was just asking myself the same question."

Pipes rumbled overhead for a moment. Toilets were being flushed somewhere. Nelson had slept in some dire and disgusting areas, but this was going to be tough one. Besides that pile of feces was a small slope and drain to be used for the bathroom. No sink meant no brushing the teeth in the morning or washing his face. Smells still lingered in this room from past occupants. Like body odor.

"You ever seen Star Wars?"

That movie was reaching it's 65th anniversary, neither of these men were born when it released. Impressed by anyone with admiration for older films, Nelson smiled, "Yep. One of my favorites."

"Me too. I always wondered about them storm troopers. You know? Like…how you going to admire and protect a crazy ass motherfucker like Darth Vader. I mean, the asshole kills his own people. His own damn people, man. And they just go around, marching like it's no big deal. Why?"

"Why what?"

"Why they so…loyal and shit?"

Comparing Darth Vader to his son Marcel didn't sit well in Nelson's stomach. But it deserved some thought. Throughout history, people obsess over those with higher stature. Especially those with magic. Were the People of Bliss any different with Sirius Dawson? They followed her every word like mosquitos to bare skin. "We just bond to people we admire. I used to have a following. There's nothing like that roar of the crowd. I never slept the night before a campaign rally. Too jittery with excitement. Now," Nelson shrugged, "they all love Marcel."

"Supreme Leader," the cadet corrected him. "He doesn't like being called Marcel. He says it's disrespectful."

Nelson touched the side of his bruised face. The captain was right handed, so the punches just kept flying into his left cheek. Marcel had been beaten like this. Beaten so badly that he became almost unrecognizable. It had been the last time he'd seen his son, in a hospital bed comatose with tubes helping him breath. So convinced that Marcel wouldn't survive that incident, he already accepted his son's death. Now that he was alive, it still took so much to accept. Marcel wasn't the same. And neither was Nelson. "I'll call him what I please."

Claw marks could be seen on each of the walls. Escape didn't seem feasible. Countless men had tried and failed. His only hope of survival was Marcel. Surely, a big reward awaited the captain for bringing the Celest family together. But at this point, could the family ever be together? The idea of eating breakfast every morning with the *Supreme Leader* seemed more raunch than that smell arising from the pipe.

Almost like the cadet read his mind, he asked, "You don't like your son?"

Being a father had sets of challenges, but no dad could ever go as far as to dislike a child. "I still love him. But I guess…I'm not sure I agree with his actions. I just don't know how I feel."

"Listen to you. You're just like Luke."

"Who?"

"Luke Skywalker, man. Still believing there's good when you know their ain't. Well, I mean, I guess there eventually was. But took a lot of lives to get that far."

Nelson nodded. "Yeah, kid. I guess so." He rested his left cheek against the cold wall, the coolness relieved his pain and he could almost hear the whooshing of the ocean. "What's your name?"

"Antoine."

"Why are *you* here, Antoine?"

After a short chuckle, the cadet answered, "For trying to leave."

Nelson shared that chuckle. Things obviously hadn't worked out for Antoine. "You tried to leave on port?"

"Naw, man. When we was out at sea."

"I don't understand. On one of the rescue boats?"

"No, I was trying to steal the jet."

He sat up a little too quickly and felt his head spin. "You can fly the jet?" Nelson peeped through the hole in the wall.

Antoine sighed. He held his hands up for Nelson to see. Wrapped in bandages, the captain must've made sure the cadet would never fly again. "Could," he corrected Nelson.

"Hammer?"

"Worse. Bible."

Confused, he clarified, "They broke your hands with a Bible?"

Antoine crossed his arms, hiding his hands in his armpits. "My grandma gave me that Bible. It's heavy as hell, but I still carried it in my duffel bag. It's cracked in half now. They probably threw it overboard. The captain likes to send messages, if you know what I mean."

Hope fluttered away faster than it had arrived. The only pilot of the jet was incapacitated. "I read a manual on it," he answered. "I tried to fly it, but couldn't figure out how to get in."

Antoine's grin was riddled with yellow teeth. "You crazy. A manual. Pfft. Going to take more than that to fly it. But, man, when it's in the air…it is a work of art. No electricity. Not even battery. Runs on fusion."

This all couldn't be a coincidence. Sure, Nelson had made bad mistakes but ultimately it led him to the man who knew that plane. Together, they had a chance of figuring this out. Adam foresaw that jet would fly in the final war. Perhaps destiny just dealt a card and the game was about to start. "Antoine. Can you teach me everything you know about flying that thing?"

"Why?"

"Because I'm going to get us out of here."

CHAPTER FIFTEEN

"We got less than an hour," Willie shouted firm and yet professional. "Where's my propane?"

His eyes followed the red dot on the computer tablet. The system had estimated a four-hour arrival time. It obviously didn't account for the lack of traffic nowadays. Now all six of his docks were occupied with fully-loaded trailers.

A young kid heaved a large aluminum tank towards the dead forklift. Age didn't seem to define work eligibility anymore. Old enough to carry big equipment without any help but young enough to look intimidated by the grown-ups, Willie guessed his age between thirteen and fifteen. With ease, the forklift driver and his apprentice secured the new propane tank. The forklift started up instantly. Before he knew it, Willie watched his team continue unloading the trucks.

Everyone worked in such unison that it made his position of supervisor seem obsolete. Smiles crossed everyone's faces instead of frowns. Being his first day on the job, Willie had felt nervous but his workers fit together like the pieces of a

Tetris game. Perhaps the Union was on to something; genes did determine the right career for them all.

Regardless, running a warehouse had its difficulties. Even though the computer system chose how to store and organize pallets on the shelves, sometimes the paperwork was wrong and the freight came in bigger quantities than expected. Incoming cargo had been mostly recovered goods from abandoned businesses after Doomsday. Today, Willie had seen a range of simple items like mulch, sod, lumber, and water supplies. Other shipments weren't so simple. Nuclear waste had been salvaged from the manufacturing plants with nowhere to put them. Some of the guys joked that touching the barrels could make you grow an extra arm; Willie didn't find that amusing. Who knew what kind of toxic mixtures Doomsday created as 400 mile-per-hour winds devastated cities and killed countless. Out of curiosity, he checked the tablet. The interface could've been handled by a four year old; it was so easy to use. Three menus displayed: INVENTORY, ARRIVALS, and DEPARTURES. He tapped on arrivals to see only one icon of a truck; at the beginning of his shift he'd seen eight here. Instead of feeling relieved that his work day was coming to end, he felt discontent. In just six hours of work (the norm now, not the eight hour anymore), he discovered this to be his favorite occupation.

Odd. Clicking on the truck's shipment did nothing. So far, this system had been flawless. Double tapping it didn't seem to solve the problem either. All that happened was a red letter X popped up over the truck icon. The Human Resources manager Rick must've saw the confusion because he looked up to see the stout balding man looking down at him. "It's Classified."

Willie looked down at the tablet as though it would somehow clarify the situation. "Classified? What do you mean?"

"It means we don't talk about it," Rick said under his teeth. Under the Union's command, it had kept the management teams very minimal. Human Resources not only hired the teams of people, they trained them in each position. All morning, Rick explained everything in true detail. But seemed to be alluding this time.

Looking around, Willie noticed a surge of Union Keepers surrounding the area. It had not only made him nervous when one had patrolled them the rest of the day, but now at least seven wandered and questioned. The last time he'd been this close to the Union's guards had been Sirius Dawson's arrest. The moment he woke up in the middle of the night dreading another dream of the voice of the People of Bliss. Her running. Union Keepers surrounding them. She cowered behind him. She told him to run. Abandon her. Let her get arrested. He hesitated. He listened. And ran.

"Roach coach!" someone exclaimed routinely. It jumped Willie out of his remorseful thought.

Rick signaled to Willie to check his watch, by tapping on his own. "Your first paycheck should be there now."

"My check already?"

"The Union pays daily. Use your palm chip to buy something to eat." He either was chipper about the money every day or the incoming hot enchiladas.

Willie scrolled his digital wristwatch. His mind froze. "300 bucks!" he spat out. If he had been drinking anything, the liquid would've spurted out his nose. For one day of work, he got paid 300 dollars? Even owning his own company, he never brought home that type of weekly income.

The food truck pulled up and blocked one of the docks. Dozens of workers flocked to it like seagulls around a basket of leftover French fries. Willie patted his gut wondering if he'd been eating too much lately. The puffed stomach wobbled back, but also grumbled hungrily. Wiping off excess ash from outside, the driver cleaned the glass casing over the lunch specials. Since the truck was arriving any minute, Willie decided on something quick and light. He ordered the ham and cheese grilled sandwich. It reminded him of the first meal he had after the nuclear crisis. From a flipped over garbage truck, Willie had felt blessed to find an eatable sandwich. It had been his only meal in three days.

"85 please," the food truck vendor politely asked, wiping black soot off the glass doors.

"85 cents?" Willie exclaimed already unwrapping the plastic wrapping from the sandwich.

A few of the guys around the truck were kind enough not to laugh, but the rest burst into a snorted laughter. The vendor said, "Nice try."

It took Willie almost a minute to realize that the vendor meant 85 *dollars*. For a measly sandwich? Suddenly that garbage truck's food didn't seem so disgusting.

One of the men said, "Heard their raising sales tax again."

Another guy almost spat out his food, "No way."

The vendor replied, "What do I care? All my housing is paid for. I'm just saving up for a vacation next year. Flights are starting to open up again."

Being so sure that the Union's benefits had been a blessing, Willie began to feel uneasy. Almost hundred dollars to eat lunch seemed as far-fetched as Michael Jordan returning to basketball. Yet no one seemed phased by this as they used their palm chips to buy lunch. Was the Union so skilled at making people smile with excellent employment and lavish livings that they became…blind?

After paying the ridiculous amount of money, Willie swallowed down the food in six gulps. A hundred dollar bill would've tasted better. And that's practically what he just ate.

His watch buzzed. Another notification. Truck 532175 approached with that confidential cargo and had less than a mile before arrival. Wanting to buy a Pepsi, he shunned at the idea of how much it would cost for that. A water fountain would have to quench his thirst.

Then he felt something cold seep through his skin. Something so instantaneous and shocking that it made him stop as he climbed up towards the dock. Standing there like he had forgotten his car keys, he contemplated what he was feeling.

At the exact same moment he tried to understand this overwhelming strange sensation, the electricity in the building shut off. Grumbles came from the workers; some noting verbally that the power had never died out before. Using flashlights, the warehouse employees scattered to open the door manually for the truck's entrance.

Since his childhood days, Willie had felt the electricity around him like the flow of air conditioning in a home. Controlling the bolts of power had been his curse and his gift. But even during power outages, he'd never experienced true freedom from the waves of energy like now. His heart beat different and he felt almost light headed. He grasped the railing, trying to take deep breaths and stay calm. What was happening?

He looked down at his tablet. The screen was pitch black. Pressing the power button did nothing so he resorted to tapping it a few times.

"Hey," someone hollered, "anyone having problems with their ear pieces?"

"My watch is dead," someone else griped.

In fact, every bit of electrical equipment in the building was off. As the workers raised the dock door, Willie could see outside. All the street lamps were black. Flashlights aided the truck driver as he backed his trailer into the warehouse. The closer that trailer got to Willie, the more his heart rumbled. Something was in there. Something "confidential". Something powerful enough to shut off power around it.

A group of Union Keepers huddled and spoke irrationally toward each other. Whatever was being said, nothing could hide their nervous sweat. Not until Willie saw one of them continuously pressing the trigger lightly on his gun did he realize the truth. Their guns had stopped working. Fingerprint scans were necessary for the guns to fire. The surge had killed their weapons too?

After the trailer docked, Willie supervised as the lock around the trailer doors was severed by bolt cutters and the doors swung open. Inside was an enormous black box; practically the same length as the 53 foot trailer. It had what seemed to be a control panel. Lots of buttons and keypads, but no screen anywhere. What was this thing?

"Oh what the hell? Where we supposed to put that?"

"It's not even on a pallet, how's the forklift gonna get it out?"

While the men complained about the shipment, lack of power, and their dead cellphones, Willie approached the driver's door. Doing some paperwork on a clipboard, the driver didn't glance up as he climbed out of the truck. "You William Cooper?"

Rubbing his head to gather his composure and professionalism, Willie answered, "Yes."

"Sign here and here," the trucker said handing him the clipboard.

Normally, he'd keep his nose out of things he didn't need to know, but this was different. Willie never before experienced such loss of electricity. He asked, "What is it?"

Like he said it for the hundredth time today, the trucker answered, Classified. Even I don't know."

As he signed the paperwork, Willie tried to squeeze anything else out of him. "Did you at least get a name of what it was?"

"Guys at that government building in Nevada kept calling it 'Project Syncope'."

"Project Syncope," Willie repeated questionably. The name didn't ring a bell.

"All I know is," the chubby trucker said retrieving the clipboard from Willie and breaking off his copy, "I am damn glad to get his off my truck. You have any idea how it is to drive around with no power? Can't even listen to the goddang radio. Had to use flashlights for headlights. Everywhere I drove, all power went out. No zaps or surges. Just like someone turned off a light switch."

Willie bit his lip. "Thanks, boss."

As he climbed into the truck, the trucker said one more thing before closing the door. "You know what's crazy?"

"What?"

"If that *thing* is that strong now…imagine what it'll do when it's turned on."

CHAPTER SIXTEEN

Different countries had lines drawn amongst them for a reasons. People liked segregation because they were...segregated. Then the Union comes along to force the defiant system to a become peaceful. For some, shaking hands amongst peers was easy. For others...not so much. Gerard took a huge breath, wishing peace wasn't so difficult.

Today, he had to train thirteen soldiers in combat. Thirteen soldiers from seemingly thirteen opposite countries.

"In Pakistan, you would be hung for such hypocrisy!" One soldier said, finger thrusting upwards.

"This isn't Pakistan...it's the *Union*, dip-shit," Another soldier, probably American judging by the hick accent, said sarcastically. "We got none of them stupid names anymore."

Partially true, but not completely. The Press had trouble explaining the new map according to the Union. Basically, the continents were what separated the Union's districts; not countries. The United States' name (the name men and women died to protect) was now merged with Mexico and Canada to become The North American Union. Or the NAU, as though who hate using long titles deemed it.

Gerard rolled his eyes. He tightened his dark blue obi, a belt well deserved for years of training in Aikido. The others wore white uniforms and white belts. Not only could the soldiers barely hold their formation, they could barely hold their mouths.

"Shut it," Gerard commanded. "Backs straight. Eyes to me."

Most of them complied, a few took longer to follow his instruction after finishing a whispered conversation. But after a minute, the dojo finally had a moment of silence.

Barefoot on the room-sided mat, Gerard paced his group of individuals ready for training. "You are here, because you ass wipes are the first batch of genetically modified Union Keepers. Swimming inside your veins are nanobots. They will enhance your body's natural strength and speed. Does this mean you can pickup a car? No. But it means you can dodge one."

Under his breath, one of the Union Keepers looked at the dark-skinned gentleman to his right. "You hear that, *Habib?* That means you can dodge a camel now." A few muffled giggles interrupted Gerard's train of thought. He stopped and sighed. This was Marcel's idea of global equality? Adult men bickering like school boys?

"I'm from Istanbul, asshole. We don't use camels," the Turk retorted.

"Oh, great, we got a damn Muslim in the room."

"The Union isn't about religions anymore, you goddamn spic!"

"Yeah, because you assholes kept bombing people over a stupid Bible and ruined it for the rest of us!"

Gerard stepped up to the student he suspected to have the biggest mouth and cockiest attitude. Judging by his missing teeth, bad hygiene, and southern accent, he assumed the jackass could've been from Alabama or any of those other south states that still flew the confederate flag on their front lawns. "We are not here to bitch and whine. We are here to learn how to control the nanobots."

As expected, the arrogant American spat back, "We know how to control them."

Quickly, Gerard threw a punch and it landed on the redneck's throat. He fell to one knee, grasping his throat. Gerard snorted, "No…you don't. Or else, you would've seen that coming." As he walked away, the student mumbled something through a bruised Adam's apple. Gerard paced the group again, "Nanos live in your adrenaline. So you must learn to control that. You must always be on the edge of…" He paused to search for the proper word.

The only student who showed any interest spoke up. "Fear?"

"Yes," Gerard nodded, "Exactly. You must always be scared shitless idiots, instead of just regular idiots."

"So you teaching us to be pussies?" Someone snickered. "Great, he's teaching us to be French."

Bickering broke amongst the uniformed officers again, like a dam shattering. Gerard couldn't make out much of the arguments. The ones he did comprehend were ridiculous stereotypes about towels on heads and gun-toting hillbillies. Gerard held up his hands. "Shut up! Jesus, things were easy when we had borders."

Then a voice echoed in the dojo. "Actually, things were much tougher when we had borders." Everyone quieted at the familiar voice.

Marcel.

He entered from the north entrance. Wearing a pure white Karate uniform and black belt reminding Gerard that he was outranked. It also reminded him of how Marcel had grown up. Even though his best friend was five years younger, he seemed five years older. Sleepless eyes left dark circles and speckles of gray showed what forty did to male hair color. Still, Gerard felt proud of what Marcel had become. In High School, he had been the shy guy, a Senator's son, in the back of the classroom secretly acing all the quizzes.

Officers' feet smacked together, backs straightened, and their right fists covered the spot on their chests where a heart beat. Better than the salute Hitler received, but still as creepy. Gerard just stood there. Saluting Gerard would've felt like saluting Nelson. Family was family, not leaders.

Marcel pointed to a wall. "Do you see that?" Hesitant heads turned. Secured to the east wall hung two weapons, each with wooden handles and extended curved steel. The tip of the blades were so thinly sharp, they looked like paper from this distance. "Those are called Kama, or some would call Double Kai. It's a Japanese weapon originally intended for slicing crops before being used to slice throats." Next to it, Marcel introduced another weapon that looked like big enough to carve a turkey for Thanksgiving and cut it in half too. The nearly foot long single-sided sword gleamed under the above lights. "That is the Butterfly Sword from Southern China, roughly the size of a human forearm is meant for stabbing." At the first right of the dojo, a beautiful practice room with bamboo walls, was a pair of black sticks with dragon imprints in an X formation. "Those are the Escrima Sticks from the Philippines. Don't be fooled by their simple style, the Escrima art has been around since the early 1600s and that weapon can hinder a man unconscious in less than four seconds." He made his way towards the front of the group and stood before the trainees. "You know why I created this dojo with such unique weapons. To prove a point. Every country…knows how to fight. It doesn't matter where you are from, but who you fight for."

The students nodded in agreement. If only Gerard could muster obedience so easily. He had to admire Marcel;

admire him for how much others admired him. He built quite a reputation and there was no doubt who these students wanted to battle for.

Gerard, finally the center of attention again, continued teaching. "Martial Arts is an *art*. When nanotechnology first started, scientists made the product but couldn't figure out to control it. Like how I can't control some of you fuckers. It wasn't science they needed to guide it, but...art. So once people were trained in Tai-Chi, Kung Fu, and all these styles...they were able to create a flow. Once the flow happens, you have an offense and defense. That's it. Cause and effect. Like a game of chess. One move at a time." He looked over at Marcel, poised and proud in the corner watching. Moments like this, Marcel showcased his passion for equality worldwide. He had once said what would the world be like if everyone became blind. A world without prejudice. It seemed improbable, not impossible. Marcel Celest's vision was what made him so popular. The most imaginative of leaders garnered the most respect, but also the most ridicule. And his opposition grew expediently. They gathered in an underground bunker with plans to end his reign, his vision, and his leadership. Maybe Gerard could warn him. Tell him where the People of Bliss hid. But instead, he decided to see the true struggles in his best friend's mind. The easiest way to discover that...was in a battle. "How about a demonstration for them, Marcel?"

A student interjected. "That's disrespectful. He's the *Supreme Leader*."

Marcel held up his hand. "I appreciate the deference, but this an old friend. He can call me what he wants." With a big smile, he answered, "And yes, let's do a demonstration. It's been a while since I spiked these nanos in me."

The students stepped back, clearing the center mat and sat down on the outer edges of the dojo while Marcel slipped on a head guard and mouth piece. Gerard preferred no safety gear, he'd taken worse punches. They both stood at opposite ends of the mat. Since this was a class, Gerard instructed the students further. "Harnessing your adrenal glands is important. With training, you can voluntarily send that signal to your mind and slow the pace of time in your mind. Your reactions will be quicker."

Then he experienced a flutter in his ear. It sounded like a palmetto bug searching for a place to land, a familiar and welcome feeling as the nanobots in his adrenaline gland rushed to heighten his senses and slow his perception of time. After a cordial bow to each other, Marcel dashed forward in a formation of punches, kicks, and uppercuts. Gerard swung out of the way of each, sweeping downward and tripping Marcel to the ground. One of the students sucked his teeth while another one booed. Gerard smiled like he'd just been knighted.

Not prepared to look weak to his strongest constituents, the Supreme Leader leapt up, his foot so close to Gerard's face he could smell it. He backed off while he watched a more aggressive Marcel, a more stressed Marcel, throw punches with fury like Brent.They were becoming alike, infuriated with the paths they'd taken. And Gerard saw this, as he did when he battled Brent, as an opportunity to show weakness. He hadn't felt a rush like this in months. The thrill of the fight. Before, the only action Gerard had was catching his pen before it fell off the desk. He blocked several punches before allowing one to slip by and hit his upper lip. Marcel stopped, catching his breath and instantly became worried. "I didn't mean to –"

But he did. The Supreme Leader meant to bust Gerard's lip, because he needed a punching bag. And Gerard was going to give him the opportunity. Because if Hitler had been aware of his own cruelty, understood it, then maybe he'd chosen a different path.

The sparring didn't pause. Marcel fought and block, Gerard spun kicks. Then at a final moment, Marcel grasped Gerard and shoved him to the ground. He began ravenously kicking his face. Gerard pretended like the hits hurt by covering his face and screaming. He shouted with a suppressed grin, "Marcel! Please!"

Marcel stepped back, sweat dripping from his head gear. He ripped it off. "Oh Jesus," he whispered, "I'm sorry. I…"

Trying to helpless, for perhaps the first time in his life, Gerard crossed his hands in front of his face. If he was talented like those soap opera stars, he could conjure up some tears and make Marcel's soul rip in two.

"Seriously," Marcel insinuated. "I didn't mean it." He held out his hand to help Gerard stand.

But something unexpected happened. He didn't like not being prepared for moments like this. Blood poured out of Marcel's right nostril. Acting over now, Gerard pointed to Marcel's nose. "You're bleeding."

The Supreme Leader dabbed it with the back of his hand and looked at the large amount of blood. "You got me good."

"I never hit you in the face."

Before Marcel could question it further, he slumped over and collapsed to the floor unconscious.

CHAPTER SEVENTEEN

Blacker than black. Darker than dark. More nothing than nothing. Marcel Celest had travelled the cosmos in dark energy but never seen anything so black. The Doctor kept talking, saying something about the treatments for cancer. How advanced the treatments have become. How in the final stages, the odds of defeating cancer lessened. Every time he said the word *cancer*, Marcel's heart skipped a beat. He never looked away from the x-ray of his lung, secured to a white light background. Still so dark. Blackness swallowed his right lung and parts of his left. His ability to heal expediently had no power against this. Because this was beyond even his capabilities of evil.

Gerard put a hand on his shoulder. A show of comfort. But nothing could comfort this. How does anyone respond to finding a friend succumbing to cancer? *You'll pull through.* No, Marcel wouldn't pull through this. *You should spend your final days with family.* No, Marcel's family hated him. *There's a chance of a cure.* No, there wasn't. He could control minds and influence the elements, but not defeat the blackness swallowing him into an abyss.

The Doctor tried to explain that smoking all those years caused the tumor. Marcel's struggle to quit cigarettes ended up another regretful decision; he was going to die anyways. But something told him, tobacco didn't do this. Darkness did. Was Lucifer aware this could happen to him? Marcel had been one of several humans in history with the ability to change the future. Lucifer told him all people had fates, except for a minute few and those progenies could alter the future. But had his predecessors experienced this same side effect? Cancer? Pain? Death?

Why didn't Lucifer warn him?

"Can I have a moment please?" Marcel said, not sure if the Doctor was done speaking. "With my friend?"

The Doctor seemed hurt by the word *friend,* then looked at Gerard as though there was confusion who Marcel meant. Gerard often got this look; the look of jealousy. It must've made him feel like a gold medal winner. The Doctor walked out the office and closed the door.

Marcel slumped back on the stool; the stool he didn't remember even standing up from to get a closer view of the x-ray. Gerard had never gotten to his feet, maybe he hadn't been as surprised. Sure, Marcel smoked but not everyone who smoked contracted lung cancer. Not in a time when the disease was practically curable.

Thankful that Gerard didn't say *I'm sorry,* Marcel enjoyed the silence for a moment. He thought about Lucifer's action, or lack of action actually, so shortly after they compromised. If cancer was a component to the power of dark energy, even a simple warning would've sufficed.

In an effort to break the silence in this already quiet white room, Gerard said, "Guess quitting cigarettes did you no good. Wow. It almost looks like…" He turned his head side-to-side, staring at the x-ray pictures as though it was an expensive abstract painting and trying to figure out what people saw in it. "Looks like a monster."

Marcel snorted, but then took a broader look at the x-ray. Two spots, not infected by cancerous cells, did insinuate slit eyes. If he stared long enough, he could almost see jagged teeth. "Yeah. Yeah, it does." But he read about this before. Often an object couldn't be seen until it's implied, sort of like the way some people would see Jesus Christ in toasted bread. It was nothing more than an illusion.

Wasn't it?

"Should we tell the Press?"

"No," Marcel said, without thinking. "This is a way to show weakness. I don't trust the Press." Gerard didn't seem to agree or disagree, he just nodded. "I don't trust anyone," Marcel whispered, "except you. I can…trust you. Right?"

They stared at each other a long time, the faint light from the display colored half his face gray. It reminded him of Brent, for a moment, battling between the black and whites of the world. Then finally, Gerard answered, "No."

After seeing a vast tumor in his lungs, nothing should shock Marcel at this point, but he was. "No?"

"You shouldn't trust anyone, Marcel. I don't. Look at my wife. I trusted her and now she's ran away to be with those hippy rebels. The less you trust, the less you'll be let down."

Sensing Gerard was just being humble, he nodded. Marcel stared at the black spot on his lungs. But perhaps his brother-in-law was right. He had trusted Lucifer and had been let down.

Lost. Somewhere, like a forest at night. Unsure of the direction. Unsure of the location. Unsure of the will to live. Marcel swallowed another glass of the whiskey. It burned. He never enjoyed the taste of alcohol, the dizziness of alcohol, and the loss of self. But loss of self was exactly what he needed. To flow on a river out of his congested mind, that swam with questions. Questions only one person could answer. And that person wasn't a person at all. Lucifer. A creature created by the dark energy of the universe. All that power and yet it still relied on deceit. It had lived perhaps millions of years. Marcel had been only this planet for 38 years, so of course Lucifer knew more. Before he found out cancer began digging a coffin for him, Marcel trusted the dark lord's words. But now...

He drank what was left in the glass and flung it at the painting of George Washington on the wall, wishing his cancer would melt away like the vibrant colors on that masterpiece. No one knew much about the awful things the first President of the United States had done. Because everyone only focused on the good in people and their image. Lucifer formed an image of sincerity, professionalism, and determination. His exact words were "I want to save the world". But did he? If so, why wouldn't he appear more often? Why would he curse the leader of the world with cancer?

Marcel paced the dining room, circling around the wooden table that could fit sixteen people but yet no one but him ate here almost every night. The curtains swayed even though the windows stayed closed; Wind enjoyed Marcel's dismay, as always.

The issue with questions wasn't the act of asking them, but hearing the answers. Because only one of two things can happen with an answer; it's either an answer you wanted to hear...or an answer you don't. Most likely, especially from Lucifer, it wouldn't be a favorable answer.

"I wouldn't say that," Lucifer said, appearing out of nowhere as usual. He sat in a chair at the head of the table. A place usually occupied by Marcel himself.

Another lie. The agreement had been that Lucifer wouldn't be in Marcel's head, reading his thoughts or making decisions. "You're in my mind…"

"Actually, the opposing factor has bound us. You are in my effervescence, my locality, my…energy. I strive to not perceive your thoughts; leaving you 'free will' as they call it."

More convoluted talk. Just like biblical lingo, Lucifer's words could be taken in several interpretations. What did it all mean? "Speak clearly," Marcel spat, "Tell me why you are here? What do you want?"

"Did we not speak of this manner beforehand? As we traveled amongst the stars and planets? Earth, as it is named, needs to be preserved. And I appointed you because it is within your competence to do so."

Absolutely, Marcel knew he had the capability to bring the dream of world peace to a reality. But the answer didn't bring him peace. Lucifer had a plan, but didn't seem too concerned with sharing it. "Why didn't you tell me there was a price to pay?"

Staring with those crystal blue eyes at him, the devil seemed to fit his title of the master of evil. For being in the embodiment of a nine year old boy in a prim suit and red tie, he looked quite terrifying. It wasn't until this moment Marcel realized that Lucifer never blinked. He had read once that psychopaths didn't blink much either. It was a predator's way of studying its prey. "You must refer to the cancer? Do you even fathom the agreement we made? Does a man with a lifejacket and umbrella jump into the Atlantic with the expectations of an elementary journey?"

Another vague response. "I'm going to die, goddamnit! Cancer is eating me alive!"

After a slight grin, Lucifer snorted, "You are not dying, Marcel. You are *living*. Becoming one with the dark energy.

You are experiencing what's beyond this realm. Understanding the elements. Seeing the shades of the Gray mist. And dancing with Death."

Beyond the point of subtle aggravation, Marcel picked up a chair and flung it across the room. "So what's that mean? I don't want to die! Not until…" He stopped and thought to himself what to say next. So many people on this planet wouldn't hesitate to find a reason to live, but Marcel just had. After a deep breath, he muttered, "Not until world peace is a reality. Not until my mother's vision comes true. I can't die. I don't want to."

"Then do not die."

Feeling exhausted from the act of throwing a chair, Marcel's lungs gasped for air a few times before he could speak again. "How? How do I cure this?"

"Maybe it is time to stop holding your breath as you sink into the quick sand. Breath it. Breath death. Breath your future. Breath the elements. Breath…," Lucifer paused, "…me.

Someone knocked on the door and opened it at the same time. Marcel turned to see his brother-in-law standing at the entrance. Usually quick and on-point, Gerard seemed thrown aback. He just stood for a moment and then finally said, "I need to talk to you."

"What is it?"

He noticed the broken chair on the floor, but chose to ignore it. "Just got a call that they found your dad."

Since hearing the news of cancer, Marcel needed to hear something positive. And this was it. The elusive thought danced in his head. "Dad? He's alive?" He could even hear the giddiness in his voice. The last time he saw his father hadn't been well. Nelson stared at him with disappointment. Marcel hated that look. "He's in good health?"

Gerard shrugged. "I'm not sure. I only heard he was captured on a ship. I'm getting together some detail and we'll be flying out soon. Better get ready."

CHAPTER EIGHTEEN

If Royal saw this, she'd ask why Adam was in *cahoots* with an enemy. He could hear her southern accent, see her sour face, and feel her scorn. Even all the way from Russia. Becoming allies with someone who only a year ago threw him in prison couldn't make this situation stranger. Neither side seemed to trust the other. Gerard kept his distance, close enough to hear but not close enough to shake hands.

A mosquito bit him again, but he didn't move to swat the damn thing away. Who knew if Gerard was armed. With his feet sinking into the marsh and the duck tape on his sneakers beginning to loosen as swamp water seeped in, Adam knew he'd better get out of this situation quick. If Janice wasn't wondering where he had gone to, surely some member of the silo would grow suspicious. They may not have known about this place. "You got it?"

"Do you?" Gerard spat out, ready with the retort.

Next to a pipe, large enough to ride a bike through, sewage pumped out of the silo and close to Adam's feet. He was covered in the gunk. Not his proudest moment, but secrecy was a must. If Gerard hadn't shown up for their weekly rendezvous in a Union uniform, black with blue trimming and several honorary pins secured to his shoulder, maybe Adam could've played it off as a recruit to the People of Bliss. Being caught right now would surely mean the end to both their goals.

From his back pocket, Gerard yanked out a Manila envelope, keeping their eyes fixed. Sneezing in this dense fog could mean a bullet in his chest by his new still-reluctant ally. He tossed the envelope and Adam looked inside. Five pages of documents was more than he anticipated. After glancing through the names listed, recognizing a few of them, Adam said, "You probably wondering what I need this for."

"Not really," Gerard shrugged. "I need my drive."

From his front pocket, Adam produced a small USB drive. He threw it too high, not nearly as swift and precise as Gerard's throw, but he caught it anyway. "I need more time to deliver the rest of the ledger."

As he expected, the husband of the woman he slept next to every night didn't seem pleased. His lip curled. "You promised."

"I know, I know." Adam held his hands up, like trying to calm an unsettled horse. "But hear me out, there's a lot of people here. *And* I have to get them locater chips in their palms. Not an easy task. I've been lying to them all, saying its a vaccine for the new flu. If we don't do this in an organized fashion, then the plan falls apart."

Gerard stayed silent for so long that Adam wasn't sure if the conversation ended. "Does she have one?"

Knowing instantly who the *she* was the referred to, Adam answered, "We haven't speaking much lately. I injected the chip in her hand when she fell asleep. It's a quick prick. She's usually such a light sleeper, I thought she would've woken up."

"I know she's a light sleeper. She's my wife. I know she rubs Vicks Vapor Rub on her chest, because the smell puts her to sleep. I know she likes to cuddle under a comforter, even when its warm inside. I know she never snores, regardless of how rough her day was. No matter how many nights you stoop her. Or hold her hand. Or hold that body. I still love her. I'm still her husband. You got that?"

He'd been in more than a few fights in his life, but Adam faced perhaps one of the toughest fighters in his life, therefore one of the scariest. If urine hadn't been exiting the pipe behind him, Adam would've questioned if he just pissed himself. Gerard repeated, in a lower voice. "You got that?"

Was he asking him to part ways with Janice? Or was he just reaffirming that Janice still wore his ring and he wore hers? Unsure what exactly the threat was, he knew it was a threat irregardless. Adam answered, "Yeah. Yeah, I got it." His socks started to get wet. He was due for a very, very long shower after this. "Can I go now?"

"How many more drives you got for me?"

"Just one. Promise."

"You better," Gerard scowled as he turned to leave.

Adam could've turned to leave too, but instead watched as Gerard climbed on a motorcycle and took off into the darkest of nights. What had he gotten himself into?

CHAPTER NINETEEN

-Taken to subway station.

-Zharkova: "For you to learn how to win, you must first learn how to lose."

-Tough Russian women surround her in subway tram.

-Zharkova speaks russian to tough women. "I told them you are an American that thinks you are the best country in the world. And that Mother Russia is nothing but a bunch of cocksucking communists."

-Tough women beat Royal until she blacks out.

Nine months ago, this subway station must've been bustling with tourists. Royal would have to use her imagination nowadays. Not a single visitor ever entered these premises. As they on a bench across from the tracks, Royal pondered if she should ask Zharkova how many Russians died on Doomsday. But surely the witch's head would turn backward and breath fire.

Zharkova tapped her shoe impatiently. They were Alfani footwear. Seems the devil doesn't wear Prada. "Finally," she whispered.

What they were doing here or what was about to happen remained a mystery to Royal. All she knew was it took almost an hour of awkward silence. A slight breeze entered the station and the sound of whistling could be heard through the tunnel. A train was coming! Royal had never rode an actual underground subway train before. Maybe they were leaving and escaping this station full of piss, feces, and death smells.

As soon as the excitement hit her, it turned into caution. Why was there a train here? Royal had lived underground for almost two weeks and a train had never passed before.

It pulled up with only one car connected. She'd seen these vehicles on television and movies, but they didn't look anything like this. Graffiti painted the vehicle with purple and pink Russian lettering. It looked old and rusted.

Still not explaining anything, Zharkova walked up to the car and the doors opened. The lights were off inside. With one hand on her cane and the other holding the door open, Zharkova's eyebrows raised. "Are you stupid, Aurora? Go inside goddamnit."

"Please don't use the Lord's name in vain."

"Goddamnit! Now!"

After a deep breath and long exhale, Royal stepped into the subway car. The lights may have been off but enough could be seen. It looked just like what she imagined: seats made of torn felt, steel bars to grasp onto that had more germs than a toilet seat, and leftover trash tossed to the ground. What she hadn't imagined: the vehicle wasn't unoccupied.

Four women stared at her. One had a shaved head with eye drop tattoo and wore a white tank top. Another had a pink mohawk. Long fingernails drummed impatiently against the third girl's crossed arms. The last girl had gold teeth and brass knuckles. All the girls had crunched eyebrows and bitter frowns.

At the door way, Zharkova didn't enter the subway car but just held the sliding door open. "I told them you are a cold-hearted American that thinks Russians deserved this chemical war. That you piss on every dead Russian you walk past."

Astonished, Royal's eyes widened. "Why?"

"Because, Aurora, in order for you to learn how to win a fight...you must learn how to lose one." Zharkova said as she stepped back and the door slid closed.

Royal tried to open the door with her fingers, but could barely get it to budge. Zharkova rolled her eyes behind the glass then snorted.

Behind her, the girl with brass knuckles tapped them against the metal pole as a way to get Royal's attention. She turned slowly to her inevitable attackers. "Look, I ain't like that. I didn't say none of those things."

"They don't speak English, stupid girl," Zharkova said behind the door.

Trying to use body language to convey some sort of mistake, Royal looked more like a drunken mime. The girl with long fingernails charged up to her. Before Royal could even cover her face, the first slap hit her so hard there were stars in front. Then brass knuckles struck her in the cheek. Royal fell to the ground, pleading. "Please! Please!"

Three or four of the girls started kicking. They had steel-toe boots on. Royal kept screaming, "Please!" Her screams became gargled by blood coming from her mouth. Long fingernails slapped several times leaving scars across Royal's face. The pink mohawk girl must've been envious of all that brunette hair on Royal's head, because she grabbed it with big twist. An uppercut crunched Royal's chin a few more times then the mohawk girl threw her into a metal pole.

Royal felt dizzy. Everything spun like she'd been rolling down a hill in a barrel. She was chewing on something, but it definitely wasn't gum or candy; Royal spat it out. It was her molar tooth. "Please! Leave me alone! I didn't do anything."

A few more punches to the face and Royal began to say the Lord's prayer. She was going to die.

Then the beating stopped as sudden as it started. The door slid open and Zharkova came in. Panic made Royal's heart jump. An evil dictator that planned this attack must've had a way to end it. Maybe a gun. Maybe a bat. Maybe a bucket of acid. Then she'd giggle as her Aurora hollered in agony. Staring up at Zharkova, Royal tried to hurry away using only her elbows to scurry backwards. "Please leave me alone! Please!"

"Silly girl, crawling away like some crab. A crab facing a shark. You've got claws that could rip my skin, gouge out my eyeballs, and teeth powerful enough to make me bleed…and yet *you* run away in fear? *You* don't want to kill me. All you want is to scurry away?" Zharkova giggled. "Can you feel that fear? The wrath of a predator casting its shadow upon you. I've felt it. As an Iraqi soldier stood above my beaten body with a knife in my kneecap, bloody right hand, and a gun in my left hand. Guess who shot first? I did. Do you think he gave me the opportunity to scurry away backwards?"

After a brief exchange in Russian language, the four girls left the subway car. Royal stared at Russia's Prime Minister until her breathing returned to normal. Though her body was screaming in pain, the woman had a point. Royal could be dead. In a fight such as the fight to be against Marcel Celest, surely she wouldn't be given the choice to get up and walk away.

She fought the urge to ask for a doctor or an emergency clinic. Instead, Royal stumbled to her feet. Being only able to see out of one eye meant she had one hell of a bruise forming.

After a short snort, Zharkova said, "Well. At least you stood up. Maybe there's hope for you. Come with me. Shower then start dinner."

CHAPTER TWENTY

The warehouse had an intricate labyrinth of storage, mainly because the facility stored what was leftover from cleanups of major cities. Mostly items that couldn't be identified or thought to be useless to the future of the Union. Willie, with tablet in hand, inspected the shelves high enough to create quite a catastrophe if they ever toppled over. He found something thinking like this, ever since Doomsday. Imagining the worse case scenario.

With his thumbprint, a lift activated and elevated him to fifth row of storage. Thankfully, Willie never had much of a fear of heights because this would be the moment to be terrified. On a wobbly lift, fifty feet in the air and tethered via a harness, he stopped at the B3 cubical area. He removed his harness, an annoyance to him not only because they crunched his manhood but because they were an essentially useless safety rule. What if the whole lift fell over? Would he really want to be harnessed to a falling lift?

He unlocked the storage container with his thumb print and opened the doors. Inside it smelled like the inside of a port-a-potty. Older items always had that stinky odor,

Grandpa's basement smelled the same. Dead bodies had that same stench too.

His job could be described as a dream job. Supervising a warehouse included scheduling import and export trucks, managing employees, and organizing stock. A dream job until moments like this. Who knew what was brought in from these container trucks. It was his duty to find out. Most times it was a single object, like a decommissioned car to be recycled for scrap metal. Sometimes it could be a piece of a jigsaw, clueless pieces to a larger structure. Just last week, Willie solved a slew of seemingly crazy metal fragments. Together it formed The Charging Bull, an art piece in the center of Wall Street. Somehow it ended up in the outskirts of Ithaca, almost 250 miles away. Scientists had said the nuclear blasts could've carried debris over 100 miles from ground zeros. That statue proved the estimates were far worse.

Crates lined up the walls of the containers. The truck driver hadn't bothered to secure them, so most of the junk fell onto the floor. It was going to be a long day logging all this stuff. He knelt down and picked up the first item. A half-charred toy, Barbie doll perhaps, but it had no head. Willie photographed it using the camera of the tablet; the computer took only two and a half seconds to recognize it. He was right. Malibu Barbie, to be exact. The head popped off, but if he could just find it he was sure some little girl at the silo would love it.

The silo. He hadn't thought of that place in over a week. Spending almost over night watching television or play video games at home made him forget about his actual home. But did any of the People of Bliss even miss him? No one, including Adam, hadn't even attempted to contact him via letter or secured phone call. He put the doll down and gave up his search.

After two hours, Willie had logged 143 items in this container. Some toys, cosmetics, torn clothing, picture frames with no pictures, hair brushes still with strands, and a few used coffee makers. But just as he went back to the container doors to shut them, something occurred to him. All these useless items had a use. They all belonged to someone. A person. A man or woman. A child. If souls stayed with everything they touched his life, he was about to lock it all away in a container forever perhaps.

Was this the Union's intention of this place? To make the past disappear, the way he made his memories of the silo disappear by throwing aside that doll? Surely the past held more importance than the future. Something grumbled in the pit of his stomach and it wasn't because he was late to lunch. His radio chirped before he could give it more thought.

"Yo," he said into the handset.

Instead of crackling from normal radio handsets, these came in loud and clear. "We got visitors. They need to see the supervisor."

Odd, because he didn't have any meetings scheduled today. "What for? Tell them we got work to do."

"Boss, it's the Tech Czar."

Hoping that the man on the other end of the line had the courtesy to be in a private area, not an area where these visitors could hear him, Willie shrugged, "Who's that?"

"Big wig. Come down. He's got keepers with him."

Willie started wondering if he wasn't the only one that got the shakes around Union Keepers. Reluctantly, he locked the container doors and descended on the lift. A Czar? From the Union? Known as the top of the ladder positions, czars had the final say in almost every decision. Except that of the Supreme Leader himself Marcel Celest. Willie didn't know what to expect. Had they figured out he had been a part of the resistance? How would they know? Even the People of Bliss barely remembered his name. It wasn't possible.

The chip! Adam had placed a dummy chip in his hand to try and bypass Union databases. It would make sense now why the technology leader awaited him down in the lobby. Willie immediately relived that moment in his past, being a juvenile delinquent in front of a judge having to answer for his crime. And just like then, he would have to play dumb.

Downstairs, he followed the long hallway of skyscraper shelving. He checked his watch. It still hadn't turned on since that machine fried all the electronics around it. Project Syncope. He checked the tablet database and it still was located at the dock. Crew couldn't get the damn heavy thing out of the trailer. Since electronics didn't work around it, the electric pallet jacks were obsolete. For now, it had to stay in there.

He met the Tech Czar outside the break room. Surrounded by six Union Keepers, the man seemed fit enough to handle any altercation without their help. His chiseled biceps nearly tore through that fancy polo collared shirt. When he shook his hand, Willie cringed at the tight grip. This man had strength, looks, and apparently to get into this position he had smarts too. "I'm Lester."

Willie had seen some muscle hunks in his life. For some reason, homosexual men set higher standards and strived for perfection. Liposuction, fitness, collagen, manicures, pedicures, whatever it took to look flawless. But Lester fell into a different category. He didn't strive for perfection, he was perfection. So much so that his name didn't seem to fit his physique. Muscle jocks went by names like Kyle, Cody, Max, or Rex. Manly names. Not Lester…

"William. Friends call me Willie."

With his cocked and smile even more cocked, Lester asked, "Can I call you Willie?"

He had been arrested many times in his youth, so he knew a situation was going in that direction. But for now, the threat didn't seem real. The Union Keepers barely paid attention, instead they circled the lunch truck buying snacks. If Willie was in trouble, it didn't seem too serious.

"Sure you can, bro. What can I do you for?"

"Well, I heard through the grapevine there's a questionable machine here. I'd like to take a look at it."

The czar was here for the machine! Though relieved this wasn't a visit about Willie's fake chip, it still made him feel uneasy. Surely the czar was a busy man, so why make time to come out here for a machine? And his office was in the Union Castle, that must've been quite a trek. "Project Syncope?" Willie asked, as though there was some other interesting machine in this building full of junk.

"Yes, can you show me it...Willie?"

As if the request could be met with a "no" answer, he answered affirmatively. Without the accompany of the Union Keepers, Willie led his guest through the corridors to the dock where the trailer was still parked. "We still haven't figured out what to do with it. If I were you, leave any electronics on the table there."

Lester didn't listen. Instead he walked toward the trailer with cellphone in his hand. And in seconds, his cellphone screen went blank. Like everyone who witnessed the power of this device, he played with the cellphone attempting to restart it. "Fascinating," was all the czar could say. "It melted the battery."

While Lester opened the doors and circled the beautiful black metal exterior of Project Syncope, Willie got that feeling again. That peaceful feeling of zero electronic waves or pulses in the air around the equipment. What did the czar want with this machine? Willie could only think of two reasons: either the Union would want to destroy it before the resistance got it or use it as a weapon against the resistance. If Doomsday taught anything, it was that governments shouldn't be allowed to get their hands on dangerous weapons. Willie wished he had hid this device or taken more interest in studying it more, but he gotten so sucked into the world of a digital home and detailed job.

"Did it come with anything else? Like, this may seem silly, a manual or something?"

It did have a manual, still in Willie's locker. Just like that day in front of the judge, he played stupid. "No. I haven't seen a manual."

Lester stared at him, reading his "Shame." Lester said. "I'm going to assemble a team of scientists to come by next weekend to study it some more. Maybe figure out what makes it tick. We don't want something like this zapping electronics."

Enjoying the peace of no electrical signals, Willie couldn't help but ask, "Why not?" Once again, his mouth was about to get him in trouble. His mother used to say maybe consider cutting his tongue out sometimes. It may have been a simple question but also a suspicious one to someone in charge of technology.

Lester squinted his eyes then smiled. "You hungry? I know the perfect burger joint."

After Lester finished ordering from the menu, Willie wasn't sure if he had ordered for the both of them. Even the waitress, in that pink checkerboard outfit, seemed confused until Lester spoke up. "What are you having, Willie?"

Certainly not three full mouth burgers, two order of chili cheese fries, and an extra large milk shake. "I'll have the hamburger meal with fries and no ketchup."

The waitress nodded and wrote on her tablet with a stylus. "Not a problem," she said way more chipper than any server he'd met in New England. Like much of the employment under the Union, people were chosen based on their genetics. And she liked her job about as much as Willie had.

Except for now.

Being a supervisor had its perks, but meeting with bigwigs wasn't Willie's style. He found himself frantically searching his mind for something to talk about like searching for an outfit to wear clubbing.

Lester broke the tone. "Why did you do that?"

"What?"

"Order a hamburger without ketchup?"

Honestly, Willie never had a fondness for the taste or the look; ever since he saw Carrie covered in pig's blood - ketchup just didn't appeal to him. But instead of ruining his boss's appetite, he stuck to the basics. "We're all different, I guess."

The empty diner played some pop music; older pop music since even the saddest of musicians couldn't find solace in writing new songs. Lester grabbed Willie's palm suddenly. He felt that warm tension rise up his neck. Either he found Lester intimidating or attractive. "You still haven't fixed it yet, huh? Your chip. It got broken by the machine." Lester's hands felt like silk sheets. "Why haven't you fixed it yet?"

Rather than be honest and say if he went to get the chip replaced they'd noticed the old one was hacked by the People of Bliss, Willie chose to lie. "No time."

"And your watch too? All your co-workers got their equipment replaced after Syncope busted them. All…except you." Lester pulled his hands away slowly.

Willie shrugged, "We're all different, I guess. What was it that man said? *Technology can do so many things, but there are many things technology should never be allowed to do. And the way you not allow it – is not create it.*"

"Hmph. Elon Musk?"

"No, Tim Cook."

Leaning back, Lester stretched out and asked. "Don't you like being connected?"

The question made Willie feel slightly guilty, like he skipped class and was being questioned if he actually cared about his future. This time he decided not to lie. "But I like being disconnected sometimes do, you know what I'm saying? Don't want to be dumb. If we keep it up, you won't need teachers in classrooms. Just put a poster up in each class that says *Just Google It.*"

A plate of chili cheese fries plopped onto the table between them. Lester smothered the food with hot sauce and ketchup. "I read your profile," Lester said with a mouthful of chili, "Born in Camden, but raised in Philadelphia right?"

Swapping between custody of his mother or father, neither of which seemed interested in caring for a boy that blew up electronics around him, Willie was raised in more than just Philadelphia. But somehow the fact that Lester knew this disturbed him. What else could someone in the Union find out? Were there even secrets anymore? Medical, dental, residences, finances, everything were stored in one place now. Some main server that all these chips connected to. The thought made Willie feel slightly betrayed. As much as he loved tech, he didn't love being watched. "Yeah. Kinda lots of places, know what I'm saying, bod...I mean *bud*." He immediately wanted to slap himself on the head for the verbal slip.

His boss made no reaction and rested his perfectly sculpted arms on the table. There wasn't even hair on them. "I'm from Jersey myself. Short Hills. See? We're not so different. We've got a lot in common. I got my master's at Rutger's then completed my PhD at Kean. We're from the same area. We are going to be good friends."

The median price of a home in Short Hills was in the two million dollar range. Willie lived under a train station in Philly. He hadn't finished High School, failed his GED test twice, worked at a tire recycling yard for six years until he had enough money to move out of his old man's place. They couldn't be more than different. "Hmph yeah, boss. Not so different."

After a long uncomfortable silence, he wished the waitress would hurry up with that burger. At the diner's bar, a quick place for a quick meal, Willie listened to a conversation with a patron and the waitress. Agitated and fed up with the patron, he could hear her repeatedly say "Chip purchases only." She even pointed to the sign. The patron, some guy with long dreaded hair and unkept beard, clasped his hands in a begging manner. Willie had met many homeless people living in Philadelphia. There were three stages of desperateness, on the verge of death, anger, or tears. That man was on the verge of tears. After a minute, a manager appeared and gently but forcefully pushed the homeless man outside the door.

With that same sly smile, Lester whispered. "Are you with the resistance?"

Unsure how to answer that, Willie paused. Blunt questions usually left him like this, with mouth half open and eyes completely open. Before he denied it, which of course he had to, Willie wondered if he still was with the People of Bliss? Sure hadn't felt like it lately. His assignment was to gather intelligence but Willie found himself every night relaxing on a comfy couch watching the game on a large screen television. And every night he slumped into his pillow top mattress, he wondered if the People of Bliss even thought of him. Perhaps he could answer this without seeming like he was lying. "No. No, I'm not."

Wiping the bottom of the empty plate with his finger and licking it, Lester said. "I think you're with the People of Bliss."

Willie could feel his chest pulse up and down. From what he heard, martial law had been declared. And to save the paperwork, Union Keepers were just shooting first. Piles of dead bodies sometimes were left on the side of the street, not because they didn't have time to clean them up but instead to send a message. "Huh?"

"I'm just busting your balls, Willie," Lester snorted. "See? I got you to smile. We're going to get along just fine."

Maybe this was an interview for a best friend. Whatever the reason he was here, Willie couldn't help but notice the seats were becoming more uncomfortable. Finally, the waitress appeared. His plate had one burger and fries, while Lester's had three burgers. "That's quite an appetite, Chief."

Lester finished the first burger in four bites. Willie couldn't help but wonder what the secret had been to staying in great shape with a devouring stomach like that. Lester's forearms looked primed and lean as his hands grasped the second burger. "I couldn't help but notice," he said, mouth still full of food, "that everyone seemed panicked by the machine. Everyone…except you." Being that it was neither a question or accusation, Willie decided not to respond. "So," the Tech Czar swallowed what was left of the food, "Why not?"

"Well, you know, it doesn't seem like that big of a deal." Willie said, barely touching the fries on his plate.

"Not big of a deal?" Lester snorted again. "Are you kidding? It's a doomsday device."

Sarcastically, Willie replied, "We already had a doomsday, am I right?"

Lester finally stopped eating and glanced out the window, watching taxis and busses pass by. "I remember when I was a kid, my grandfather told me this story. He said he used to work this crappy job at a hotel when he was a teenager. The job was to go down a list of names and room numbers, call them, and wake them up at the specified time. He hated it. Said that people hung up on him, grumbled, were bitter and rude. But then, technology comes around and he got replaced with a machine that dialed the numbers for him and played a recording more polite than he could ever sound at five in the morning." With his elbows on the table, he sipped on an empty cup of soda loudly as though wasting even the ice cubes was against the law. He continued, "There's so many jobs that technology has taken from us, to ease our lives. Can you believe there used to be people that bagged food at grocery stores? Tellers at banks? Check-in personnel at airports? Tech has saved us from utter boredom. My department at the Union has created a convenience cloud system. Health records, you can bank and bills from one credit card, single payer system for all utilities, one grocery chain, one communications company for emails phones texts and letters…I mean, the world is much better. Even the Press has been replaced with computer systems, reporting *accurate* news for once."

Hearing about the Press just reminded Willie of her. Sirius Dawson was a reporter and she became the voice of the resistance. If she had been replaced by a computer, the People of Bliss would've never been born. The Press, no matter how people felt about it, was important. Willie shoved aside his plate of food, no longer hungry.

Lester continued, excited like a jockey talking about horse racing, "I used to be this fat tub of a man, in a wheelchair. I broke my left kneecap from the weight. Diabetes had caused me to get Peripheral arterial disease. So, to say the least, I am grateful for the Union. We have a department focused on the science and technology of stem cell research."

Willie lost an uncle to heart disease several years ago. Doctors had told them stem cells could save his life, but unfortunately due to governmental regulations, they couldn't perform the procedure. Flip-flopping back and forth with the legal restrictions, depending on the leadership, stem cell research showed signs of become a life changing science. Now, without those governmental regulations gone, Lester was a prime example of how the "perfect" someone could become.

Wiping his mouth with the back of his hand, Lester continued, "You would be a good candidate. I could put in a referral for you."

"Me?" Willie said, poking himself in the chest that used to be rock hard at a younger age but became a flappy at an older age.

"Sure! Why not? We could fix that balding spot. I mean, what are you 42? 43? And you're already balding that bad? We could remove the fat around your waist. Straighten those teeth too. Even fix that acne scarring on your neck." Lester put food in his mouth so the next words came out muffled, "Fix your sexuality." He awkwardly put more food in his mouth.

"Uh. What did you say, boss?"

"Your sexuality. I mean, come on! You glanced at my crotch the moment I walked in the door. Look. I'm not saying you have to give up having sex with men. Hell, I've had a few steamy nights with the same sex myself, if you know what I mean. But we can fix your genes so that you're bisexual. So that you're at least reproducing."

Willie swallowed back vomit. The world around him felt different, like a veil had just been pulled away to reveal darkness. It all felt so fake, like Lester's perfect bony cheeks. Everything had been structured; rebuilt to suit the needs of the Union. He could think of nothing else to say. "I have to go. It's been a long day."

"Oh, okay, buddy. Well, here's my card. Call me when you're ready to see someone better in that mirror." Lester said sliding the card across the table with ketchup-stained fingers.

Willie took it, trying to be polite, and stood up to leave.

"One more thing," Lester said, "Stop by the Union Institute to get that chip rebooted, would you?" He smiled. "It was nice meeting someone from the same neighborhood. Don't be mad at me. Friends are supposed to be honest with each other. Isn't that how it works?"

Without another word, Willie rushed out the front door.

This was all like that World Series game in 2016, everything going so right until the end. Willie stared out the window, as the taxi sped along the freeway. He was talking hockey again, but Willie kept his mouth shut and just watched the city pass by; Lester's words still repeating in his head.

In his days, the digital land had a wall around it. Net neutrality, data caps, speed limits, government regulations; all these kept barriers up. But Doomsday and the rise of the Union knocked those barriers down like buckets of hay. Science could accomplish anything, even beautifying a man like Lester. Spying would be broadened and no one would defy that, because Marcel Celest was adored and respected.

But Project Syncope could stop that. An apocalyptic device to end the apocalypse. In theory, anyways. That's why Lester was so interested in it. For now, the device would stay put. Especially since Willie was the only one with the capability of activating the machine. But should the resistance know about it? Willie wasn't too sure.

"Hey, you listening?"

"Yeah," Willie lied, "Say, where we headed? This is different."

"Uptown. That's what the dashboard says. Union Institute?"

They were supposed to be going home. Lester must have changed their destination. Being that this was Willie's regular cab driver, he didn't feel uneasy about being truthful. "They want to implant a new chip in me. The old one don't work."

"What's the big deal?"

"It was fake."

The cab driver bit his lip and could only say, "Oh."

"They find it, I'm in a heap of trouble, know what I'm saying?"

"Yeah. Yeah, I got you," the driver exhaled, "But the vehicle is self driving. Mostly. I can't take you home without them knowing. I gotta stay on route."

Willie looked out the window again. Scar from baseball still discolored the bottom of his chin, tummy that Connor used to fall asleep on, the tattoo of his grandmother, and baldness that reminded him of his father. These were memories implanted on his body, physical memories, and Willie wasn't prepared to erase them like an old hard drive. Why? Aging was the best part of living. Memories meant everything. Memories that he could tell others. Something familiar blossomed in him. "Can you pull over?"

"That I can do."

The smart car pulled along the edge of the road. A female voice and flashing touchscreen asked if there was an emergency. After pressing a series of menu options, the driver chose *Bathroom Break*. "Make it a number two." He joked.

Willie stepped outside, the chilly air making him rustle in his jacket. Since the sun could barely be seen through tainted clouds, he had learned to judge the sun's location by the level of bitter cold. It definitely disappeared over the horizon somewhere. He wished he could see it. No one else drove by, the roads empty as usual. Sometimes he missed traffic. Facing the forest, Willie contemplated something. The burnt tree branches were shaped like the veins of lungs, wobbling slightly with the wind. Earth breathed. Its voice sang through the music of birds. It cried from the sky. His boy taught him all this. Camping trips were his thing, but eventually Willie grew fond of it because the fascination of a little boy. "This is near Scotland Run park. I know where I am. Where I gotta go."

"Go? You mean walk?" The driver questioned through the open passenger window. "Where?" He paused. "To *them*? They out there?"

Around the metropolitan areas, the People of Bliss faded into rumors after the death of Sirius Dawson. News outlets reported the movement died. Willie knew the truth. They were all alive and well, ready to fight a war at Marcel Celest's door. A war that Willie needed to be a part of. "Yeah, man. I'm going to *them*."

"How? You ain't got no GPS."

True, but Willie had knowledge of the area. "You know, boss, we didn't always have GPS. I know my way around."

"Okay, well, what about water? Food?"

"Forest has it. Hell, I know how to make a water container out of birch bark. Make a knife from rock. Hunt. I don't need anything."

Again, hesitant, the driver looked out into the dense forest more afraid than Willie. He'd watched too many horror movies. "But…but…" the cabbie frowned, "Who else am I supposed to talk to about the Phillies?"

Suddenly feeling sorry for the man he rode with everyday after work and still neglected to ask his name, Willie offered. "Come with me."

Disagreeing with the government always caused this reluctant step forward than a skittish step back. Being a fighter took more than brawn, it took an internal confidence the way that Willie was confident about his trek through the forest and dangerous roads for forty miles. The cabbie leaned back in his seat. "It's too late for me." Willie's prison mate, a New Yorker serving life, said that phrase too. Were the prisons so different? A steel prison versus a digital one? The cab driver extended his hand out and Willie shook it, suddenly realizing there was no turning back. He was leaving the Union's home to go to the silo's home. And as the cab drove away in a trail of dust, Willie couldn't help but sense relief.

Technology is suppose to replace the
meaningless jobs not the meaningful.

-Victoria Celest
First Lady of the United States
2033-2038

CHAPTER TWENTY-ONE

Depression had sunk into Nelson's mind again, telling him thoughts. *Why bother?* Learning how to fly a jet that was out of his reach did seem pointless. The only way he could escape this cell was if he could walk through solid walls, a feat even his miraculous son Marcel couldn't do. This same solidarity cursed him to the confines of the Oval Office after his wife's death, wanting nothing more than to be left alone. Now, he wanted nothing more than companionship and family.

Antoine did his best to keep them entertained over the past week, but their three decades apart. The more they spoke, the more different they appeared. Music, movies, politics - the only thing they shared in common was flying. Training on the jet progressed repeatedly. Having little visual interaction except through a finger-sized hole, Nelson often got bored like listening to self-help tapes. Those things never helped him.

One morning, he'd been awoken to Antoine silently speaking to himself. It wasn't the first time he heard the whispered conversation, but the first time he heard it so clearly. His cell neighbor's amplified voice seemed to be asking that his family stay safe in these hard times. Though they've spent night and day together, Nelson realized he knew so little about Antoine besides his expertise with piloting. His wife used to say, when you can't get out of your head - get into someone else's. "What is that? Praying?" Nelson scoffed.

"Oh right. Last thing I remember hearing about your presidency was you got something against God."

Denouncing religious freedoms in the Union agreement wouldn't exactly be the pivotal moment in his presidency, but at least it was something. "Let me ask you something. How long have you been in that cell?"

"Sixty-three days, four hours and sixteen minutes."

"And have you prayed every single one of those days?"

"Hmph," Antoine mumbled. He finished his prayer with a murmured *amen*. "I get what you're going with that. Why hasn't He found the key, opened up this door, and let me out yet?"

"Maybe you can read minds better than my son."

Antoine turned on his sink and sipped some of the water. "You ever been so thirsty that drinking water gives a sorta sense of satisfaction? Ever been sick and enjoyed that feeling when the recovery begins? How about taking a bite of sweet red velvet cake after an amazing meal? It all feels good, right? I think that's God. It's a feeling. We all share it. Even me and you."

Though there wasn't much to look at except endless water, Nelson took this moment to peep out the open slit above the sink that served as a window. "My wife used to love the ocean. We'd go out, just the two of us, on a boat and do nothing. Those were the best days of my life. Now? Well now, she's buried in a cemetery. There's a God? I don't believe that horse shit. If there was a God, he wouldn't have let her die. Do you understand? I'll *never* see her again."

"You sure you won't see her again?"

Facing sideways so his nose could fit through the opening, he smelled the ocean air. Much cleaner than the air on land. "I'm sure I won't."

Talking about this didn't make him feel better. If he had sheets, he would've concocted a way to hang himself. Anywhere was better than here. Even death. But he knew, because the moment had crossed his mind before. "A week after my wife died and the media lost interest, so did the world, I swallowed a handful of Somas. Even before it made it's way to my stomach, I chickened out and hurriedly grabbed a glass of water and added salt. I guzzled the salt water and vomited instantaneously. Never been sure what caused me retract my attempt at suicide. It wasn't my family, my children hated me after Victoria died. It wasn't my loyalty to the country. Or my minuscule fan base. I…just…couldn't do it."

"Maybe something *else* stopped you."

Nelson rolled his eyes and paced around the cell, forcing himself to do this pathetic exercise every day to avoid atrophy to his legs. Besides, he enjoyed walking. Since Doomsday forced most of them to walk miles, he found it not only good for his body, but good for his mind too. "So what do you think? You blame me for Doomsday too? That my stance against religion sparked an apocalypse?"

"We both know damn well that many reasons sparked the war, but Marcel Celest let it happen. So he could push his Union agenda. Of course, NAN never mentions that theory. They put the blame entirely on you."

Nelson stopped to squint his eyes. "NAN?"

"What? Have you been living under a rock, my man?"

Considering that the missile silo entrance was hidden behind a rock, Nelson could affirm that statement but decided not to. "Never heard of it."

"NAN. North American News. Press is now per continent and is supposedly unbiased."

Nelson bent down to do push-ups. He hadn't done them in the ages, but the confines of these walls were driving him insane. After only three push-ups, he collapsed onto the ground. Half his face still resting on the cold floor, he asked, "When was the last time you spoke to them?"

"Seventy-eight days, two hours and thirty-three minutes."

Getting off the floor, he realized he should've cherished time when it was on his side.

"Promised them I'd be home by now," Antoine added. "Military families are trained to be patient, but this... damn captain won't even let me send an email to let them know I'm even alive."

Footsteps echoed outside in the walkway. It was much too early for that slop they called dinner. The tension from Antoine could be felt even through the four-inch thick steel walls. "If they are coming for you," Antoine whispered, "Act you like it."

"What?" Nelson said, his imagination going in several directions. "What's happening?"

The footsteps stopped in front of Nelson's door. Antoine said again, "Act you like it. It turns them off."

He wobbled back as the crew unlocked the door with a key, and grasped onto the sink. They rammed their way into his cell. Nelson couldn't get a single punch before they knocked him to the floor. Trying to bite at an ear, or head butting, had no effect. The guards locked their arms around his arms, but it did little to keep him from struggling. Not until one of them bashed Nelson in the back of a head with the barrel of a rifle did he finally cease fighting.

Dazed, he went from moments of being dragged on the walkway to being dragged upstairs. Muffled words from the crew made no sense. With no idea what cruelty he was about to endure, Nelson thought about praying. Even at a time like this, maybe it could give comfort.

His face smashed onto another floor. Cold air chilled his face and body immediately. Wind swashed his clothes about. Since being in that cell, he'd wanted more than to be outside. But now outdoors, he found himself more terrified than that cell. Stumbling to get up, he couldn't get a sense of his surroundings. He was certainly on deck. But why? His vision cleared slightly when he shook his head.

The captain sat on a barrel, cutting an apple with a sharp blade. "If you're thinking of running…good luck."

Nelson swung around to see endless ocean in every direction. Under other circumstances, the view would've been quite breath-taking. "What do you want?"

Before he could open his mouth, the captain was rudely interrupted to the sounds of screaming. He rolled his eyes and chewed the first slice of apple. Assuming the high pitched and panicked screams were a woman, Nelson was surprised to see them coming from a man. The man, naked below the waist and wearing only his crew uniform shirt, ran up the stairs. "She shat on me!"

Crew members, scattered around the deck, pointed and laughed as the pant-less man grabbed a garden hose outside and washed his genital area that was covered in brown liquid. "She fucking shat on me! Jesus Christ, what if she got AIDS."

"That's not how you get AIDS, fuck-tard," the captain said sarcastically.

Three more crew members exited the door the half-naked man just exited, holding a prisoner tightly. A prisoner Nelson hadn't recognized. Old enough to have children, but not grand-children, this woman didn't bother to fight back like Nelson did. Blood stained her panties down to her ankles. Fresh blood.

Without even hesitating, the humiliated man punched the woman in the face like a boxer. Even from their distance, Nelson could hear her jaw crack. "Fucking cunt!"

Feeling helpless, Nelson thought of lunging forward to protect this innocent woman, but the half dozen men on this deck would surely insure he lost that battle. So he stood, shoulders sagged and swaying with the boat.

The captain smirked. "Caught her a whiles back. Three ports ago. She snuck in, like you. Except she wasn't trying to steal multimillion dollar equipment. Oh no. She was trying to steal food." He cut off a large chunk of apple and swallowed it after two bites. "I'm gonna tell you two stories, Mr. President." He stood up and inadvertently Nelson squabbled down to his knees. "Jessica was this fine girl, born in a Bible-thumping town outside of Jackson, Mississippi. In Middle School, she wrote letters to the Armed Forces overseas. In High School, she worked a second job and gave all her money to charity. She went on to college to become a nurse, you know because she loved helping people. Fell in love with a patient, an army vet who lost both legs in the war. Jessica asked him to marry her, if you can believe that….women never ask first, right? But she did because she's a strong woman. A kind woman."

He chucked what was left of the apple in the ocean, right past the railing. "The second story ain't so happy, now. We got a girl named Margie. In Middle School, she flunked twice and got put behind with the retard class. In ninth grade, Margie was giving BJs to the boys under the bleachers right before cheerleading practice. Sometimes even teachers. Not long after, she got knocked up by the quarterback. When the bastard cheated on her, Margie keyed his truck and busted the tires. Literally her only reason for having that baby was to collect welfare checks from the good ole' U.S. of A. She got hooked on smack and almost burned the trailer down when she tried to cook her on meth, with the baby in the crib on the other side of the room. One night, if it wasn't for her nosy neighbors, the baby would've died. It kept crying and crying that night. You know why? She forgot to feed it and passed out thanks to a good taste of the Brown Betty."

He bent down to Nelson's level, licking the end of his knife. "Which story you think is true about our lovely, shit-smelling whore here?"

Not sure where this was going, he decided he didn't want to play anymore. But watching the captain's wild eyes and the sharpness of that blade in his hand, Nelson knew he had to give some type of answer. "I don't know."

A smile streaked across the captain's face. "Well, I'll be… That's right, Mr. President. The answer is…you don't know." He stood up briskly, walking toward the woman. She gave a slight sob as he grabbed her arm. Showing his strength, he hoisted her up like a bride on her wedding day.

Then the captain strolled over and slung the woman over the railing into the ocean.

"NO!" Nelson screamed. Crew immediately grabbed Nelson and held him down as he lunged for the captain.

Eyes as round as snow globes, the captain stared. "Would you have reacted like that if I told you that she wasn't the kind, loving nurse, but the neglectful, druggy girl? Or maybe it was the other way around? But what's matter, right? She could've lied about her story."

"It doesn't matter which story was true! It was still a life! And you just ended it!" Nelson felt a hard thud from someone's elbow into his back. He fell to his knees.

The captain removed the map, the map Nelson shouldn't have brought, from his back pocket. "See that red X, boys?

That's where the People of Bliss are." He glanced at Nelson. "You know what's the difference between everyone under the X and the rest of the world…you *care* about lives. Was she Jessica or Margie? Or both? No matter what their story is, you didn't know. Maybe that bitch deserved to be thrown off a naval ship to her death, maybe she didn't. Did it matter? This is what made you a mundane leader, you cared about human life. Like one of them peace loving liberal hippies." Shaking his head, the captain said disappointedly, "You are *not* the President I voted for." Looking to his men, he ordered, "Get him out of my face."

CHAPTER TWENTY-TWO

Babies needed sunshine. At least, that's what a baby magazine at the grocery store line had said. That was many moons ago, when Janice had decided not to be a mother but still found herself leafing through the magazine. It was a different time then; when deciding to be a mother had been a choice, being at a grocery store had been a choice, and even getting some sunshine had been a choice. Every day, a group of people from the silo would travel outdoors for what they called fresh air. Fresh air still poisoned by ash and filth. No one ever said it, but most missed the sunlight. The last news, Janice heard on the radio, was that ideas floated around for how to clean the clouds. Turbines attached to planes, add chemicals to weigh down the filthy particles, seed the clouds more so that it rains. Bu they were just that…ideas. Marcel's new government still took years to make a decision. Not much different than the old government.

Until the sunshine came back, her child would have to get Vitamin D from another source. Madley's concoctions of vitamins and minerals from plants worked. For now, anyways.

They had been outside all afternoon, walking around the scarred forest, before the rain started up again. Nothing more disgusting than smokey colored drops from the air. She brought the baby inside, noticing how much stronger her right arm had become since getting used to holding him there. The People of Bliss supplied her with a baby carriage (with a wobbly leg) and baby sack (which hurt her back); yet, Janice preferred holding Colin. He still weighed less than ten pounds, which mothers here had promised her was an ideal weight for a twelve week old baby.

Inside, she still felt like Colin needed more exploring time. At this age, his eyes darted everywhere as his little mind took in his surroundings. It wouldn't be apt to place him in his boring crib and room again. Besides, Janice liked the idea of exploring together. She wondered what went through his head. If he found a missile silo so amazing, imagine how he would've reacted to the cities before nuclear weapons demolished them. The Saint Louis Arch. The Freedom Tower. Disney World. Colin would've loved them.

So instead of a walk to their bedroom, she decided to go a few floors down. It hadn't occurred to her that much of the silo was still unexplored to her too. The elevator, shaky yet safe, took them down to far underground levels. Hundreds of rooms had been made into bedrooms, but down in the lower levels they had remained mostly unchanged. These larger rooms must've been where state officials met to discus war strategies. Little did they know that World War II had been a pebble in the water compared to events of the last year.

Up until this point, Janice enjoyed being barefoot as everyone else did. But the steel mesh on the walkway made her feet sore. Tempted to leave, her eyes were drawn to a room all the way down the walkway.

It pulsed. Something pulsed behind the door. At first, she thought it was her lack of sleep playing tricks on her mind, but even baby Colin's eyes stared at it. He even stopped nibbling on the pacifier for the first time in awhile.

"What's that?" Janice said in that high-pitched mommy voice she had perfected. "Looks like pretty lights, huh?"

Then again, perhaps it could be something dangerous. The silo had been tested for nuclear fallout and searched for weapons already. It was safe. According to Adam, anyways. The more time she spent with him, the more shattered she realized his mind had become since Doomsday. But who's brain hadn't?

The pulse stopped behind the door followed by an applause. An applause? There were other people down here? Now, Janice couldn't withhold her curiosity. Colin gave an endorsing *coo* sound. She walked them towards the door and leaned her ear against it, remembering when she used to do this same thing growing up at the Baltimore Adoption Agency. Perspective parents would chat with the headmaster about how boring and nerdy Janice was, not a fit for their active lifestyles.

People chattered for a moment behind the door, but the muffled dialogue made no sense. Quiet came and then, the glowing began. At first, a long pulse lasted nearly a minute then faded down. Another pulse started, lasting even longer. What was going on?

Maybe she could sneak in without anyone noticing. Or even just open the door a peep. Colin agreed, giving a pitch that sounded almost like a cackle. Janice pushed slowly on the door, but it swung open more than she intended.

What she saw had no words.

Sitting on mats in meditation poses with legs locked and hands resting on knees, thirteen men, women, and children faced a leader. The leader was Pierre. He too sat in the dark room with his eyes closed. And every person in this room glowed. Glowed! Janice's mouth dropped. It looked like they sat on significantly high-powered light bulbs. Something inside them shined outwards, showcasing their cardiovascular, nervous, and skeletal systems. Janice had studied these in biology classes but never like this. How was this possible?

The glowing stopped. Janice had been in such shock that she hadn't heard Colin's cries. Since everyone turned to face them, apparently the group had. Instead of being angered or flustered, the people seemed completely calm like waking up from a long nap.

How did they glow like that? Reaction to nuclear waste in the water? No, that would only happen in Adam's silly comic books. Contrast liquids, or dyes, can be used during MRI's to glow, but that was under a computer screen and not visible to a naked eye. She'd heard of tattoo dyes that could be seen under fluorescent lights. But none of this explained this phenomenon.

"Would you like one of us to hold him?" Pierre asked politely.

"Hmm?" Janice said. Then realized Colin was still upset. She didn't blame him. If she wasn't an adult, she would've been crying at the sight of glowing people too.

"Do you want to join us?" Pierre smiled. "I can teach you how to do it."

Memories of previous foster parents surfaced; none as kind as the Celests.

Would you like to try a drink, little girl? What's your name again? Janice? When do I get my check for fostering you? Know how to cut up coke? I can teach you how to do it.

Panicked, Janice turned and hurried out the door, feeling her heart pound as she made it to the elevator.

As in every situation, whether the outcome could be productive or non-productive, Janice figured it was worth researching further. Colin had finally calmed down, falling asleep in her arms. She wished she could fall asleep like that, without the need for pills, herbs, alcohol, or all the above.

In Popular Science magazine, she remembered an article explaining the phenomenon of the body creating light. Every species, big or small, emitted small amounts of bioluminescence as a result of chemical reactions in the body, there was no debate over that. But what she just saw could be considered extreme. Most light emissions were invisible to the naked eye, except of course deep sea creatures that have evolved to utilize this for survival. Lipid and proteins collided with fluorophores to radiate light. But those people, somehow, intensified the reaction. The scientist in her, an MSc graduate in Biology, had to know more and Colin needed his nap.

When she got to the room, the door was completely shut. Odd, considering Adam hated a stuffy room and often left the door ajar or entirely open. She thought of knocking, but it was her room too, and she couldn't help the audacity he had sometimes. Swinging the door open, she found Adam, as usual, huddled in the corner of the room sitting on a crate with the computer on a dinner stand-up tray ahead of him.

He rapidly switched screens when she interrupted, but she got a long enough glance. Whatever he was working on took some intense programming language, she could make out three columns. Though most of the coding she couldn't decipher, Janice could definitely see a ledger of names. Possibly thousands of names since the scroll bar next to it was minuscule. There's only one list she could imagine to be that long...The People of Bliss. What was he doing with that?

Immediately after the changed screens, he closed a small tin Altoids can that rattled with small chips. Very small chips. In the months they'd lived together, Janice had never seen that canister, but he sure was in a hurry to protect it as he stuffed in his pocket. "Hey, Janice." He hardly ever called her *baby, hon,* or *sweetie.* And that bothered her.

Already knowing he wouldn't answer, she asked anyway. "What are you working on?"

"Nothing. Just a computer game," he murmured.

With a snort, Janice went to the baby's crib and laid Colin down softly like a sack of potatoes ready to break through the bag. "You mumble when you lie," she commented.

"No, I don't." He mumbled.

Trying to hurry before the group of glowers left, she hurried through a set of simple instructions. "He needs to be fed soon, my breast milk is in refrigerator." Janice popped open the small refrigerator, a most generous offer from scouts since she had a child to care for. Inside the appliance, she found four bottles of her breast milk. "Only one bottle and…Seriously, Adam? Why do you put cereal in here? Who does that?" She demanded, holding up a box of the morning breakfast. "And you're a grown man eating Lucky Charms?" Not only that, but the leader of an opposition; she didn't bother bringing that up.

"The sugar helps me think," he shrugged.

Feeling a headache emerging in her temples, Janice decided she had enough. "I'm taking a walk. If Colin wakes up, don't ignore him."

She stomped out of the room and purposely left the door open. Sure enough, he called out, "Hey, can you close the door?" But she didn't.

He's up to something secretive.

Losing count now of how many conversations with Adam had left her dumbfounded, Janice decided to investigate this glowing phenomenon further. Free from the confinement of motherhood felt simply odd. Carrying Colin on her hip most of the day, she'd grown accustomed to the weight and now seemed off-balance.

She made her way back down the elevator to the classroom, only to find the area empty and the door left open. Either the people vanished into thin air (which didn't seem so implausible nowadays) or they had left the premises (which seemed plausible). With no idea of where they could've gone, Janice was relieved to run into a familiar face roaming the hallways.

"Matley, hey," she said.

The crazed woman had jellybeans wrapped into her dreadlocks, presumably allowing the children to play with her again today. Matley grabbed Janice's hand and held it, like she was reading a fortune. "What you doing down here, child?"

"I just saw a sort of…class going on here. Like a meditation, of sorts."

"Oh yes, it is phenomenal."

"Where did they go?"

Matley looked to the sky, as though she had x-ray vision and could see through the walls. Holding her wrinkly hand for this long went from polite to eccentric. "I believe they must be doing the ritual, child, for our newcomers."

Slowly releasing her hand, Janice squinted. "Ritual? As in sacrifice?"

"No, my no," she answered, giggling. "They be dunking them in the oasis."

In the several months since Janice arrived here, she couldn't recall ever hearing of something called the oasis. Putting two and two together, she assumed Matley must be referring to the lake, a few hundred yards outside the silo. Peculiar stories had been told about the effects of that water. "Is that how they got the ability to glow?"

Like Janice had been the only student with the correct answer in class, Matley clasped her palms together triumphantly. "Yes! Lloyd and Nina blessed the waters before they departed this world. The Frenchman discovered its true power. We can conjure the glow without the aide of our angelic leaders."

Janice had seen it with her own eyes, so she couldn't be skeptical, Lloyd and Nina's corpses had erupted into specks of lights before drizzling back into the lake. Ever since then, she hesitated to even take a swim. It would be like climbing the tree her mother Victoria had been buried with. Most traditions were silly notions built from generations, but she couldn't help her constant respect for the dead.

Matley's hand gently touched her and they walked toward the elevator. "You must bathe in the light, child. Please. Go see. It will change you."

Once inside the elevator, the botanist fanatic closed the gate and Janice ascended the rickety shaft. *It will change you.* What was she about to see?

Outside, there were a couple dozen people standing about, not usual since Union Keepers' often flew in choppers over these forests and always kept the People of Bliss hidden inside like gophers. Janice knew a lot of these faces, but never knew how to speak to them. That shy woman inside, often mistaken for being prude, always came out of her in crowds.

After a brief walk through the bland woods of brown cracked tree stumps, Janice noticed a few dozen more people had joined this *ritual* around the lake. She watched from a distance as a tall and wide man stood at the shore. It must be Bruno, the German Adam spoke highly of, that had to duck through every door of the silo. The conversations were so low and so far, Janice struggled to hear.

"But Bruno no swim," she heard him say.

Pierre grasped onto a cane, looking at the German's mouth instead of his eyes which blind people often did. With that pencil thin mustache and long face, Pierre looked more like a man ready to steal Dudley Do-Right's girl rather than a blind man seeking tranquility. "You will be fine, my friend. It's a little over a meter deep."

Hesitantly, Bruno stripped off his clothes and removed even his underwear. Janice watched uncomfortably while others gazed on; forgetting Europeans disregarded nudity much more than Americans.

Jumping up and down desperately, Janice noticed the burn-scarred Victor that Adam warned her about. He spoke so fast that she couldn't hear or understand him as he begged Pierre for something. Finally, the Frenchman answered. "Yes, you can, but do not use too much kerosene again, my friend." Victor rushed to light up the already darkening afternoon, staring at each tiki torch as if it was a gold brick being presented to the gods.

Absolutely terrified of the temperature of the water, or the water itself, Bruno held onto two men as they entered the lake. Once inside, they stopped and he dunked his head into the crystal clear waters and emerged gasping for air like he'd been under for three minutes and not three seconds. Everyone applauded. Janice had seen baptisms and found them utterly confusing and ridiculous, but found herself joining the applause. After the clapping ending, everyone bowed heads like it was supper time, including Bruno.

Frankly positive she was losing her mind, Janice watched incredulously as everyone at the shore began to glow. The energy of it all made her back away and clutch her chest. Sweat began to slide off her forehead from the striking warmth and bewilderment. Seeing even the skulls and brain tissues, this phenomenon could only be explained as the soul igniting. A soul that no scientist had ever proven. She wished her group of colleagues at the University could see this now and explain, because she had none.

The glowing teetered off and the day returned to the normal dull sun-less sky. Internally giddy, Janice wanted to see it again like that time in college her professor made marbles in his hands with gallium metal. Next to her, another person she knew so little about spoke. "Never seen it before, have you?" Willie asked. Besides the occasional passing by in the hallways, this was the most words she'd heard out of his mouth.

"No. How do they..."

He slid his winter's cap off, obviously feeling the hot flash she'd experienced. "Happy thoughts."

"You mean like...Peter Pan?"

"Yeah," he exhaled, "sorta like that. I did it once, months ago, but can't seem to do it again. They make it look so easy, am I right?"

Teaching classes about evolvability, biological engineering, and evolutionary algorithms, Janice still felt stumped like one of her students. They did make it look so easy. But how? Happy thoughts? She tried to reflect back on her happiest moments. "Right after nuclear strikes everywhere, I pondered my existence. What had saved me that day? Luck or...something else. Me and my husband were brought to a medical tent, where I was the least of their worries with just a simple cracked rib and minor stitches needed. While I waited, I wandered the tent watching all the injured. Men with severed arms, some with partially severed arms still dangling by the tendon, children with debris slicing through their bodies, and...well, you get the idea. In my half-drunken state, I wanted nothing more than another drink so I could convince myself it was all just some hallucination." She paused and could see Willie staring at the ground, as though he experienced such trepidations, but didn't interrupt. "Anyways, I stumbled upon a medicine cabinet and applied bandages myself. In there, I found one of those quick blood-prick pregnancy tests used before population control mandated the removal of them. Just out of boredom or…something else, I decided to open the case. After a swift needle and single drop of blood, the pregnancy read-out only took about twenty seconds to confirm my pregnancy."

"Is that your happiest moment?"

She shook her head, watching as Bruno practiced glowing. Little sputters of light formed inside him, still wet from the water. Pierre spoke to him. "No. I was positively frightened. How could I bring a child into this world? How could I keep it safe? But now, I watch him intuitively. So thrilled I brought him into this world."

"Happy?"

"Oh yes. But. Is it enough? Trying to concentrate on a single mass of land in the far distance when you've been thrown into an irate, blackened ocean? Have you heard of Cherophobia? Is this human condition where the subject avoids moments of happiness, out of either fear of the consequences of it or fear of the credibility of it."

Nodding his head, Willie said, "I know what you mean." He spun a wedding ring on his left hand. "I can't keep my mind off him. Don't know how to be happy sometimes."

Janice watched the people glowing and said, "I don't know how *any* of them can be happy sometimes." Before she could muster another tear, another useless tear that usually soaked her pillow every morning, Janice gave a polite nod goodbye to Willie and walked back towards the silo.

CHAPTER TWENTY-THREE

Having the crap beat out of her, for the first time ever, Royal was unsure how long it took for a swollen cheek to recede. She had placed a bag of peas on it every night since Zharkova's girls taught her a lesson in that subway car. The swelling still reminded her how horrifying and humiliating the situation was. Anton never asked questions, though Royal wished he would so she could state how awful his mother could be.

Not far from the entrance to Moscow's busiest subway station, she sat at a round table. Anton had done an excellent job of preparing a nice dining experience. In the center was a red rose that Royal assumed had to be fake since flowers didn't grow in toxic fumes. The table cloth had a peculiar pattern of chickens with a white background. He set out a series of plates as his headphones boomed the music of some rapper she didn't recognize. All this seemed like a moment of celebration. But celebration of what? Certainly not of the situation. Outside, humid air kept the chemicals at a dangerous level. Royal's broken nose still bled from time-to-time. And Zharkova was still coughing and alive. There didn't seem to be much to celebrate.

The cranky old troll hadn't said much since she sat, besides that Royal looked like *shit*. She avoided the mirror for this reason. A week after the brutal beating in the subway car, the only scar that had disappeared was the black eye.

Anton mouthed the lyrics to his song as he brought over a large silver plate with three soup bowls on it. Royal's stomach grumbled. Finally, a decent meal. Then she saw the sloppy mess in the bowl, as Anton set it down before her. Royal stared at the plate for a long moment, trying to make sense of what she could. The meal was some type of soup...but not. It was like Jell-O. Leafs, black pepper corns, and something that seemed like dog food had been mixed together into this solid gelatin. Before Royal could ask if this was actual food, Zharkova was nearly done devouring the bowl.

Using a spoon, Royal poked it. Zharkova's hand slammed the table so hard that she nearly fell out of her seat. Without saying a word, Royal interrupted Zharkova's stern face and curled upper lip. *Eat it!*

Maybe it would be like that Olivye salad they had last week; it tasted a lot better than it looked. After the first bite of the meat gelatin meal, Royal became immediately surprised. The meal actually tasted *much* worse than it looked. Anton sat down, tossed his elbows on the table, and began to munch on the dish. Again, Zharkova's hand slammed the table. But this time - the angry facade was directed toward Anton.

The wanna-be gangster immediately sat up and turned into a wanna-be butler. He removed his elbows faster than he removed his headphones. With his hands in his lap, he awaited a silent instruction from Zharkova. After a brief nod from his mother figure, he stiffly grabbed his fork and took tiny bites of the grub.

Even with a busted nose, Royal still had some sense of taste. She didn't know if she could eat this. Starving didn't seem all that bad. But Zharkova's quick glance gave no indication that the decision was Royal's. Reluctantly, she took another bite of her food.

Thirty minutes past, maybe more, of complete silence besides the clank of a fork hitting the plate or Royal's stomach giving a rebellious groan. Finally, after the last bite, Zharkova spoke. She said something in Russian. Anton's reaction made Royal wish she spoke the native language. He seemed torn between concern and obedience. "Now," Zharkova whispered.

Anton nodded and walked away. The Russian leader faced Royal. "Alright, Aurora, follow me."

"Where we gonna go?"

"To watch television."

Royal's forehead crunched into what must've looked like a question mark over her head. *Watch TV?* Zharkova gave no further details, she sat up and used her cane to walk away. Royal followed.

They walked through a series of spiral stairs past a door that said something in Russian. But the emblem of straight metal bars translated it for her. It was some kind of holding cell. The room had an enormous television set attached to the wall. Royal noticed the room had several speakers attached around the cell. In the center of the room was a single chair. The far corner had a toilet and sink.

"Sit down, Aurora."

The only other choice would've been to run out of this room. Whatever the woman had planned couldn't have been good. Royal weighed out her options. If she ran, the air outside was so dense with green gases that it would make her choke to death by the time she made it out of this Godforsaken Hell. Even with a cane, somehow Zharkova would catch up to her and probably beat her dead body with the cane. That was no way to go. Being gullible was an option too. Maybe this was just a simple television and Royal could watch some old episodes of Full House.

Reluctantly, she sat on the chair and faced the television. Anton appeared at the door with a remote control and blue mop bucket. He said something in Russian, probably about the blue mop bucket because Zharkova snatched it and threw it next to Royal. Thankfully, it was empty and not full of nasty mop water.

Zharkova used the remote control and turned on the television. "You've only experienced a pimple on the face of evil. Americans and their goddamn censorship haven't seen the real side of war. I'm about to show you the true face of evil."

The surround speakers popped as a video started. With the remote control still in her hand, Zharkova walked to the door. "And try to aim in the goddamn bucket, Aurora, or I will make you clean it up."

"There's a toilet. I don't need a bucket –"

"It's not for your piss and shit, stupid girl!" Zharkova grabbed a set of keys from a worried Anton. "It's for your vomit."

Zharkova slammed the door closed and locked it.

At first, the video started with just a series of war images. Nothing that couldn't be shown to a class of sixth graders. Black and white pictures of World War II. American soldiers prepared for battle. The famous photo of a man standing in front of a tank in

   ***

If this was Zharkova's shot at scaring Royal, she might as well just turned on the History Channel. Was this the Russian leader's way of showing violence? Royal scoffed. She knew the true face of violence by watching every episode of 'Walker: Texas Ranger'.

Then the blood started to appear. First on a soldier's uniform, right around the knee where he had been shot. The next image showed a dead body lying on the ground in a jungle with a Vietnamese uniform. Then the photos became more modern by showcasing the brutal actions of American soldiers in what so many called the most devastating war. The Vietnam War brought out the worst in both sides, because no one could understand the point in fighting. It drove men mad. Soldiers took pictures with severed heads on stakes. The image made the meat gelatin delight rumble in her stomach.

The video went black for several minutes. Royal snorted at the bucket. She made it through the graphic images with ease. But then a video started. A man sat on a chair, which eerily like the one Royal sat on at that moment. The man had been stripped naked besides a blind fold around his eyes. Mucus and tears ran down his chin. There were several slashes across his skin; some scabbed and others looked fresh. Perhaps caning or whipping, whatever the case may be...no man deserved this. Royal covered her mouth with one hand. His whimpers came crystal clear through the surround sound system. She felt in the middle of the action. What fear this man must've felt.

A lamp hung above the victim and glistened the amount of sweat on his poor body. Looking at how thin the man was, he would've surely devoured that meat gelatin without any remorse.

Two middle eastern men entered the video's frame, armed with AR-15 rifles and bandanas to conceal their faces.

Whatever they were saying into the camera, Royal couldn't translate but the sheer rage in each syllable made it clear they weren't happy. She prayed they would just put a bullet through this man's head and end his suffering quickly. But instead, one of the armed men tied a rope around the victim's torso and tightened him to the chair. "No! Please! No!" the victim screamed. It was an American. Before Royal could figure out what was happening, the other middle eastern man pulled out a machete and swung it into the back of the victim's neck. Royal cried out and covered her mouth with both hands. The victim's neck didn't sever completely. He was still alive and screaming at the top of his throat! She'd never heard a cry like that. The machete came down again and cut only a few more inches. Beheading wasn't a quick, clean cut. It took several swings before a human's head released from the rest of the body. Thump after thump, the victim continued to plead for mercy. Finally the machete made it to the throat. The victim began to choke on his blood, but kept crying out.

Then the head fell off and landed in his lap. Blood spewed in every direction. Even hitting the lamp above.

Another video clip began to play. A woman was being stoned in the middle of a town square. Each stone thrown ripped off skin and tissue. Blood soaked her clothes until they turned red. By the end of the movie, the poor woman looked like a chunk of wet ground beef.

The next video showed a homeless man sleeping. Kids giggled quietly as they sprayed lighter fluid all over him. The homeless man mumbled to be left alone. Too drunk to stand up, he tried to kick the kids away. Suddenly, one of the brats threw a Molotov cocktail. The homeless man ignited immediately and hollered in pain. Royal felt a tear roll down her eye. The kids' giggles grew louder and they filmed this murder triumphantly.

Screams echoed through each of the speakers around the room. It seemed to have gotten louder. Royal covered her wet eyes, but the noises seemed worse. Every sinister cackle and every traumatic wail traveled through her ear drums clearly. Royal closed her eyes and covered her ears. It only sounded muffled; not nearly enough.

Panicked, Royal grabbed the chair and tossed it at the television set. There was a tough glass blocking it; the chair didn't leave a dent. She ran to the speakers and tried to rip them out, but they were bolted to the wall. The sounds of children screamed through the speakers. Whatever was happening on the screen, she didn't want to know. Royal dashed to the door. Until now, she hadn't noticed a door handle was missing. Using her fingernails she tried desperately to open the door. Even cracking one of her nails was no use.

"Please! Anton! Please! Open the door! I got the message! Please!" Royal kicked at the door. "I get it! Alright! This is war! I get it! Open the door!"

On the television, a woman chased a youngster with a bat. He was no older than five, maybe six years old. He kept crying out, "Mommy! Please don't! Please!" Royal watched in horror as the woman smashed the youngster's head until the brain became exposed.

Royal hurried to the bucket and vomited her dinner.

CHAPTER TWENTY-FOUR

Even though blisters reminded Willie of all the miles he had walked, he continued on. Leaving the Union and its incredible benefits for a dangerous trek to the missile silo and its non-existent benefits seemed stupid. Last night, sleeping under a tree to hide from the torrential downpour, he had thought about going back to a delicious meal from his refrigerator or comfy mattress to sleep on. But whatever compelled him away kept his feet forward on the long path.

The missile silo's entrance had been hidden so well, that often the residents of the colony would circle miles without seeing it. Thankfully, Adam came up with a clever plan so that unwelcome visitors (such as the drones that periodically scanned for any signs of the rebellious People of Bliss in the woods) couldn't find them. Paint would be too obvious and so would any insignia, so he opted to use an optical illusion. Three trees, which branches had been cut to create the illusion, needed to line up a certain way to create the look of a real big tree. The left tree had its right branches cut, the right tree had no right branches, and the center tree had no branches.

With squinty eyes, Willie finally saw the three trees and aligned them. Dead center of this was the missile silo's entrance. Hidden under a blanket of leaves was the circular doorway and lock. He twisted it and opened the door. After a short climb down a ladder, usually he'd be greeted by an older man with a cane in one hand and a pistol in the other. Rumor said the guard had great aim. But Willie didn't find the man in this first room before entering the establishment. Instead, someone entirely different sat the chair next to the door.

The younger man, maybe in his early 30s, scanned the air. His crystal blue eyes reflected from even the dim lights overhead.

Willie swallowed and said, "How's it going, boss? I know you?"

Instead of just looking directly at him, the new guard seemed to be looking everywhere else. He smelled the air a few times. "I'm Pierre," he answered in the thickest of accents. Whatever the mystery man was from, Willie didn't care because he loved accents. He felt the sweat build up under his collar even though the room was cold enough to chill ice cream.

"Willie…William…Cooper. That's me," Willie said correcting himself. Pierre seemed too humble and proper to use a name such as "Willie".

"Hello, William," the stranger said with a smile that made Willie melt. "By now, I would've sensed some danger from you and taken you down. But I almost feel you are worthy to enter. How did you hear about the People of Bliss?"

"Oh, I'm actually already with the group."

"Strange. I don't remember letting anyone exit today."

"I left…a while ago, boss. Just coming back now."

With a cocked head, Pierre seemed to be using his ears to place Willie's position. "Why did you leave in the first place?"

To sound mysterious, because all men loved mysterious, Willie muttered, "I was on a mission for Adam."

Smirking now, Pierre stood up. In his right hand, he used a device that dog trainers used. The clicking noise echoed in the small room. Pierre's ear moved about and then he began to walk toward Willie.

"You can't see me?" Only after he said it, did Willie realize how rude and ignorant the question had been. "Oh, you're blind. Sorry. I just –"

Pierre wore a tight black turtle neck and even tighter blue jeans, leaving little to Willie's extensive imagination. No Union department had created this perfect human being, nature did all the research. With a hint of hairy chest through his shirt and long thick mustache, Pierre looked like a human version of a weasel.

"Wondering why they'd put a blind man to watch the door?" Pierre said, finishing the sentence. "Because I can see much better than most people here. You know why?"

Pierre stepped closer, now only a foot or so in front of Willie. The sweat grew profusely, dripping off the tip of his nose. Willie hadn't been this close to such an attractive man since Adam sleptwalk into his room and cuddled next to him. "No," he squeaked.

"Because it's not only about *seeing*, but about *feeling* too."

Without asking, Pierre lifted his hands and touched the sides of Willie's cheeks. The fingers were callused yet so gentle. Just like his husband's hands. Pierre ran his fingers along the wrinkles on his cheeks, pimples on his forehead, and receding hairline on his head. Willie really wished he'd gotten that plastic surgery now and morphed himself into the Union's definition of a perfect man.

"Hmph," Pierre giggled, "you've got dimples."

After a brief heart flutter, Willie could finally speak. "You too."

Pierre nodded, "Come inside. They are doing a play in the auditorium. You should see it."

"Sure," Willie squeaked again. "I mean, sounds fun. See you...around?"

"That would be nice," Pierre said, turning to the large wheel that opened a metal door to the missile silo. He turned it with ease and the entrance opened with a clank. "See you around, William."

He didn't realize until it was time to walk that his knees had been nervously locked. Willie walked slowly and entered the missile silo.

"Goddamnit, where have you been?" Adam said breathlessly when he saw Willie at his doorway.

Greeted with a hug, he suddenly felt less rigid. Willie had been thinking about what to say the entire walk here. Should he admit the truth, that the Union nearly sucked him into their technology black hole? Or should he lie and say testing the farce chip had been more time-consuming than they planned? Without having to make up an excuse, Adam immediately changed the subject of the month long delay and looked at Willie's palm. "Did the chip work?"

"Yep. Worked like a charm."

Ecstatic, Adam threw his fists in the air like he was Tom Cruise talking about his perfect life. "This is awesome! Best news I've heard all day. We need more people chipped."

Whatever strategy Adam had planned for this final war, the chip seemed to be the key. But how? Instead of asking, Willie just absorbed the gratitude for his role in it. He wondered if the rest of the people here would be so welcoming. After Sirius Dawson's death, many accusing eyes had pinned the blame on him of letting Union Keepers kidnap her in the first place.

Adam returned to his computer desk and manically typed at the laptop.

"Hey, boss, there's a play going on? Mind if I go watch it then we can go through the details?"

"Hmm? Yeah sure," Adam answered without turning around. The moment reminded Willie how he looked slouched in front of a laptop for hours.

Once he dropped off his supplies back in his room and changed out of sweaty clothes, Willie made his way down the hall to the spiral of stairs. No one seemed to be around. The stage play had drawn in the People of Bliss like a dry sponge.

He could hear laughter, then clapping, followed by the voices of children reciting lines. The Wizard of Oz. Willie already knew the dialogue of Dorothy disobeying her Aunt and Uncle's wishes.

The stage had been setup the largest room of the missile silo. What probably used to be a computer room for rocket scientists had been transformed completely. Hundreds of chairs with hundreds of citizens all faced the small, yet adequate, wood stage. Not only had the chairs been filled, but even the floor. Sitting on the floors with blankets, no one even turned to see Willie as he entered the room and shut the door behind him. Having to stand since there didn't seem to be a place to sit, he crossed his arms and leaned against the wall.

With the straight brown hair tied behind her, the star of the show had the cutest of cheeks. Willie wondered how much they had been pinched to make them so red. A flashlight, from a stagehand in the distance, shown on the little girl like a spotlight. The room quieted as the young angel began to sing "Over the Rainbow".

So pure and serene, Willie wished he could record this girl's voice and play it to help him sleep at night. It sent a shiver up his spine. Would the Union Transmogrification Center be able to genetically replicate such a voice?

Looking around, he noticed a few eyes glance back at him. Eyes that had squinted angrily at him were now excitedly wide open. A few people waved at him. He waved back.

Willie closed his eyes and kept them shut as that gentle voice melted the hearts of everyone in this room. Maybe Pierre had been right. Maybe there was something more to what was seen. Maybe feelings, a natural component built into every human being, meant more. Willie experienced an energy in this room. A grateful energy. A joyful energy. A peaceful energy. More peaceful than any government could offer. And technology didn't craft it.

CHAPTER TWENTY-FIVE

Cured Salmon with Horseradish. Tex-Mex Deviled Eggs. Spanish Ham with Olives.

Marcel suddenly realized this long table of tasty hors d'oeuvres didn't have any options for vegans. Of all these adoring fans, surely someone didn't prefer to savor animal by-products. How could he had been so blind to his loyal followers? How about his best friends, Joey and Joseph? Did they eat meat?

The castle looked incredible from this view. Towers cast a shadow even in the cloudy sky. Sometimes he thought of that sun, hidden behind blackened clouds. His journey of the universe with Lucifer crept him closer to the ultimate light in the solar system. Then invisible rays led him toward the star, soft voices repeated *Come into the light,* his skin began to ignite, fire surrounded him, the place of peace seemed to be more the place of fear...

Giggling passerby broke his concentration. Two girls grabbed a few of the snacks and smiled in his direction. Hundreds walked around, shopping the tents and meeting representatives of the new world government. Thankful for this opportunity to clarify all the misconceptions, Marcel's throat had nearly gone dry from all the questions he'd answered for the last three hours. He rubbed his hands together, not to keep warm in the chilled breezy air. But to wipe away the nervous sweat from his palms. His dad never got sweaty.

The thought of the former President of the United States, his father and his role model, sat in a cell on a ship. Had the Light blinded him? Blinded him? Lied to him? Then began to yank him slowly into a fiery demise?

Looking around again, he couldn't find his best friends Joseph and little brother Joey. They promised to be here. For the last two weeks, they stayed in the castle with him. Every night was a different board game, Marcel thrilled at the challenges. Joey didn't care for games, but loved movies. He almost seemed like a little brother to Marcel too. In the theater room, he brought in old reels of his favorite films. Both of them enjoyed edge-of-your-seat actions movies. Neither of his new friends even saw the *Transformers* films and munched on popcorn with wide eyes. Even classics like *Forest Gump, Saving Private Ryan,* and *Titanic* were new to the brothers. Joey loved *Pulp Fiction* the most. So did Brent.

Another unexpected handshake and congratulations of the Union's success. Before Marcel even had a chance to see the face or even pose, a camera flashed and the fan shyly ran away with friends to the pavilion. They disappeared into the mass amount of casually dressed patrons. Nelson would've enjoyed this crowd of well-dressed, well-groomed, and well-educated people. Most of all, he would've enjoyed the attention Marcel got and deserved.

"Can we take a picture with you too?" a tiny voice asked. He looked down to see brown curly hair combed over to the side. A boy, no older than six, tugged at the bowtie around his neck. "Mom says I can grow up to be like you someday. Be a leader and stuff. Can I?"

Marcel got on his knee while the child's excited mother held tightly to a camera. He wondered what Janice was doing now. Was their child as precious as this boy? Was it even *their* child? He whispered, "Of course you can. With the Union, you can be anyone you want to be."

Those words gave the kid a bigger grin than if he had told him they were going to Disneyland. The child posed next to him and Marcel gave a grin to the camera. After a quick flash, the boy ran away and grabbed his mother's hand, then used his other hand to wave to Marcel.

Nothing could ruin this moment of honor. Not the image of Janice's petrified face at Brent's dead body. Not Nelson's poor performance at pretending to be "in shock". Not the abundance of protests against the Union.

Nothing.

He circled the table of scrumptious snacks. Then a familiar face stood at the end of the table. "Joey!" Marcel called out and waved.

Seeming to not hear him, Joey continued to stare at the table of foods. Strange thing was that the teenager never picked up any of it. He just stared. Something was wrong. Marcel could sense darkness, but couldn't decipher it.

He approached and patted Joey on the back. "Hey, buddy, everything okay?"

Not turning around, Joey mumbled, "Hey."

"We got lots of food. Stop by later, I brought another one you might like. Ever seen *Man of Steel*?"

"No."

"You like superhero movies?"

"Yeah."

These one words answers were making Marcel even more nervous. He patted his friend on the shoulder. "What's the matter?"

With his head down, Joey turned and said nothing. In his right hand, he grasped a plate of uneaten chocolate java cakes, red velvet squares, and lemon cupcakes. His other hand held something in his pocket.

Dressed in a suit and tie with his hair slicked to the left, Joey stared at the concrete pavement of the pavilion. The plate of snacks shook as he spoke. "Joseph says I don't need to talk to you. Joseph says stand near the table. Joseph says I need to just hold a plate so I don't look suspicious."

"Suspicious?" Marcel asked. He thought of what could possibly be suspicious. It did seem odd that his older brother Joseph was nowhere to be seen when the two seemed tied at the hip. It also seemed peculiar that Joey's coat was way too bulky, even in this weather.

Joey whispered, "Joseph says the Union is up to no good. Joseph says Mr. Declan didn't finish the job. Joseph says we have to."

Mr. Declan? "Charles Declan? The maniac that shot up innocent people and blew up the nation's capital?" Marcel squinted, knowing that had to be the reference. "Charles Declan? The leader of the terrorist group Servo Clementia?" He gulped. "Were…are you…followers?"

Joey nodded, shamefully.

Slowly, Marcel used the tip of his finger to pull Joey's trench coat back a little. A device clung around his body like a weight belt. Connected to pounds of explosive C4, a clock timer circled around to midnight. Joey's entire body was covered in the gray clay. His last words came out a faint confident whisper, "Joseph says we doing the right thing."

Wind burst and wrapped a bubble around Marcel microseconds before the clock ended. The C4 activated. An explosion melted away any existence of his friend Joey. Not even an ash. Fire circle around him and devoured the hundreds of followers that had came to support the Union. And support him. Screams of joy had turned to screams of terror. Laughter turned to wails. Flames dissolve all the voices around him. He watched in horror, in his protective bubble, helpless to what was happening. It occurred so fast that his brain couldn't contemplate what to do.

Every settled as fast as it had detonated. He felt something he hadn't felt all day. Alone. His people...dead. His servants...dead. His admirers...dead. The bubble created by the wind element faded away and flakes of ash touched his face. With a shaky finger, he wiped a smudge of ashes from his face then looked at his blackened finger. This was all that was left.

Marcel took a step back, but hadn't realized the shock made his legs not work. He fell backwards onto the pavement. Black dust flew up. Rushing to stand up, Marcel hastily wiped away all the ash on him. People. It was all that was left of these people. He circled around. Through the mucky air, he couldn't see any sign of life. A few fires still burned. Trees burned slowly, but nothing else survived.

How could he do such a thing? Joey. One of the kindest, shiest men he'd ever met couldn't have done this alone. No. Men like Joey were blinded. Blinded by the Light. And his light was his brother.

"Joseph," Marcel whispered to himself. There's no way a scandalous liar like Joseph would leave such a task up to his brother. That meant he must've been in a stone's throw length.

Marcel walked toward the bridge, thinking of the boy. The boy with a dream of the future. Where was his ashes? The Light had stolen them. Again, a rebellious attack on him had ended the lives of innocent people. Marcel's hand clenched as he walked. Then he heard the screams of people. The panicked voices were coming from across the bridge. His walk hurried to a sprint. Sure enough, on the bridge's entrance to the pavilion, people had escaped the explosion.

Then the sounds of sharp gun shots echoed. He was too late. In the distance, he saw a few Union Keepers on the ground with bullet wounds in their heads. In front of their lifeless bodies, Marcel began to slow his dash because he found who had exchanged the gunfire.

Joseph, holding his bleeding side and very much alive, scurried to one side of the bridge. He pointed his gun at Marcel and fired without even a hesitation.

But Marcel didn't feel a bullet hit any part of his body. He stopped and waited, expecting his body to go weak. Nothing happened. Slowly, he looked down. A bullet spun in mid-air, inches from his chest. Joseph fired more ammo. Each bullet stopped an inch before its fatal entrance into Marcel.

The air had ceased the trajectory of the bullet. He realized almost immediately. Wind. Just the way the element bubbled him from the explosion, it had also stopped the fatal shots. The bullets fell and clanked on the ground.

He heard more clicks. Joseph continued pulling the trigger on his gun, but the chamber was empty. This man, that only days before, seemed on a path to becoming Marcel's friend had transitioned into Marcel's enemy. Marcel demanded, "How could you?"

Joseph didn't answer. Instead, he unstrapped the device around his waist and began to try to clumsily pry the clock off. The story unfolded before Marcel's eyes, apparently his bomb hadn't gone off. Joseph tried desperately to fix it by rewiring the clock.

"There were children there!" Marcel shouted. "Children!"

Blood pooled out of from Joseph from his wounds. His bloody, shaking hands began to connect the clock back to the device.

"No," Marcel shook his head. His pupils widened and he grasped the darkness in Joseph's eyes. Going limp, the deceiver gave up on repairing his failed bomb. Then he faced Marcel like in the presence of a god. Which he sort of was.

To the right of him, Marcel saw a slight fire from the explosion still burning a wooden table. He smirked. "Open your mouth."

Joseph shook his head, sweat poured out of him more than blood.

"I said 'open your mouth'!" Marcel screamed. His power clenched onto Joseph's soul, hypnotizing him.

Widening his mouth, a tear trickled down his cheek, knowing his fate. From the nearby inferno, a blaze rose like a snake. It slithered toward Joseph's trembling body. Then the igneous apparition motioned towards the liar's throat. Joseph began to cry out, mouth wide but unable to fight Marcel's grasp of his physical skills. The snake swam down Joseph's throat. His body convulsed and muffled cries for help became muffled as he burned from the inside. Flames exited out his chest.

Marcel had never intended to murder Brent, so this felt different. This felt…relieving. That man, who could've someday been Marcel's best friend, had planned this attack from the beginning and brought his innocent brother into this devious plan. Unlike Brent, Joseph deserved death. In fact, Marcel did a favor for the future of the Union. He watched as Joseph's body burned and his ashes mixed into the air with his victims.

CHAPTER TWENTY-SIX

It had been eight years since Willie had been awoken by a baby's cry. After adopting Antoine, him and his husband questioned their abilities to be parents. No matter what, their boy wouldn't stop crying at night. Trying different techniques eventually worked though; they found a way to be at peace and be parents. Willie turned over in his floor mattress to the side where his husband used to sleep. It sometimes helped him fall back asleep.

He thought it was one of those strange dreams where the sounds seem so real, but in fact...it wasn't. There was a baby crying. Being a father for eight years created this sense of heroism in him; that he could sweep in and save the infant from his pain.

Standing up, his back cracked and knees popped like firecrackers. Getting old sucked. He read somewhere that life began at 40. Too bad the body didn't agree. It was chilly again. Damn heaters must be down again. Wearing his A-Shirt (or his man used to say "wife-beater" shirt) and striped boxers wouldn't keep him warm as he ventured to where the baby cried. Out of bed now, he immediately covered himself in a heavy hoodie sweater and gym pants.

Across the hall, the babies crying was evidently coming from behind Janice Celest's door. Still catching up on all the missile silo gossip, he hadn't heard the President's daughter had a baby. Now that the fatigue began to wear away and Willie realized the miracle that had woken him up. Population Control departments decided parents and where children were born. But somehow, she'd became pregnant on her own and had a child. Curiosity overshadowed his need to be father superhero. He knocked softly before realizing the baby's cries were louder, then he knocked louder.

"I'm working on it!" she shouted from the other side.

Coming from Jersey, attitude like that was met with Willie's crude mouth. But this time he decided to be polite. "I can help."

It didn't take long before the top lock snapped open and the door swung just a few inches. She didn't even look to see who was at the door, instead she walked away and left Willie opening the door the rest of the way. Janice, much more thinner and sickly than he'd ever seen in those New York Times photos, slumped into a rocking chair. Frustrated and visibly stressed, she crossed her arms to warm up in that ugly pink robe. "He won't stop. I'm sorry. I'm trying."

"Don't apologize. No big." Willie turned to the baby's crib. Wrapped in several blankets was what he remembered made life so precious. Big blue eyes squinted as the boy cried even louder at the sign of a stranger. So angry, the infant's hands clenched together more than his eyes as it wailed into the empty room. "He's beautiful."

Janice's face smirked on one side. "Usually." She sipped on a cup of steaming hot tea. "I'm a terrible mother if I can't figure out what's wrong with my baby."

Vividly remembering his own self-loathing moments as a father, Willie replied, "No. You're not." He had an immediate idea. "I'll be back. I bet I know what's wrong."

After a minute digging through his still unpacked satchel in his room, he returned with a set of pricey headphones. He had borrowed them from the warehouse and didn't have any intentions of bringing them back now. Janice stared strangely at him. "Ear muffs?"

"These puppies will block out any noise. Used them in the warehouse to shut up those forklifts."

Reluctant, Janice stared at the yellow clunky ear muffs. "They resemble headphones the workers use on airport runways."

"Yes, exactly." Willie said, realizing how different they were. A politician's daughter had flown countless time while him, a janitor's son, had only flown twice in his life. But this made him respect her more. She went from riches to rags and yet prevailed.

"I don't follow," Janice said. "You want me to drown out the sound of my baby?"

He nodded. "Yeah. Get this. My ex was into all this body-science mumbo-jumbo. He said that we're going to stress out when we hear a baby cry. But if you can relax, then so can the infant. Put them on. I'm going to hand you...what's his name?"

"Colin."

"Colin. Okay. Great name. Anyways, relax for a minute and hold him. Sing a song. You like Green Day? My son loved Green Day. Know the song 'Good Riddance'?"

She didn't answer, just nodded. "But I can't sing."

"Good! Then you won't hear it either. You see? Win, win!"

After a long moment, she shrugged. "Okay." Janice placed the headphones on and Willie quickly, yet gently, lifted the baby from the crib. It was a cold night, but maybe the number of blankets might've been extreme. He kept only three layers of cloths wrapped around the precious child. Slowly, he put Colin into Janice's lap. Her motherly instinct immediately grasped the baby correctly and she held him.

Willie mimed, knowing that Janice wouldn't be able to hear past the top-notch ear muffs, for her to close her eyes. If she hadn't started singing, Willie would've thought she fell asleep by how peaceful she seemed with shut eyes. The lyrics flowed out of her mouth rehearsed like a stage performance. For someone who said she lacked in vocal talent, Janice sang like that woman vowing for attention at a church choir. Memories resurfaced of his husband Connor and his attempts at singing. His voice may have been so bad that even the American Idol judges would've walked out of the room, but baby Antoine loved it. Trying not to tear up in front of someone he barely knew didn't work out well. Willie wiped a droplet from his eye.

Once the song was done, Janice seemed to be frozen in some type of invisible cocoon and awaiting to be awoken anew. Willie reached over, removing the headphones. She looked down to see her child dead asleep. This time, her entire face smirked. Without another word, Janice lifted the baby and gradually place him in the crib. It was like little Colin had become a doll because he didn't even budge.

"Thank you," she said, her back to him, "What's your name?"

"Willie."

"Ah. The electrical conduit. Adam talks about you like you're some kind of superhero."

Funny, because he just felt like one by saving another life. He rubbed his head and then awkwardly said, "Alright then. Nighty night."

"You like red?"

"Huh?"

Janice looked to the table at the far end of her room. Next to a photograph of the Celest family, including the First Lady that passed away several years ago, was a bottle of red wine. Perhaps drinking at this hour of night with a baby nearby seemed a bad idea, but maybe not so much. Surely the child would sleep for a while and Willie did have a weakness for Pinot Nior. "Sweet."

"He actually told me once: 'You're like Superman, baby.' And I just grunted: 'What?'. Then he says: 'Because your eyes melt me like lasers.'"

Red wine nearly shot out of Willie's nose as he covered his mouth and cackled in laughter. Janice joined him in their mutual hushed bit of drunken stupor. Baby Colin barely stirred in the last hour, even after all the noise they made. Hearing stories about her relationship with Adam seemed so amusing. The goofy college kid turned Servo Clementia assassin turned rebellion leader was still...goofy.

Being the President's daughter seemed to be a curse of reckless drinking behavior. Janice downed most of their bottle of red wine like a pro while Willie felt the effects almost immediately. Red wine brewed naturally here in the silo was quite potent. So potent that he realized that his giggling had turned to snorting, which made Janice laugh even harder.

After the laughter died, Janice must've felt guilty and quickly added, "He's sweet though. He tries. I just...haven't figured out how to tell him."

"Tell him what?"

She glanced towards the baby's crib. "Colin's eyes are blue."

The odd statement took a moment to make sense. Then Willie uttered a short, "Oh."

Before he could ask, Janice answered. "I'm not sure who the father is. But I have my suspicions. The last time I got this drunk..." she swung back the wine glass to let even the few drops at the bottom touch her tongue, then said, "...was with my adopted brother Marcel."

Again, she left Willie to speculate. Even hammered he knew what she meant. He uttered once more, "Oh."

Janice put her finger to her lips in a *shhhh* motion. Some of the People of Bliss, the few radical ones anyways, called Marcel Celest an "Anti-Christ". If word got out that his possible child lived in the premises, a Lynch mob would surely be pounding on this door.

"Got it," Willie nodded. "Who else you know that could be the dad?"

"Well, honestly, I guess I hadn't put much more thought in it." Janice admitted. "I'm content with Adam not being the father. He's too immature. I remember when I first met him. I was teaching my Evolutions class about a very interesting study done by a woman named Michelle Rigina. He kept giggling every time I said 'Rigina' because it sounded like 'vagina'."

Willie snorted as he laughed which made Janice giggle along with him. After it died down, he asked, "He taught Evolutions?"

"It was my way of changing the world. There's a lot to learn in adaption and evolution." Janice dug through a box underneath her bed and pulled out one of those large tin canisters of caramel popcorn. She offered, but Willie declined.

For some reason, the thought returned to him of that machine in the warehouse. A machine so powerful that it shutdown all electronic equipment without even being turned on. Curiosity got the better of Willie as he questioned, "Ever talk about technology? Like...does it help us evolve?"

Eyebrows raised quizzically, Janice shook her head as though everyone should know this. "Heavens no. The exact opposite."

"For real? How so?" Willie grabbed for some popcorn now.

"Well. Humanity has shared information for thousands of years through genes. Genes, essentially, are building blocks. Building blocks of accomplishments and mistakes. But…add technology into it and essentially we cannot make mistakes. Gadgets stop us from learning to adapt and therefore evolve."

Barely passing High School and struggling through trade school, Willie found himself easily overwhelmed by this conversation and his face must've showed it.

Janice turned the popcorn canister over and the kennels fell to the rug they sat on. Showing him the empty can, she explained, "See this? This represents humanity. Pretty plain and boring, right? This was the start of our kind. Then…" she trailed off, tossing one kernel of popcorn back in the canister at a time. "…we began to learn things. The wheel, fire, hunting, gathering, etcetera. Now, open your mouth…" Willie listened. From the can, Janice began to toss one piece of popcorn at a time for him to catch with his mouth. They laughed at the few that missed. "Then technology comes along, represented by you, of course. We start feeding it all this information. Making our lives easier, but…" she trailed off.

Holding up the tin can, Willie could clearly see it was empty. She continued, "We haven't learned anything. You get it?"

"So, it makes us…stupid?"

Sitting Indian style, Janice brushed her hair back. "We gather knowledge and we spread knowledge. In fact, we *love* knowledge. We learn from mistakes." She stared at her empty wine glass and glumly repeated. "We learn from our mistakes. Then we spread this new knowledge to our kin, family, children…whomever. That's how evolution works. But something more powerful has sucked us in and stupefied us. Then ended our capability to evolve."

Fascination and fear took over Willie's mind. He immediately pictured that trailer with the strange device in it. Project Syncope. Something so powerful that it shutdown all electronics. He looked down at his watch. Still dead. How addicted he became to all his gadgets and computers made him sick to his stomach. The silo had become his rehab center. Now officially sober, Willie could finally see straight. "I'm not alone."

"Huh?"

"My addiction. My addiction to all of it. I'm not alone. The Union. The Union is using this addiction to reel people in, huh?"

The sentence was stuttered and confusing, but Janice seemed to understand by giving a subtle nod. "I was there too, you know. Conversing with the Union and its propaganda. You're correct. Technology is mankind's weakness and eventually we'll all succumb to it. Because beating it is nearly improbable. I sometimes wish we could just…reboot it."

"Reboot?"

"Yeah, like start over. From the beginning. Before buildings, infrastructure, electronics, and government. Reboot the entire world."

"You mean like Spiderman?"

Janice squinted his eyes. "Like what?"

"Spiderman? The movie? They've rebooted that movie like four times. But the original was the best, you know what I'm saying?"

"Um. I guess so. Never seen them. But yes. Wouldn't it be amazing? To start a new world? And do it *right* this time?"

Willie imagined Project Syncope. His idea of how to create a digital detox around the world. Since his arrival at the silo, he struggled with himself if the idea did work...what it would do to the planet. What it would do to him. It would certainly reboot this planet.

"What if," Willie started, knowing that someday in the future he may regret this conversation, "What if I knew how to get rid of it?"

Janice sat silent for a moment before she giggled. "I'd say you drank more wine than I did."

"I'm serious. What if I knew a way...to end technology...on a global scale?"

Since Willie kept a relaxed face for the first time this evening, Janice ceased her laughter and stared at him. "Are you referring to cellphones?"

He nodded.

"Guns?"

He nodded.

"Nanos?"

He nodded.

"Internet?"

He nodded.

Janice stared, waiting for Willie to crack a smile or something. "All of it? All electricity? Everywhere?"

After a slight nod, Willie whispered. "Yeah, doll. Yep. I know how to get rid of all of it. And give the world a digital detox. We could start from the beginning."

"It's called 'Project Syncope'," Willie said the group.

Adam slid over from one side of his room to the other on his computer chair. He typed rapidly into a laptop.

Willie sat on a chair, getting that familiar feeling of a police interrogation. Above him, Janice stood at the doorway with her arms crossed. On the other end of the room, looking like he had just been woken up abruptly, which he had been, was Adam typing quickly on his computer.

"You're not going to find anything on the 'net, boss. I tried." Willie affirmed.

"This isn't the internet. It's a back door to old archives. You're talking to a bad ass hacker, remember? When I worked with Servo Clementia, I bypassed FBI, NSA, and all those other departments that use lazy initials."

After a minute, Adam stopped typing and began reading. From his view, Willie could only see strings of computer code that he knew nothing about.

Janice broke the timid air. "What did you find?"

Adam spun around. "Holy shit. He's right. It's real. Project Syncope is an explosive NEMP." Blank faces must've stared back at him because Adam sighed and explained further. "Haven't you guys seen any cool movies? Star Trek? The Matrix? EMP stands for Electronic Magnetic Pulse. NEMP is at a nuclear scale. Very powerful stuff that was banned in 2021." He moved the mouse around the screen with no intent of clicking anything. Perhaps he was fascinated by the computer and also dumbfounded by the fact that it would be obsolete when the EMP triggered. He mumbled, "This is it. This is how we bring the Union down to our level. Their guns, fleet, communications - all of it gone within a tenth of a second. It'll cover a ten mile radius."

"But," Janice asked Willie, "I thought you said it would knock out power globally?"

No one could question Adam's computer skills and no once could question Willie's power skills. "It's not the device you need to be worried about, doll," he shrugged, "it's the 98 issues scattered across the US."

It took several minutes before his words made sense to anyone in the room, but Willie knew. He'd been next to the nuclear warheads in the center of the country's largest cities. The nuclear warheads that denoted with devastating winds and killed hundreds of millions. Still glowing with internal power, those weapons of mass destruction were scattered everywhere. Willie had seen one on his travel back here to the silo. They were tall like skyscrapers and terrifying as a crumbling one. He knew, or perhaps felt, from the beginning what would happen if Project Syncope activated.

Adam asked, "Shit, he's right. The nukes will make the signal blast around like a pinball, gaining more force as it retracts. By the time it ended, the world would be without power."

Being the only uneducated person in the room made Janice physically uneasy. "I don't understand. The nukes aren't live."

"Yes, they are," Adam corrected her.

Many nights Willie had thought about this very scenario. What he experienced with the power of electricity was different than others. He knew using the nukes as amplifiers to the signal of Project Syncope would work, but he let the others figure it out for himself. Turning on the machine meant a global blackout. He kept silent until now but Janice's speech changed him. Technology's quest of world domination meant the end of humanity. Even hidden under the guise that we controlled it, eventually we wouldn't. Now, the idea settled deep into the trio's skin just like it had Willie for all these weeks since he saw Project Syncope. The world would be without electricity.

"How long would it last?" Janice asked as though she already didn't know the answer.

For someone as hooked on his gadgets as Willie was, saying goodbye to all the possibilities brought him to the verge of unexpected tears. He had been six years old when he touched the first model smartphone. The surge of information felt like a flower growing rapidly in his hand and at this moment it felt like he planned on spraying bleach on the botanical wonders. "Forever," Willie answered. "The machine fries it all out. Get what I'm saying? Everything will be gone forever." He pointed at his his palm. "My chip got friend by Project Syncope. Still dead. And we didn't even turn the device on when it happened. Imagine what that thing can do when it's activated."

Arms crossed still, but now pacing, Janice asked, "Adam, why was the project scrapped in the first place?"

After typing more vigorously into the computer, he answered, "Activating Project Syncope also shocked anyone near it. Shocked them to death actually. Killed four scientists in Zimbabwe."

"Well," Janice admitted, "it's good we have someone who can withstand electrical discharge."

Suddenly feeling like the most important man in the world, Willie sat up. It was true. Only he had the capability to activate Project Syncope and live to tell about it.

Adam leaned back, bending the already wobbly chair. "This doesn't make sense. My precognition showed electricity in the future. Well. Sort of electricity. I was on a train run on something else. Like a light source or something." Realizing neither of them would be able to comment on what was his inside his head, Adam changed the subject, "We should put this up to a vote, let the People of Bliss decide –"

"No," Janice stopped him with her hand up, "Willie is the only person in the *entire* world that can do this. Doesn't matter what others say, he makes the choice in the end. The whole purpose of escaping the Union was because we didn't want to be governed. And you are suggesting governing Willie? The way I see it, it's his decision."

The weight of the world fell on his shoulders. William Cooper, a lightning strike survivor from the poor side of Philly and ex-con, had to make the most important decision of humanity. He balanced the bad and the good.

The bad: technology had aided humanity. Thousands of people live thanks to the help of pacemakers, dialysis machines, and blood transfusions. Would his decision end those people? What about how far humanity had gone because of technology? Traveling to another planet or seeing outer space would certainly not be capable anymore if the world transitioned to the Dark Ages. And what about communications? Phones, internet, laptops, watches…everything would be obsolete.

The good: technology had ruined humanity. Just like Janice had said. And wars would end. Can't fight without guns or nuclear weapons. The chip wouldn't work so the Union would die with it. And the locusts, the worldwide nano killer insects, would shutdown essentially saving millions. Willie nodded to himself. His decision could save millions, if not billions.

The decision should be simple, but he still hesitated realizing his mouth had been open for nearly a minute.

Janice walked over and bent to his level. She looked so pale and sickly from this close. "Willie, I know this is a big decision but think of it this way. Humanity could reboot. Just like a computer system. Start over again. And do it right this time."

Reboot.

Willie shook his head. "Yeah, you're right. Start a reboot. We'll do it right this time. Rebuild a better system. Technology that doesn't own us, but we own it." He rubbed his hands together. "Let's do it."

CHAPTER TWENTY-SEVEN

When someone gets beat to the ground, verbally and physically, they fight to rise back up. But not Nelson. His butt had gone sore from sitting on the solid ground of his cell. He'd only gotten up four times in the last three days since he watched the captain of the boat toss an innocent woman into the icy ocean, each time to use the restroom. Food collected at the doorway. A few grumbles from the crew about his lacking of eating made no difference, Nelson just wasn't hungry. Unlike his friend and colleague Declan, he never devoured his troubles down to the pit of his stomach with more food. He would starve himself, as a sort of unwarranted punishment for his actions. After Victoria's funeral, he'd lost sixteen pounds in two weeks until his advisors put him in a diet plan to beat his depression. At the time, he thought his advisors actually cared for his well being, but he was now convinced it was because the Press constantly nagged about his lethargic appearance.

How did a man like him become President? The captain was correct, Nelson lacked guts. On several occasions, as Commander-in-Chief, he should've blasted away his foes off the face of the planet. Instead, his foes blasted his country into oblivion. He did care about human life, because no one deserves to die. Especially Victoria.

Antoine's prayers aggravated him. It used to be just a morning prayer, but turned into a nightly and daytime prayer. The soldier never quit believing in hope and his god. So far, neither had gotten that cell door unlocked.

One morning, Nelson awoke to the ship surging backward. Saliva stuck from the ground to his lip as he stood, feeling his stiff neck begging for a mattress. "We stopping?" He asked, sure that Antoine was awake because the soldier never seemed to sleep.

"Yep. I can't see much, but I think there's Union choppers coming in."

The day he dreaded arrived. Marcel finally made his way out to the middle of the ocean. All these days and he never planned what to say to his son. But maybe this could spell his freedom. It was also spell the end to plans for that jet to be in his possession. In the rebellion's possession.

Crew hurried down the stairs and corridor. Whoever slid their meals through the bottom slit of the door arrived. "Captain says no new bruises. Unless you fight back, of course."

Nelson could barely lift his body, worse yet throw a punch. Either he'd been beaten so bad that the toll on his muscles became critical or self-loathing was responsible for his weakness. Maybe both. "Okay," Nelson said, grumbling as he stood.

"Hey," Antoine whispered from the hole. "Come here. Quick." Whatever he wanted, it sounded urgent. Nelson placed his ear against the hole. "Don't look in his eyes."

"What? Why?"

"No one wants to talk about it, but he can get inside your head, my man. Not like controlling minds, but influencing them. Just like what he does with fire."

Influencing minds didn't seem like such a stretch, since he'd seen Marcel controlling a tunnel of water with his hands. Magic existed and his son, of all people, conjured it. Nelson recalled his first born son's obsession with the stories of wizards, castles, and kings. Every night, before bed, he read Harry Potter to him, always wondering which side of magic Marcel was on. With that, Nelson took Antoine's advise seriously, feeling a chill scurry up his spine.

"Hey! I said let's go," the soldier behind the door shouted.

Knowing the routine, he pushed his hands through the open slot and felt a zip tie secure his wrists. After a minute, the door swung and the soldier grasped him by the collar.

Corridor after empty corridor, Nelson wondered how many other people were on this ship because every room seemed unoccupied. Besides Nelson and Antoine, he suspected no other prisoners, except that woman the captain tossed over the edge. They stopped at a steel door marked MESS HALL.

Straight ahead, past that entrance, was his son. Next to cell, through a peep hole in a concrete wall, was a stranger named Antoine. How did he trust the stranger more? He couldn't help but sense the peril he was in and if he had enough water in him, he might've pissed on his jeans. On one hand, he knew his son wouldn't lift a finger to hurt him. But on the other hand, would he try to convince his father to join the cause? Through that mysterious power he had over minds? Could Marcel force him to lead the nations, side by side, like the king and princes in his childhood books. With no other choice, he had to go with his gut. And his gut was saying the same thing Antoine demanded. *Don't look in his eyes.*

When the door opened, sitting at a table next to vending machines, Marcel leapt up and hugged his father before he even entered the room yet. Nelson couldn't remember the last time they had hugged. Perhaps at Victoria's funeral almost two years ago. Things had changed, but most notable was the coldness of Marcel's body. Could it be his son had died in that coma, like he had accepted over a year ago? Marcel pulled back and looked at him with wet cheeks. "Dad, I can't believe it's you. God, what happened to you?" He asked, inspecting the bruises and cuts.

The captain, legs propped on a table and leaning back on a chair, interrupted. "We caught him trying to steal the plane, Supreme Leader." He stood up, a toothpick dangling out of his lip. "After a heavy scuffle, we realized who he was."

Nelson kept his eyes on the captain. Trying to avoid Marcel's gaze turned out more difficult than he expected. Panic crushed his chest down. All his life, he was trained that politicians looked each other in the eyes, but that habit needed to be broken quickly. He glanced around the room. Near the vending machine, holding an open can of Coke, was Gerard.

Gerard? Why was here? Their eyes met, but his son-in-law gave no indication his true intention.

"Dad? Can you hear me? Is what the captain said true?"

Being in such a daze of stress, Nelson hadn't even heard Marcel ask the question the first time. He just kept staring at Gerard, waiting for help maybe. Even without locking eyes, Marcel could read Nelson's expressions. "We both came as soon as we heard the news. Can't believe you're alive. Dad? Are you okay?"

Just like that time Nelson arrived at the White House State Dinner without a speech prepared, he found himself unable to formulate words. What should he say to Marcel? He could take the route of his deceased son Brent, spout angry words and then kick, punch, and scream his way out this situation. Or maybe take the approach Janice would say, try to talk sense into Marcel about his actions causing massive deaths worldwide. If Victoria were here, she'd say to just hug Marcel and love calmed even the darkest of raging oceans.

"He seems in shock," Gerard assured Marcel.

"Yes," the captain affirmed, "This was why we threw him in the cell…to keep him from harming other crew members. As you can tell, he's mental. With all due respect, Supreme Leader."

Marcel swung around, "My father is not mental! He's the smartest man I've ever known! You should be bowing down to him."

"I apologize, Supreme Leader," the captain said, staring at Nelson with that look that showed utter disappointment.

"And he's not going back in a cell!" Marcel commanded. In all the years he'd raised his son, Nelson never heard such authority in his voice. As parents, they both taught him respect led to admiration, not oppression.

Gerard interrupted the brief quarrel between the captain of a ship and the leader of the world. "Marcel, let me offer a suggestion. Maybe keep your father here? There's food. Plenty of light. A bathroom. A phone. I'm sure the captain can provide a cot and pillows. And they can lock the door to keep the crew safe."

As soon as Marcel turned to Nelson, he looked to the floor avoiding the eyes. "But I want Dad to come back with us. Wouldn't you like that? Dad?"

"I'm not so sure about that," Gerard insisted. "It's an over eight hour fly back to land. A very uncomfortable ride back. Nelson needs medical attention. We can bring that here. Let him get some rest, that'll be the first thing a doctor suggest. Rest outside of a cell, of course." His son-in-law locked eyes with Nelson, still holding that Coke can tightly. "You need rest. Don't you?"

Sensing Gerard taking control of this awkward situation, Nelson nodded. "Rest." He whispered.

"Make sure he's taken care of," Marcel snapped at the captain. "I want him looking healthy when I return tomorrow. And cut these damn handcuffs. He's the President of the United States, for crying out loud!"

The captain walked up, as Marcel and Gerard stepped away. He stared Nelson down, saying under his breath, "Not the President I voted for." With one swipe, he yanked up a knife and cut the zip tie.

Having to play the role of a man in shock, Nelson stared down to the ground and sat slowly at a chair. Marcel came up, kneeling down to hug him. For a moment, Nelson wanted to hug back. He also wanted to cry, remembering how close their relationship was and, yet, how far it was. But instead, he did nothing. "I know you hate me, Dad. Brent was an accident. I didn't mean to kill him. I don't expect you to forgive me. I just…hope you will."

With those last words, Marcel turned and hurried out the door. Gerard patted Nelson on the shoulder and placed the Coke can in front of him, "Stay hydrated." Then he followed the guards out the door. The captain, being the last one to leave, said aloud in the most fake of tones, "I will make sure our prisoner will be treated like a guest." He slammed the door closed and locked it.

Gasping for air, Nelson released all the stress he just held in. His leg shook and head pulsed for several minutes, until the sound of choppers overhead began to leave. After a minute, his breathing returned to normal. He saw the Coke can. *Stay hydrated.* Why did Gerard say that? The statement seemed so out of place; a bottle of water would've made more sense. Slowly, he reached up and grabbed the soda.

Something jingled inside.

Nelson turned the can upside down. Some liquid spewed out, coating the plastic table. But something else dropped out. A gray small box, the size of a lighter. Hands wet from spilled drink, Nelson opened the box.

It was a lock pick.

Locks were very easy to pick…with steady hands. Nelson found his hands shaking so uncontrollably, especially when a noise that sounded remotely like footsteps could be heard.

Since abandoning him at the Mess Hall, no crew member, even the captain, hadn't bothered to check on him. Maybe it was laziness or bitterness. Either way, Nelson had been given plenty of time to refresh his memory of how to use a lock pick.

Every old-fashioned tumbler lock had five hanging pins, upper and lower. One portion of the kit had a hanging hook to hold the lower, while the other part of the kit would test each upper pin for the right combination. He recalled the hours of practice him and Gerard had that winter in the mountains when Nelson accidentally locked his keys in the cabin. Whatever caused Gerard to handover a way for Nelson to escape, either pity or another plan altogether, wasn't important at the moment. He just needed to get that jet and off this ship.

Over an hour of missteps and retries, Nelson finally popped the door open. He waited and listened before making his escape into the hallway. Freedom seemed much more frightening when it wasn't your right to be. At every corner, he expected a soldier to jump out and grab him. Judging by that captain's insanity, he'd surely be thrown off the boat into his abyssal graveyard.

After a few miscalculations in the direction and walkway, Nelson found himself near the cells. He decided the moment he got that lock pick in his hand, that he'd get Antoine out of here too.

Next to his cell door, Nelson whispered. "Antoine? Can you hear me?"

The sounds of rustling and crawling then Antoine's voice whispered through the door. "My man, is that you?"

Now that he had some practice, Nelson immediately started working on the lock. This door had more pins, but confidence ensured him that it could be done; confidence he hadn't felt in weeks. "I'm going to find a way for you to get out of here. Can the jet fit us both?"

Strangely, Antoine didn't answer immediately. "Are you going to use that jet to defeat the Union?"

"Just answer the question."

"Answer mine."

Something was keeping his cell neighbor from answering. Did Antoine want to stay here? Did he feel there was no purpose outside of this cell? "Yes," Nelson assured him, "With that jet, I'm going to blow the hell out of the castle's army."

After a moment, Antoine answered, "Yeah, there's two seats in the jet. But you gotta fly. My hands....remember?"

"Yep," Nelson answered dishonestly since he actually had forgotten the captain mangled Antoine's hands. If he was going to fly a supersonic high-powered vehicle, breaking a lock seemed minute.

A few minutes later, the lock hinge loosened and the door opened slowly. Nelson stood back. Peeping through a tiny hole in the wall didn't give him the entire clarity of Antoine as this lit hallway did. The young man stepped out, wrinkled face and darkened eyelids. His hair, uncombed for quite some time, was shaped like the corner of the room. He stepped into the hallway and took a breath, as though it was different than the air inside his cell. Maybe it was.

"Thank you," Antoine said, rubbing his face with pasty hands and long fingernails.

"How long have you been here, Antoine?" Nelson demanded.

"I lied. I don't like people feeling sorry for me."

"How long?"

"102 days, six hours and..." he looked at his watch, "thirteen minutes."

Looking at the scabs and torn clothes over his body, Nelson asked, "How many times have they," he stopped himself from saying rape or tortured. "...have they hurt you?"

After a quick snort, Antoine said. "I lost count."

With determination he hadn't felt since the Presidential primaries, Nelson said, "I'm getting you out of here. Got it?"

Antoine nodded slowly. "Follow me. I know the quickest way."

Ducking, Nelson followed Antoine's lead hastily. Every so often, a troop of armed men would pass. He had to hand it to Antoine, the man not only knew the ship flawlessly, he also knew the times people would wander. Breakfast called a large group to the mess hall, but it also left a few wanderers sipping on coffee. They hid, sometimes for thirty or more minutes, waiting for just the moment to dash to another hiding spot. His heart would sound like a car riding over a series of speed bumps anytime someone would pass by. A shadow more frightening than Marcel's hovered over them as they sheltered themselves. At least his son's shadow had no intention of killing him upon sight. The shadow moved along.

Realizing he'd been holding his breath, Nelson took a breath of fresh air. The jet was within grasp. If only he had hid correctly, then he wouldn't have been in this situation.

But this was no time to beat himself up. Another officer passed by while Antoine held Nelson back from moving. The officer wore a similar outfit like the captain, the Union's new wardrobe for the military. Black seemed to be the fashionable choice of Marcel, because everyone seemed to wear it. Or at least some form of dark colors. Another thing that was so strange about his son's behavior. When he was a boy, his coloring books were filled with vibrant colors. Marcel died in that coma and some parasite had taken over his body. It was the only explanation. He had to accept it.

"Okay," Antoine whispered, the first words he'd said since they made their way to the deck. "I'll remove the chocks. You climb in the front seat."

"And then you climb in the back seat."

"Right."

That seemed to be the easy part of the plan. They've been practicing the procedures for take-off and operations for the jet. Simulation flights prepared pilots for this. As much as Nelson wished it was, in fact he wished all this was, he had to be responsible for flying the plane. He took this moment to look down at Antoine's hand. Knuckles swollen, and fingers missing, the cadet had been put through Hell by the captain. At least Nelson's scars would heal.

"Alright," Antoine said, "Follow close."

Both hunched over and ran quickly across the open deck. Last time Nelson was this close to the jet, he couldn't figure out how to open the hatch. Thanks to his training, the button seemed so obvious. He popped it and the glass slid ajar. Antoine removed the chocks before Nelson even had a chance to climb in the front seat.

He sat down and it felt strange at first, the seat propped up for Antoine's smaller stature. Touchscreen buttons lit up. Automatically, the seat adjusted itself. Nelson stared at the dashboard, overwhelmed by all the options. It was like all the training for over two weeks went out the window. Antoine said, "You can do this."

Nelson nodded. He looked out to see Antoine out in the tarmac. The cadet reached inside with his hand and pressed one of the buttons, then climbed off. The hatch began to slide closed. Just then, Nelson realized there was no other seat besides his.

Panicked, he stared into the cadet's brown eyes. "Where's the other seat? There's no other seat!"

"I know," Antoine smirked, "I lied."

The glass slide closed and locked. Nelson screamed out, "No! We can both fit!" Antoine never had the intention of coming. He stepped back. The jet's engine whirred to life. Nelson's fidgety hands couldn't remember the controls for takeoff. Rising up, the jet's wheels retracted. "Damnit, Antoine! You're coming with me!"

"Save our nation!" Antoine called out. Then saluted.

Blood spouted out his chest. Then another bullet penetrated his neck. Then his arm and stomach. Behind him, guns fired continuously and Antoine's body collapsed to the ground. Nelson's lips quivered. In the distance, walking toward the ascending jet, the captain held a semi-automatic weapon. Its barrel still smoking. In his other hand, he put a walkie-talkie to his mouth.

From the dashboard, the captain's voice came through a speaker. "Now, Mr. *President*, we are going to need that jet back. Don't kid yourself. You don't know how to fly that thing. You're not a hero, remember? So stop pretending."

The jet ascended higher in the sky. Up there, Antoine's dead body disappeared to the size of an ant. But that didn't make the memory disappear. Soldiers didn't murder other soldiers. This new Union military wasn't the military at all. The true sense of protecting the nation died along with Antoine. He stopped, midway, and floated in the air.

"Oh, I get it now," the captain snarled over the speaker, "You mad because we shot that kid? Let me ask you something. What if I told you that cadet murdered the pilot and tried to steal that plane? Would that change your mind? Huh?"

Could it be true? Antoine? But they were all just words. Words could be manipulated. They were all just words. Victoria repeatedly told him actions spoke louder than words. Antoine sacrificed himself to save Nelson and get this jet in the hands of the rebellion, while the captain and the crew murdered, raped, and disemboweled prisoners.

Calmly, Nelson pressed a few buttons on the control pad…and aimed at the bottom hull of the boat. Without hesitation, he fired four missiles.

Over the speaker, the captain whispered wildly, "Now, *there's* the President I voted for."

The missiles hit the hull and exploded. Fire, so hot he could feel it inside the jet, covered the center of the boat. He made sure to hit it perfectly. His aim flawless. Nelson watched as the structure cracked down the middle like striking a log of wood with an axe. Frightened passengers jumped out, only to be consumed by the fire. Whether they did it on purpose or by accident, it didn't matter. Nelson wanted every single one of these soldiers dead, because they were no longer soldiers. Patriotism was consumed by the Union, the same way the fire consumed this vessel. Pretty soon, he'd like to see the castle, a vast symbolism of the Union, drown too. Drown for not teaching its followers to swim. Swim in the ocean of dignity.

Surprisingly, the boat took longer than expected to sink. The two halves separated and drifted apart. Nelson thought about turning away and flying off, but he didn't. He watched. Watched as smoke choked the lives out of survivors. Oil leaked out the bottom of the hull, spreading the fire. Bruises on his face felt the heat and it soothed their pain. Memories of what Nelson experienced here wouldn't heal completely. But that was alright. Scars toughened the skin around them.

Sometimes a lifeboat would try to slip away, with battered and tearful officers. Too late for tears. Calmly, he'd float the plane that direction and use the side Gatling guns to fire at the lifeboats. No naval military would be allowed to live this day. No humanity would survive. Not without his permission. And Antoine was the only humanity left on that ship. He kept firing until the water around the survivors turned dark red.

It took almost two hours for the damaged ship to be swallowed by the Atlantic. Nelson remained emotionless every minute. Personnel with life jackets would try to swim away. With no chance of actually making it to shore, Nelson thought about leaving them be. But instead he sprayed down bullets on them, then watched their yellow life jackets get stained red. He imagined the captain had died immediately. Too bad. It made him smile, picturing the captain choking on his goddamn toothpick as his one precious boat crumble in two.

Hope was a difficult state of mind to destroy. Even after the vessel had none, people still tried to escape. Pity. Because that hope was met with further missiles and bullets from his hands. He pictured the panicked faces of the rapists as they had lost all hope. Just like he had inside that cell. But hope blossomed within him. Antoine's spirit didn't die on that deck. His spirit lived. It strengthened. And it would be in Nelson's mind forever. Until it would be his time to sacrifice for the greater good.

Smoke blanketed the sight where the boat was, leftover debris lying on the surface of the water. Remains of a satisfying journey wobbled before sinking. The ocean wanted more, just like Nelson. More destruction. More death. He circled around, but saw no more bodies trying to leave their impending graves.

With the excitement over, he overwhelming needed another taste. At this moment, Adam planned a large scale assault on the Union. Those dead bodies wouldn't be swept away by the sea, so he'd get longer to gawk at evil's painful deaths. It gave him pleasure.

"Goodbye, Antoine," Nelson said aloud. His steady hands turned the jet and flew away.

CHAPTER TWENTY-EIGHT

The long train ride through Russia only cemented Royal's distaste for the country more. It wasn't very pleasant looking. Even though nuclear weapons decimated the United States, Russia had no excuse for these ruined cities. Looting after the chemical attack on Doomsday left many stranded and citizens murdered. Being that much of her country ran from the nuclear disaster, not many knew a green gas spread from the Kremlin through much of Russia, as if any American would've cared anyway.

She watched train stop after train stop of refugees attempting to board the train. Without tickets, they got kicked or punched to the ground. In the seat next to her, Zharkova didn't say much, her face always scowling like she'd been sitting at a slot machine for an hour without a single win. Their destination had been discussed briefly. *Shut up, Aurora. We are going far. That's all you need to know.*

Anton kept quiet, as he always did around his mother, listening to music on an iPhone with headphones plugged into his ears. Everyone once in a while, checking to make sure his mother wasn't watching, he'd show his cellphone to Royal looking for approval. Not knowing a single musician or album art, she'd still give a nod of affirmation. Anton would go back to keeping his eyes closed and head back against the soft seat.

By the time the train traveled to its last depot, no one was left on the train. Even the creepy gentleman in row A that kept ogling her legs departed two stops ago. The little girl in row B got off with her father at the last station. Too bad, because she enjoyed seeing the little girl giggle at the funny faces Royal made. Also at the last stop, most of the crew left. So now, as the train slowed to its final destination, it was just her and the Russian equivalent of *Mommie Dearest.* Thankfully, Zharkova, didn't attempt to make small talk. She didn't even tell Royal to follow her as the train halted and she stood to exit. There would be no cordial gathering from the witch, Royal doubted Zharkova would ever lift a finger to help anyone; the only finger she'd lift was the middle one. With a quick pat on the shoulder, Royal had to wake Anton or else Zharkova would've abandoned them both.

They traveled down the walkway to the exit. Zharkova wore her Tuesday brunette wig that had even been topped off with a red ribbon, like her mind was a birthday gift. Royal wondered why women who donned wigs made it so obvious. Either because they thought no one would notice or they just don't care about other opinions; assuming the later. Royal couldn't see much out the windows anymore, which meant it must've been nighttime. So many luxuries faded out on Doomsday, including a simple watch. With hardly any sun, the time was either slightly dark time or non-slightly dark time.

Without any luggage or personal items to bring, they stepped out of the train and into the dry chilly air. Immediately she found herself surprised at where they arrived at. Obviously, she hadn't expected Zharkova to take her to a theme park, but a shipping yard was far beyond Royal's expectations.

The train personnel were already locking down pins and releasing air brakes by the time they walked onto solid ground. Amidst the heaps of various colored trailers and rusty old scrap metal there was an office trailer on cinder blocks. Zharkova scratched the back of her, causing her wig to shift with every shovel of those crusty nails.

"How long we going to be here?" She asked, intending for Anton to answer, but Zharkova spoke louder.

"All you goddamn Americans always in a rush. Just because Chicago burned down in a day, didn't mean it only took one to create it. Creation takes time, annihilation does not. So keep your mouth shut, Aurora. I'm in charge here." She said, banging on the office trailer door with the palm of her hand. Her words stung, Royal hated not being in control and even worse, not having a clue what was going on. Everyone should stick to plans, but something told her that the Russian witch didn't have one.

Some sound that Royal could only assume was Russian lingo came from behind the door. Zharkova entered. The inside was more filthy than the outside, loads of coffee paper cups, empty bottles of Smirnoff, and stacks of paper nearly covered the only desk in the room. Sitting behind the desk, his chub sticking out over the arms of the chair, was some sweaty man. Without coming close to him, Royal could tell he must stink. Flies circled around a plate of leftover food.

Not even a simple hello, Zharkova immediately started barking at the man in Russian sharp dialogue. She kept slapping his desk like there was a mosquito on it, hard and direct. Royal looked to Anton for some direction of what was happening, but he kept his head low. "What in tarnation is going on?" She asked him. He awaited permission from his mother to speak, but got none. Starting to feel useless in this endeavor, Royal stressed again, "If we gonna combine forces against the Union, I need to understand what's happening."

"Do you see," the stranger behind the desk muttered, interrupting Zharkova's rant and leaving her speechless, "those containers out there?"

Thrown aback, it hadn't occurred to Royal that the man had spoken to her. Not only did it surprise her that he spoke flawless English, but that he also had the nerve to interrupt Zharkova. She looked out the yellow stained window in bad need of Windex. By the dock, waves wobbled a large cargo ship with stacks of those same metal containers that were in the yard. "Um. Yeah."

"They are filled with people," Anton said, suddenly feeling a sense of confidence since his mother's mouth had been shut.

Containers filled with people made sense now. That was how rebels were being transported. "Well, what are you all hooting and hollering for then? This is great news. We can get people out."

"They aren't alive, stupid girl. They're dead!" Zharkova spat out. "Thanks to this man's incompetence."

With a smug face, the Russian shrugged, "I said the protests were a bad idea. We had guns, but they had better guns."

Royal peeked out the window, reminding herself how many containers she saw outside. Blue, red, green, and yellow containers large enough to fit half a dozen cars were now caskets. "How many?" She whispered.

"Eight thousand," Anton answered.

Feeling faint, Royal slid into a seat, stacked with papers, by the window. This was what defeat felt like, the strength stolen from your legs. It didn't need to be said, the Union military was unstoppable. Without a clear plan as to how they would storm the castle, and not be murdered like all these people, Royal could only sense hopelessness.

"*That's* what happens, Aurora, when you defy a government!" Zharkova said, snatching up her purse off the desk and exiting the trailer.

Was this how rebellions fell? With thousands of lives dead and no report of it?

"Look," the stranger said, "I don't usually do this, but I can arrange for your safe passage back."

Royal turned, "Sorry?"

"I've been smuggling Russians out of this country for months. I'm sure I could get an American back home…to where you belong." He lit up a cigar and took a big, sad puff. "The Union doesn't have a military of one country, but of all of them. Do you have any idea the arsenal they possess? We can't win. Might as well enjoy what's left of this life. In your own goddamn country." He reached in his drawer and pulled out a fresh bottle of vodka, snapping the cap open and pouring the liquid down his throat like it was water.

Every morning Royal was awoken by the screams of Zharkova, she dreamed of going home. At least the silo made her feel welcome. Besides Anton's attempts at hospitality, Royal was imprisoned. A long boat ride across the Atlantic might be what she needed. "Please don't use the lord's name in vain," she whispered out the window. Adam's plan didn't take into account how to get passed the military to enter the castle and essentially dethrone Marcel Celest. Praying wouldn't stop a bullet from entering the skull.

"Hurry up!" Zharkova said outside in Russian, which Royal actually understood since she said it a lot to Anton.

Her son held the door open for Royal. "I'll bring you back in the morning to take the morning ship to America."

Royal nodded and stood to leave.

The train ride back seemed more lonely than the first. Zharkova had finally fell asleep, so Anton had done his best to comfort Royal with nonsensical chatter. One moment he talked about the influences of Rock and Roll music, then the next moment he'd talk about music as though it was dead. Maybe it was. Free speech got squashed by the Union, surely entertainment would be next.

No one boarded the train in the first hour. In that time, Royal routinely spun a speech in her head of what to say to Adam. Things were different when Lloyd and Nina were alive, they had powers beyond what most could comprehend. She once saw Lloyd conjure a ball of bright light in his fist. Whoever they were, wherever they were from, they started the idea of a rebellion and Sirius Dawson strengthened it with words. Now all three of those people were dead. Maybe their idea was supposed to die with them.

The train slowed to a stop. Even though it wasn't a peculiar action for this vehicle, Anton perked up and tried to glance out the window. Royal, just starting to get cozy enough to sleep finally, sighed, "What's got you all wound up?"

"No one lives at this depot. Why are we stopping?"

Before Royal could let the question sink into her head, the answer appeared before her. As the train pulled up, four black SUVs crowded the station. The words "Union Keepers" printed in plain white letters on the side.

"Shit," Anton said. He immediately tried to shake his mother awake, but she kept slapping him away spouting Russian bitter words.

Royal tried to think of what to do. Hiding seemed like an option, but surely they had access to tickets and who was on board. Running could work, but how far could they really go, especially with a crude elderly woman who'd probably complain the entire time. Growing up on an 80 acre farm, Royal had faced some dangerous animals. Coyotes used to circle the woods sometimes. If you ran, you were the prey. Sometimes standing your ground was the only option.

"What should we do?" Anton asked Royal, as though he noticed her mind working to find a solution. Zharkova was already awake, her wig backwards and a bit of slobber still dangling from the lip.

"They only bite if provoked," Royal said.

"Stupid girl, I hope they gouge your eyes out first, Aurora!" Zharkova shouted.

If the Russian leader kept calling her Aurora, the name of the sleeping beauty, one more time then Royal might gouge her eyes out. "Would you just sit down and shut your mouth, you old bat!"

Zharkova gasped, her cane not nearly long enough to reach across the aisle way and hit Royal. If it was, she might've had second thoughts about verbally combatting the surrogate of evil in the form of a kindly old woman.

The door to the cab slid open. Anton sat next to his mother; Royal hugged the wall closer like it was invisible and she could run out.

Union Keepers always wore all black, with a slight hint of gray colors on the trim of their uniforms. Such a simple design, yet so much more terrifying than if they'd just dressed up as killer clowns. So far, only one entered with his eyes glued to the trio and his right hand resting on the firearm on his hip. Behind him, one more entered. The second was dressed different, beige colored turtle neck sweater with rolled up sleeves and blue colored jeans. Must have been someone important to forgo wearing the required textile.

"Don't bother pulling out the firearm...they would've ran already." The man in charge said.

He sounded like a robot! His voice computerized, but different than old man Albert who used to live across the farm that lost his voice to cancer. The man in charge stopped in the aisle between them. Royal wished that Anton had sat in the empty seat next to her and not to his mother, now she had no one to clasp too.

"They could have guns, Sir," the Union Keeper said.

The man in charge shrugged, "Search them, tie them up then. We don't need reasonable cause, remember?"

Being a typical man, Anton tried to retaliate. He yelled something in Russian, but immediately got tackled against the seat and bound with handcuffs. He may have been a lot of things, a hippie, a vegan, and a musician, but that didn't mean he was a fighter. Being a typical woman, Royal tried to push and shove while screaming, "Leave him alone!" It didn't work, because of the butt of a gun knocked her down to the ground. In minutes, all three of them were cuffed to the back of the train cab. She'd never been cuffed before. Criminals were right, they did hurt.

Certain that her death was imminent, Royal kept kicking as hard as she could, injuring the Union Keeper. If she was going down, one of the pack was going with her.

"Everyone calm down," the robotic voice insisted. "We just want to talk. You've been a hard one to track, Mrs. Zharkova."

She'd never seen the Russian leader scared, perhaps no one had. "General Vanderbilt, I assume?"

The man in charge nodded. "Our reputations are well known, I take it." The general looked at Royal. "I know you, don't I? Secretary Declan's daughter. I actually listened to that podcast of yours. Maybe we wouldn't be in such a heap of trouble worldwide if you had just kept your mouth shut about government conspiracies. Building up resistance before a resistance was even needed."

General Vanderbilt? Royal did recognize the name. Radio said this madman had been acquitted of killing Sirius Dawson. Sirius Dawson, the voice of the movement and Royal's best friend. She tried to kick at him, but the other Union Keeper kept her at a distance.

"Feisty," Vanderbilt commented, "just like your father. What's it like being the child of a mass shooter?"

"You murdered my best friend!" Royal shouted. Trying to calmly handle this situation went out the window awhile ago, either she got beat by Keepers or got beat by Zharkova with an old bat for calling her an old bat.

He snorted, "Sirius Dawson? Yeah, I did. And it didn't stop you a-holes from trying to shut the Union down. Maybe we gotta try something different?"

The Union Keeper sneered, "I say we torture them, Sir. Send them back to their people with a missing limb. That'll send a message." Biting his lip, the Keeper seemed as excited as an empty stomach on Thanksgiving Day.

"Maybe we should," Vanderbilt instigating him. "No one would know."

"Can I have my way with the girl, Sir?" He requested, ogling at Royal.

Vanderbilt shrugged. "Sure, why not?"

With no use of her hands, Royal could only use her words. She felt daring at this height of total fear. "Bring it!"

The Keeper's eyes bulged out as he approached Royal. Still attempting to be the hero, Anton lurched forward with arms cuffed behind him and slammed the Keeper over, but he was no challenge to the military's training. The Keeper did some swift kicks and punches, leaving Anton bloody and on the ground. Royal had seen first hand that their enemies had more than weapons, they had fighting style. Her bravery melted away.

Then a gunshot boomed in the cab. The Keeper's brains splattered over the carpet and Royal's jeans. Everything happened so quickly, she just sat there with her mouth half opened. The Keeper's body crashed to the floor, with only a partial skull left. If Zharkova hadn't forced Royal to watch those gruesome videos, this might've made her vomit.

At first, she assumed Anton had somehow gotten his hands on a gun. Or maybe Zharkova. But she was wrong in both guesses.

Standing above the dead Keepers, with his revolver still giving off a bit of smoke, General Vanderbilt took a deep breath and sighed. "So difficult to find any sane ones. They all don't get the *big* picture." The maniac took out a napkin and wiped the blood off his gun. "You must have wondered, more than once, why I sound like a robot. Well, let me tell you. My windpipe was cracked and my vocal chord dislodged; there's a metal box in my throat to help me speak and breath." He wiggled and scratched his throat. "Very uncomfortable. You know who did this to me? Brent Celest. You want to know why? Because my actions caused the death of Sirius Dawson." He put away his gun into the holster. "I've had a change of heart recently. No, I'm not joining your ignorantly named movement. Actually, it's more of an acceptance rather than a change of heart. Stricken for the rest of my life to sound like I'm inside of a trash can, I've come to accept that I'm trying to stop a movement that builds from somewhere we can't kill…inside the heart. This isn't uniformly dressed opponents, like the Syrians. The People of Bliss could be anybody. So, instead, I need the rebellion to come to *us*. The Union Castle is well guarded, but perfect for a final brawl, wouldn't you say? I bet that's been the plan all along, huh?" Vanderbilt stood over Royal, down on the ground he looked twice as tall and intimidating. "Well, all

I've got to say is...*bring it.*" He smirked and turned to walk to the door out.

Zharkova, not saying or doing much besides huddling in the corner the entire time, finally crawled over and consoled her beaten son.

"Oh!" Vanderbilt said, door somewhat ajar, "One more thing." He gazed into Royal's eyes. "You want to know *how* Sirius Dawson died? I mean, not the act of it...but *how*?"

Royal gave no answer, still trying to catch her breath.

Vanderbilt smirked, "She gave up." He left, tossing a pair of handcuff keys in the walkway and closing the door behind him.

She gave up. Royal drowned out the sounds of Zharkova and Anton talking, desperately trying to sit up. They spoke in their language, presumably planning on crawling to get the keys to un-cuff themselves. But Royal, her breath finally caught up, didn't move. *She gave up.*

Moments later, Anton had crawled over to the keys and unlocked himself. His mother demanded he free her next, which he did hastily. After he loosened Royal's cuffs, she didn't bother to stand up. "What's wrong? Are you hurt?"

Hurt could mean many things. Physically, no. Royal had taken a worse beating than that, thanks to this awful visit to Russia. She didn't answer him. "Do you know how me and Sirius got so many followers? We traveled around and gathered people. This will be as difficult as making a good bowl of jambalaya, but not nearly as bad as trying un-make jambalaya."

He stared, "Okay."

"Me and you are going to need to do some traveling. Trains, buses, walking, whatever. But we need more followers. Not protesters...followers. Do you understand the difference?"

At first, he didn't seem to, but after a moment he nodded. "Yes. But what about taking you home?"

"I'm not going anywhere," Royal said. "They want to kill eight thousand of us? Then next time, we bring twice that."

CHAPTER TWENTY-NINE

Slamming his laptop lid down, in the middle of a heat argument online, Gerard tried not to seem too suspicious. But his visitor, the fat guru turned fit guru, Lester still showed concern. "What were you doing?"

"Watching porn," he replied glumly from behind his desk, hoping the Tech Czar would leave the subject alone.

"Hmm," Lester said, swiping and tapping through menus in his tablet, "I don't see anybody logged into our 'net."

The best way to get out of a blunt lie was to make the instigator seem foolish, Gerard's old man taught him. "Are you saying I'm a liar or there's a bug in the system?"

It worked. Lester, in that awful tie with short sleeved shirt that a person who worked his way up to that handsome physique would never wear, immediately became apologetic. "No! Of course not! It's obviously a bug in the system. Duh."

From his desk, ergonomically shaped like a crescent moon with a chair he could sleep in (and he did often), Gerard opened a drawer and placed a titanium-shell flash drive on the glass surface. Lester's eyes widened, staring at the flash drive. "Is that it?" He asked ravenously.

Between his fingers, Gerard wiggled and tapped the drive on the desk. He liked his office, even though he assured it to be plain and unflattering, it became his second home. What he was about to do would put an end to all this. It felt like saying goodbye to a grandfather who wouldn't shut up about old time stories, but when gone - the room would get too quiet.

"Is that it?" Lester repeated. "The decryption code?"

"Yep. With this, you have the location of everyone on the rebellion registry."

"They've all been chipped? Like planned."

Gerard nodded, finding it hard to handoff the flash drive. "All of them."

Lester held out his hand. "Let's get it over with. I can upload it now."

"Yeah," Gerard breathed, "let's get it over with."

He handed the flash drive to the Tech Czar. Even though it was smaller than a regular thumb, it felt like a humungous weight lifted. Lester grasped it firmly. "Come on. Follow me. Let's go to the mainframe."

Following Lester, he couldn't help but notice the way the former obese man walked. He still gave too much room to people strolling by in the hallway and still gave that annoying snort, that gene therapy couldn't get rid of. "So now," the Tech Czar continued his *latest technology rant* that Gerard never asked about, "pre-crime algorithms are a reality. See, before, we had the programs to do it, but you know all that government BS wouldn't let it happen. Our Supreme Leader, on the other hand, is totally for the idea of tracking possible criminals and stopping them before any crimes are committed. Sort of like that old movie with Tom Cruise. But we don't have magic, just plain algorithms. The mainframe can do this all. It's quantum."

"I don't know what that means," Gerard grumbled.

"Quantum? It's like super fast, noob. This system is even working on creating genetic therapy formulas. We got ways to prolong life. I brought this same plan to your father-in-law years ago. But with such an enormous population, making people live longer wasn't in the best interests of any country leadership. The funding fell through. But thankfully, the Union is making it reality. Now that we got a smaller population, it's possible."

Sarcastically, Gerard muttered, "Yeah, thank God billions of people died."

"Oh, you what I mean! Of course that's not cool. But at least we can make something of it. Once you and all your staff move out of our Tech building and into the castle, we're making your office into a testing facility."

The last he heard, the castle was still partially under construction but safe enough to begin moving personnel into it. Gerard would've liked working in a castle.

The entry to the mainframe was heavily guarded, four men with semi-automatic weapons. Dressed more like Armed Forces rather than Security Guards, Gerard could sense the urgency for protection. They both pressed their thumbprints to scanners for the turnstile to release. "Where's Marcel?"

"When you going to stop calling him that? It's disrespectful," Lester said emptying his pockets into a conveyor belt and walking through a metal detector. "Our *Supreme Leader* is already inside waiting. I texted him when you gave me the drive. He's so thrilled."

"I bet," Gerard said under his breath as a guard frisked him too close to his crotch.

Once inside, the talking died down. He couldn't help but be mesmerized by the machine. Centered in the room that took up the space of two stories, was the quantum computer. Being used to massive storage shrunk to the size of a key, he was taken aback by the structure. Circular, with four chairs and monitors around it, the computer probably cost a great fortune.

Marcel said nothing as he clasped Gerard's hand for a shake.

"I know," Gerard smirked, "we did it."

"Yes we did. We can finally put an end to this battle and save lives. I have Union Keepers ready to find and arrest members of the People of Bliss. God, I hate saying their name, don't you? It makes them seem like they aren't savages."

Gerard counted a total of eight people in this vast room with them. Two women with lab coats attempting to look busy with tablets they were probably playing Tetris on and six armed men standing in spots for no apparent reason but to protect their beloved leader. Gerard placed himself in the room, behind a steel desk with computer junk and his back to a large window.

Lester didn't hesitate to rush to a computer connected to the quantum structure. He plugged in the flash drive and began typing vigorously. Marcel secured both hands onto the back of Lester's chair. Together, they looked like proud parents peering through a glass wall at their newborn.

It happened.

Lester's face went from raised eyebrows to squinted eyes. From the other side of the room, back to the window, even Gerard could see the lines of code on the monitor go haywire. Lester whispered something and yanked the hard drive out. The lines of code increased, being devoured by new lines of code. Panicked, Lester stood up, "Jesus Christ! It's overwriting the system! Linking to every file Gerard's ever uploaded since the day he started!" The Tech Czar turned to face Gerard, eyes wide and sweat forming on his temples. "He's been fooling us this whole time!"

Marcel swung around, giving this look of disbelief, dismay, and disgust at the same time. "It…he…no…he wouldn't."

Smiling, because truth finally revealed itself. Gerard had infiltrated the Union with Marcel's greatest weakness: trust. And now, with Adam Durham's help, they just overtook the most powerful computer in the world. "Hey," Gerard shrugged, "I told you not to trust me."

All his life he'd done awful things: stole money from drug dealing foster parents, got the Vice Principal fired for smoking weed with him under the bleachers, and even made sure his dorm roommate (an acquitted rapist) failed all his classes by memorizing his computer password then changing all the answers on his tests. None of these he felt guilty for. But as Gerard saw that look on Marcel's face…he felt guild. He just spent a year collapsing this system's surveillance chip system, an idea that he gave Lester in the first place. All so he could get access to the Union Keepers and their locations, therefore helping the People of Bliss.

His heart pumped adrenaline and time slowed. He didn't have much time to face guilt because four armed men were ready to fire at their Supreme Leader's command. Ready to fire on a traitor to the Union. Gerard kicked over the steel desk he purposely had placed here, with a window behind him. From the holsters on his belt, he yanked out two revolvers and began firing in Marcel's direction.

Two guards rushed in and pulled Marcel to the ground, the bullets missing and shattering the mainframe's monitors. The guards fired back. Gerard slumped behind the steel desk and listened to the bullets ricocheting off its surface.

The gunfire ceased for a moment. While reloading his guns, Gerard snickered, "Can you guys *please* move out of Marcel's way?"

"Fucking traitor!" One of them yelled.

Gunfire ensued. Glass from the window shattered and sprayed to the floor. Covering his face from the debris, Gerard started contemplating how long this desk could withstand the bullets. Bending outwards like goosebumps, his shield wouldn't last long.

"Take the leader out of here!" Another one yelled.

"I can handle him!" Marcel said.

Immediately disagreeing, another guard commanded, "No telling what the traitor has planned. We got to get you out of here."

From the reflection of the glass, Gerard could see Marcel being rushed out of the room with three bodyguards around him. Good. That's exactly what he had planned. Sure, Marcel could magically destroy everyone in this room, but he wouldn't risk hurting his followers. With three guards gone, it meant only three left. Once Marcel was out of the room, Lester and the two lab coats followed.

In the reflection, he could see the three guards, arms forward and guns pointed, approaching the desk. "You're obviously out of bullets," he stated, "or else you would've kept firing."

"Yeah." One of them admitting, "You?"

Gerard sighed, "Yep."

He stood, facing the three guards, each sharing this determined bitter face. One by one, they re-holstered their guns. The first guard, much taller than Gerard, cracked his knuckles. The next guard, much slimmer would be a faster fighter. The last guard, with a cocky smirk and perfect teeth, spoke first. "Ready to get your ass kicked?"

"Wait a minute," Gerard said, holding up a finger. "I just spent nearly a year…manipulating a man that, rumor has it, can read minds…therefore, proving I'm quite possibly the best liar on this planet…and you believed me when I said I was out of bullets?"

He pointed and shot three bullets, each one hit each guard between the eyebrows. Thanks to years of visiting the gun range, Gerard couldn't be more happy to have ignored Janice's objections to guns.

Once the dust settled, he inspected the computer system. As planned, his bullets had destroyed any access to it. He pulled a small headset from his inside pocket and secured it to his ear. On the other line, Adam's voice was heard. "It worked! I have it all uploaded. Worldwide maps! All the chips of Union Keepers! All the chips of our people! We can even inform our followers! Give them access to food, medical attention –"

"Yes, I know, dweeb. That was the whole point. Where's Marcel?" He said, yanking off a leg from the table and using it to remove all the rest of the shattered glass from the window edges. Like it had been rehearsed before, Gerard removed a rope from a duffel bag hidden behind a filing cabinet in the room.

"Just like you said he would, he's following the escape plan. Elevator B Service. Should be in the garage in four and half minutes."

Gerard peeked out the window. It must've been a fifteen story drop, the farthest he's ever repelled. "Get the chopper ready. And you better have given me enough rope."

Adam, sounding overly thrilled and happy, said, "Of course! You ready to do this?"

"Are you?"

Gerard tied one end of the rope to a carabiner and secured it to the window ledge. After a few tugs to make sure it held, he removed his shirt to reveal a harness underneath then secured the other end of the rope to his body. With one big breath, he leapt out the window.

Marcel punched the wall of the elevator three times. This must've been the release Brent felt when he'd lash his ire out on inanimate objects. "He betrayed me! Gerard! I can't believe it."

Feeling the nervousness of the three guards in the elevator, Marcel ceased his show of outrage. He'd have to center all that pain, just like Brent would, and unleash it when he saw Gerard again. Never the violent type, this new sensation thrilled him. Maybe he could draw fire into his mouth, just like the last man to betray his trust. Maybe he could influence water to bubble around his head, drowning him no matter where he ran or tried to hide. Maybe he could cause a gust hard enough to tear Gerard's flesh from his skin.

"Supreme Leader?" The guard said, as though he had repeated himself. "Do you understand the evacuation plan?"

Rehearsing these scenarios seemed as dull as a fire drill. Now, in the situation, Marcel wished he paid more attention. "Yeah. We use the direct service elevator to the ground level and ride the limo to the nearest safe haven." At least he remembered that much, but recalling what the safe havens were surpassed his memory.

"Yes, keep your head down at all times. We will create a barrier fence around you."

The thought made Marcel realize the sacrifice these men were about to make. Rebels could be in the garage, camping out with automatic weapons. One of the guards, pale and too young to be in this situation, nodded his head rapidly. Marcel used to do the same thing, in the days when he succumbed to fear instead of embracing it. "What's your name?"

"Brad," his voice squeaked. "I'll be the driver."

"Brad," Marcel said, placing his hand on the youngster's shoulder, "I promise nothing will happen to you. I'm a god. Understand? They should be scared of me."

The pep talk worked, Brad nodded more slowly.

The elevator dinged. All three guards readied their guns and pointed. Marcel was ready to block bullets if he had to, his bond with wind could stop any projectile. The elevator doors opened.

Nothing.

Besides the musky smell and three cars in the parking garage, nothing else occupied the space. The guards stepped out, regardless, and surrounded Marcel as he kept his head low. Using hand signals to communicate amongst themselves, the team checked behind dumpsters, cars, and dark corners. Nobody else was here.

Relieved and yet suspicious, Marcel made his way to the limousine. Looking through windows, the driver Brad gave a hand signal for all clear. He opened the door and let Marcel inside the back. Even though he could control the elements around him, at will, Marcel still felt his heart beating his chest. Inside, the sense of safety calmed him. Bullet-proof glass, semi-automatic guns protruding the windows, and hidden blades in the seat definitely guaranteed security. Instead of grabbing a weapon, he banged a compartment between the seats and a drink bar slowly began to emerge. Too slow. Marcel yanked the drink bar, hearing the bottles and ice rattle around. He grabbed a small bottle of vodka and chugged it. Something Janice would do.

The third guard, who he just noticed never spoke once, sat next to Marcel. Then the limousine lurched out and skidded through the parking garage, bouncing over a speed bump. Marcel ripped the cap off another tiny bottle of vodka, letting the liquid burn away his stress. How could Gerard do this? Everyone that he loved turned against him. Why? He was only trying to do good. Trying to create peace. Why did no one want peace?

"Supreme Leader, the closest safe haven is less than fifteen minutes. I'm notifying General Vanderbilt of the breach."

Marcel could already hear his general's response. *I told you so.* His thoughts were interrupted by the loud sounds of chopper blades. As they sped through empty streets and tall skyscrapers under construction, he could see a shadow on the ground. A shadow of a helicopter. He peeked out the window. High above, in perhaps one of the most corroded vehicles he'd ever seen, the chopper followed their every turn. Noticing no Press logos or Union emblems, Marcel assumed the worse. "It's them," the quiet guard said finally.

"We have counter measures," the guard in the passenger seat said, but that didn't make the driver Brad's sweat stop pouring off his chin.

A screen on the dashboard lifted and the guard tapped a few buttons. The chopper above descended closer. From the bottom, a wire dropped with a hook attached to the end. "How's he plan on hooking us? We're going too fast." Brad mumbled with a tone of confidence finally.

The guard in the passengers continued to tap a button marked EXECUTE. Nothing happened. Unsure what the limousine was supposed to do, maybe fire missiles or guns, Marcel assumed the button did nothing. "It's not responding," the guard stated the obvious.

Then it occurred to Marcel. He asked, "Who designed this vehicle?"

Without answering, the guards glanced at each other. "Shit," Brad gasped.

Suddenly, the trunk door popped open outside. Marcel watched out the window behind him as Gerard climbs out of the trunk. Before they could even react, Gerard grabs the hook from the helicopter and clamps it to the back of the limousine.

The vehicle flipped forward. Bottles, ice, weapons, crashed to the floor. Marcel couldn't grab anything to hold onto. His face smacked the back of the driver's seat. The guard next to him kicked open the door and began firing his weapon, bullets not even close to hitting Gerard grasping onto the cord. Outside, Marcel could see them rising high off the ground. Still attempting to compose himself, the two guards in the front seat struggled even more. As they rose, the wind became harsher. Marcel couldn't even concentrate enough to control it all.

Swinging like a mid-air pendulum, the guards bounced around. The guard in the passenger's seat was crunched near the windshield, unconscious, with blood pouring from his nose like a leak in a garden hose. Suddenly the driver door swung open. Marcel reached his hand out, but was too late…the driver Brad screamed as he fell out of the vehicle. Trying to concentrate, control the wind to save them, made the situation worse. The limousine swayed faster. With no time to even grieve the loss of a guard, Marcel had to compose himself to dominate this chaos.

One of the guards fired at the back window, shattering the glass, and showing Gerard's struggle to control this situation too. All that resentment returned to Marcel when he saw his brother-in-law. Grabbing tightly to the seats, he hoisted himself toward the broken back window.

The wind calmed. Marcel could see darkness envelope him, demanding cooperation of the elements. He stared Gerard in the face.

His brother-in-law sighed, "Okay. I get it. You're probably *a littttlllle* angry with me."

Marcel thrusted his hand palm and wind shoved the chopper backwards. Gerard spun in circles, clasping the cord. Unbeknownst to Marcel, the vehicle hit the side of a skyscraper and spinning wheels cracked the windows of the building. Shattered glass flew in his face. Instinctively, he covered his face and lost his grip. He fell backwards down the inside of the limousine and banged his head against the side. Spinning like the wheels outside, his head wouldn't stop the sensation of vertigo.

The wind outside returned to normal.

Wiping blood from his chin, Marcel regained consciousness and began another ascent.

"No!" Gerard screamed outside, "I'm not doing it! That's not the plan!"

Presuming he was talking into some earpiece, Marcel ignored the conversation and hoisted over the backseat. This time, he'd conjure enough wind to blow Gerard to the next city. He lifted his hand up. Darkness grew.

Gerard released a pin in the hook.

The limousine fell.

Marcel bounced around, smashing into every window and door handle. Gravity tossed him around like a pinball machine. If he could concentrate enough to stop a nuclear weapon explosion, surely he could handle this. They had maybe seconds before the vehicle would hit the ground in a fiery end. Drowning out all sound, he meditated. Picturing himself somewhere else.

Oh, you're no fun, Wind whined.

The limousine began to balance itself straight. Attempting not to think about how close they were to the ground, Marcel grasped his hands and demanded air to level the vehicle.

Before long, wind slowed the decline. Eyes still closed, he could feel air pushing the bottom of the limousine upwards and cradling it to the ground.

They landed, harder than he would've wanted, on the side of the vehicle. Marcel immediately rushed out the sunroof onto the street. He looked up, but the chopper was gone.

Gerard's legs touched the surface of the rooftop and he moved away as the chopper landed next to him. While the chopper blades slowed down, he caught his breath. He'd been in some wild situations, but never thought he'd be dangling in the air with a limousine and a bitter sorcerer-of-sorts.

Adam climbed out the driver seat. "Jesus Christ! Did you feel that wind?"

Sarcastically, Gerard widened his eyes, "Yep."

"Do we try again to capture him?" Adam said.

Being in the safety of a helicopter, the naive college kid didn't understand the severity of the situation. Having no intention of risking his life yet again, Gerard answered, "There will be Union Keepers swarming this city in minutes. No doubt Vanderbilt will send tanks. It's not safe here." He climbed into the passenger seat and buckled himself in.

Shoulders sagging, Adam said, "But…well, that sucks. The plan failed. He can't be killed, he can't be kidnapped, this escape was just…useless."

"I wouldn't say that," Gerard said, leaning back in the seat. "Did you happen to notice the whirlwind stop instantly?"

Adam tapped his lip for a second, "Oh yeah. It did. Why?"

"Marcel banged his head. Hard. It broke his concentration." Gerard nodded, "His magic has a weakness."

CHAPTER THIRTY

Bobbling and weaving through the sky, Gerard asked Adam again how long he'd been flying choppers. And again, the answer was *awhile*. Whatever that meant. For an hour, they flew low on radars but high over trees. Trees that even with a lack of sunlight, still managed to grow. Gerard could say he related. Even settled in such discomposure as the Union, he still found strength to stay focused. And even grow. Repeatedly, Adam said during the trip how relieved he was that the possibility of winning this war seemed achievable. On the other hand, Gerard was relieved the possibility of living a future with his family as achievable.

Or was it?

How would Janice react at his presence? Did she even want him around? Would she even let him touch their child? And she couldn't possibly be in love with the idiot sitting next to him flying the chopper…could she? Didn't she still wear her wedding ring, like him?

The computer in his lap gave a series of beeps. Gerard looked down. Blue dots covered the GPS map of their location. Adam spoke loudly into the microphone headset, even though just whispering was good enough. "Remember the blue dots are our allies. Red represent the Union Keepers."

"I know."

"You just look confused."

The only thing Gerard felt confused about was why he didn't just simply kick Adam out of the helicopter and laugh as the moron fell to his death. But then, he reminded himself not only that he didn't know how to fly helicopters…that it probably wouldn't be a good start for his new life at the silo if he murdered the rebellion's leader. "I was just wondering if I tossed you out the door, if we were high enough that you'd flatten like a pancake."

Adam giggled, "Oh, Gerard. You're so silly. We're going to make great friends. I just know it."

What an idiot.

Gerard gazed out the window as the sun rose, casting its hazy and boring brightness over the horizon. What he would do to just get a chance for one single sunrise. When he first married Janice, they spent every weekend at the beach watching the sunrise followed by a light lunch and hard love-making. But that spark dwindled just like the sun. If he couldn't fix his marriage before Doomsday, how would he afterwards?

"Are you listening?"

He wasn't. "Yeah."

"Everyone chipped, on our side, can be warned where nearby Keepers are. We get messages out to them. I can finally get this battle organized. Royal will be thrilled."

Funny how Gerard's mind was on Janice, while Adam's mind was on Royal.

He landed the chopper not far from where the blue dots gathered. This felt like changing schools, new people to meet and new people to be jealous of. "What are we going to tell them? About me?"

"The truth?"

Gerard shook his head. "If they find out I've been manipulating Marcel to gain his favor, just to betray him...do you honestly think they'll trust me?"

"Uh...hmmm...guess I never thought of it."

Idiot.

The chopper thudded as it landed on a bare hill. If Adam's leadership was as good as his driving, then the People of Bliss were in for a rough ride. After pressing a few buttons and triggering a few knobs, the chopper's blades slowed to the point they could remove their headsets. "Well," Adam huffed, "I guess we can just tell them you deflected from the Union. And I trust you because you're my *best* friend."

Gerard's stomach felt uneasy from either the radical ride here or the way Adam said *best friend.* The last person to call him that was Marcel. And perhaps, in many ways, he was his best friend. "How about just saying we're friends? Maybe acquaintances? Or co-workers?"

"Oh, you," Adam giggled, climbing out the door. "Gimme a hand, would you, buddy?"

Even the word *buddy* made a chunk of vomit travel up Gerard's throat. He climbed out and landed on the faint green grass. From the back seat, Adam yanked out a large green colored sheet that looked more vibrant than the grass but did its job at hiding the vehicle from prying eyes.

"So, our plan worked out great! But um...what about Marcel Celest?" Adam said, losing his breath after only a third of the way through covering the chopper.

Admittedly, the plan for ending the Union's database worked but not for ending its Supreme Leader. Marcel, undoubtedly, was peeved with his best friend. Gerard had kept a secret for nearly a year. A secret that he planned on gaining trust and obliterating it when the time was right. It seemed cruel. But so was declaring martial law upon innocent people. Sympathy never lingered long in Gerard's mind. The future mattered, not the past. And the future couldn't revolve around the Union.

By Gerard's long silence, Adam knew there was no answer. "Well, then we wasted our time trying to take him out, huh?"

Gerard pictured that moment, fighting with Marcel high up in the sky on top of a vehicle, when his brother-in-law's concentration broke. And so did the wind. His control of the elements had a weakness. "Not necessarily."

Using the excuse that he needed time to prepare himself, Adam finally left Gerard alone. Daybreak reminded him how much he needed coffee. But somehow he assumed the missile silo didn't have a Starbucks. Unable to decide which would be more awkward meeting, the People of Bliss or his wife, he concluded on both. So now he had to decide what to say to both. Honestly, he thought he wouldn't make it this far. It's like when his father-in-law ran for President, so much energy had been applied to the journey that the end result seemed surreal.

Since the truth coated him as such an awful person for siding with the Union, Gerard kept going over and over in his head what to say. Adam already warned him that every new member got vetted. Part of their agreement was Gerard would help Adam upload his virus to the system and he'd stay inside the Union as a mole. Plans changed. Especially when he had no yearning to stay and be some kind of *Bard* to *King* Marcel Celest in a castle.

The longer he stayed in this tight passenger seat of the chopper, with empty pizza boxes and napkins on the floor, the sooner he wanted to leave. But a headache was growing.

Lack of sleep, or worse yet lack of a decision of what story to tell, made the headache balloon like a cake. He heard a repetitive clank, like metal hitting metal. That sound definitely didn't help. To his right, down a hill covered more by moss than grass, were four teenage boys. Judging by their attire of dirt-soaked pants, socks with no shoes, and shirts too small, it was safe to say they were children of the rebellion. The youngest one, probably juvenile enough to be a freshman, threw an empty soup can while the other boy, probably old enough to be a senior, hit the can with a metal bat. This was the worse display of baseball Gerard seen since he watched the Astros play in Houston. He could've ignored it, but forcing himself to address other people's problems could help him escape his.

What if the People of Bliss didn't admit him? And they kicked him out on the street? What then? The Union couldn't take him back. Would Janice even be able to look him in the eye?

Gerard shook his head and hopped out of the helicopter, landing on both feet. Halfway down the hill, the senior noticed him and froze in place. Visitors didn't come around here often, he could tell, because all three boys said nothing as he approached. All frozen like statues, Gerard decided to break the ice. "It's in the stance."

The trio looked to each other for some kind of non-verbal agreement of what to do. The senior said, "We ain't supposed to talk strangers out here."

"Well," Gerard shrugged, "You technically just did."

Caught off guard, which the truth often did, the boy took a step back. "We were just wandering the woods, decided to play some ball."

More lies, like the creases in a uniform that would never go away permanently but could be ironed out. Gerard bent down to the ground and with his finger drew two circles diagonally from each other. "Your feet are the most important part. You a leftie or a rightie?"

Again, the senior looked to his naive, and yet just as clueless, peers for instruction. He turned to Gerard, "Leftie."

"Good! I hear *left* handed people are in their *right* mind."

Not getting the lame joke, the boys nodded their heads. Gerard continued, "Put your left foot here and right foot here."

The senior listened, holding the bat with a firmer grip than before. Already understanding these boys didn't want their backs to a stranger, Gerard turned to face the kid as he positioned himself. "Back is important too, keep it aligned to the center of those feet. Your head and hip too. When it's time to swing, make sure the arm is bent and palms are down to the ground. Prepare yourself for the worse. Because, let's face it, you have no idea what is about to happen."

The senior nodded and raised the bat up to his shoulder. Gerard, like he was a supermodel photographer, took glances from different areas. "Perfect. Now," he said grabbing the can from the freshman and holding it up, "don't look at anything else besides this." Jokingly, he moved the rusty object around in zig-zags to ensure the boy listened. The middle kid giggled, at least someone had a sense of humor. Sure enough the boy's eyes never left the goal, an inanimate object that meant everything at that moment. Gerard tossed it and the senior hit it with all his might. The can flew across the yard, higher than they could see.

"Woah," the boys said in unison.

"You see, it's all about the preparation." Gerard whispered proudly. "So...What gives? You boys practicing for the World Series, because I hate to break it to you...doubt its ever gonna happen again."

"We're not playing baseball," the freshman said. "We're practicing."

Throwing objects with the intention of smacking them away sounded like baseball to Gerard. Wasn't it? "Practicing for what?"

The freshman opened his mouth only to be interrupted by the senior. "It's a secret. Secret mission."

Gerard wasn't used to information being withheld from him. The last person to keep a secret from him was his neighbor and the recipe for quite possibly the best lasagna Gerard ever tasted. Determined to find out the ingredients, he decided to just break into the neighbor's house to steal the receipe rather than accept someone was better at cooking. "A secret?" He answered glumly.

"Yes," a female said from behind. He knew immediately who it was, for he'd known her voice since they dated in High School. "A secret. You should know about that," Janice said standing by the open door to the silo.

Expecting to see his wife, Gerard still didn't know if he should run up to hug or kiss her. Or do nothing at all. She seemed fragile, if he held her too tight she might snap like these tree branches. Maybe she didn't want to be held in the first place. It had been almost a year since they parted and who knew how she felt. "Hey," was all he could manage to say. Janice looked tired, more tired than her hay days of partying and boozing all night. Something was wrong, but he couldn't put his finger on it.

"Hey," she answered back, about as unemotional as his greeting. "Follow me. I'll take you to the check in office." But he couldn't help notice she looked him in the eye. Already off to a good start.

As Gerard left, he tossed the can and the senior hit it nicely with the bat. Practice made perfect, but they were on the right track for whatever they planned on doing with those bats. It bothered him, the Capital Policeman still in his blood had to understand this situation. What were kids doing playing with bats and tin cans? But not doing it for sport?

Only halfway down the corridor, into the silo, did he realize. The boys outside were practicing swatting away tear gas canisters.

After a brief visit through the corridor, where a blind Frenchman guarded the door, Gerard was led by Janice into circular walkway. Hearing the clank of each footstep on the metal grated catwalk sounded like an alarm. It smelled like musty old tavern that his father would drink and pass out in. Underground silos weren't known for excellent air quality, but Gerard could still hear the mum of vents pushing air throughout the silo. Water rushed through the pipes. Everything here needed a desperate upgrade, but as soon as that thought sparked in his mind, he distinguished it. Upgrading and lavish living belonged in the realm of the Union. Gerard was just going to have to get used to this new lifestyle. That's if, the People of Bliss even accepted him.

As he followed Janice into a side room and hallway, he remembered what Adam had prepared him for. First, the medical room. Second, the search room. Third, the vetting room.

The medical room was what he expected. Everything was white. White floors. White tables. White chairs. And personnel dressed in white. Why are doctors so obsessed with the color white? The only thing Gerard hadn't expected, was children. Besides a head nurse, the other three people in that room were children aged between 9-12. As uncomfortable as Gerard was with a kid that should've been in school creating a volcano project for the science fair and not sticking a needle in his arm, the girl did an exceptional job of drawing three vials of blood. The nurse guided the children much of the way, explaining the difference in needles and how to operate the machinery to test the blood. Each of them fascinated and taking notes. Gerard only found video games fascinating at that age.

While the blood circulated in the machine, Janice finally spoke for the first time in the silo. "Union agreement included something similar, if I'm not mistaken, right? A procedure to find who is more compatible with what position?"

Gerard nodded, feeling himself falling in love with her again. Though her pale face and sunken eyes made Janice seem ill, she was still the most gorgeous woman he'd ever met. "They used genetics to determine what job you belonged to. What about here? How do they do it?"

Janice smirked, "They ask."

The door opened and Adam entered. "Sorry, I'm late," he said almost too ecstatic.

Not expecting him to join the entrance examination, Gerard just scoffed. Janice gave a short smile before coughing frantically. Not some sort of too-much-pollen-in-the-air cough, but a deep permanent phlegm hack. Afterwards, he asked softly. "Is something wrong? You seem…I don't know…sick."

She shrugged, "I'm fine."

"I can always tell when you're lying, because you curl your hair."

Looking down, Janice noticed her finger twirling a bit of her long golden hair. She let go immediately. Adam's arms crossed.

"O-negative." One of the nurses-in-training said.

"That's right," the nurse said, rubbing the child's back triumphantly.

"What a minute," Janice interrupted. "He's o-negative blood? Like Colin?"

The teacher nodded and checked over the paperwork, "Everything else came out good. Just a few vaccines we will administer and then you're free to go."

While the pupils dug through cabinets to prepare for more needles, Gerard studied Janice's face. She did this when something complicated was ahead of her, eyes reading an invisible formula on an invisible chalkboard. Something was bothering her and she couldn't solve it. Her eyes met with Adam's in this silent conversation. "Who's Colin?" Gerard asked.

"Oh," Janice responded, "The baby."

"Oh," Gerard mimicked, picturing the baby in his head for the first time in months it felt like, though he honestly had no idea what he would look like. "So. It's a boy, huh?"

Stumped by that invisible equation, Janice looked down. "Yes."

As he suspected on several occasions, his wife had doubts on who the father was. Gerard didn't need a tracker to know Janice snuck out many nights to party and escape the confinement of a perfect life. It hurt. But that was the thing about Janice, she liked experiences. Learning experiences was how humanity evolved, she would say. In a time when pregnancy became a rarity, so did monogamy. He let it go, as he always did. But now, he wondered if she was positive of the baby's father. That would explain the look of doubt that both her and Adam shared. Did she suspect the dweeb could be the baby's father?

After eight vaccinations, Gerard felt like his arm had punched but it didn't hurt nearly as much as his heart. Janice hadn't been faithful, and worse, the baby's father was still unknown.

They travelled to the next room where Janice stood outside the doorway. As a detective, he supervised many criminals being admitted into jail and knew the routine. A man, maybe known as a giant in medieval days, asked him to remove his clothing. His name was Bruno and spoke in third person. Bruno's fist was bigger than both of Gerard's fists put together so he listened to every word. Only fifteen or so minutes later, the brute had checked every pocket of his jeans, underneath the pads in his shoes, and any other hiding spot on his clothing. Criminals had become clever over the years of sneaking contraband into jails, so Gerard was impressed the giant knew where to inspect. The strip search procedure made him understand why his arrestees were so uncomfortable afterwards. When all was complete, Gerard walked out of the room to a sly smile from Janice.

"Was he polite?" She asked.

"You mean ask me out to dinner? No, that was the least he could've done after."

As nervous as those two rooms made him, Gerard felt bubbles in his stomach grumble at the third room. Interrogations were easy for him, being the cop. But how about being under the spotlight?

Expecting a room with concrete walls with only one aluminum table and two aluminum chairs, Gerard was pleasantly surprised to enter a quaint room with flowers at one corner, cabinets at another, and two leather seats like Grandpa had.

The interviewer, with a child assistant in his late teens, were standing at the doorway. An older woman with tied back gray hair and thick glasses greeted him with a handshake. "Hello, Gerard, please come in." She walked in high heels with ease and dressed like a realtor. "You like tea?"

"No," Janice answered for him. "He hates it. I'll make the coffee."

The assistant wasn't used to someone invading his drink counter, but Janice never asked permission. She opened an overhead cabinet and grabbed coffee grounds, a scoop, and filter. Making him proud she remembered, Janice poured six scoops of pure black coffee grounds into the filter and started the coffeemaker. The assistant, confused what to do next, awaited instruction.

"Would you have a seat?" The interviewer asked, hinting the boy to lead Gerard to the chair like he couldn't find it on his own.

The situation felt like a meeting with a psychologist, which he'd only experienced once after his father drank himself to death. Perhaps the interviewer was a therapist at one point, because she used the monotone polite voice that they all used. "Hello, Gerard. My name is Dr. Richards."

"Hey." He said, folding his hands in his lap. Police work taught him that flailing hands can often be misinterpreted and needed to stay in one spot.

"Adam and Janice have both briefed me on your situation, but you must understand even though we are a loving group of people...we are also a skeptical group of people. This isn't like signing up for a gym membership or applying for a home loan. We aren't money, we are after something else."

He felt like this is the same speech Marcel gave him before joining the Union. "What? Loyalty?"

"No, Gerard. We want to know what you want."

Janice handed him the cup of coffee, black. He took a sip and thought it wasn't so bad. "Okay."

She pulled up a clipboard with scribbled notes. "I'm going to be asking a series of hypothetical questions. Answer quickly, because we want honest answers."

"Okay." He said slowly, realizing that the boys outside preparing to bat away gas canisters or the blind man guarding the doorway weren't the craziest situations he'd been through today.

Slowing putting on a pair of reading glasses, Dr. Richards asked, "If you could sell your soul to the devil, what would you sell it for?"

An appropriate question considering that he was sure Marcel did exactly that. But now Gerard had to imagine what he could have, if anything was possible. "I've been a detective, security guard, and police officer. I'd sell my soul for a world where people like me weren't needed."

Blank and emotionless, Dr. Richards glanced down at her clipboard again. "You've been diagnosed with a memory disorder. Would you rather forget who *you* were or who *everyone else* was?"

That was easy. He answered quickly, "Forget who I was."

"If you were given the power to abolish one of your fears, which one would it be?"

Nothing worse than being asked such a question in front of a wife of twenty years. Even worse, in front of a snot-nosed college hunk named Adam that stole her away. Gerard took a little longer to reflect on this. Honesty was always the best policy, Janice would appreciate it. "My fear of not being accepted."

She turned to the next page, writing notes. Without looking up, she asked, "You are stranded on an island from a plane crash with no source of food. Would you eat the dead bodies in the plane?"

Considering he left the riches of the Union to join the slums of the rebellion, Gerard wouldn't be surprised to find a buffet of dead bodies. "Yes, because life takes sacrifices to endure."

The interviewer's assistant made a grossed out face. Gerard shrugged. Dr. Richards remained unfazed. "Would you rather put an end to world wars or world hunger?"

Since his stomach hadn't stopped growling the entire flight here, the answer was obvious. "World hunger, so we would have the energy to fight wars." Adam nodded, liking that answer.

"You're God for a day and given the ability to remove one worldwide emotion, what would that emotion be?"

He glanced up at Janice, just noticing she'd been staring at him with those sullen eyes. For some reason, he pictured her in that white breathtaking dress on their wedding day with her eyes filled with admiration. After all they'd been through, he may never see that again. "Regret."

Janice looked down at the floor and closed her eyes.

"Do you believe in God?"

Gerard sighed. What a cliche question. Falling asleep during church and Sunday school, he already made his decision a long time ago how he felt about an entity that could control everything. But if Nelson, a President who publicly denounced religion, could be accepted into this movement...so could he. So he opted to be honest. "Nope. And if I ever met the guy, I'd sock him in the face for putting us through this."

Dr. Richards remained expressionless while Adam shook his head. She placed the clipboard on her lap and sat down. "So, what made you decide to come here today?"

Besides the fact if he'd return to the Union Marcel would surely slice his throat, Gerard was at a lost on how to answer this supposed final question. This would be the deciding factor for his acceptance. It was like being interviewed for a reputable college, sure they knew you...but they didn't *really* know you. He could say many things to make himself out to be an asset to the rebellion, but something struck him at that moment. Janice had a secret. So it seemed like everyone did nowadays. It was hard not to. And Gerard held the longest secret of them all. He could lie now, welcome himself as a hero to this new home and deceive them as he deceived Marcel with that new home. But somehow he felt enough of it. No more false or altered stories.

She repeated, "Can you tell us what led you here?"

"Sixteen months ago, nuclear weapons hit over 90 cities in this country. I remembered finding Janice underneath rubble, in our basement completely wasted on booze. I squeezed her so tight and never wanted to let go." He didn't need to glance at Janice to hear her take a deep breath of disdainful, yet fond remembrance. "That night, she told me in a medical tent she just learned about her pregnancy. I knew then, looking around at the havoc the Supreme...I mean, Marcel...could've stopped. He could've stopped it," he said reassuringly. "Something had to change. As if a gift, low and behold, I run into Brent Celest. If anyone could stop Marcel, it was him. I told Brent where to find Marcel, but ultimately he failed at defeating him. It bothered me, someone trained to assassin anyone couldn't take down the almighty Marcel Celest. The only other choice was to gain his trust and betray him. Somehow take out the Union from the inside. I tried to keep this cover, a person interested in joining the czars of the Union. Marcel bought into it. Janice didn't. Unfortunately, it led to me having to make the toughest decision to date...I had to let go of my wife."

Janice stood up, arms crossed, to face a painting on the wall. With eyes still awaiting the end of his story, Gerard continued. "Shortly afterwards, an idea sparked in my head, ironically given to me by the Tech Czar, Lester. He said that in order to create a war, both sides had to know where their followers were. I gave the idea of chip implants."

What kept most of these people from getting food or holding jobs was now revealed to be Gerard's doing. Dr. Richards nodded, "Go on, please."

"Well, needless to say, I'm not good enough with computers. I tried to infiltrate their systems and track users of the chips, but fell short. So I turned to the only man smart enough to create a virus that could control the Union's database and give us access to chip locations of both sides of this conflict."

Adam bobbed his head to some invisible, silent triumphant music in his head. He didn't mind taking the credit and would probably remind everyone daily of his virus that saved the day.

Gerard finished what felt like an interrogation, because it practically was. "I'd been forced to play this role of a Union supporter, until the time was right that I would become a Union defector." He stared off, watching the clipboard. "And I've seen some shit, let me tell you. One time, in Chicago, Union Keepers got so fed up with protestors that they tied a bunch of them to these posts and poured wet cement up to their knees. Once the cement dried, they untied them, but of course...they couldn't move. 'Let's see if you guys really can stand your ground', one of them said. They drove a tank," Gerard had to stop to bite his shaky lip. He didn't cry, his father taught him it was for pussies. But holding tears back now took all his effort. After a brief throat clearing, Gerard said, "They drove the tank over the protestors. A few got away by breaking their legs." Though the story, one of many grotesque stories, didn't end there, he decided to stop. His point had been made.

Trying to read the face of the interviewer, he could only see mixtures of disgust, confusion, and admiration. She put her clipboard in a drawer, then said, "Welcome to the People of Bliss."

CHAPTER THIRTY-ONE

The limousine rattled and swayed as it climbed through the familiar debris of most road in the United States. Consensus on how devastating the nuclear weapons were to the United States varied from winds exceeding 300 miles per hour, 500 miles per hour, some experts even saying a thousand miles per hour. However much it was, Marcel never seen wind that could curl up the concrete layer of the road like a shape of a hurricane.

"Are we afraid, Supreme Leader?" General Vanderbilt whispered, staring out the window.

Marcel always thought the same issue when he saw destruction of this magnitude, as he was safe, cozy, and drinking wine in a limousine while others chased rats for dinner. But no doubt, Gerard's deceit made him question loyalty more. Even Vanderbilt could turn sides on Marcel. Anyone could. He turned and faced his bald-headed commander. "Should we be?"

His deep breaths stained the window in a slow succession. "I believe you when you say the soul of Brent Celest still haunts you. Sirius Dawson's voice awakes me every morning. She caught me, when I was torturing…she caught me shaking. And laughed."

"Why were you shaking?"

"The same reason I am now." He held his hand jiggled as he lifted it.

The limousine approached the stadium. As in the last six rallies, thousands of protestors had awaited aside. A two months ago, Marcel's vehicle almost got turned over by all those angry bodies trying to push their ways in and strangle Marcel's throats. Against all objections, he decided on another rally. His supporters, and loyalists to the Union, needed guidance and news. News from his own mouth. He needed to remind his fans that he loved them.

Four armored vehicles ahead of them climbed the hill while the limo ceased to a halt. Per protocol, they awaited until their escorts scanned the perimeter and mapped a route; per the protocol that Gerard implemented. Marcel's hand clasped tightly and his heart raced. Never before had he felt so deceived, even when he discovered that his own brother was part of a terrorist organization and tried to assassinated him. At least Brent didn't fake the love, like Gerard did. Did anyone truly love him?

One of the armed men, wearing a helmet and thick bulletproof gear walked up to their limousine. Vanderbilt stepped out and spoke to the officer before returning to sitting next to Marcel. "Well, I have excellent news, Supreme Leader. Looks like they are finally more scared of us."

"What do you mean? How many protesters are outside the stadium?"

With an enormous smile, he answered. "One."

One? Did he mean one thousand? "One person?"

Vanderbilt nodded affirmatively. "We will escort the man out and –"

"No," Marcel held up his hand, "I want to meet him?"

"But, we haven't searched him or –"

"I want to meet him." Marcel said as he stepped out of the limousine, signaling the conversation was over.

Soldiers swarmed around him, even his father never received this much protection as the President. He walked up a lime-stoned road, past the perimeter fence, and gatehouse; all the while surrounded by armed men with guns pointed ready to fire at the slightest sight of danger. After passing through the parking lot of junk vehicles and busses, Marcel could see the lone man outside the door to the massive stadium. Wearing one of those massively bulky signs that secured around his neck and covered nearly his entire body, the protestor seemed in a half drunken state as he swayed trying to pace back and forth. On the other end of the parking lot was the entrance where his supporters waited in line to enter the already-full venue; the idiot was on the wrong side of the building protesting.

"Sir, I suggest we –" Vanderbilt never finished his objection, knowing it was futile.

Marcel's presence made the drunk pause, as he approached. Skipping the formality of a greeting, he asked the protester, "Can I ask you something?"

His politeness always shocked his opposition. Marcel didn't hate them, just wanted to educate them. The man reminded him of his father with fuzzy, stressful gray hair extended out of his head and face. And just his dad, they a shared a common blindness to the truth; the truth that Marcel wasn't the enemy. The protester, yellow teeth and stank breath, answered, "Okay."

"How long have you had that sign?"Around his body, written in faded red marker were the words JESUS IS COMING SOON. "In fact, how long have we all seen that sign? The second coming? I mean…there is billions of people on this planet. How do you know it didn't happen already?"

Taken aback and unsure how to answer, the protester's eyes darted around.

Marcel continued, giving a shrug, "Maybe the Messiah already came and went again, but just didn't get any media coverage. What would you need as verification anyways? Even Jesus himself was called a liar for stating he was the son of God. How many have said those exact words? What would you, personally, need to see in order to verify the Messiah returned?"

"I…I…don't know." The old man said.

Marcel nodded. "Exactly. How would you even know? Maybe…just maybe…I am the Messiah?"

The protester reached for his pocket, but made the mistake of staring into the Supreme Leader's eyes. Souls locked together by darkness, Marcel's mind traveled through the protester's convoluted thoughts, leaving the old man in a gaze. Drunken minds were the easiest to hypnotize.

Marcel whispered, "What do you have in your back pocket?"

"I have a Beretta 92FS semi-automatic pistol." The drunk answered in the same monotone.

"You planned on shooting me?"

"Yes, Supreme Leader."

After controlling so many minds, the guilt practically vanished. Men like this needed to be freed from their ire. "I'm going to need you to remove that gun and hand it over."

General Vanderbilt must've heard the word *gun* and approached the two. From behind Marcel, he asked, "Is he –" Like everyone else who saw the rumors were true of Marcel's mind control ability, he didn't know what to call it.

"Yes, he's under my command."

The protester yanked out his gun slowly and tried to hand it to Marcel. "Not me. I hate guns. Hand it to my general here." Practically an automated mannequin, the man listened and Vanderbilt went to grab for the gun, but Marcel interrupted. "Wait." They both stood still, his hypnotized puppet and naive puppet, awaiting instructions. "Sir, I want you to put that gun to your head."

"Yes, Supreme Leader," he said and placed the barrel of the weapon to his temple.

"What does that feel like?" Marcel asked, knowing the man would answer truthfully since the darkness cleared his thoughts.

"Terrifying," the man answered.

"Imagine what that's like for a world leader. Constantly knowing, at any moment, someone is ready to fire a gun at you. Like, any day, you could be dead by a radicalized patron." Not until this utter silence did Marcel actually hear the crowd inside the stadium. It roared excitingly, chanting and waiting impatiently for Marcel's late appearance. "Do you hear that, my friend? That's love. Love for me. Love for the Union. Love for the future." He smiled at the protester, "How about you join us? Hand the gun to the general, then throw that sign in the dumpster and go inside. Be a part of that love. Tell everyone in there that you met the Messiah."

The protester nodded, handed the gun over, and turned to stumble into the stadium.

Vanderbilt took a breath. "We have nothing to fear anymore, do we?"

"Not exactly. We do have one thing to be afraid of. And I'm going to change that tonight." Marcel entered the stadium.

It didn't matter what he said. He could call Jews a curse to this society, African-Americans deserved no special rights, and same sex marriage should be illegal. Not that Marcel believed any of those things, but he could say them and the crowd would still roar.

He looked to the TelePrompTer for his bullet-point notes. Four colossal sized screens above him televised his face to the thousands on his left, right, straight, and behind. No world leader could amass this crowd, maybe because for the first time, not only did he feel safe from the opposition, but so did his supporters. The stadium could fill 21,834 people. Marcel assumed there was way more since people sat outside the stadium to listen to his speech too.

"And no longer," he paused for dramatic effect, something his dad taught him, "will people go hungry or live on the streets. We have established centers where you can find jobs, food, and shelter." Another pause. "At no cost to you."

The crowd cheered so loud, he couldn't hear his own heart racing. This is what it must've been like for his father, President of the United States, as his adorning fans followed him to every state for campaign rallies. In the hour since he entered the stage, a couple dozen individuals attempted to run to the stage, not to try harm against him, but the opposite. They just wanted to touch the Supreme Leader and thank him personally. As much as he objected to the security, they refused to allow the worshipers to approach him.

"This is not your typical government, with long spirals of red tape and regulations, making you wait and wait. And wait. You know why they made you wait? Because you all meant nothing to those world leaders. They only told you what you wanted to hear so you can re-elect them. But not in the Union. The Union cares...for...you."

Chants continued, signs were held up, cheers blasted the stadium. He knew they couldn't, but wished the People of Bliss could hear it.

"The age of politics is over. Now is the time to do what is right. Clean energy will save our planet, no more fossil fuels. Transit systems will take you anywhere you need to go, with little energy consumption. And I promise, folks, we are working diligently to solve the air quality and get things back to normal." Marcel listened to the applause with a sense of guilt. The last part of that bullet-point was a lie, they weren't solving the air quality issues because it was way beyond the means of scientists still. And beyond the funds available. But hope, as an archangel once told him, was the most powerful entity in the universe. It could change everything. He swallowed hard, "No more being kept in the dark." The dark. It had such a different meaning to him, besides some cliche statement.

As the applause continued, Marcel looked to his left and right. More vast than the television screens above him, six Union flags with the emblem of a dolphin hung from each corner of the stadium. Sections had been roped off for his personnel. Gerard's seat was empty. All his staff had their loving partners, suited and dressed for the moment. They looked so proud. Someone's wife wore a lovely purple gown with a bodice that hugged the woman's curve. Purple is Janice's favorite color. He pictured his father in this standing ovation, with that proud half-smile.

The last time the public saw President Nelson Celest was the State of the Union address where he condemned religious provisions to the Union agreement. Would Marcel receive that same reaction with the next bullet-point on the TelePrompTer? That same awkward, gapping mouth stare? The next part of his speech, the final subject, was going to cause a stir, either a bad one or good one. He could chicken out, leave after a brief farewell, but if President Nelson Celest had the courage to speak the truth than he could. Marcel swallowed hard and cleared his throat, praying the crowd wouldn't turn on him and start exiting the rally. "There's always been a sort of danger, lingering in our society. For over a thousand years. Their origin is believed to began with Chinese fire lances, the first official use of gunpowder in weaponry. Bred from war and violence, guns have became the most lethal invention in humanity, killing more than all diseases combined." He stopped speaking, awaiting people to leave at the word *guns*. But no one did. "I hate that saying: *guns don't kill people, people kill people.* Wrong. Guns do kill people. How? By giving them an opportunity." Surely, objecting fans would've left by now but the crowd stayed. Stay away from sensitive subjects, his father told him five years before Nelson challenged the rights of religions organizations. Marcel took a breath. "Opportunity. I want to stress the importance of that word. When I was in college, my roommate started experimenting with heroin. Most mornings, I'd find him passed out on the toilet or in the shower with cold water spraying his clothed body. We used to live across the hall from a drug dealer. I made sure to stay clear, but some of us are stronger than others. Before he died of an extreme heroin overdose, I asked him a simple question: why did you do it in the first place? His simple answer was: because the opportunity was there." Silence and nods from the crowd made him convinced the fans were listening. "What is the purpose of heroin but to ruin lives, even end them? Makes you wonder what is the purpose of guns? It's to ruin lives and end them." Before he continued, Marcel reminded himself that what he was about to say could obliterate his goals for the Union. If this crowd didn't like what he was about to say, he could expand the network for the People of Bliss, rather than shrink it. But this was the only way to reduce the threat posed by the opposition. "From this moment on, the Union will ban the use and purchase of civilian handguns and assault weapons."

He looked down with his eyes closed, expecting the crude shock his father received after he said that if religions want to act like businesses then they would be treated like business. That crowd didn't even have the time to boo the President, they just left the chambers without another word. Marcel looked up.

The crowd yelled and clapped, cheering in agreement. He let go of the breath he'd been holding.

CHAPTER THIRTY-TWO

The story behind Chuck had been different depending on who told the tale. He didn't speak, Adam had been forewarned. Some said he vowed silence to avoid persecution. Some said he refused to talk to people because he was racist. Some said he wasn't racist, he just hated everybody. Whatever the reason, Chuck didn't talk. And this would make Adam's mission here intense. The only thing he hated more than silence was uncomfortable silence.

He entered Chuck's room. Three posters were taped on the walls, all rock bands Adam didn't know well. Metallica's lead singer held a golden guitar and eyed Adam as he walked in, like he was the room's bodyguard. Chuck sat in one of those rolling stools that doctors liked to use, useful if blood squirts out and it needs to be dodged.

His arms, neck, and even a quarter of his face was masked in tattoos. As expected, Chuck said nothing. Maybe he was deaf. Adam made sure to speak slowly and directly into Chuck's eyes, just in case he was. "I hear you're the person I need to talk to." Clearing his throat, he immediately regretted using the word *talk*. "I don't have a design, but eh…" Not

317

sure what the next step was of this process, Adam lifted out his hand to deliver a manila envelope. The same envelope Gerard handed him outside the sewer system. It had been weeks and now it was time for Adam to get over this fear.

Chuck's burley gray eyebrows crunched up and he grabbed the envelope. His thick neck tilted as he looked at the papers inside. Adam glanced at the sketches Chuck had drawn, scattered and taped to the walls. With black pencils and no color, the drawings varied from simple tattoos like a heart to more complex ones like faces. "I like to draw too. Just not good at this stuff."

Using the word *stuff* made Chuck's lip curl up. Adam cleared his throat again as the artist sifted through the papers in the envelope. He clarified, "They are names of victims. Victims of the Union Keepers, since Marcel Celest turned his militia into Judge Dredds." Chuck's mouth frowned and he gave a blank face. "Judge Dredd? It's a, um, comic book…silly movie…I am the law…you know, never mind."

Chuck rolled his chair to the other side of the room and placed the papers on the table to inspect them more with reading glasses. A neon sign hung on the wall over the table. It read: CHUCK AND BUCK'S TATTOO. Adam recalled the rumors he heard about this other name on the wall. Buck was Chuck's brother. One rumor told a story that Chuck turned his brother in to get freedom. Another rumor said Chuck ate his brother when food was scarce. And the last rumor he heard was Buck joined the Union Keepers. Whatever story was true, Buck definitely wasn't helping his brother run a tattoo shop anymore.

From a cabinet filled with tattoo supplies, Chuck pulled out a small whiteboard and pen. He scrawled something on it then held it up.

Lay down.

318

Adam took a deep breath. Of all the time he'd taken on this, he came up with nothing. No idea of a design. Yet, Chuck took only a few minutes. It worried him that the tattoo artist didn't ask where he wanted it on his body. Adam removed his shirt, looking at his bony chest peak up and down. Breathe.

About to lay on the table, Chuck held up his hand. He erased the whiteboard with a cloth and wrote on it.

All off.

Being that the list was over two thousand names, he felt silly for not realizing this could cover his entire body. Having second thoughts again, Adam took a step back. Obviously not being his first time dealing with a hesitant customer, Chuck leaned back against the wall and waited.

Adam asked, "Gonna need the whole body, huh?"

Chuck erased the whiteboard and wrote.

Yep.

Realizing he was about to ask another mundane question, Adam whispered, "This going to hurt?"

Chuck erased and scribbled.

Yep.

A little perplexed as to why Chuck would clean his board just to write the same thing, Adam decided to ask a more important question. "Got clean needles?"

After clearing the board and scribbling, Adam was certain that the whiteboard would say *yep* again. Chuck held up the board.

Nope.

"Shit," Adam sighed as his shoulders fell. Trepidation swelled up in the back of his throat. It was like seeing red and blue lights in the rear view mirror and having a backpack full of weed. He pictured if Brent were there, in this tight four sided concrete room. Probably asking him why he decided to do this in the first place. There were several ways to be reminded of what the Union, and Marcel Celest, had done to the country. To the world. Why a tattoo?

"Got anything that can calm my nerves? Opiates? Painkillers? Sedatives?"

Chuck answered on the board.

All the above.

Maybe all the above would be needed. Adam and Janice vowed together to never touch another illegal substance, since much of their time together seemed hazy. But sacrifices had to be made. Adam's heart thumped like a jack hammer, he needed relief. Sometimes small talk helped. He nervously chuckled, "So what's the deal with you? Why don't you talk? Cat got your tongue?"

After a quick erase and rewrite, Chuck showed the board.

No. They do.

Suddenly, Adam's heart slowed its selfish panic. His anxiety settled like sand at the bottom of a calm sea. He felt his chest stop the useless heaving. Something devastating slapped him and woke him up. He stared into Chuck's eyes. "*They* took it?" Adam said under his breath.

Slowly, Chuck nodded.

Even as he spoke, Adam could hear the difference in his voice. Not squeaky or squeamish, it held an authoritative tone. "Why did the Keepers take your tongue?"

Talk too much.

Good answer. It gave Adam solace that others fought back as much as he did. That sacrifices were made. More of a sacrifice than any person, including himself, could make on this tattoo table. "They cut your brother's tongue too?"

No. His throat.

Chuck slid one of the pieces of paper from the envelope and held it up, pointing to a name on the list: BUCK RICHARDSON.

For moments like this, moments Adam felt like crying, he'd close his eyes and count to ten. Brent taught him that technique used to control rage. But that's where his tears flowed from. Rage of all that the Union had done. And if Brent were here, asking why Adam was doing this tattoo in the first place, he'd answer back that he needed to experience more than reminders. He needed to experience pain.

After counting to ten, Adam's throat didn't feel swollen and his body remained calm. As Adam locked eyes on the artist, he wondered if those swollen yet sunken eyes were how his looked. Every morning, he stand in front of a mirror for ten minutes before he'd start to brush or shave. Reflections lied, he learned that in his Psych class in college. Brains tended to interrupt only the good in a reflection, not the bad. No wonder everyone would ask him if was okay, dozens of times a day, it seemed. Truth be told, he wasn't. No better than Chuck. External pain could heal, while internal pain never really did. It wasn't just Brent, but all those he lost to the maniacal idea of a unionized government and those that would do anything to protect it.

Chuck scratched out his whiteboard and held it up.
Still need drugs?
Adam answered firmly through glistening eyes, "No."
Chuck's nod affirmed he understood. Words could only say so much. Perhaps that's why their silence seemed so deafening. He barely knew the tattoo artist, but trusted him with everything. Adam began to undress.

Mixtures of red and black spiraled down, winding down with the clear liquid into the drain. Adam watched it, knees on the shower floor. His body ached, covered in names tattooed with dark ink. Names that curved, twisted, and circled all over his skin in maniacal beautiful designs.

For over an hour, alone in the shower room, he'd sat in this prayer position below a spray of water. The hot water had already come and gone, leaving him with the frigid leftovers. Adam stared at his arms. *Cody Anderson. Herald Bushner. Loretta Matters. Kimberly Evans.* All these names didn't mean much on paper, but meant everything on his skin. Their souls were with him now. He could never forget. And he never wanted to.

Visions of battered bodies flashed in his head. Piles of dead bodies instead of graves. Some were even children. Raped by Union Keepers, stoned by Marcel Celest's followers, most of these people suffered more than he had. Or ever will. *Michael Peters. Danna Collins. James Fernandez.* Hung on streets to remind rebels how powerful the Union was. The Union was the only option. Rebellion meant death. But so many fought back. *Shelly Asher. Madeline Illner. George Turner.*

Remnants of the black ink washed off like tears. Blood traveled in droplets from his scars into the floor. He looked at his palms now, asking them for relief. Any type of relief. Wash away his sadness. Adam buried his face into his palms and sobbed loudly. The sound of rushing water drowned out his cries. It was the only place he could. No one could see him like this. Leaders don't show fear. They don't show anguish. They don't show doubt. This was the only place where he could release all that down a spiraling drain.

The biggest mistake that can be made
is not learning from your mistakes.

-Victoria Celest
First Lady of the United States
2033-2038

CHAPTER THIRTY-THREE

After all the abuse of mankind, trees thrived. Royal looked up and wondered how tall they were. At a young age, her mother told her trees reached out to the beautiful lights of heaven. What Royal would do to see a decent sunrise or sunset. Just to see the sun for even a peak would be satisfactory. But Russia seemed darker than the United States.

Anton must've read her mind because he glanced upwards from his guitar. "Who's idea was it to use goddamn seeds to stop global warming? Now they'll be up there forever." With that deep accent and pearly white teeth, Anton seemed the kind of man ready to capture James Bond not save the world.

"Don't use the Lord's name in vain," she replied. "Just play me another song."

Sneaking out in the middle of the night from Zharkova to play campfire songs sounded like something from a teenage romance movie. But here they were, sitting across from each other and soaking in the warmth of the flames. Anton could play the guitar like a rock star. He had said his mother loathed the instrument so he had done many midnight rendezvous when she fell asleep; gin and vodka knocked her out for several hours. Listening to the sounds of car alarms would've been more pleasurable than Zharkova's aggravated comments.

She watched Anton with admiration more than infatuation. In Sunday School, Royal remembered the stories of Jesus Christ. How he hung around the lepers and the whores. How his teachings were so different than the rest of them. How he stunk and bathed in filthy water. Yet, one thing life taught her was that it's the "weird" ones that make a difference. For example, Anton was a peace-loving, Earth-giving, barefoot hippy. Yet he made her life easier.

The guitar drummed. Anton kept to just the strings and not the vocals, admitting that his voice sounded like an ox humping a rhino. His song faded into a whisper in the night. Royal clapped her hands, "Bravo."

She blew on her marshmallow before taking a bite. Anton scoffed, "Any idea what's in those marshmallows?"

Figuring one of his vegan rants couldn't possibly ruin the taste of the good old-fashioned snack, she humored herself. "No. What?"

"It has gelatin." He said it as though it had been brewed in a witch's cauldron.

"Jell-O? What's wrong with Jell-O?"

"It's made of animal byproduct. Remnants of being with a soul." He looked up at the clouds. "Just like that. The byproduct of humanity. There's ashes of humans, animals, buildings...all floating up there like it all meant nothing."

Her appetite sank the longer she stared at those clouds. Admittedly, Royal never thought of the ash like that. "Is it too late?" she asked aloud to more herself than to Anton.

The guitar strummed for a bit before he stopped to munch on white crackers with filthy hands. This coming from the man who scolded Royal for flushing the toilet after she peed.

If it's brown, flush it down – if it's yellow, leave it mellow.
"We just need someone strong enough to defeat the government and erase further toxins being released. Mother Earth will heal herself. I hope."

Nodding, Royal placed the tree branch with the marshmallow into the fire and listened to it sizzle. She listened to Anton play another slow tune filled with sorrow. The branch eventually turned black and crumbled away into a stronger force. Was the Union stronger? Could they defeat the fire that tore them apart and melted them into ashes?

Anton finished the last note on his guitar. But something odd happened. Something that made Royal stay absolutely still. The noise of the strumming didn't cease. It transformed into a frightening sound she'd never heard before. High pitched and uniformed together, the clatter came from all around them. Anton's eyes scared her more than the phenomenon, because she'd never seen him scared before.

"They're coming," he shuttered. "Locusts."

Killer locusts bred from government labs in Africa had escaped the same day nuclear mayhem spread around the world. From what she'd heard, no one had ever survived the sting to tell about its effect. Apparently not being his first encounter, Anton spat out orders as he stood slowly. "They detect breathing. You'll have to hold your breath."

The nightmare of thrown into a pool by her father came back to her. *You have to learn things the hard way.* Instead, she nearly drowned and a lifeguard had to perform CPR to loosen the water in her lungs. "I can't do this," she whispered as the sound got louder. Not far from her was an over-turned tree with a hallow inside. With her tiny body, Royal suspected she could squeeze through the truck of the tree and hide.

Anton must've read her mind. "Don't run. You're breathing will exhilarate."

Her breathing was already exhilarating. How long would she have to hold her breath? What if they didn't keep passing? What if they're stingers accidentally hit her? Would they get stuck in her hair? She knew she should've worn her cap.

"Take a deep breath," he demanded.

She couldn't be less prepared for this, much like her daddy's attempt at teaching her nine-year old self how to swim. Thankful for making the decision to quit cigarettes and spouting ugly anti-government rhetoric over the radio, Royal could take a deep breath without coughing. But lung cancer sounded much less painful than a sting of locust venom. Attacking the nervous and muscular system, reports said that the stinger stiffens the body so it's victim feels every bit of pain without a way to react. Royal never imagined the day would happen she'd face these tiny monsters.

She held her breath as the swarm approached. It seemed like a king sized comforter floating in mid-air. The yellow blob had hundreds, maybe even thousands, of the mechanical insects. Her heart raced and begged for air. Piercing her lips, Royal stood still. The swarm moved past Anyone, blanketing him to the point she felt alone. What she thought was the size of a king sized comforter turned into the size of a King's room. The swarm spread out hunting for prey. If only they liked marshmallows, she would've been happy to toss the entire bag at the sinister insects. But they didn't feed on sweets. They didn't feed on anything. Manufactured to kill anything breath, their purpose was just to murder.

Air was running out. How long were they going to linger? She saw that tree trunk, lying sideways with a hiding place. Maybe Royal just needed to time it right. Even though she couldn't see Anton, she felt his disapproval. But what else could be done? Eventually, like all humans, she needed to breath. And her lack of swimming skills also meant her lack of holding her breath.

One of the curious nano machines made its way toward her; its eyes (or sensors more like) darted around. It stared in her direction. Panic raced her heart passed the point of beating and sounded like a steady strum. Matching the steady strum of the locusts about to kill her.

She fled. Faster than she'd ever ran. Faster than any human ever ran. Without looking behind her, never look behind she learned from horror movies, the locusts no doubt chased her. Royal dashed then slid like a game of softball and the hollow trunk was third base. But the satisfaction quickly faded. In her race to escape certain death, it never occurred to her that the open end of the tree trunk had no type of plug. The locusts could still get inside. She scurried backwards. The manhole sized open end of the trunk reminded her of the failed attempt. Her ears stung as the sound of locusts became louder as they approached.

Zzzzzz....zzzzzzzzz.........zzzzzzzzz.........

Someone blocked the other end of the trunk. Anton. His body covered the hole. He looked directly in her eyes and said, "You're stronger than me. Stop the Union."

Before he could say a final goodbye, he screamed at the top of his throat as hundreds of locusts. He froze and blood poured out of his nose. Her cries muted the screeches of the locusts. She yelled so loud her throat hurt immediately. Anton's frozen body bled from the ears and mouth. He was still alive, blinking every so often. Blood popped out of his eye sockets and ran down his face like tears.

It might have been several minutes or several hours. Royal wasn't sure. The locusts had left a long time ago. Even the scavengers, feeding on the tainted leftover blood of Anton, had left. But Royal still stared. Every once in a while, she hoped Anton would give some sign of life. Maybe a twitch or a blink of the eyes. Then she could tell him sorry. Like that would somehow undo the mistake she had made. A mistake that cost a life.

When the tears on her face had dried and her tongue stuck to the roof of her mouth, Royal's body had suffered steep dehydration. It passed her mind to maybe just die here. Then Anton's voice, in some ghostly recording in her head, would whisper *Stop the Union.*

Growing up in the South, the television always showed commercials about military heroes. The people that sacrificed every day. But they never showed what those sacrifices looked like. Anton's corpse turned into a something Mama would put on the porch during Halloween with a Tupperware full of candy. The locusts had sucked so much of his blood, that his skin went even more pale. Almost to the color of pure white like freshly bleached linens. With a gentle shove, she pushed Anton's body out of the way and sneaked out of the tree's hiding place.

After spending an hour digging a hole with bare hands, she dragged Anton's body in and covered it with dirt. It was the best she could do. Anton wanted to be one with the earth someday. Without a doubt, the earth wanted to be one with him too. How had she survived? Why did she survive? Did she deserve to survive?

The long walk back, Royal kept her head down in deep thought. But when she made it to the front door and entered the subway station – she couldn't remember any of it.

Wearing a pink flowery and sun hat over that brunette wig, Zharkova looked as though she should be on a beach somewhere not inside a subway station. She sat on the bench with her nose stuck in a novel. Royal never seen her read.

Without looking up, she spouted, "Where have you both been? It's been all night. I can't sleep until I receive a warm cup of hot cocoa. Anton knows this." Not until she glanced up did she realize Royal was alone. Once again, their eyes met and Zharkova just stared. Royal heard once that psychopaths stare a lot to interpret human reactions. "What happened?"

Three explanations came to her head as she faced Zharkova. The first speech in her head explained everything: we snuck out, we sat around playing music, we ate marshmallows, we flirted, locusts appeared, I overreacted and Anton sacrificed himself to save me. The explanation seemed too long, so she came up with a shorter version: we were out in the woods and locusts showed up; Anton protected me from certain death and lost his life. No. Telling Zharkova that her only son gave his life to save Royal's pitiful American life...well, that would be like telling Zharkova that the United States was better than Russia. Instead, Royal settled on shrinking the large explanation to a short one. A very one. She whispered only one word. "Locusts."

The Russian leader paused, pulling the fake strands from her wig out of her face. "Okay. And my son..."

This time, Royal said nothing. That explanation had no words.

Zharkova pressed her lips together and her head bobbled a little. She probably had a long rant forming in her, but instead...she slapped Royal across the face. Royal's head swung to the right and she immediately pressed her palm to the red cheek. It didn't hurt. Not really. Not as much as Anton's absence did.

No further words came out of her mouth. Zharkova bookmarked her page in the book with a leaflet and walked away.

Trying to contemplate all that happen, Royal felt weak at the knees and sat on the bench still warm from Zharkova. She only thought of Anton's heroism. How he just dodged in front of those locusts with no fear while Royal panicked like a squirrel in the middle of a highway. It took a certain control, or maybe acceptance, to do such a thing. Was she ready to do that? Ready to hop in front of danger at a moment's notice?

Soldiers could train to be heroic without actually being heroic. Which meant there was something else. Something inside the soul that had to make that decision. Royal closed her eyes and concentrated.

Then she made a vow. A vow to never be afraid of death ever again.

CHAPTER THIRTY-FOUR

Mashed potatoes with smooth brown gravy, vibrant green beans, carrots smothered in warm butter, and sliced ham with crispy skin sat on a plate untouched. Janice admired the food, almost as perfect as a Christmas dinner at the White House. But yet, she felt the least bit of hunger. She'd literally starved herself the whole day in anticipation of the holiday gathering at the cafeteria, but still couldn't touch the stuff. Something inside her stomach gnawed and twisted her. It would be day three without eating.

Adam noticed, practically finished and pulling up the bowl of cranberry dessert leftover from Thanksgiving a few weeks back. "Not going to eat?" It was the most caring comment he had made in months.

She pushed the plate aside and kept the fork planted in the potatoes, in case one of the cooks passed by, she could pretend to be in the middle of eating. Considering all that had been done to get this meal, she should have been grateful. Which she was. Grateful, just not hungry. Changing the subject made her feel less intimidated. "Who are they? The names?"

Streaming in unique patterns around his arms and body had been several names. Her husband would've, at least, spoken with her about it before making such a drastic move as a body tattoo. Then again, Adam barely understood how to be a boyfriend, much less a husband. Janice's eyes scanned the room, hoping that Gerard would have joined the feast.

Adam, reading a notepad with what she assumed was a string of algorithms for his program, never looked up. "What was that? Sorry. I'm still working on some coding to get messages through to our people in other countries."

"I understand," she said. And she actually did. "My father was the President of the United States, I know what it's like when someone is distracted." Janice wanted to say she understood what it was like to be ignored.

He brushed aside the empty bowl of dessert and pad of paper, turning his attention to her. Nelson used to do the same thing, guilt clearing the mind. "Is it your stomach again?"

"It's everything."

And he genuinely looked sad and helpless. "Maybe I could get you a decoy chip and get an actual doctor to check you out."

"I'll be fine," Janice said unsure why she didn't want anyone to fix her.

Looking for something else to chat about, Adam twirled his thumbs. Either he couldn't find something else or didn't want to talk about something else. "So is…um…they still green?"

Janice nodded.

"No chance they change?" He said, staring with those perfect brown eyes.

Janice shook her head. "99 percent probability." There was no telling what was on his mind, relief or repentance.

Everyone sat at tables, grinning with mouths full of turkey, and yet she didn't feel much to celebrate. In just a couple months, the one year anniversary of Doomsday arrived on January 7th. Maybe some saw a reason to be thrilled at how much had been accomplished, and there had, but Janice still felt alone.

In the distance, past three tables of mothers singing and clapping to a melody with children, sat Gerard. He too looked alone, munching on cranberry sauce while picking at the vegetables. He hated vegetables.

"Ask him," Adam said.

Janice hesitated, going to stand but sitting back immediately. "Don't you ever get scared."

"Scared of what?"

"Decisions."

Adam picked at a scab starting to form on his forearm from the tattoo. She read the name Brent Celest in black letters. "Brent actually was the one who gave me the courage to speak to you the first time. Can you believe it? He was always protective of you, but he knew that if I spoke to you…it would alter the future. I ponder what life I would be living if I didn't approached my sexy married Professor and asked to her party with me." Party they did. Too much partying. If they hadn't met, Janice wouldn't have committed the some-would-call sins. Long nights of psychedelic adventures or blackout Bliss. But on the other hand, she wouldn't have ended up here. Adam had led her down a distinct paths, but a path nonetheless. Sometimes, when not content with the trail, it was necessary to return back. "Hey, can I ask you something? Did you…hate Gerard when you first met him?"

"Oh God, yes. He drove me insane. So cocky and rude, we argued constantly. Then one day…it just slipped away."

"I have this theory," Adam said, "that the best relationships are the ones that start with all the anger, hurt, and frustration. That way, you get nothing left but love, admiration, and friendship. Maybe its a side effect of our evolution to sex."

Janice smirked, "Well. That's your new writing assignment for this week. I want it on my desk by Friday."

Returning the smirk, they both shared a silent memory of better times when college was the only stress. "Ask him," Adam repeated. "I know you want to."

She laid her hand on top of his. "I'm always going to love you. You know that, right?"

He nodded and gave a slight smile. "Ditto."

Without much more to say, their relationship had came to end before it even reached a satisfying beginning. Much too naive for her and she too mulish for him, Janice and Adam never connected in the way opposites did. She stood up and walked towards Gerard. He sat alone, chewing slowly on the juicy turkey. When she went to sit down, he stopped chewing and stared at her that way he did in High School.

"Hey," he said with his mouth full, an aggravating bad habit but something she missed.

Janice twisted her finger where her wedding ring, lost somewhere in these long travels, used to be. The wedding ring she'd worn for over twenty years. "Would you like to see him?"

He finished chewing and swallowed. Putting down his fork, he seemed genuinely confused. "See who?"

Letting the mystery that had been resting on her chest, keeping her from breathing, finally come to fruition felt relieving. The mystery that started with a pregnancy test that showed a plus sign. Janice said, "*Your* baby."

Doing her best to make the concrete four-walled and no window room more homely, Janice grew some plants. Without light, they didn't grow much. Neither did Janice. She felt wilted most days and malnourished the other days. Gerard had asked if she was okay, during that awkward walk to her room; her reply was the usual *Please stop asking that.*

Though her living quarters wasn't much to look at, she kept it clean and tidy. So Janice couldn't understand why Gerard had stopped at the door, almost frozen in time. Not until he looked at the crib. Nestled, on his back with plenty of blankets, Colin didn't make much noise. He was always so quiet, like his mother. "He's not asleep."

"I know," Gerard whispered.

Her shoulders slumped as the right side of her mouth smirked. That wide-eyed stare looked familiar. Nelson had that same pause right before entering the Oval Office for the first time. Things were going to be different, not just now but forever. Janice placed her hand on his arm. It had been the closest they'd touched in almost a year. "It's going to be okay."

Again, he whispered unnecessarily. "What if he doesn't like me? And...and...he starts screaming. What if I'm one of those dads that can hold a baby right? What if I drop him? Jesus Christ, Janice, what if I drop him?"

"It's fine," she giggled. "You'll know what to do, it's instinct." Though she wouldn't admit it took her hours to practice tying on a diaper. Janice tugged at his arm and he entered the quiet room.

Colin stared at the visitor with those breath-taking green eyes. His legs danced in the pajamas that probably too big for him, but he'd eventually grow into. She only hoped he wouldn't grow too fast; babies were so innocent and uncorrupted by this world. Being a mother was her only relief.

"He likes to make people laugh," she commented.

Gerard gave a nervous chuckle, as if he didn't believe her. But right on queue, Colin began to coo and swing his arms with a gigantic smile on his face. "Wow, no kidding. He really does like it. He's going to grow up to be a comedian. I know it."

Janice agreed with a solemn nod. "Pick him up."

Gerard swallowed hard. Having served over a decade in the Capitol Police force and another decade in Secret Service, she found it amusing that holding a baby scared him. Timidly and cautiously, he lifted Colin from the crib. They gawked at each other in this sort of silent agreement. Then Gerard held the baby close to his shoulder and closed his eyes, savoring this moment. So many lies, misgivings, and lonely nights had he endured to get here? To this very minute where he could hold his baby. And how many deceits had Janice endured?

"I'm sorry for -" She began to say, but was interrupted before her list of apologies started. Sorry for cheating on him with Adam. Sorry for sleeping with her adopted brother Marcel. Sorry for drinking too much. Sorry for partying and acting like a fool.

"Don't apologize for anything," he said finally opening his eyes to stare at the giggly trophy in his arms. "Don't apologize ever. We make choices in life, whether they are good or bad, it doesn't matter. What matters is that we keep going."

"That's inspiring," she nodded.

"I read it in a Sports Illustrated magazine."

Janice rolled her eyes and snickered. The three of them, together finally, felt right. She gazed into his green eyes as he melted into hers. Then she moved in and kissed his soft lips.

Without an alarm or sunlight, Janice often depending on the internal clock to wake her, but most times Colin woke her demanding his bottle. Instead, this morning, she awoke by herself. Three uncanny occurrences happened.

First, Colin didn't angrily cry. She thought the worse, until she turned over and saw Gerard feeding him. It was like watching a mechanic assemble a car without any knowledge, but just hope. The baby batted away the bottle while his father fumbled to keep it from falling to the floor.

Second, Janice genuinely experienced happiness. Sleeping next to Adam meant either an empty side of the bed or an awkward conversation about the plans for the day.

Third, she dreamt. Janice never had dreams. Theorists would say that's impossible, that some are better at remembering their night journeys than others. But she remained firm that her brain wouldn't allow dreams. Not until last night anyways. In it, Janice was with Brent and Victoria. They were on a raft, coasting along a quiet river, before ravishing waves took them on a wild rush. Grasping tightly to the edge, Brent and Victoria tried to paddle out of the mess. Water smacked her face so hard, she felt it even now. Victoria told her they'd have to lose someone off the raft, to keep it afloat; instructing Janice to push Brent into the river. Moments before they approached sharp rocks and an incline of the water, Janice looked towards Brent. Then she jumped into the freezing river.

"You alright?"

Janice snapped awake from the awful recollection of the dream. Or nightmare. "I told you yesterday, don't need to ask me that."

Gerard nodded his head. "Yeah, but you look more pale than yesterday."

Changing the subject, Janice pointed at the bottle. "You're holding it too vertical."

Quickly, he adjusted his stance while Janice put on a robe hastily as though her husband hadn't noticed her naked body last night. "I've lost a lot of weight, I know." After she said, she immediately hated herself. Janice wasn't one of those girls who fished for compliments. The way Gerard touched her in the middle of the night, and the way his hands slide across her hips spelled out his attraction. They made love for over an hour. Men don't do that with women they find unattractive. So why did she need a compliment?

"You look amazing," he said.

With a smile, Janice grabbed a plastic box with shampoo, conditioner, and body soap. At one point in their lives together, she had a shower with four different shampoos and conditioners. Much had changed, but the idea still stayed the same.

"Janice? Did you hear me?"

She was holding one of the bottles in her hand, staring at it with no knowledge of holding it. Before she could ask what Gerard had just said, her throat tightened and stole her voice.

"Janice?"

The silo felt like it begun to spin, slowly at first. Judging by his lack of reaction, Janice assumed it was in her head. She held onto the shelf.

"You alright?"

As much as she wanted to react angrily that she was fine, Janice couldn't. Because she wasn't. Something terrible was wrong. The world around her spun faster and faster. Thoughts couldn't correlate. Everything began to sway like that precarious water ride. Her plastic box of bathroom essentials crashed to the floor, but she didn't remember letting it go.

"Janice!"

Then she lost consciousness.

CHAPTER THIRTY-FIVE

Snow piled up enough to build snowmen. Not the snowmen Adam remembered from his childhood, but at least the children tried to have fun outside. The sense of urgency stepping outside the missile silo disappeared, thanks to his virus that corrupted the Union's mainframe. No longer did they have to worry about snooping eyes, because Adam knew the location of every Union Keeper in the world. Using chips to track their soldiers, the Union made a mistake in their confidence. In his back pocket, Adam kept a tablet Gerard gave him. The app he coded alerted him of any intruders nearby. There was peace in security.

Adam attempted to help the children construct a snowman, but the gray stained snow didn't stick well and the head fell off. Just in time to break the awkwardness of destroying the kids' snowman, a van pulled up. The familiar logo of Willie's old electrician business was caked in mud. Willie slid open the door to reveal his vehicle stacked with grocery bags. Without the need to even ask for help, others rushed up to carry food inside the silo. "I take it the decoy chips worked," Adam asked, grabbing the lighter grocery bags.

Willie, out of breath from excitement or from grabbing heavy bags, said, "Yep! And we didn't have to pay a dime or show ID."

He followed him into the portal door hidden behind rocks and bushes, then through the entry tunnel Pierre guarded. "No chance you could find ammo?"

"No can do," Willie answered, smiling at Pierre as they past by, "Marcel Celest's ban on weapons also meant a ban on ammo. Once we fry their guns with Project Syncope, we're gonna have to use what we got."

Even the greatest of wars at least had bows and arrows. This news didn't settle well with Adam. After dropping off some of the bags in the kitchen, he snuck off to meet with the man in charge of their limited gun supply.

Six levels down, he knocked on the door marked ARMORY with a sharpie over the knob. Knocking was useless, since he could already hear the sounds of gunshots inside. Adam walked in to see Bruno, ducking to keep his head from hitting the ceiling light, wearing earmuffs to block the sounds of the gunfire. In three separate rows, three men practiced shooting rounds at far away targets.

"Bruno like your aim!" He clapped when the shooting finally stopped.

Adam didn't like to interrupt, but he felt it was important. "You're using rubber bullets to practice, right?"

"Of course!" Bruno said, slapping Adam's shoulder as a friendly gesture, but only leaving it pulsing painfully. "Bruno no idiot! I count! Not much ammunition."

"And we can't get anymore. I'm going to trust you to come up with some good weapons to use on the field. Understand?"

He beat his chest and nodded. "Bruno understand."

One day, he promised to teach Bruno to stop referring to himself in third person, but today wasn't the day. He gave a polite nod and left the room.

The next room down was a gym. Usually empty, Adam was pleased to see people inside using the equipment. Jogging on the treadmill, lifting weights, and boxing with a punching bag were all good techniques to practice before the war. Thinking about the war knotted Adam's stomach. The only obstacle, which Zharkova rudely brought to light, was their lack of organization. Now that hurdle had been overcome. There was no other path besides their march to the castle, so vividly dreamt in his precognition. It was going to be a bloody battle on both sides and there was a good chance someone in this room could be dead in a week. Adam gave a polite nod and exited the gym.

Cackling and laughter could be heard in the room across from the gym. The area had been designated by Victor to build his weapon, a suit of fire cannons Adam had seen in his vision of the war. Scouts had brought what they could to the pyromaniac's request and he had been locked up in this room for seemingly weeks, only appearing to eat and refill his tumbler of coffee. Adam tapped on the door lightly before opening it. Victor stopped his welding and lifted the mask to stare at his visitor with wide eyes and drops of sweat from his nose.

Victor had made quiet an advancement of the suit. Hanging from the ceiling via coat hangers and rods, the uniform would make Victor even tower above Bruno. Gas canisters had been welded onto the back, as well as a host of other wires and containers marked HAZARD.

Wearing a welder's apron made of leather and that constant maniacal smile, Victor looked ready to cut up bodies. Always at odds of how to speak to the man, Adam chose his words wisely. "How's everything?"

Suddenly, Victor busted into a sudden laughter making Adam jumped back a little. After the hilarity was over in the psycho's mind, he smirked, "I...burn...everything."

Not turning around, Adam felt for the knob and quickly opened the door. "Good chatting with you, buddy." He rushed out into the hallway and slammed the door shut, the sound of Victor's sadistic chuckling continued through the thick walls.

Adam walked down the circular a little further until the snickering noise stopped and was replaced by something more relaxing. A humming sound. It was coming from one of the classrooms. Adam looked at his watch and knew exactly what was scheduled. He couldn't help but peek through the window of the door, because no matter how many times he'd seen it...it wasn't enough.

Dozens of people, sitting in mediation positions on mats, were glowing. They hummed in unison. Their skin brightened from whatever magic had been in left in the lake by the Light's teachers, Lloyd and Nina. Adam had experienced the sensation, the warmness of that inner peace as it expelled out of you and made your skin illuminate. He would've liked to join them, but it took concentration. Concentration he just couldn't do. Especially not with Janice constantly in his mind and the stresses of an upcoming battle.

Across the hall, Adam stopped at the plant nursery. Perhaps Matley and her ingenious concoctions could carve up something to calm his nerves. She had become the premier medicine woman for the People of Bliss.

Unfortunately, when he opened the door of the misty and humid plant room, he didn't find her. Instead, strolling through the aisles of plants like at a grocery store, Gerard held his baby. Little curious Colin tried to grab for one of the plants, but his father quickly snatched it out of his hand.

"That's a no-no. Eating that will probably give you the urge to eat Funyuns and drink Mountain Dew."

Seeing Colin sit so well with his actual father, Adam wished he felt jealousy, but he didn't. Because fate had placed everyone in the right positions of this immense board game.

"Hey," Gerard said, noticing Adam. "Happy New Years."

"Wow. I actually forgot that was today. So much on my mind." In fact, he'd forgotten almost every holiday. The only reminders he had was the different tastes at dinner time.

"Me too," Gerard said, handing a dandelion to Colin he'd plucked from under a set of grow lights, which the child immediately put in his mouth. "Never saw the point of the holiday, except to make new resolutions."

"I can only think of a resolution to end the Union, once and for all."

Gerard wiped the drool from the baby's mouth with a cloth. "We finally got something in common."

"We also have *someone* in common. How is she?"

Even with the baby around, the mood went rapidly from cheery to gloomy. "She's in and out. Doctor says she'll be fine." Gerard said, swooping Colin over a series of plants like he was Superman. Colin's giggle made even Gerard laugh. Come to think of it, Adam couldn't remember ever seeing him laugh, the baby or Gerard.

"You're really good at that." He said, feeling guilty immediately for ruining the mood between father and son.

"What? Being a dad?"

"Lying." He answered bluntly, sensing the spirit of Brent telling him to be bold and get answers. "She said you blink a lot when you lie."

"Well, look who's balls are starting to grow in. Doctor says an infection. She's bleeding internally. But we are going to fix her." As if somehow Colin could understand, even though it was highly improbable since the child hadn't said it's first word yet, Gerard explained in that high pitched tone that rewarding fathers had mastered, "Mommy is going to be much better soon! She just needs lots of sleep. Even more than you do!"

Adam touched the petals of a lilac flower, Janice's favorite. Their bond wasn't meant to be, but didn't change the way he valued her. "How do you do it? Remain so positive?"

Gerard sighed, either annoyed by his presence or annoyed by the conversation. "Let me ask you something," He paused to wrap Colin in a sarong on a table, "What tastes better, kid? Water that has been wallowing in place, collecting impurities, and harvesting filth? Or water that's been rushing through difficulties, running over obstacles, and pushing forward to keep itself pure?"

The answer was obvious. But easier said than done. "Thanks for being a friend, Gerard."

He grabbed the baby, wrapped in the sarong and then secured the cloth around his waist and neck. Adam would've never figured that out with the help of a YouTube how-to-video. "Look, I know you lost your best friend, don't get me wrong I admire the friendship you had with Brent, but I'm not going to be the one to replace him."

Placing his hands in his pockets, Adam's head bowed and shoulders sagged.

Lip twisted and eyes squinting, Gerard said, "You're good at that."

"What?"

"Making people feel guilty." If that was an apology, it seemed the best Adam was going to get. Gerard added, "I mean, I get it. You want love. Family."

"But every time that life starts for me, I feel like I'm not ready."

Colin tugged at Gerard's beard. "You'll know when you're ready. I wasn't for a long time. But you'll just...know."

Hands still in his pocket, Adam smirked. "It's not about the aim, it's about the timing."

"Huh?"

"Just something Royal says."

The door swung open hastily.

"There you are!" Willie shouted, grabbing Adam by the arm. "We gotta go! Now!" All the loud commotion and hurried energy made the baby began to cry. "Sorry," Willie immediately apologized, "We got one of *them* out there!"

"Them?" Gerard asked, trying to bobble Colin to make him stop crying.

"Union soldier!" Willie said, running out the door.

It was impossible. Adam yanked his tablet out and checked. "No one is in the area besides us."

Both of them immediately sensing their plan had failed, hacking the system of palm chips, went into a panic. Gerard, wide-eyed, said, "Show me where's the armory."

After only a few minutes, chaos erupted in the silo. People rushed hallways into their rooms. Alarms blared over the speakers, something they've never had to do before. Finding a woman to babysit while Gerard joined the fight didn't take long, Matley took Colin and calmed him down as Adam and Gerard rushed to the armory.

Inside, Bruno handed off magazines of ammo to men entering and exiting. Gerard went for the rifles section, handing Adam a long rifle with a sturdy wooden stock. "You ever shot a Ruger 10-22 with bump fire technique?"

Adam shrugged, "Yeah, of course."

Gerard rolled his eyes. "I mean, not in a video game."

"Oh! Then no..."

"Aim through both the front and rear sights, hold the butt of the rifle to the left side of your chest, and be mindful of the trigger guard."

Panicked and already sweating, Adam hurried behind the other men up the corridor and to the entryway. Willie hung just below the ladder and exit door. "I don't see any men yet. It hasn't moved. It's just floating there."

Being the leader of this establishment, Adam had to keep the situation controlled and calm. Judging by his incoherent statement, Willie seemed the most worried of the group. "What do you mean *its* just floating there? What is it? Drone?"

Willie didn't know how to answer, he stepped off the ladder and let Adam climb up.

Peeking slowly through the slit of the ajar door, Adam tried to see what was out there, but his view was shaded by trees. This was his moment, surrounded by men who were on the verge of fighting for his promise of a better future without the Union, to show strength. Gerard gave him a nod.

Adam climbed slowly out and squeezed through the door, remembering to put the rifle straight ahead and secured to his chest.

Hovering just over the trees, the flying vehicle seemed like a billboard attached to the sky. No brushes swayed around it, meaning it had some type of propulsion system that needed little air. It didn't move. Surely, at first sight, anyone that saw it would think it was a UFO and alien soldiers were here to capture humans for testing. But it wasn't. Adam recognized it. Regardless of how many precognitions came to fruition, he always had the single chill climb up his spine when he recognized something from his visions. A smile formed on his face.

The jet began a slow descent before landing on an open field, barely disturbing the corn growing on the field. Black with gray glowing lines and a sleek nose, it was exactly the way Adam pictured.

From the top of it, a hood popped open and Nelson Celest stepped out. After he walked down the hill, he approached Adam. "Didn't mean to scare everyone."

Adam immediately hugged him, his father figure was alive and well. People from the silo, including Gerard, came out to shake hands, pat backs, and hug the President of the United States. This was the second time today he'd seen abnormal reactions from the men he knew, Nelson was genuinely happy to receive this admiration. His grin slowly faded. "Where's Janice?"

Just as his smile went away, so did everyone else's. He repeated, more concerned, "Where's my daughter?"

CHAPTER THIRTY-SIX

"Aurora!"

Royal gave a long drawn out groan as she awakened from whatever little sleep she'd actually gotten. Since her time aiding and caring for this malicious Russian woman, Royal barely slept. It took her nearly three hours just to fall asleep and then in less time than that - Zharkova would be screaming her name.

"Aurora! I know you can hear me!"

Maybe if she stabbed herself in the ears with pencils, she wouldn't be able to hear her. Then Royal could get a decent night of sleep. Her back had gotten even stiffer than this rock hard bed. The only comforting item in this shaky boat was the pillow. Made from goose feathers, it felt like what Royal would imagine God's shoulder to feel like. Just when the pillow put her into a deep slumber, she'd hear the sound of -

"Aurora! Now!"

Royal took a deep breath and opened her eyes. According to her Swatch watch, it was time to get up and start breakfast. And Zharkova got even more cranky without her maple syrup and waffles. That woman was so frightening that even the Wicked Witch of the West's sister would climb back underneath the house. "Yes, ma'am. I'll start breakfast."

When she sat up, her eyes felt stuck together and the left cheek felt crusted with saliva. With all her willpower, she stood and went to the kitchen. Living on a boat sounded more exciting than it actually was. For instance, cooking. The plates would sway to the side, butter didn't melt in the right places, and silverware never stayed organized in the drawers. She opened the cabinet to find an empty bottle of maple syrup. Great. What would Zharkova say to this predicament? *Stupid Girl, walk six miles to the maple trees and extract some!*

"We're out of maple syrup," Royal said to the wretched woman's closed door.

"Come here! Now!"

Another deep breath prepared her. She cleaned Zharkova's room daily and made sure to get rid of anything sharp that could be flung at Royal. But what's the worse the weakened world leader could do? She walked to bedroom door and knocked slightly. The usual locked door swung open when the boat swayed. Lying in her bed, Zharkova barely moved to fling something at Royal. *Weak* wasn't a strong enough description of the prime minister. Frail, fragile, fatigued. Darker circles than Royal's hung underneath the eyeballs. Pale as a Precious Moments doll, Zharkova barely looked human anymore. Death drew a blanket to keep her warm. Even Royal's mother didn't lose that amount of weight on the chemotherapy; Zharkova looked like a Halloween house prop.

The IV cord was wrapped in her hand. She rolled it gently between her fingers. Whatever it meant, Royal's mother used to do the same thing. Zharkova whispered, "I've tried and tried. I just can't do it."

Royal walked slowly as though it would prolong what little lifetime Zharkova had. "What do you mean, ma'am?"

Without answering, the ill woman looked up with dried lips. "Take a seat."

From the corner of the room, Royal grabbed a stool and sat. The boat's rocking seemed to slow.

"Closer. I want you to smell the death on my breath."

Royal scooted up and sat inches from Zharkova's bed. The IV tube dripped its last drops. "Is there something I can –"

"So courteous. Even to a woman like me." She stared at the IV drip until the last drop fell. "Take this tube. Unplug it. Then from that end…blow as hard as you can."

It took Royal a full minute to understand what was being asked. Blowing air into an IV tube? Why? Then she remembered an episode of Chicago Hope. A large air bubble in the tube would stop the blood flow to the heart. Zharkova may have asked too much, but this even seemed out of her league. "I can do no such thing, ma'am."

"After all I've done to you? Please. You wake up every day looking aggravated. Why? Because you want to murder me and throw my body into the ocean. Why so scared of killing? You've already killed an innocent animal and my faithful assistant. Accident or no accident, you caused their demises. And they didn't deserve it. I do."

With a shaky hand, Royal shook her head even faster. "No."

Zharkova scoffed then laughed. She took a deep breath and sighed. "Fine. It seems there's too much light in you. We'll have to fix that now, won't we? Close your eyes."

"Why?"

"Because I want you to enter darkness." Zharkova hissed. "Now, close them."

Whatever that meant, Royal felt hesitant. But arguments with the Russian Prime Minister could never be won. Royal shut her eyes slowly.

"Listen to my voice, Aurora. I have made you wax my floors all night, because I like seeing your knees red and scabbed. You've spent hours cleaning quarters I don't even use. I cackled inside when you wiped the shit off my bed pan; I missed on purpose."

Royal could smell the feces. Her breaths began to slow.

Zharkova continued, "I've made you kill animals to eat when there's plenty of meats stored in a freezer below. You've got bruises still from where I watched you get beaten to a pulp. I enjoyed every minute. Because you are the stereotypical arrogant American. I watched planes hit the World Trade Center and giggled. I watched nuclear missiles ignite your landmarks and I laughed. Because you all deserve death."

Her fist tight, Royal pictured an amused Zharkova munching on popcorn as the best country in the world got obliterated on television.

"In my eighteen years of leadership, I've worked with intelligence agencies to gather Muslims and have them gassed in chambers. Just because I don't like them. I don't trust them. We would cover up the rumors about what we were doing. Muslims missing? That's strange! Russia knows nothing about it. While secretly, they were gathered underground naked and cuffed to each other. Women. Men. Children. No matter. I had my vengeance on the radicals and their suicide bombings. Right before we gassed them, we would tell them that they'd be free in just a few hours. I like to give hope and crush it. Do you know the sound a child makes when its throat swells up? Do you know the sound a child makes when it throat swells up after hours of hope? It so much sweeter."

Royal ground her teeth so hard, her jaw began to throb in pain.

"Now, open your eyes and stare into mine." Zharkova whispered.

When Royal opened them, she felt different. She didn't know the saying "*so angry you saw red*" was literal. Everything she saw seemed a tone of red. She felt like swimming in a humid, sticky steam room. And so confident. Like the world belonged to her and no one else. As the ruler of this world, Royal could decided who lived and who died. She decided the fate of the female monster dying in this bed. Why not slay this dragon? Make her world a better place? Isn't that what life is? The stronger crushing the weaker?

Zharkova smiled. "There it is. Finally. No longer the damsel Aurora, but the powerful sorceress Maleficent. Keep staring into my eyes. I can see the difference. The dark quicksand has swallowed you whole. You are…at this moment…Secretary Charles Declan's daughter. Capable of anything necessary. Now, grab that IV tube."

Slowly, Royal took the IV tube.

"Unplug it."

She unsnapped the tube.

Zharkova's bottom lip trembled. But it didn't change her fate. "Now, Maleficent. Blow into it. Blow as hard as you can."

Royal took a deep breath, then put the tube up to her lips. Without a second thought, she blew into it. A large air bubble travelled down the tube like a train about to roll over a tied-up damsel in distress. Zharkova smiled. "Very good. One last thing." The air bubble was inches from the prime minister's vein. "Don't be like me. Learn to climb out of that dark quicksand."

The air bubble reached Zharkova's vein and Royal continued to blow into the tube. Her eyes locked onto the witch's gaze.

Then Zharkova's lurched and screamed in pain. Royal kept blowing. Spasms overtook her body, sending the world leader's body into convulsions on each side of the bed. Zharkova's teeth were clenched as she groaned through them. Royal stopped blowing so she could watch. Watch Death remove the blanket and carry away its new recruit.

The convulsions stopped as sudden as they had started. Zharkova's eyes were wide and glazed like a donut. Her lungs gave out a long sturdy breath, but never rose back up for another breath.

Royal stood up slowly. The world around her still seemed like a daze. With her back straight, she walked to her room on the other side of the boat. The pillow on the bed looked so comfy. Royal laid down.

Then she fell asleep instantly.

CHAPTER THIRTY-SEVEN

Was this what world leaders felt at all times? Fear of being assassinated? Fear of deceit? Fear of loneliness? But Marcel Celest shouldn't be afraid of anything. Especially humans. Humanity lied beneath him in a grave; Marcel decided the tombstone and the flowers because he was a step above this so-called existence. But yet, it all felt like swimming with cement shoes on. He swallowed another shot of the imported Scottish whiskey. Years ago, alcohol used to burn as it dripped down the back of his throat. Now, it seemed to soothe a burn.

A knock on his office door made him spin his chair. Unfortunately, when the chair stopped spinning his head didn't. Being a drunk could be difficult at times. Marcel waited a moment for the spinning sensation to stop before he answered the door. "Come in."

The double doors to his office swung open with a strong thud. Centuries ago when those castle doors would open, a king's council would enter with silk robes and steel armor to discuss finances across the kingdoms. Today, a puny man with a brown suit entered with thick horn-rimmed glasses and a mustache that made him look much older. As if the Financial Czar's last name Goldman didn't stereotype himself enough, the long-term accountant wore a Yam-aka and tightened his tie maybe too tight. He sat at the end of the table. Without even a polite greeting, the Financial Czar opened his briefcase and got down to business.

"We have a lot to talk about. So let's get down to business. The Union dollar." Goldman said nothing for a moment, maybe expecting a reaction out of Marcel. "We've spoken over and over again about this. Yet, I don't think you understand it."

"Have you ever heard the verse: *Money is the root of all evil*? Maybe it is. How significant is it really?" Marcel poured himself another glass of whiskey. "For instance, did cavemen use credit cards? Did the neanderthals apply for business loans? When did it become so…important?"

The Financial Czar didn't answer and just stared at Marcel. "How much have you had to drink…You know what, not my business. I'm here because you hired me to implement a worldwide currency –"

"Want something to drink? I hate drinking alone. Makes me feel like an alcoholic. It doesn't have to be whiskey. How about just some coffee? You must be sleepy from the trip here, right?"

Goldman nodded. "Sure, I'll have some coffee."

"Let me guess, no cream or sugar right?"

Goldman nodded again. "Just black. Thanks."

Marcel stood and went to a temporary kitchen in the side of the room. One small refrigerator, coffee maker, and a hot stove was all he needed. He poured a glass of the searing liquid into a cup and placed it gently in front of Goldman.

"This currency is becoming a problem, Marcel –"

"*Supreme Leader.*"

"Sorry, Supreme Leader. I applaud the idea of forbidding income tax, but to counter-balance that...sales taxes have increased upwards of 30%. And that's still putting us into deeper debt. We are going to have to begin an income tax –"

"Absolutely not."

"Then how do we shrink the world's debt numbers? The money has to come from somewhere."

When Marcel first established the idea of worldwide union, he promised himself to focus on simplicity. And adding more taxes just didn't fall under the category of simplicity. He thought about this for a moment, enjoying this wavy rollercoaster in his drunken head.

"Sir?"

"Alright, Czar Goldman, I have the solution. Use the stock market."

"The...stock market?" the accountant said inquisitively. "I don't understand."

"Well, the New York Stock Exchange was nuked on Doomsday. The NASDAQ went broke. China's market fell apart. Why not just simply get rid of the stock markets?"

After staring for maybe too long, Goldman said, "How much have you had to drink, Sir?"

Marcel raised a finger up. "That's the plan. We pull the funds from stock markets, trade at –"

"Have you lost your mind? You are talking about pulling from retirement funds, stocks, businesses and essentially peoples' futures? No, that's insane."

"*The Peoples' future is with the Union*," Marcel drew out the words on an imaginary marquee in front of him. "That's what we will advertise it as. There's trillions in the stock market."

Taking one deep breath, Goldman asked calmly, "Supreme Leader, can I ask you one question? Are you crazy?"

Marcel leaned back in his chair and thought about this for a second. It was a simple question and deserved a simple answer. "No. But everyone else is. Now, Czar Goldman, can I ask you one question?" The financial advisor didn't answer. Marcel sat up and put his elbows on the table. The steam from Goldman's coffee grew magically, only a few inches but enough for the czar to notice. He froze, his mind screaming to run but his body unable to move. "There's been rumors I'm capable of magic. I can not only influence the elements around you, but influence your mind also. Place your hand on the table." Goldman's glasses slid to the bottom of his nose as sweat formed. "I said, place your hand on the table." The steam wave grew more and circled around the accountant in his chair. Goldman slowly placed his hand down on the table. The steam wave rose high than fell onto the accountant's hand steadily. It may have not have been hurtful at first, but the increasing heat as more steam fell made Goldman flinch. "My question to you is this…Why is no one afraid of me?"

"Please, Marcel –"

"*Supreme Leader*. It's disrespectful to use my first name."

Stuttering, Goldman pled, "Supreme Leader, I was out of line. Please. This hurts." The steam from the coffee made the accountant's hand turn red and begin to blister.

"*That* hurts? Wounds like that can heal. Try taking on some mental wounds. Now, answer my question. Why is no one afraid of me?"

"I don't know."

"You do know the answer. I can feel it. Just answer me. Seems only fair since I answered your question honestly."

The accountant stared at his hand. His glasses slid off his face as sweat dripped off his nose onto his pants. "It's because you're too soft."

Marcel raised his hands triumphantly. The steam flew away into the air. Goldman clenched his shaky hand. "Finally! An honest answer around here. Yes, Czar Goldman, I've been worried about that too. I've...been...too...soft. The day after nuclear missiles destroyed my once-happy country, I told myself that I would need to use fear. Perhaps I do." Their eyes met for almost a minute before Marcel said, "Is our meeting done now?"

"Yes, Supreme Leader," Goldman spat out; his bottom lip quivering. "I'll work on deconstructing the stock markets right away."

Marcel smiled and took a sip of his whiskey.

CHAPTER THIRTY-EIGHT

Waking up from going abruptly unconscious isn't like waking up from a terrible night of booze. Janice couldn't remember who she was or the words being repeated to her.

"Janice?"

"Janice? You okay?"

"Janice?"

The bitter cold struck her first, so she pulled up the wool blanket that gave little warmth. Who's Janice? Oh, right. The adopted child of the famous political family that covered Time magazine; the orphan who strived to be the best and bottled up the worse. A perfect life with a perfect husband and perfect father that somehow imagined herself imperfectly.

"Janice?" The male voice said.

Just then she realized not only was her memory hazy but so was her vision. Blinking several times, she tried to make sense of the world. It wasn't the orphanage with that one teenage boy who kept sneaking into her bed to touch her breasts. No. She was an adult now. Though this place did have that familiar stench of sweat and unbrushed teeth.

"Janice? Baby?"

Baby? The baby. She sat up. Her infant. "Where's Colin?" She demanded.

"He's fine." The man said, grasping her hand. Steel surrounded his finger. A ring. *Their* ring. She helped him pick it out. Her husband came into view. He looked worried. He never looked worried. "Honey? You took a nasty fall. Don't stand up or move, okay?"

No muscle in her body would've allowed it anyways. Everything hurt. She remembered the fall, but not the actual fall, just the moment beforehand. The moment she felt truly content. And, once again, her troubles put a stop to it. "What happened? How long have I been out?"

Faces began to take shape. Adam shared that same timid look like they just broke the family vase and mother was on the way home. Someone else was in the room. The doctor, the only one with survival training in this facility, stood over her. Both men looked to the physician for words to say. "Hello, sweetheart. I'm the facility doctor. You fainted and have been suffering sporadic comatose states for eight days due to an infection that spread to your central nervous system and spinal cord. I just need to verify you haven't suffered long term memory loss. Can you tell me your full name and date of birth?"

A bad taste made her stomach uneasy. "Janice Nancy Celest. March 31st, 1998."

The doctor's raised eyebrows turned to Gerard. He nodded in confirmation.

"How about short term memory? Can you tell me where you are?"

"A missile silo rehoused for a rebellion called the People of Bliss."

"Good! Janice, do you remember me? Dr. Harper? I helped remove your clip so that you could bear your child."

"I remember," she said. In fact, Janice did remember everything now up to this point. Though she wished she could remove the egregious ones like sleeping with other men, chugging vodka like Gatorade, and swallowing illegal pills like candy. Whatever kept the room so mum went beyond just her simple tumble. Something serious was about to be uttered from the doctor's mouth, it could be the only explanation for the distressed faces. "It's okay. I know what you are going to say. I've been sensing it for weeks."

Dr. Harper looked on the verge of tears. It must've been difficult being a surgeon, knowing that a patient couldn't survive; no matter the skill training. He scratched his head, even though he had less than a dozen gray hairs to scratch. "I've removed several female pregnancy clips, but without the proper equipment –"

"You did your best," she assured him.

"The infection," Adam spoke up with a quivering lip, "has gotten so far out of control. We just don't have the medications here."

Seeing all these watery eyes, Janice suddenly realized how loved she actually was. Adam and Gerard hovered over her, both with those same sullen eyes. That even with the news of her approaching death, they seemed more stressed than her. "How long do you think I have?"

That sort of question to a doctor always got an exaggerated response, because any medical professional knew it better to tell a patient too little a timeframe than too long. Too little meant the patient got this invisible will to live longer and often strived to fulfill it. "Days. Weeks maybe."

Strangely, Janice hoped to hear she only had hours to live, then there would be an eventual relief to this incredible pain. She tried to sit up, ignoring her husband's visual pleas not to. Head against the cold concrete wall, Janice could almost feel where the infection in her uterus planned to end her time on Earth. It pulsed between severely hot to moderately hot.

Now propped up, she could ask for something to drink or perhaps some food. But she could only think of one request. "Can I see my baby, please?"

Matley, the medicine woman, with long dreads and even longer neck beads, walked in carrying the sleeping infant. Janice remained strong instead of letting the tears form in her eyes. She grasped her child, pleased that he was always so obedient and quiet; it didn't hurt that he slept so much. Active minds needed rest. She wished she didn't have to let him go, but her shaky arms could barely hold the weight. Matley could see the distress. "Let me hold him, child. You need the rest. We gonna get you the medicine. Get you better."

Cherophobia is a medical condition where the patient literally feared happiness. Janice read about it after Victoria died and she became motherless, wondering if she suffered from this rare phobia. She lacked the will to see things on the bright side, even though love surrounded her daily. Hearing the positivity gave Janice no further hope, because she none to begin with. For months, knowing something was wrong with her, she allowed the sickness to worsen.

"Someone else is here," Adam smiled. Nelson entrance. Holding tightly, she could feel her adopted father sinking into her. All this was too much, staying strong became a struggle. Janice's eyes watered. Nelson never cried, spouting that Presidents never cried. Sniffling, he turned his face and put his cheek on her shoulder. "I can't lose all my children."

He sat up and she used her thumb to wipe a tear traveling towards his beard. "You of all people should know, family isn't just blood. Isn't that what Mom used to say?"

Nelson nodded.

Janice confirmed, "Everyone here is family. That's what so great about this place. It's all love and respect for each other."

They shared grasped hands and a moment of silence, before Adam whispered, "Not all your children are dead yet. Marcel Celest isn't –"

"That's not my son," Nelson abruptly interrupted. "I saw him. Aboard the naval ship. He's…changed."

"He's the only obstacle we haven't solved yet," Adam reminded them. "He certainly can't be killed. It's his fate. He'll always survive."

"So then," Janice added, "the question is: how do you stop him?"

Gerard intervened, "I've already said that I will take care of him."

She lifted her body up while Nelson put a pillow behind her back so she could lean against the bed frame comfortably. "So Marcel can control minds, conjur weather, heal quickly, and slow time. And what's the plan? Kill him?"

Adam sat on a stool, cleaning his fingernails nervously. "But…in my vision of the future, Marcel specifically said he would have to die in order to weaken the darkness."

"Wait a minute," Gerard shook his head trying to make sense of it. "You can see the future?"

"It's very complicated," Janice said, still trying to wrap her head around the fact that Adam was technically seeing visions transmitted from a future form of himself.

"It was the whole basis behind Servo Clementia." Nelson explained. "Secretary Declan helped build a terrorist-style network to target and kill people that would bring about Armageddon."

Gerard rubbed the spot between his eyebrows, "Okay, so you saw Marcel alive in the future, so that means he doesn't die?"

Adam clarified, "I found out the future can be changed. He said we have to stop him from absorbing all the darkness, free it, then kill the darkness with light."

"What on earth are you talking about? None of this makes a lick of sense. We kill darkness with what…a flashlight? And what does that even mean? I'm telling you guys, I've been there. I've seen what Marcel can do. He *can't* be killed. He *can't* be stopped. Marcel decides his own fate…not any of you." Gerard slumped down in a chair, holding Janice's hand. "Whatever connection he has with this other side, he kept mentioning Brent. He said Brent haunted him all the time. And I don't think it's the drinking. I think he really sees him. He even mentioned he saw your mother."

Janice's eyebrows raised. Even Nelson stood. "He saw them? Like ghosts?"

Gerard didn't answer, perhaps he couldn't find an answer. Adam took a breath and asked, "What happened to her? It was kept out of the papers. Just said a car accident. Nothing more."

Giving a massively bitter look quickly, Gerard said, "Seriously? You've got some nerve."

Nelson added, "We don't talk about it."

Feeling cornered, Adam crossed his arms after placing the hood of his sweater over his head. It reminded Janice of how he showed up to her class, practically every week, in a hoodie. He was shy then, fearful he would say something stupid. Students like this often had a point, maybe things that shouldn't be discussed…should. Coming to his defense, Janice said, "Maybe we should. Some memories need to be relived. Even the awful ones. Adam, I'm going to tell about the night Victoria Celest, the nation's First Lady, died December 24th, 2039."

I've relived this moment so many times in my head. Not because I had to, because I wanted to. Because not only did she die that day...we all did. Christmas Eve, 2038. I remember specifically realizing that after seven years as First Daughter, I never fit the title. We were at a gala. Dozens of men eying my dress more my face and dozens of women prettier than me. Confidence extinguished any form of awkwardness in a room of unfamiliar politicians. As I sipped on a glass of champagne, Marcel spoke to a group of tycoons, bankers, and congressman. They always looked alike. As much as women strived to attempt different styles and gowns, men just stuck with the traditional tuxedo and bow tie. That night, Marcel's idea of the Union proposal started floating around. He created quite a following as campaign manager for my father. Before he could create hypnosis with his mind, he did it with his charm. People loved him. Handsome, smart, and wealthy. While others suggested a run for President, Marcel insisted on something larger.

On the other side of the room, instead of speaking to exquisite men, my brother Brent spoke to exquisite women. He always seemed determined with some type of purpose when he had no purpose; Marcel had a bright future with the U.N. and I was a professor for Baltimore University. But Brent had no degree, no goals, and no concept of his future. That always fascinated me. Knowing what I do know, it was all an act. Brent, at the time, was an assassin for the terrorist organization Servo Clementia. For all I know, he could've been researching a target that night, with his commander Secretary Declan in the same room.

I took another sip of champagne, remembering that I didn't enjoy the taste of alcohol or enjoy the loss of control. Before I could take another forced swig of the bitter drink, a delicate hand placed hers on mine. My mother, stunning as always with a floor length white dress and silk top decorated with floral designs, said, "Getting drunk on champagne gives you the worst headache. Here try some white wine." The First Lady Victoria Celest said in her slightly hoarse voice that sounded strong and calm simultaneously, handing me a glass of sparkling white wine and it tasted sweet. "It helps me get through the night," she whispered, bumping me on the hip. "You see Senator Kelly over there? Bad breath, which makes no sense that a six-figure-a-year senator can't afford a decent dentist. Senator Madison? Well, he's obliviously to the fact the comb-over look died sixty years ago. Right there is business tycoon, Mrs. Swanson with over a billion dollar net worth and stinks so bad it's like she uses bug spray for perfume. And over there...Secretary Declan has packed on thirty pounds in the last couple months and finished all the hors d'oeuvres we had tonight. But none of that bothers me, you know what bothers me?"

I shrugged, realizing that my shoulder strap had been dangling on my purple gown making me look sleazy. My mother quickly fixed it. "What bothers me, sweetie...is that the most gorgeous individual in this room, with good breath, a nice set of hair, smells nice, and isn't hogging all the food...is just sitting in this corner talking to no one."

With my cheeks blushing, she spun me around to look at my dress. "My God. Lilac is your color." She wrapped her arm around mine and lead me towards the ballroom. "Keep me company. These people scare me. I'm afraid, at any moment, they'll rip their masks off to show their androids. Seriously, it would make sense. They lack character. They do and say only what their voters tell them too. When I had children, I decided to let you embrace your differences. And I was going to love you, no matter what."

I felt a lot less intimidated with her there. She introduced me to several men and women, always calling me her "daughter" even though we both knew I was adopted. Everyone in that room knew I was adopted. But I was a Celest, just as much as her.

Marcel's posse of ass-kissers eyed me up and down with either contempt or attraction. They carried on about his wonderful idea of a unified government. One of the politicians, dead now, specifically said it was time for simplicity in this world. I remember Marcel touching my arm, like I was his date to this party. His soft hands stroked my bare arm. It felt good. "Where's your husband?" He had asked. I never answered, because I had none besides the typical Gerard is busy excuse.

The night livened up, I met several people thanks to the confidence of my mother. I watched her with curiosity, like they way you can watch a freeway and wonder how there can be so much calm in such chaos. Mom out-shined Marcel's charisma at every corner. People acted different around her, more genuine smiles and shy handshakes.

Joining our group, arm around Brent, was our father. No, he wasn't drunk. Drunk in happiness perhaps. He joked. He laughed. He was the most important man in the room. We were the most important family in the room, planets orbiting our star for life and direction...our mother.

The time was 10:32 pm. I know the exact time, because this is the time the truck driver passed the weigh station at mile marker 22. It's barely visible from I-495. Trucks pass it everyday.

"What's next?" Brent said excitedly.

"National Cathedral," Marcel answered, always in charge of the family schedule, "Christmas Carolers are going to love a visit from the First family."

Victoria clasped her hands. "Oh, the little angels are so cute."

I always enjoyed these little meetings before leaving. Placing coats on and Secret Service briefing Dad about new routing procedures. It felt like a huddle right before the first ball is kicked in a football game.

Marcel continued his conversation with Dad, "We have several supporters on this idea. I'm telling you, a unified government could work." Noticing his father's skeptical smirk, he turned to my mother. "Don't you think so, Mom?"

Putting on her fake fur coat, she refused to wear anything with real animal, my mother answered, "I think simplicity leads to peace and complication leads to chaos. If there's anything I want more in this world, is that feeling I share with my family. No hate, only love." She said pinching Marcel's cheek.

My father said, "It's Christmas Eve. Let's just concentrate on what's it's about. This is the day we celebrate our savior Jesus Christ. He was born this day. We have a lot to be thankful for. No politics or unified government talk. It's all about God's son tonight."

With that, they said goodbyes to several people. I shook hands and received hugs from people I'd just met, but I could never get sick of it. It took me years to accept being First Daughter and took even longer to embrace it.

Dad grasped my mother's hand, looking at her through relaxed eyes. "Brent, when you going to find the right woman?" He asked my brother, without losing his gaze on my mom.

Brent snorted, "No way. I'm perfectly happy being single."

"But," my father said, eyes drawn to Mom, "you don't know what this is like. Looking into the eyes of the one you love and feeling complete."

My mother rested her head on my father's chest and he closed his eyes to hold her. All those years together, and they just couldn't get sick of each other. I remembered being so jealous, because my bond with Gerard, our marriage, didn't seem so omnipotent.

As we made our way outside, waving to the crowds past the barriers, that truck unknowingly carrying too much weight exited the freeway, taking the wrong intersection.

"I think we should change seating," Marcel said. He probably lives with that regret everyday, because those words altered the future. "Instead of us riding together, how about you two take the second limo?"

Sarcastically, Mom answered, "Good idea. Let the men talk about their boring sports or whatever." After quick kisses on both Brent and Marcel's faces, she grabbed my arm and waved. The crowd cheered and Secret Service yanked us away before Mom and Dad could have an embrace. They never got the chance to say goodbye. I didn't realize that until now.

Before we got in our vehicles, I heard Marcel instruct the drivers to take an alternate route to avoid traffic jams. None of us objected considering we were running behind schedule. I wish one of us had.

The semi-truck, carrying over 40 thousand pounds of sand, pulled aside realizing his GPS was taking him the wrong way, according to his later account.

We were off in minutes. After all the waves, my wrist felt numb. I sunk into the cool leather seats, removing my gloves as the vehicle began to finally warm. "How do you do it?"

Already understanding what I meant, my mother answered, "Because they look up to us. To these people, we are the future. We can make the changes they so desperately need. I'll smile, wave, give them confidence all day if that's what it takes. It's a little price to pay."

"And...how do you do it...with Dad?" I asked, twirling my hair and staring out the passenger side of my window.

"Oh," Mom smiled, "You can't get him off your mind, can you?"

"Is that a bad thing?" I responded.

About that time, 11:18 pm, the truck driver returned to the road and began the ascent onto a fourteen percent grade hill, vastly steeper than recommended for a vehicle that size.

"Well," Mom answered, "to be honest, sweetheart, it's a great thing. Means he's really the one for you."

Sometimes I caught myself speaking to her like a best friend instead of a mother. "But how do I know if he's the one for me? Especially when I can't keep my eyes on him."

"Hell, there's nothing wrong with looking at the dessert menu, as long as you keep ordering from the same entree." She paused to pat my hand. "Have you ever jogged around Lake Montebello?"

"No," I replied.

"Well," she said, "it's about six and half miles around. Quite beautiful and the landscape is spectacular. But, Lord knows, I'm in no shape to be running that. I told our personal trainer to start me off easy, that trail was too long. I'll never forget what he said to me. 'It gets easier'. Well, I told myself, let me just try just a brisk walk. The first day, my brisk walk ended half way. Oh, I felt so light-headed from the summer heat and exhausted. I told myself, never again. Then one morning, I told myself 'it gets easier'. I put on my pink running shoes and jogging clothes. And again, halfway through, I gave up. All those years of smoking and battling lung cancer finally ruined me forever. But no, the next morning I reminded myself that 'it gets easier'. Fourteen tries later, I could briskly walk that lake and enjoy the nice breeze every morning. Now…I can jog it. You know why? Because I forgot all the pain, anguish, and fear that trail put me through. It's true…it gets easier."

About this time, the tractor trailer began its descent down the steep hill. With all that weight, the brakes began to overheat only a quarter of the way down the two mile hill. Smoke bellowed out the back end, the driver recalled slamming his brakes several times but the truck didn't stop. That was about the time we made our final turn towards the freeway.

I remember the last advise Mom gave me. "Don't over complicate life, stick with what you're familiar with and get damn good at it."

Secret Service noticed the vehicle barreling down the hill and immediately took it as a threat, halting our limos and firing at the incoming truck. The driver, unintentionally becoming a death trap, ducked the bullets and lost control of the tractor trailer.

From the passenger seat, all I remember were the lights. The lights so bright, that they seemed like some aura glowing around my mother.

The truck smashed into us, flipping us three times before crashing into a set of trees on the side of the road. After a crash, you don't get up right away. It's because you are so confused. I didn't understand what was going on. Blood dripped off the side of my head, and being so disoriented I thought it was ketchup. I was thinking, did I eat something and drop ketchup on my head? Vision being so blurred, I stared at my right hand wondering why I felt a stabbing sensation. A glass shard had penetrated clean through it.

My hearing was muffled. I kept listening to a word being repeated except I didn't know what I meant. It sounded like "jump on". Jump on? Jump on what? Once the sound came closer, did I realize that word was "Janice". That was me? Or was that...

Mom.

I looked over to my right, but could see nothing but crunched metal. That word again, more frantic this time. "Janice!" It was Marcel.

Reaching out my arm, I realized I couldn't. I'd been cocooned this massive steel and leather fist. Above me, light poured in. I looked up to see the street light. Just then, I figured out we had been in a crash. "Janice!" Marcel said, his arm reaching through the hole that once been the back window. At first, he grabbed me by the hair and yanked. I screamed, not only did it hurt my scalp but sent streaks of pain down my body as metal scraped me. "Climb out! You can do it!"

It hurt so bad, every movement I made just dug something deeper into me. But I had to get out. I had to rescue Mom. I had to live on. It gets easier.

I climbed out, blood covering my lilac dress and heels. None of it mattered; the ruined dress, the months of physical therapy I'd need for my damaged sciatic nerve, or even the massive amounts of scrapes and blood loss. None mattered more than my mother. Stumbling on my heels, trying to circle the crushed vehicle that resembled a smushed soda can, I didn't even had a moment to marvel at what I had just survived. On the other side, next to the truck mushed into the driver side of the limo, was my father holding something.

Covered in massive amounts of blood, my mother didn't even look the same. It looked like Dad was holding a mannequin. Mom was already stiffening. This wasn't like the movies, where you get a final goodbye. No need to check a pulse or repeat her name.

She was dead. I covered my mouth, wanting to bellow something. Some word. Some cry. But I held it in with my hands cupped over my mouth.

Secret Service tried to grab Dad, but Brent pushed them away. "Leave him alone! Leave us alone! Leave!" He screamed over Secret Servicemen's pleads to get them to safety. Without hesitation, he punched two of them and fought one other. Tears flowing down his face, I'd never seen Brent that enraged. He looked at me. It took me a moment to realize, it wasn't me he stared down with scrunched eyebrows and ground teeth. Brent was staring at Marcel next to me. "You did this," he growled.

Hands shaking over my mouth still, I looked to my right and saw Marcel no longer able to stand and slid down the side of the wreckage. "I did this," he whispered.

Dad kept repeating the same question, rocking the body of my mother. "Why God? Why?"

I couldn't take it anymore. I ran. Ran towards the woods. Ran as fast as I could. No. No. This wasn't happening. No. It was a nightmare. Mom wasn't dead. No. No. No. I kept running, keeping that word locked into my mouth until I was far away. Far away, hiding in a corner where no one could see me. No one could hear me. Weak. I felt so weak.

I let go of the cupped hands around my mouth and cried out at the top of my lungs. "Mom!"

Nelson handed Janice a tissue, needing one badly for himself too. Both their faces wet and sore from the sorrow of a family's death. And the sorrow of a family that shattered the day a car window shattered. Janice buried her face in Nelson's chest and they held each other, praying their faith would heal the wounds. But it wouldn't. Everything Janice did, nothing erased that day. Not only was Marcel just a shadow of his former self, so were they.

She wanted to continue the story but couldn't. Explain how the nation reacted. How the media reacted. How all the outpouring of love didn't seal that wound.

"You all should've died." Adam whispered.

Wiping his forehead, Gerard scowled, "Jesus, you never have the right thing to say."

"I'm just recalling what Marcel Celest said, in the future." Adam clarified, "He said in my vision they should've died that day. It changed everything."

Janice sat up, "What do you mean?"

Delicately, he answered, "Your brother, I mean the future version of your brother, said he changed fate. That he had the power to do that."

Whipping her runny nose, Janice said, "It's called Fatalism. It states we all have a predetermined destiny."

"Yes," Adam nodded, "except him. Well, that's what he said anyways. So, he basically changed what was supposed to happen that night. You were all supposed to die in that be limo together."

Gerard sucked his teeth and crossed his arms, but Janice wasn't so skeptical. It didn't seem so far-fetched that everyone's purpose could have an interruption. Theories about fates always concluded that knowing choice was a facade meant a chaotic order to humanity. While some might be okay with releasing the wheel of their ship and letting an outside force decide where the wind blows…others might not be okay with this. So the subject remained controversial to investigate further.

But what if?

Thoughts swung around in Janice's head. She asked, "He said that? That fate is real?" Her eyes darted around faster than the neurons in her mind. It all suddenly made sense. She stared at Nelson, like she could telepathically communicate with him. Her father gazed into the distance, contemplating what he'd heard too.

Janice whispered, "We should have died that day. Or else none of this would've happened." She then turned to Gerard with timid eyes, "I know how to stop Marcel."

CHAPTER THIRTY-NINE

Royal had nightmares of this place. The endless subway tunnel with white and maroon walls. Paintings of Russian leaders stared back at her. Surely, they had gone through much worse circumstances than her brutal days in Russia. In order to survive, they learned what Royal had learned: fear was a weapon and not a state of mind. Nightmares were for the weak.

The air began to suck away as a subway car approached. Perfect timing. Sitting patiently on the bench, Royal reached down and turned her rings so that the pointy ends stuck out. Then she cracked her knuckles.

When Zharkova had brought her here, it was a test. Today would be the final exam. Royal had studied and intended to pass. When the subway car pulled up, she briefly remember her nightmare being much worse. The Russian tough girls had been red-eyed demons with sharp teeth and even sharper claws. This time, when the doors opened, the succubus monsters weren't so terrifying. That one with the pink mohawk smacked her gum like it was all the food she had that day. Probably was.

Royal didn't hesitate. She threw a hard punch into the mohawk's chunky nose. Blood spurted out. Another girl appeared, that one with long ugly fingernails. Like all rough 'n tough women, she grabbed for the hair. Royal anticipated that and clasped her hand. She ripped out one of those fake fingernails, then stabbed it into the bitch's knee. She screamed. Another jumped on top of her. Whoever it was, didn't matter, Royal just bit as hard as she could onto the ear lobe. The girl screamed. Now, it was time for Royal to throw some uppercuts. She locked her arms around one of the girls and kicked another one away. Even for a horny teenage boy, this scene wouldn't have been very alluring. Blood covered most of them. Royal continued to punch one of them until she was pretty sure the jaw bone broke. Getting up, she intertwined her finger through the matted hair of the gold-toothed skank and smashed her knee into the girl's face until the tooth broke. The fourth girl tried to jump on her, but missed. Royal shoved her into the subway car metal pole. A loud thunk ended the fight.

Royal stood over four girls that couldn't stand. She took several short breaths before her breathing returned to normal. It sounded like relaxing music hearing the painful groan from girls who had beaten her to pulp almost a month ago. In each of her nightmares since that awful day, Royal woke up in sweat. Yet she hadn't even broken a sweat this moment. Being feared had its own sense of satisfaction. One of the girls tried to grab her foot, but Royal kicked her in the head.

Calmly, she removed a subway map from her back pocket and sat in a seat to read it. The pink mohawk girl leaned up against a pole and began to use her shirt to wipe the bloody nose. Royal looked at her, then pointed to her map. "Ugolnaya gavan'," she said butchering the Russian language.

The mohawk girl frowned. She seemed disappointed that she lost the brawl, but respectful. "Da."

From her other back pocket, Royal pulled out a notepad. Listening to Russian music helped to learn the language; she learned that from a friend. Looking at her notepad, Royal said, "Take me there. Voz'mi menya tuda!"

The girl with the gold teeth spat out a tooth and slumped into a seat. The other girls didn't attempt to continue the fight either. There's no point. The mohawk chick nodded and said, "Da."

"Now!" Royal barked.

Slowly, but quickly as she could muster, the girl stood and walked to the driver seat. Royal watched as the long fingernail chick yanked her nail out of her knee. The last girl pulled out a pair of brass knuckles from her pocket; they still had Royal's blood from the last brawl. She extended her hand and offered them to Royal. Without saying anything, Royal grabbed them and put them in her pocket. A peace offering didn't deserve a response because actions spoke louder than words.

It was time to go to the port and gather everyone up for an even bigger fight. As the subway car rolled away, Royal took one glance out the window. Those painting in the subway tunnel would forever be instilled in her mind. She imagined a painting of her someday. But first, she had to win the war.

I enjoy music but I enjoy the beat of
my children's hearts better.

-Victoria Celest
First Lady of the United States
2033-2038

CHAPTER FORTY

Drenched in sweat and shivering in the cold, Janice opened her crusty eyes to the sound of knocking. Three knocks, to be exact. Strong and deep, the noises almost sounded like knocks on a wooden door and not the steel one of her room. She heard this superstition before; it meant certain death. It meant a creature in long black clothing knocked three times before entering. Silly, yet she also thought the accusations of Marcel controlling minds and weather were silly too. She closed her eyes, hoping the Grim Reaper would scrap its sickle on the ground as it approached, hold the weapon inches from her throat, and swipe quickly. She closed her eyes and prayed. Prayed to a myth. Please end the pain, please end the suffering.

When she opened her swollen red eyes, the Grim Reaper wasn't there. A 28 year old man, who looked more like 22 with those baby cheeks even through the bushel of a beard, stared down at her. "Did you hear me?" He said, sounding desperate and hurried.

"No," she groaned, sounding a bit disappointed that the knock wasn't coming from the Grim Reaper.

"Your idea, Janice. You...can't. It's...no...no, I won't allow you to leave."

Instead of arguing, she nodded. Honestly, the thought of leaving the silo with such little energy seemed infeasible at this point, but when it was feasible...Adam wouldn't be the person to stop her. It was an abortive promise.

She sat up, because lying down made her more nauseous. Pulling up her shirt, stuck to her in sweat, she glanced at her abdomen for only a second. Turning black and yellow, like a large bruise, Janice couldn't stare at it any longer. On the other hand, Adam gawked at it. "Tomorrow night, we are going into town for medicine."

Another abortive promise. Janice knew walking into a pharmacy demanding prescription medications without prior authorization would be as fruitful as trying to grow lilacs without light. So again, she played off his attempt at reconciliation with a nod. "Let's talk about something else."

"Like what?" He said sitting down at the edge of her mattress.

"I don't know. How about telling me about Brent? You never told me how you knew each other."

Adam looked down at his arm, the tattoo was beginning to flake and he started picking at it; picking right where the name Brent Celest was on his forearm.

She objected, "You know you aren't supposed to peel it off. Just let it heal."

"But it itches."

Feeling like his mother, which she could practically could be, she reached for a basket of lotions next to her bed. "I have Aloe Vera. Nature's best cure. Give me your arm."

He reached over and rested his arm on her leg. She poured the thick clear goo into her hands and rubbed it gently over his scabby skin.

"Well, I knew Brent because of Mr. Declan. We met…ah, that feels so good…anyways, we met when I was about thirteen."

"I wasn't aware you had known each other so long."

"Yeah. Right. Long time, huh. He helped me with my science studies. Mr. Declan used to home school me. I used to think I was privileged until the truth came out that I was a being studied for my ability to foresee the future."

"Figures. Brent loved science and space subjects." She replied, wondering if heaven was in space somewhere and how happy her brother would be at this moment, if it was.

"He taught me everything I know and I taught him everything I knew. You know, deep down, Brent really did care. I mean…he *really* cared. So much, that it made him angry to disappoint anyone."

Janice nodded, accepting the truest description of her brother. She continued smoothing the aloe on his skin. "I can't believe you covered your skin in tattoos. Are you ever going to stop being so imprudent?"

He smirked. "No promises."

She returned the smirk and put away the lotion as he rolled down his sleeve. "Can I ask you something?" Adam asked. "Did you hate *him*?"

Obviously, referring to Gerard, Janice shook her head. "No. Disappointed. But never truly hated."

"I mean, not when you guys separated, I mean like…" Adam's eyes wandered off, whatever he was trying to ask…it was very diluted. "Did you hate him when you first met?"

Janice snickered, "Oh yes. Very. He tried to sweep me off my grounded feet. I couldn't *stand* Gerard. Three years in a row, he told everyone I was going with him to the Homecoming Dance, even though I firmly said no." She grinned, "Finally, in our Senior year, I said *fine*. Mom bought me this dress that hung so low on my cleavage and so high on my thigh. God, I felt so embarrassed and relieved at the same time in that dress. He showed up at our door step in a tuxedo two sizes too big, he said it was his step brother's suit. The *limo* was a black spray-painted Sudan from the late 90s. It died at four stop lights before we got to the dance." Janice leaned her head on the wall. "All these pretty girls at the dance, and he never looked away from me the entire night."

"How did you know? Like...how did you know he was the one?"

Suspecting this wasn't a conversation over jealous, but a genuine inquiry, Janice answered as best as she could. "When no one else matters, that's how you know."

Adam nodded. "I wonder if that's what love is about. Getting all that hate and bitterness out of the way at first, that leaves nothing but love. Right?"

Just a year ago, she remembered having an affair with Adam and thinking he was another horny college student. It had taken her this long to affirm he was much more than that. "I've spent so many years teaching and teaching. But never *learning*."

"Sorry. I don't understand."

"It's the complexity of life that has drove us all to understand every aspect. We can teach, but to *learn* is another path. I tried to teach how to create peace by avoiding the mistakes we've made in humanity. A spiral of repeated history has evolved us to what we are today. But teaching can only go so far. You have to learn on your own." Janice touched his cheek softly. "That's what was fascinating about you. You've taught yourself everything, but *learned* so very little."

He sniffled, doing a terrible job of hiding his tears. "Don't die on me."

"No promises," she whispered.

Hours past, reminiscing and chatting. Gerard had popped his head in every once a while, always the jealous type. She reassured him they were fine. Even though nothing constituted *fine* in this matter. Janice was going to die. She knew it. The only thing she didn't know was *when*. When would that knock on the door not be a visitor, but the last visitor...Death.

Adam had tried reading to her, helping her fall asleep as the clocks struck midnight. After several pages of the book, Janice looked up, "Are you reading me a comic book?"

"Ahem," he cleared his throat, "it's a *graphic novel*. And I have no other books."

She giggled, "You are such a geek."

A knock on the door startled them both. Maybe Adam was expecting a deadly visit too. Instead, Willie peaked his head through the door. "My turn."

Adam looked at his watch. Only now did Janice realize they were taking shifts, caring for her. Like this room was some sort of hospice. The jester made her feel more like a burden. "I'm gonna get some rest," Adam said, "I'll finish this tomorrow. I bet you can't wait to hear what happens to Supergirl when she confronts Eclipso."

"Can't wait," Janice said, kissing Adam on the cheek, knowing it would be the last time she saw him. He left the room, while Willie sat cross legged on the floor. After opening up a paper bag, he pulled out a cup of cheeses and a bottle of red wine.

"Okay, it wasn't easy, but I got you covered. Cabernet, your favorite." He whispered as though prying eyes watched him in this closed room.

Before she could ask did he bring glasses, he whipped out two small jars from inside his trench coat. "Oh and I got,"

Willie said, reaching in his coat pocket, "Something to help you sleep, like you wanted." In a clear plastic baggie, a white powder jingled around. Given they had no way of manufacturing pills, powders made from plants and mushrooms, had to mashed down. Except for the brownish color, it looked like cocaine. It reminded her of those drug-induced days, where she felt the sky wasn't the limit. After emptying out napkins and toothpicks from his coat, Janice was convinced he would've made a perfect partner to sneak snacks into a movie theater.

"Thanks," she whispered, grabbing the powder. "Could you check the door is locked?"

Without questioning it, Willie got up and locked the door. "It's weird, you know. Growing up in Philly, my grandma would've killed me for leaving the door unlocked. Ever since that one time someone walked in and stole the television while she was doped up on Ambien. But since I got here, I trust people, you know?" He listened at the door. "Coast is clear." He quickly sat down, Indian-style, on the mattress across from her. "So. You going to tell me?"

"Tell you what?" Janice said, sipping from her wine glass. "How drinking alcohol is probably the worst thing I could be doing to my body right now?"

"Naw, it's fine." Willie grasped his wine and drank a few gulps. "I'm talking about what your *plan* is. I keep hearing Adam and Gerard arguing about it. They just keep calling it *the plan*. Remember Harry Potter? It's like when the kept calling the bad guy...oh what did they call him?" He asked, snapping his fingers in the air.

"The-one-who-shall-not-be-named," Janice said.

"Yeah! That. It's sorta like they were afraid of saying it. So you gonna tell me? What gives? You got a plan to stop Marcel Celest?"

Janice sipped the rest of her wine and stared at the glass. "I'd rather talk about how bad this one is for my body right now."

"It won't kill yeah."

"You're right. *It* won't."

Willie shook his head. "I'm sorry. About the...you know. But Adam says we are going into town tomorrow, grabbing some meds. Then you'll be like 'Infection? What infection?'. Forget about it!"

"You talk a lot when you're nervous," she smirked. "Don't worry. I know you aren't here to keep me company or clean out my bedpan."

After emptying is glass of wine, he poured another for the both of them. "I feel bad, you know. But Adam told me I can't let you leave." He eyed his glass like it was magic and could show the past. "I let Sirius Dawson go. She wasn't supposed to leave either. We went to the lake. Keepers showed up. She told me to run. I did. Now she's dead."

Chewing slowly on some cheese, surprised that the food stayed down in her stomach, Janice said, "I have to stop Marcel. I need your help escaping."

As though he was prepared for her plea, Willie immediately shook his head no. "I can't. I can't."

"I know what needs to be done."

"If you leave, I'll never see you again. You'll die there. Just like Sirius. Just like Brent. The Union is cursed. Trust me."

Janice stood, feeling good to stretch her legs but feeling awful to stretch that infection growing in her abdomen. She opened up the drawer in the side of the room, searching through the limit clothing. Jeans or slacks. Blouse or t-shirt. Jacket or coat. "I do trust you, Willie. I trusted you would do the right thing. I trusted you to follow orders. I trusted you to not allow yourself to make the same mistake twice. The problem is…you shouldn't have trusted me."

She turned to see Willie leaning forward, eyes drooping. In his hand, the glass of wine tipped over and splashed to the ground. "Aw shit. You didn't?"

"I drugged your drink," she said, leaning Willie's weak body backwards and placing a pillow under his head. "Marcel has to be stopped. I had no choice." Her voice became high-pitched, holding back a tear. "I'm a horrible person."

Willie interjected, voice mellow and distant. "Naw. You're the best. Just like Sirius. So damn smart." He whispered, eyes closing. "I'm gonna miss the hell out of you, you know that?"

Janice kissed him on the cheek and combed his thinning hair with her hand, as he began to snore. "I'm going to miss you too."

It took her only a few minutes to get dressed, choosing something more incognito like Gerard's baseball cap, light slacks, and a simple t-shirt. She wiped more Aspercreme on the infection, which seemed good enough to numb the pain for a few hours. And she guzzled what was left in the wine bottle to numb the regret.

In Willie's front pocket was a key with a rabbit's foot keychain. It was her lucky day, the key belonged to the ATV vehicle outside.

After unlocking the door, Janice made her way into the quiet hallway and closed the door behind her. Even more risky than the decision she just made to leave was to visit Colin. She accepted the fact she may never say goodbyes to her father, Adam, or Gerard…but not saying farewell to her child felt inhumane. The only other crib in the facility was in the nursery downstairs; a nursery built with faith that more children could be born someday without the aide of the government population control department. Her miracle, so far, seemed to be the only one. And what a miracle he was.

Being the middle of the night, the amount of traffickers remained small. A teenage boy experimenting with a teenage girl in the shower room were too busy to notice Janice pass by the door. She climbed down the stairs sluggishly, because her legs weighed a hundred pounds and she strived to remain invisible in this place of thousands.

Painted with pink and blue flowers, it was obvious which door led to the nursery. She peeked in. Amongst six cribs, Colin slept in the center. He never moved when he slept. On a few occasions, Janice had been sure he had died. Children had all sorts of complications, before the Department of Proper Procreation *fixed* genes. Perinatal asphyxia or SIDS ended the lives of many infants. But Colin showed no signs of dying. He was a fighter.

As she hovered his crib, she could only wish it was possible to bring him. From the side pocket of her pants, she pulled out the pedal from the lilac in her room. Barely thriving and colorful, Janice placed the lilac next to Colin's head. "I'm going to be honest with you," she whimpered, "I use to loathe the idea of being pregnant. Having to be that woman everyone would stop to help up the stairs, or step out of the elevator to give room, or smile at inside the grocery store. Then having to deal with the back pain, the breast pain, and the constant internal nagging. Not being able to sleep on my stomach. When I was young, I saw babies and thought *how disgusting*. Babies poo everywhere and droll constantly and sneeze globs of mucus. How on earth would any woman want to be a mother?" Janice grinned. "I loved *every* minute. I just had to stop by and thank you. Thank you for giving me meaning." She reached down and kissed his forehead, then pulled up his blanket. He got warm easily. "Mommy loves you. I hope one day you'll understand why

I'm doing what I have to do. Your future means more to me than mine."

Wet-faced from tears and hands shaking, Janice took a step back. It was better to leave now. Leave all this behind. And go to Marcel.

Besides the crawl through the sewer exit Gerard told her about, the journey hadn't been as difficult as she anticipated. Finding where the ATV was hidden took awhile, but she found it buried in bushes. Janice had never driven a four-wheeler before and found it more daunting than convenient. Perhaps, she should've just walked to the road.

Starting the vehicle was easy enough, but it was manual shift so it stalled constantly. Not sure exactly where the road was, Janice kept going straight, driving along what seemed like tracks on the ground. Expecting to feel guilt, she felt nothing but determination. Was this what Brent experienced, traveling toward the castle he knew he wouldn't leave? Just like her? If only her brother could've stopped Marcel's blind endeavor of domination. Then so many lives could've been saved. It was up to her to end further deaths. If her plan worked, that is.

Riding in the dark had its fair share of obstacles. Hills seemed to appear out of nowhere, giving her no time to swerve. On three occasions, she contemplated abandoning the ATV in the ditch. But, as if the vehicle heard her, its wheels would turn and get enough traction to back out. After an hour of proceeding the forest, she saw a deer and stopping. With brown short hair and spots of white dots, the doe looked at her, more still than a statue. Victoria bought a painting, for her office in the West Wing, that hung above the desk. It was a painting of a deer.

Unsure how to react, the deer didn't move. Neither did Janice. If it was there to stop her, it made no attempt. If it was there to aide her, it made no attempt for that either. She was an observer. "Hey, Mom," Janice said. In most circumstances, it would be silly to assume spirits inhabited animals. In most circumstances… "I have to stop Marcel. In this world, or the next."

The deer looked away, then walked the other direction. She watched, expecting the animal to poof away into some magical dust or something. But drifted away into the dark woods. "I'll see you soon, Mom."

Janice drove on for about an hour, stopping twice to apply more ointment to her wound. Just a little longer and it would all be over. Finally, street light could be seen. A road approached. Willie's description wasn't wrong, the road was dull and empty. She sat at the edge of the street, not sure if the whole thumbs-up or showing-leg thing still existed because no car ever stopped. Six or so cars had past before she decided to force someone to stop. Janice parked the ATV in the center of the road, hoping it wouldn't cause an accident because a dead motorist did her no good.

Before long, a truck pulled up and stopped, throwing his hands up in frustration. She trudged up to the driver's window, his angry face melted at the sight of her. "Oh, Jesus Christ. Are you okay, miss?"

"You have a radio, right?"

"Yeah. Yeah. You need an ambulance?"

Janice shook her head. "No. I need you to call the police, or whatever their called nowadays. And tell them you have Janice Celest. She needs to be arrested for crimes against the state."

CHAPTER FORTY-ONE

Governing the world had several advantages and disadvantages. Making decisions to create peace and harmony were simple. Making decisions on how to decorate the castle were not. Marcel regretted his demands to structure the Union's home. Oftentimes so mundane, he wished the staff just knew his taste in architecture. His office looked it had been constructed six days ago and not six months ago. Boxes blocked one corner, making him have to squeeze by to reach the bathroom. His desk had finally been finished. Marcel packed away file folders and neatly stacked pencils of different colors in the drawers before another knock interrupted his progress.

"Yes?" Marcel said sarcastically.

Two men, carrying what looked like a large fish secured to a wooden plank. Before he could ask, one of them answered. "It's a koi. From the people of Japan."

The first gift he'd been grateful, the second gift he'd been honored, the third gift he'd been pleased, the fourth gift…

"Just put it somewhere, I don't care."

The phone rang, he specifically asked the secretary to hold all calls. How was he supposed to unpack when the damn phone won't stop?

"Anywhere?"

"Yeah surprise me," Marcel shrugged. This went against every moral his mother taught him. Gifts were from the heart. So why didn't any of it matter?

He lifted the phone and hung it up without answering while the two stammered to find a place in the office to hang an ugly fish. The phone started ringing again. He lifted and hung up. Without even a second passing, it rang again. This time he walked away and tried to distract himself by emptying another box of paper files. Why did he ever resort to printing everything?

The phone continued to ring. He rubbed the temples of his forehead, watching the two men place the statue in quite possibly the worse place. Hammering and hammering, they at first hung the koi too high, then too low. For whatever reason, the secretary hadn't given up calling him and the phone continued. The room felt stuffy, like the inside of a hot balloon. Marcel would burst if he didn't get a moment alone.

He dug through a box labeled *Media*. Throughout the years, he remained nostalgic. When he was ten, MP3 players were the norm but he stuck with CDs. Scratched and constantly skipping songs, he never gave up touting that someday digital formatting would implode without any physical backup. Lo and behold, the apocalypse happened and the internet got a fresh start and erased everything left behind. In only a minute, he found the CD player and a pair of headphones. For Christmas, his mother made him a mixture of movie scores on a single disc. There was something about movie score, the building of a scene whether action or romance.

Just as he placed the headphones on, he could hear banging at the door and visual permission from the two men if they should open it. "Sir," the secretary's high pitched voice said from behind it. "It's very important -"

Marcel scrolled up the volume key and drowned her out with the orchestra of John Williams. Leaving the two men glancing back and forth from the door to Marcel, he squeezed between cardboard boxes and entered the restroom, where he collapsed on the door and locked it. Silence finally.

Without warm running water in the complex yet, Marcel tossed the idea of a bath. Instead he sat in the tub and closed his eyes. Brent used to do this, when he got so irate that Mom couldn't get a word in. School did that to his brother a lot, made him so peeved at the useless teachers, useless counselors, and useless principals. Maybe Marcel should train himself to fight back to all the bullies. Fear worked for Brent, so why not? Why did Marcel always back away and feel the guilt holding him from unleashing full hell on Earth? Was it that light his mother said that flowed through Marcel but struggled through Brent?

"Sir!" A robotic strong voice commanded behind the door. Only Vanderbilt would have the audacity to interrupt Marcel.

"What?" He screamed, ripping away the melody of Hans Zimmer and hurling the headphones at the wall. At least Brent would thrown them hard enough to break.

"We have her in custody. Janice."

Marcel shot up and nearly slipped on the porcelain surface. "Janice? Where!"

"Downstairs."

Floor ties had been completed in some places, but not others. Like playing a game of hopscotch, Marcel hurried through the hallway trying to reach the goal. His sister! Here? Why? How?

The last time he matched her stare, it was atop this very castle as he stood over the bloodied body of their brother. With the murdering blade in his hand. Never imagining the day would come where he'd be forgiven. Maybe she finally saw the true future, the safe future…with him.

Resorting to only wearing jeans and t-shirt because he couldn't find his box with more formidable attire, Marcel realized in the hurry to the infirmary that he'd left his flip-flops on.

White hallways lead the way to the hospital wing, nurses behind him tried to keep up and instructing him which turn to make. He eventually ended up at a room marked ADMISSION. Inside, lying face up and connected to a white bag via IV, was Janice in a white gown. There was so much white in this wing, any bacteria would practically be visible to the naked eye.

"Hey," he managed to whisper.

Janice looked up, her hair wet. He pictured what it must've been like to be a nurse bathing her. "Hey you," she said emotionless. In all these years together as adopted siblings, he'd never seen her like this, with such sunken eyes and colorless skin. One time, during a winter storm, she suffered a flu that put her in the ICU. Marcel aided her back to health and he intended to repeat history. Before he could ask, she affirmed his suspicions. "I'm dying."

Before their mother died, Marcel often wondered if the news would be easier to handle if it came unexpectedly or expectedly. Both seemed brutally equal. The idea of Janice slipping out of this world was unacceptable. "Not on my watch," Marcel shook his head.

Amused, Janice stood up and sat at the edge of the cot. "I'm okay," she told the nurse, asking for a moment alone.

Looking to Marcel, he nodded affirmatively. She said once the room was empty, "Gerard told me. He told me everything. About Doomsday. He saw you, alive and well, moments before the attack. When the whole world, including me, thought you were in coma. Or worse, dead. You instructed him to tell no one. And warned him that something bad was about to happen." Marcel found himself looking about, attempting not to make eye contact. "You knew, didn't you? That the apocalypse was happening? That nukes were going to fall, lethal locusts were being freed, and a debilitating virus was about to spread. Did you know?"

Lying was a possibility, but Janice always had a knack for discovering the truth. So, Marcel answered, "Yes."

"Dad was your idol. You learned politics better than any of us. World leaders worshipped you. And you couldn't have made a phone call to stop it?"

Realizing this was the first time anyone had brought up this moment, nearly a year ago, where Marcel had made the most difficult decision. But if she had seen what Lucifer showed him, an end to humanity because of overpopulation, maybe Janice would seem so condescending. If he believed his decision had been the right one, then why did he feel a bead of guilt sweat droop from his eyebrow. "I could have stopped it."

"Why…How could the Marcel I know, do such a thing? Was it the Union? You wanted to be the Phoenix, rising from the ashes to save the world?"

His body stiff, he decided to move and relax. His father taught him during debates, a slight pace helped blood flow and made you look in charge; a fast pace made you look guilty and antsy. Marcel pulled up a stool and sat across from her, noting that she didn't back away fearfully. "We were just kids when it happened, but I remembered watching the television over and over again during 9/11, when terrorism showed its ugliest face. Something drew me to it. Not the fascination with the attackers or how the buildings fell," he took a breath, giving his debate opponent time to soak in what was being said, "but of the people who survived. Hell, all the people. It didn't just change the city, it changed everyone...around the world. Citizens were kinder. Neighbors checked on neighbors. Hugs were tight. Kisses lasted forever. An energy surged from the darkness that day. You know what it was? Light. Light bleeds from tragedy and bonds humanity. Every time. Wouldn't you agree? Wouldn't you say that Light blossomed around the world after Doomsday?"

She didn't say no, she didn't say yes.

Marcel continued, "It's the real Phoenix rising from the ashes. And I allowed it to be born that day."

"Let me guess. And that Phoenix goes by the name...the Union."

"Maybe we are after the same thing, ever thought about that?" Marcel retorted.

Without asking for help, Janice stood and limped over to the wall. For fear of it being slapped away, Marcel didn't offer a hand. Surprisingly resilient, she was able to walk almost upright as she poured a cup of tap water and swallowed it.

"We can fix you," Marcel proposed.

"Funny," she said tossing away the styrofoam cup, "I came here to fix *you*."

Against the objections of Janice, the doctor insisted she be confined to a wheelchair until the morning when further testing could be done. Besides photo-ops at charity hospitals, Marcel had never experienced wheeling someone around. Janice kept silent as he gave her a tour of the castle. They traveled through a long corridor with a floor so waxed it looked like glass. While he explained the statues on pillars, where they from and who they represented, she stared at her reflection on the floor. What was meant to showcase the life she could have with him here came off as bragging.

He stopped midway through the foyer, underneath a chandelier larger than the mobile home the Celests started in. Next to him, inside a glass case, there was a porcelain statue of a boat. On this boat, nine Egyptian figures and two children had been captured in formations dancing to the music of a harp player while supposedly sailing at sea. Marcel removed the glass casing and presented the statute. "This is called the Queen of the Nile by Lladro. It's worth one point two million dollars, last I checked. For me, it points out the happiness companionship can bring."

He held it up a few feet away from Janice. And then dropped it. The porcelain shattered into pieces, Janice flinched for a second and then opened her mouth. "Why..."

"Because its pointless. Meaningless. It's only money. Money doesn't buy happiness. Happiness isn't an easy journey. But simplicity is. Simplicity like the world around you is becoming." Realizing how much he sounded like a therapist and a propagandist for the Union, Marcel decided to change his point. He leaned back against the wall. "You remember that Friday after Mom died?"

Janice collapsed her hands together in her lap. "How could I forget the phone call from Dad? All I could get from it were the words: Marcel, bathtub, and blade."

Hearing that reminded Marcel how much his father loved the family. *Used* to love him. He said, "Death was something I had always been terrified of until Mom died. I remember, so clearly, how I felt that night. The fear was gone. I didn't think about anyone who still loved me or the outcrying support from the nation. All I thought about was how much I wanted the pain to end. I couldn't sleep, concentrate, or eat. I

just remember feeling…inconsequential to the world."
Marcel held up his wrist, showing a scar along his vein. A
deep scar. "It doesn't heal." He rubbed it some more before
putting his hand in his pocket. "I know how you feel. But
unlike my experience, you have a choice. You don't have to
be so," he looked at the shattered figurines, "broken."

Darkness grew. He caught her eyes for a moment and
began to tunnel into her soul.

Janice quickly looked down, severing the trance. "Don't."

"Don't what?"

"Try to hypnotize me." She swallowed and glanced at the
broken art piece. "Some things just can't be glued back
together."

People change, Mom taught him that. But in his wildest
dreams, he'd never seen someone change as much as Janice.
As much as he did, the day after his mother died. If he could
climb out of that dark hole, surely the most resilient woman
he'd ever met could do the same. He bend down and reached
out both hands, but she backed away. "I realize that night
shouldn't have happened. It ruined *us*. I should've kept my
hands to myself –"

"A night of booze and sex was the *least* of our issues."
Janice spat. "You murdered our brother."

Images of Brent gasping for air as blood trickled from a
knife wound in his chest flashed in Marcel's head. He
relaxed his shoulders, tired of feeling guilt. "This is
something wrong with humanity. As soon as someone dies,
their sins are erased. You weren't there the night that he
attacked me. I was frightened. An assassin coming for me?
But everyone loved me. It's terrifying, isn't it? Knowing
Death is coming for you? My Death wore a black suit that
meshed to the bathroom. My Death hid his face. My Death
beat me, broke every rib, shattered three bones, tossed me

off a balcony, and shot me in the head. My Death…was my own brother."

"So it was justice then?"

"It was an accident. I didn't mean to kill him." Even after all he'd said, Marcel couldn't convince himself. It sounded cliche, like the ending of a cop show. He meant to kill him and spill blood on the castle's roof. Facing the truth now, he realized it was justice. His brother deserved to die.

"You know what's easier than an explanation? An apology. You could at least start with that." Janice said, turning to wheel herself away. Surely, she had no idea how to navigate this wing, Marcel followed. "Do you know who they were?" She said in spite. "The couple you attacked? In the woods?"

How could he forget? The Light had chosen a couple, Lloyd and Nina, to gather forces against Marcel with the powers of light. He'd survived the spectacular fight; fortunately for him, they hadn't. "I was defending myself. I didn't murder them. They died because of their wounds. If they'd been with the Union, we could have helped them."

Janice stopped and spun the wheelchair around. "Do you know who they were? They were my parents. I mean, my *real* parents. You've taken so much from me. And all I ask if you tell the truth."

Honestly confused by the statement, Marcel's eyes squinted. "Tell what truth?"

Slower than before, Janice wheeled away and stopped at a glass display. Inside was a copy of the Union agreement, all two thousand pages of it. She struggled to stand, but was eventually on her feet looking through the glass display. "Can you take it out?"

Normally, Marcel would've refused such a request; it was the only copy with all world leaders signatures. That's why it lied inside a bullet-proof case. But he trusted her. With a press of his finger on the electronic lock, the glass case lifted. He picked up the agreement, realizing it weighed more in his hands than it did on his shoulders.

Janice thumbed through it, stopping on the section about Education Reform. Originally, he'd written that section with her in mind. All her ideas about building our future through educating the young were in it. She read it briefly, before continuing. Finally, she stopped flipping the pages and she held it up so Marcel could see. It was the signature of the Vice President of the United States. She didn't need to explain because Marcel understood almost immediately. "Oh God," he whispered.

"The Vice President signed."

This was the truth she spoke of. "We all assumed Dad was dead."

"He's not. He was President of the United States. *His* signature is supposed to be here."

The Union agreement was null and void.

Marcel glanced around to make sure no one heard the conversation and placed the treaty back inside the glass case, as though that would make the reality disappear. "Legally, we could say the Vice President was acting-President. There's loopholes here. It's fine," he said. "I can't tell the public that the treaty is voided. You know I won't do that."

"Yeah I do, but a girl can hope." Janice said disappointingly, slumping back into her wheelchair. "Don't you feel bad? At all? About any of this?"

Creating a force field against all guilt, Marcel couldn't answer the question truthfully. He looked at Janice's tired eyes. "Your room is right here. Get some rest."

Morning arrived. Even after a long night of comfortable sleep, Marcel still felt restless. His king sized bed didn't seem apt considering he slept in it alone. How was he going to convince Janice to lay here? How wonderful life could be when no one can hurt you?

Today would be the day.

The clock said 6:14. Considering he woke up at five a.m. Most days, if he even slept at all, this was a late start. For whatever reason, his automated system didn't wake him with soft subtle lights and rising music. Technology, for all the work that had been done, still wasn't reliable. Hopefully one day it would be, because Marcel needed a perfect palace for a perfect bride.

He turned on the bathroom and showered to the uplifting teachings of a love guru, preparing to be the ultimate lover and partner. *Smell your best.* Marcel would have to settle for a lesser brand cologne, but it smelled better than the homeless stench of the People of Bliss. He shaved. *A smooth face means a smooth attitude.* Blood trickled down from his chin, a slight misstep meant a deep cut. He watched as the wound sealed and molded closed, the blood began to coagulate. Amazing. Staring at his reflection, Marcel slowly took the clean blade out from the shaver. It wasn't the first time he'd done it. About to start cutting horizontal from one end of his throats to the other, he was interrupted by a knock on the door. With a shaky hand, he placed the blade flat on the counter. "Yes?"

Through the door, his secretary blurted, "Your first interview is here." The problem with having so much control was how little memory it garnered. Judging by his pause, she assumed he didn't understand. She clarified, "For the Security Czar position." Marcel sneered at being reminded he had to replace Gerard. "Cancel all appointments today. I'm spending the day with my sister."

Thirty minutes later, he was primed and ready. Walking toward the kitchen area, Marcel tried to remember Janice's favorite breakfast. Was it waffles? Yes. Mom made them every Saturday morning before cartoons started. But what kind? Blueberry? Strawberry? His special breakfast-in-bed moment would be ruined if he couldn't remember. Before Marcel would have to flip a coin on that decision, his plan was already ruined when he entered the kitchen. Sitting on a stool in the corner with a cup of tea and have eaten plate of waffles, Janice looked up. His romantic morning would have to be for another day. He sat on the stool next to her and glanced at her plate. "Strawberry," he said.

"Huh?"

"Nothing." *Talk about her,* the love guru reminded him. "Did you sleep?"

She reached in her pocket and wiggled a bottle of pills. "The painkillers *are* good here."

"What about the antibiotics?"

Without saying so, he could tell she was refusing to take them. Not only did she dismiss the idea of treatment earlier, she got her stubborn behaviors from Marcel himself. Janice changed the subject. "His name is Colin and he's the most beautiful baby I've ever seen. " She said and turned to a paper in her hand, a pamphlet of the castle.

"He wasn't mine, was he?"

Janice shook her head, not taking her eyes off the pamphlet. Too bad. The idea of a predecessor to Marcel's throne stayed in his mind since the months he found out her pregnancy. Now it brought into question why build an empire when there was no one to leave it to. "He's so innocent, not scarred yet by the world. It seems we all manifest evil, through all the evil that has been done to us. I see what Dad meant. There is good in this world, I see it in Colin's eyes. It must be saved, no matter what. We need to get rid of this…darkness, Marcel."

Marcel thought about his travels with Lucifer in the black matter. It lingered everywhere. But maybe it could be diminished. *Find a common ground*, the Indian guru's voice echoed in his head. "I could absorb it. All of it. I have the power to do it, I think."

Janice stopped halfway through raising the cup to her mouth, in this bewildered state. "So strange. Adam's precognition. It was about…never mind. Just promise you won't do it," She demanded. "Promise me."

Whatever she knew didn't fair well for Marcel if he absorbed the black matter. He recalled the name Adam, the new leader of the rebellion and if rumors were true…also clairvoyant. Did Adam foresee the coming end? Admittedly, Marcel never pondered that situation. This must've been how his father felt; trying to negotiate with world leaders that had their mind set on only one outcome. Janice wanted to die and he didn't have to see her soul to know that. She wanted to join Brent and their mother. If he was to be honest with himself, Marcel marveled at the idea of being in the family again. "Okay, I promise." Marcel shrugged. They both needed a more calm environment to release tensions. "Hey, you want to see something neat?"

Climbing up the spiraling staircase, Janice hadn't said much besides the questionable where-are-you-taking-me quibbles. They walked through a long hallway of a dozen sparkling chandeliers, elaborate patterned wallpaper, and past red doors with brass knobs. Marcel twisted one of the knobs and opened a door, being gentlemen-like. She entered, brushing her hair behind her ear.

Inside, Janice froze in place, as he knew she would. Like most people, she was probably dumbfounded by the room. The walls of the library, lined with book after book that almost seemed like murals. Gold plated ladders aided in the climb up, the opposite of the escalator idea contractors first introduced. Because he knew Janice loved nostalgia.

She entered and took several minutes to scan the shelves, remaining silent. The first vacation the Celests took with their new adopted sibling Janice was to the zoo. That same look of fascination and admiration shined on Janice's face again. Marcel sensed warmth inside, having difficulty recalling the last time he'd experienced it.

"Now I can comprehend what Belle felt like," she commented. He frowned. With that analogy, it meant Marcel was the Beast.

Without asking, she opened the double French doors and stepped out into the balcony. Someone was there. Someone in the gray. Someone staring.

Brent.

Marcel closed his eyes tightly, regretting his forgetfulness. He must've missed a dose.

"Something wrong?" Janice called out.

Nothing was wrong, except that their dead brother stood amongst the living on that balcony, with that same blank stare and emotionless expression. Marcel fumbled through his pockets. Where did he put that inhaler? "Nothing, just taking in the cool breeze." Deep in his pocket, he found it and yanked it out. He inhaled the medication through each nostril. Brexpiprazole tasted like what dung from a beetle would probably taste like. The medicine dripped down in his throat in to his blood stream. Reluctantly, he squinted and opened his eyes. Brent was gone.

Janice faced away, gazing over the ocean view. Outside, it seemed like going to the beach during summer just to be met with rain clouds. Pure, yet ruined. "You saw him. Didn't you?"

Not sure how to answer, Marcel's stayed half open. He could make her reflect the silliness of it all. Ghosts don't exist, at least not in her perspective of the world. But anything was possible. She must've accepted it as much as he had. "Yes."

"Is this where he died?" She asked, knowing the answer since she had been on that helicopter that hovered over the crime scene. The crime of murder.

He didn't answer and approached the edge of the balcony, holding the railing. Wind got harsher here. One strong gust could push either of them down hundreds of feet into the splashing shore below. Looking over the cliff and visually entwined with the sharp rocks, Janice must've read his mind. "Sure is a far drop."

They both watched the waves grasp at the rocky cliff, as though it wanted to climb up it. "Beautiful though, right?" Marcel asked.

"There's something common we share with every species, something bred into our everyday lives, and it's the need for survival. Would you agree?"

Unsure where the conversation was going, Marcel answered. Anything to keep to his mind off the fact that just months ago this floor was masked in Brent's blood. "Yes."

"Everyday needs to be a fight to live on. But, as I look around in this luxury you live in, I wonder to myself…are you fighting for survival here?"

He couldn't help but notice her struggle to not look him in the face. "Isn't that the point of trying to better ourselves? So we don't need to fight for our lives?"

She surprisingly shook her head. "No. Let me give you an example. After Hurricane Katrina, when some had spent months trying to survive, were brought to a habitable environment with nothing to fear…they reported feeling *unhappy*. That the camaraderie created amongst peers and the will for survival made them feel alive. Similar studies have been done on armed forces overseas for months at a time. We are physically built by genetics to travel by foot, rip foods with our foods, even taste when something is unsafe to eat. But then the idea of convenience came along and sucked us into this vacuum of independence. We've had a hundred thousand years of evolution to teach us to survive. Without that yearning, depression has peaked. I'll ask again, are you fighting for survival here?"

Marcel's throat swelled, not from the medicine but from something else. A confession. "No. I guess...I don't really have the need to survive."

"There's finally something we can agree on."

Whatever that meant, Marcel was driven to change this mood and add light to their darkness. "Want to see something neat?" He stared up at the clouds, hearing the apathy of the wind element.

Suddenly, air began to tear apart the dark clouds. Janice panicked as sunlight began to pour in from the morning star over the horizon. "Marcel, what about your allergy –" She stopped cold at the sight of rays hitting his face. "I don't understand. You don't –"

"No migraines, blotched skin, painful spasms. My allergic reaction to light is gone."

It took her a moment to soak in this development. Marcel had lived in darkness for so long, that everyone who loved him had to live in it too. She turned and smiled at the sunrise. Light glimmered off her lips. Her eyelashes fluttered slightly. How can such allure be filled such anguish? It all just seemed so unfair. With all the power Marcel had in this world, he couldn't fix Janice's depression. Perhaps he couldn't fix his own either.

Her hands cupped over her mouth, Janice watched the sun settle over the ocean, painting the water shades of red and orange. A tear wiggled down the side of her face and splashed to the ground where he'd dropped the blade he had stabbed Brent with.

The dark clouds gathered back together and brought in a chilly breeze. Janice's shoulders dropped while Marcel's shoulders straightened.

"How?" Janice asked.

"How what?"

She only stared ahead, over the endless sea, and repeated. "How?"

Lucifer had a strict set of rules and one of them was to never tell of his existence. Marcel had already broken that rule, telling his brother, but family should always be an exception. The Celests vowed decades ago to never hide from each other. "When I went into the coma, I awoke in the gray."

"The gray?" Janice repeated, as though the word was foreign.

"Just…nothing but gray. It was this world, just…gray." He said, feeling precarious already. This wasn't like his confession to Brent, Janice instigated and got answers. "The leader of the Dark found me. Helped me to learn. Gave me the power to persuade even the elements." After saying it, he realized he couldn't have uttered it more simpler. He always kept things simple, because that's where peace laid - in a sand of calmness and rest.

Her hair blowing in sync with the wind, Janice looked up at the clouds as though they had just taken her best friend away. "Look at them. The clouds. So riddled with filth. Will they ever be clear again? Able to roam without being reminded of what happened?"

"Its because of the explosions worldwide, we have to –"

"No, Marcel. It's because of *you*."

He pierced his lips and took a deep breath. She still wouldn't look him in the eyes. After a few seconds of reminding himself not to react the way Brent would with

such a derogatory statement, he said, "I can't take
responsibility for other people's actions."

"That's the problem…you can't take responsibility."

Marcel left it at that. Women loved having the last word
and Janice was no different. He could feel his quest for her
love failing, sinking down into the horizon just like the sun.
Both hopeless and hopeful, he was running out of options
besides locking into her eyes and her soul, devouring any
fear of their future together.

"Where did she die?"

So many had died in recent weeks here, but she could only
mean one. "Sirius Dawson died in the chambers." Maybe he
could get the opportunity there to see her soul through the
tunnel of the eyes and dig out that animosity. "Would you
like to see it?"

"Yes."

Sliding her fingers across the plank, Janice remained
mostly silent when they had entered the chambers. What
looked like a table to operate on, had a vastly different
purpose. On one end of the slanted discolored wood was a
crank connected to a winch. Janice turned it gently, while
Marcel tried to guess what was in her mind since he couldn't
a glance into her gaze. Did she respect what the laws and
leaderships had to accomplish in order to gain control of the
populace? Or did she misunderstand it, as those liberals
always did?

The vast room could room enough bunk beds for fifty
prisoners, but it wasn't about housing. Instead it was about
torturing. Janice moved onto three other machines, the Iron
Maiden, the Brazen bull, before stopping at the simple and
effective guillotine. She reached past the bloody basket on
the floor, to the top of the device's blade, and then lightly

touched the edge. Blood trickled from her fingers, but she didn't flinch. "Still sharp."

Perhaps bring someone, suffering a melancholy, into a place like this was a bad idea. Marcel looked at the clock, "It's almost noon. We should have lunch on the –"

"Remember the ISIS extremists?" Janice interrupted, eyeing the Judas Cradle, a ghastly device where the victim would be tied above a wooden post that entered the anus.

"We were kids then. Mom didn't let us watch the news much. She was afraid we would be wound up in the media circus."

She nodded. "I probably shouldn't have watched it, but this boy at the orphanage used to bring in those videos to watch on his cellphone. You know? The ones where they would kill people in the name of their god? I was only fourteen, not even old enough to drive yet and there I was watching brutal killings. You know what struck me the most? Not the grotesque moments of throwing men off high rises or beheading with a dull machete, but the moment before. Right before." She paused like staring at a hovering picture in the air. "Something every victim had in common was that seven seconds, I know because I counted it. Seven seconds right before they died. Seven seconds of acceptance. They're not even wide-eyed or shaking…they were so…placid." She turned, but still stared at the floor. "Is that peace? That seven seconds?"

Answering what he thought his father would, Marcel immediately said. "No."

"But…how do you know? Peace isn't simplicity, Marcel. It's acceptance. Accepting your fate. Accepting that people have unbalanced decisions which harbor good or evil intentions. Accepting that not everyone is compatible. Accepting that you cannot always control the outcome of complex situations. Accepting that people live and that people die."

Marcel strolled, hands behind his back, thinking about what she was saying. He touched the rusted wall of knives and stopped to stare at the coffin torture machine, like it would move. Meant to be hung over crowds of people and mimic the confinement of a casket, it became a symbolism of internal torture. It had been constructed to look like a cell, steel bars and a locking mechanism. But did its prisoner, presuming his death would be momentarily, experience peace? "No." He said, his back to Janice. "I can't accept that. Mom isn't dead. She's in the…gray. With Brent. And they'll be so proud of me when I accomplish what they only dreamed of. I'm sorry. But there are tough decisions that must be made and we can't just simply accept what life gives us."

"You're right," Janice said from behind, "There are tough decisions to make. And I've just made one of them."

She shoved him inside the cell and locked it.

Marcel grasped the bars and shook. The bars didn't budge. He couldn't presume the worst, that his sister purposely locked him in here, so he spoke calmly. "Janice, this isn't funny. Open it."

Staring at the floor still, she stood just feet away from the entrance of it. Saying nothing.

"Janice. Unlock the gate." He said slowly.

She did…nothing.

He shook the bars, harshly, the blood boiling in his veins. For such an ancient device, the steel structure still hold. His hands got cold, clammy. Fear pumped through his heart, the same fear that manifested for every prisoner in this coffin cell. Janice made no movement to his aide. She had deceived him. He growled, "After all I've done for you?"

She uttered under her breath, "This is…because of everything you've done to me."

Janice lifted her shift halfway. Duct taped around his waist, she removed a gun. A Ruger LCR Revolver. For such a small gun, it looked big in her petite, frail hands. She held it, not pointing or grasping it correctly, but inspecting it like one of the torture devices in the room.

Instead of sympathy, he wanted to spit in her face. First, Brent tried to kill him. Then Gerard. Now his loving sister. He could plead for mercy or beg that she listen to his healing words, but not this time. This time he'd do what the darkness in him wanted to do. He threatened her, through gritted teeth, "You know I can stop bullets now, right?"

Lip quivering and tears dripping down her cheeks like pedals falling from a dying rose, she said, "I know." After swallowing, she muttered, "The bullet isn't for you."

His face, scrunched and bitter, lifted. The realization of the situation made his heart race. His chest, heaving from immediate anxiety, mushed up against the cell bars. "Janice. No. Don't. Oh God. Don't."

"I won't do it here. I'm not a monster."

He grasped the bars, even tighter, and rattled them harder. "Janice! No! Don't! Please!"

She stepped backwards, her voice breaking from the sobs. "I…I'm…dying…anyways. I've been dead for a…long time…Marcel. We all have. Don't you…see? We all died with Mom. We are just ghosts…walking around aimlessly without her."

He didn't listen, using his shoulder to slam the cell door, kicking and punching, as the predecessors in this cell had done centuries ago. "Janice! Don't! Don't! I need you! Please!"

Wobbling, Janice turned towards a door in the back of the room. A measly, filthy janitor's closet. That would be her coffin. "If I can't get through to…you in this world…then I will in the next. I love…you…I really do."

Marcel screamed, "No! Don't do it! Look at me! Please! Janice!"

She walked away, opening the door to the closet room, then stopping to take a deep breath. An orgasmic breath. "There it is," she said satisfactorily, "Seven seconds. That's all I get. Oh Marcel, it feels amazing." Slowly stepping inside, she closed the door behind her.

"Janice!" He shouted. "Please!"

I'm here! The water element shouted. *Let me help!*

Marcel circled around, trying to figure out the water source in the room. The pipes! He quickly focused, his blood pumping so fast he might faint. A tunnel of water crashed out of the wall and grasped the cell's door. Within seconds, it froze solid. Marcel kicked and kicked the ice. "Janice! Janice!" Eventually the block of ice shattered, along with the bars of the cell. Free now, Marcel dashed across the room. He could make it. He could stop her. He could save her. There was hope. "Janice!"

The sound of a gun shot deafened his ears.

The sound of a body crashing to the floor stopped his heart.

Blood slipped out the bottom of the door.

His head spun. His breath slowed. His feet felt numb. His hands shook.

Before he could cry out, Marcel tumbled to the ground and everything went black.

CHAPTER FORTY-TWO

Lately, first thing in the morning, Adam would feel a
sense of purpose. Hope created by Gerard's sacrifice. Every
morning, he'd walk briskly to the cafeteria, skipping steps,
tell the kids to slow down in the hallways, wait until
everyone exited the long queue for the breakfast buffet
before grabbing a plate, and ending his morning with a warm
cup of joe at a table alone. But he awoke with dread, sorrow,
and despair. His knotted stomach skipped breakfast and went
straight for the coffee table. He drank it with six sugars and
three creams, like in college. Final semester would've been
coming to an end soon.

Without bothering to get dressed, he wore a robe that one
of the scouts found in a trash can. No one dared to wear it,
because it smelled like rotten tangerines. Skipping the line of
people for coffee at the cafeteria, he poured it black. After
slumping in a chair, not acknowledging the greetings from
others, he sipped his coffee and sighed. It must've been the
afternoon because lunch was being served. Or maybe even
dinner. He stared at the white plastic table, watching
whatever was floating on the top of his drink. Could be

anything, even flakes from the kitchen staff's dandruff. Adam took a long sip, before he got interrupted.

Willie sat down slowly, as though he didn't want to wake up Adam even though he wasn't asleep. Dark and swollen, his eyes looked like they had been crying all day. Vying for worst dressed in the cafeteria, he wore a white tight tank top with food stains and his hair uncombed looked like a dead animal. After swallowing back some mucus, Willie said, "Radio is saying another death reported at the Union Castle."

Without understanding how, Adam replied, "I know." He didn't just feel her missing body next to him in bed, but her missing soul. "I'm going to have her name tattooed."

"Where?"

Adam pointed to the place above his heart. That made the tear wobbling at Willie's left eyelid slide down and hit the table. After wiping his nose, he said, "The radio says *Another Celest Dead.* I was hoping it was Marcel Celest."

Wiping his upper lip of the leftover coffee, Adam grumbled. "It will be soon." He leaned back in his chairs and crossed his arms. "Tonight. Midnight. It's the anniversary. January 7th was the day it all ended, and now it'll be the day it all began." Trying to picture the march toward the castle became blurry, he could only see Janice and Brent, the two most important people in his life, both dead in puddles of blood. The Supreme Leader would have to pay. "Boats here yet?"

Willie nodded. "Arrived this morning. Royal called."

"Let's start transporting. I'll go with the first batch. One van per hour." He took a breath. "You getting the truck today?"

Willie's nod was so slight, he couldn't tell if it was affirmative. His unshaven face added ten years to him. Adam slammed his hand on the table so hard that Willie jumped and the people around paused mid-bite. "You need to focus. *We* need to focus. Understand?"

"Yeah. Don't sweat it. I'll get the device. I know where the trailer is."

Without another word, Adam stood and left the cup at the table. He wanted to collapse to the door, shield his face and weep into his palms. But it wouldn't solve anything. Janice wanted the plan to continue. A war to end the war.

Until people were ready to depart, Adam needed something to do. Getting dressed took him less than five minutes. Loose pants and a loose shirt gave him the mobility he would need. But every moment he had of complete silence, his mind went back to Janice.

Visiting Nelson wouldn't put him in a better mood. No doubt, the father was mourning his daughter. And Adam couldn't bear to see anymore tears. Checking on Gerard wouldn't help either. They weren't close and besides, his door had been closed since Janice left yesterday. He didn't even step out of his room to use the bathroom.

Adam walked down the hallway until he reached the gym. Inside, as usual, the only person working out on the rusted equipment was Bruno. Lying on the weight bench, the giant lifted the bar which must've had all the weights available connected to it. After three reps and three deep breaths, the juggernaut stood. "Friend!" He said, when he noticed Adam in the room.

"Hey, Bruno."

He stood up, towering above Adam. The two barely spoke. Ever. And they both knew so little about each other. Small talk didn't seem like an opener to either of them. He decided to get to the point. "Bruno. I need you to punch me as hard as you can."

The room got so quiet that the sound of air conditioning became deafening. Bruno squinted his eyes. "What?"

Saying it slower, Adam repeated, "I need you to…punch me…as hard as you can."

"But. Why?" he replied in that thick German accent. "Bruno love Adam."

"Love?" He scoffed, spouting out quickly. "Love is bullshit. It'll just rip your heart apart in the end. It sucks. Alright? It sucks. Everyone dies. And it fucking sucks. Would you just hit me? Hit me square on the jaw. Break bones, give me bruises, just anything to make the pain go away. Do it!"

They shared a moment of silence. He could see Bruno thinking, glancing around the gym like he had answers there. "It help. Yes? Bruno punch…Adam better? Yes?"

Adam nodded.

The brute stepped back and paused before slapping Adam lightly, the hit barely swung his head. Feeling the surge of Brent in his blood, Adam shouted. "Goddamnit! I said punch me!"

Another light slap to the face. Bruno's hands were almost as big as Adam's head. The slap made him stumble barely, but he regained his posture. "Bruno no like this game."

"It's not a goddamn game, you Nazi bitch! Hit me!"

Bruno punched him so narrow, that Adam's head swung backwards. He saw several stars before his vision regained clarity. The giant's cheeks drooped angrily. "Not nice. No friend. Friend no say that."

It wasn't enough. Adam could still picture Janice, her long golden hair gathered on his side of the bed. He choked back saliva and spat it in Bruno's face.

After wiping the spit off his face, the brute soaked Adam in the face twice. Blood dripped down from his nose to his mouth, leaving a bitter taste. He stumbled backwards and fell to the ground. His jaw pulsated, his cheek burned, and his tooth felt loose. Adam took deep breaths, focusing on the external pain.

"Feel better?" Bruno asked, softly.

Adam nodded. "Yes. Thanks."

Still dazed and weak, he could feel Bruno lift him up to his feet. Mimicking his accent kindly, Adam said, "Adam love Bruno."

"Bruno know."

The van ride there was bumpy. Adam yanked out the toilet paper swabs he made for his nose. Less blood was a good sign. He rolled down the window and tossed them out.

In less than an hour, they had arrived at the ports. Not until the pier started to approach did Adam realize he never looked back, saying somewhat of a goodbye to the missile silo. As a kid, he used to leave one foster home and go on to the next. After a while, saying goodbye was moot. While others in the van brought whatever weapons they could think of, Adam brought nothing. How could anyone prepare for this? No one spoke during the ride. The only familiar face was Pierre, sitting in the back, his fingers skimmed over a Braille book.

"You alright?" Adam asked him.

Pierre didn't answer. He said, "When I was a little boy, my mother gave me this book. Born blind, the world was a scary place. I read when I'm scared. It helps."

Before the ports, they descended a steep hill. He could see no lights at the docks but plenty of shapes that looked like boats. "Wow they are big." He wiggled his tongue on the loose tooth and it finally broke free. Calmly, Adam rolled down the window and tossed out his molar tooth.

The van stopped and parked along the side of the road. Adam peeped out the window but saw no one outside. Did anyone even show up? Royal promised a big armada.

Everyone got out of the van. "We have to walk the rest." The driver stated.

Once they got over the hill, Adam had to pause for a moment. The crowd was enormous. Thousands upon thousands flooded the docks and surrounding areas. It was so quiet, it felt eerie like he was amongst a bunch of zombies. They pushed their way through, following the driver who seemed to be the only one with knowledge of the ports. Before long, they met up with a familiar face.

Royal Declan, hair tied up behind her in that dull but effective Jodie Foster look, turned. Adam's heart skipped. "Hey." It was all he could think to say after nearly three months separated from each other.

"I just gathered an army and your response is 'hey'?"

Was he supposed to offer a hug? No, too awkward. A handshake? No, even more awkward. A fistbump? Twiddling his fingers, Adam replied, "I…was just…yeah…I was getting to that. Just wanted to say hello first. Thanks…for your work and stuff."

Though a cordial greeting may have been in order, it didn't mean there was time for one. Royal scoffed. "We've done a head count. Roughly 18 thousand, give or take, since we can't get an accurate one." Something was different about her, she was more blunt, bitter than usual.

Adam's wide eyes peered over the masses. "Okay," he whispered. "I…mm…" he almost said *missed you* and quickly corrected himself, "I mmm…managed to get transportation for everyone at the silo. Should be done in a few hours."

Arms crossed, Royal asked, "What's with the shiner? Already started before the rest of us?"

He dabbed the side of his face wondering if Bruno's fist left a dent in it. "First of many tonight." She moved in, closest she'd ever been to him and traced her soft fingers along the names tattooed on his skin."You like them?" He asked, wondering why he would even need her approval.

She nodded, "Love them." Directly in his eyes, she gazed and said, "We are going to make those bastards pay. You understand?" Then she spun and faced Pierre. "What's with you? You look pale." She said. The Frenchman did, indeed, look white enough to faint.

"I'm...I'm...just a wee bit...scared, mademoiselle."

Royal's mouth dropped. "Scared? Are you kidding me? Scared?"

Pierre didn't say another word, his head down like a puppy that just made a mess. Royal looked around to see that same twiddling of fingers with others. One man puked into a bucket, another man chewed his fingers until they bled, and yet another sat on a tree hump with his leg shaking like an earthquake occurred under his foot. This was the warriors against the Union? She didn't seem pleased.

Next to her, a porter from the South Asia boat spoke into a bullhorn. "Will everyone with ticket letters H through J please line up in –"

Before the porter finished, Royal snatched the bullhorn from his mouth and spoke into the loud speaker. "Scared? Really?" Pierre looked away, even more embarrassed now. She turned to other people. "Are you scared? How about you?" No answer. Royal nodded to another passenger from the boat. "You? You scared?" No answer.

She stepped on top of bundle of crates to elevate her small stature. "Who else is scared?" Her voice echoed in the silent wave of fighters. No answer. She put her mouth closer to the bullhorn and shouted. "Why are you all scared? Me? Well...I'm relieved. Relieved that tonight, we are getting the opportunity to fight for something we have never really had before. We finally are going to receive our freedom. Our freedom from government. Our freedom from control. Our freedom from the more privileged. So then…why are any of you scared? You know who is scared right now? Those that take the side of the Union!" She shouted, pointing over the horizon towards the castle, which was just a dot in the distance.

Royal stared then nodded, "Yep. I can see it. You *are* all scared. And I'm going to prepare you not to be. Everyone remembers Lloyd and Nina; their power. With just simple words and concentrate, they could get a group of us to glow. Magic that no one could explain. A light shooting out of our skin that made us feel invisible. But that's not what we need right now. We need the opposite. We need *darkness*." She said the word *darkness* with such indignation that after a good, hard swallow she was ready to continue. "Everyone close their eyes."

It took some longer than others, but eventually everyone listened and squeezed their eyes closed.

She continued, "You're worried about numbers? How many we got versus how many they got? Let me give you a list of numbers."

Royal cleared her throat. "2004. A colossal corporation by the name of Enron completed its bankruptcy. After loads of accounting lies, its stock crashed and millions lost their retirement funds. The government saw the corruption and did…nothing.

"2005. Hurricane Katrina tore through Louisiana. 53 breeches caused an enormous flood. 1,577 people drowned to death. Over 60,000 were stranded to live amongst dead bodies and crushed homes. Only a little over half were saved. That means 30,000 were left to perish by the leadership we pay taxes to. For you to understand how many people that really was…that's the *same* number of you folks here. The government saw the corruption and did…nothing.

"2008. A housing market bubble was discovered, that when it burst would put millions of people in mortgages they couldn't afford. Instead of stopping this burst, several banks invested in the chance that they would fail! And sure enough, it failed. Millions and millions of people were left homeless. Someone should've gone to prison, right? Maybe the agencies that reported the bonds were 'just fine'? Maybe the bank CEOs that did nothing? Nope. No one went to jail. And all along, the banks knew there was going to be a bailout so they…let…it…happen. Billions of dollars lost. The government saw the corruption and did…nothing.

"2008 again. As though the market crash wasn't enough, the bipartisan '9/11 Health and Compensation Act' failed to pass through congress. You know what it was for? It called for research, medical monitoring and treatment for those exposed to Ground Zero toxins in the air after madmen crashed planes into the World Trade Center buildings. Common sense wording and budget to save millions of lives…failed to move through the House. And then it was slowly forgotten about. Since that day terrorists attacked our homeland, air pollution has killed more than actually died those buildings. The government saw the corruption and did…nothing.

"2013. Edward Snowden exposed the National Security Agency for recording millions of your phone calls, folks. They hacked servers and stole information from all of us. The government saw the corruption and did…nothing.

"2014. Eric Garner was accused of selling cigarettes. Put into a choke-hold. He muttered, 'I can't breathe' eleven times. He died. The officers got a slap on the wrist. The government saw the corruption and did…nothing.

"2016. A gunman entered a nightclub in Orlando and opened fire on innocent men and women. 49 people perished before police stopped the asshole. It was revealed he was on a terrorist watch list. Yet, he bought guns and ammo without any issue. Common sense laws were introduced to prevent suspected terrorists from buying weapons. The laws failed to pass. Common…sense. The government saw the corruption and did…nothing.

"2017. President Donald Trump was the second United States President to be inaugurated without the popular vote. We didn't vote for him, he lost by three million people, but we got him, folks. Our vote didn't count. It doesn't matter what we have to say. We get the leader *they* choose. Not you. We protested, they didn't listen."

Royal was about to continue but stopped. Adam opened his eyes. There was no need for her speech to continue. Instead of worrisome faces with their eyes closed, he saw only crunched eyebrows and biting of lips. The People of Bliss were infuriated. But she decided to add just one last ingredient to this stirring of anger. "In just the last year, 98 nuclear missiles have been fired on the United States. Government-engineered locusts were freed in protest of the Union proposal. Bitter world leaders released a lethal flu on its citizens. Moscow was chemically attacked. The Union took the place of all governments. Its military have been given the right to execute us with prejudice. Protesters are being banned and shot. Retirements funds have been yanked from us. Sale of guns has ceased and pretty soon – we will be disarmed, folks."

He found himself breathing even more heavily. An out-of-control monster, like that one he saw clawing itself out of Marcel in the precognition, in him begged to taste the blood of him enemies. Without seeing it, he suspected everyone else here had that similar monster. One that had been brewing for decades. "Open your eyes, everyone." As they did, he could see the darkness in the audience. Their breaths were in sync; a quiet, furious huff of impatience.

Royal said, "It's not just the events of the apocalypse that worry us, it's that the government doesn't care about our lives. They...don't...care. And even worse, it could happen again. All these things...in just *my* lifetime. I'm young. I can't even imagine what most of you gone through in *yours*."

There were no tears; no sense of anxiety. Everyone was ready. "Now you're pissed. Good. Tonight, we confront that corruption. That government run by just one man. Take all that hate, intolerance, rage, and frustration – focus it all on...*goddamn* Marcel Celest," she growled.

CHAPTER FORTY-THREE

Join us.

Her words echoed.

Join us.

Begging. Desperate.

Join us.

"Why, Janice? Why?" Marcel pled through the gray mist. "We could have been happy."

The wine bottle rolled off his lap and shattered on the concrete floor. He didn't even remember grabbing the bottle or even getting out of bed. Caught between a dream and reality, Marcel had lived this nightmare before. When his mother died his blackouts were even worse; sometimes hours would pass. Just like Victoria Celest, he never imagined a world without Janice Celest.

Had he heard a voice a moment ago? The room remained empty and yet a woman could be heard. Janice? Her voice calling from the gray between light and darkness, dimensions forever she'd be lost in. But he had many voices in the last year.

She's gone. The element of water, as always, spoke sympathetically. It rose from the spill of wine on the floor, leaving behind a swirl of colors from the red nourishment. Pure water glimmered, the fireplace grew behind it. This was the first time Marcel had sensed jealousy from the most loyal of elements, fire. *I'm truly sorry, Master.* Water said circling in the former of a bubble.

"We could have been so happy together," Marcel said staring into the peaceful abyss of liquid flying before him.

She's trying to make you understand that the only you can stop this madness. The water element stressed again, *only you.*

"But how?"

Don't you see, Master…you are the madness. Water stated.

Suddenly, the fire lashed out from the fireplace and devoured the bubble. *No!* The element of fire shouted, *It's all lies! THEY are madness.* In a rage Marcel had never seen before, a plume of flames ran around the room like a nice irate childhood tantrum. The air element snickered in the wind, *Here it goes again. They've been bickering like this since the planet created us.*

Fear should've gripped him, but curiosity did instead. Marcel watched as the flames left trails in his bedroom as it danced around. It bellowed, *Your own brother attempts to murder you. Masked like a dark creature. Beating my master with his fists until he bled than threw him off a balcony.* Marcel knew this story already and hated reliving it. The United Nations on a cold night and a shadow assassin attacking him; a bullet entering his brain and eventually leading him to a coma. A coma that led the way to an afterlife. An afterlife hosted by the lord of darkness. None of this would've happened if his brother Brent, hiding as an assassin, hadn't nearly murdered him. *It was his fault! He deceived you! He's madness!* Marcel tightened his fists; the fire grew lighting his bed into a massive flame. Brent's ghost appeared for only a moment before it ignited in the fiery rage.

Did you forget about Gabe? That's madness! An archangel from the Light posed as your friend. For years! Marcel pictured the older man, a better friend than any man he'd ever know. Then he pictured himself, humiliated, when found the truth…it was all just a lie. *A rouse to lead my master in the direction of the Light and their devious plan.* The room filled with smoke, but he didn't feel short of breath. The fire's tantrum circled more and devoured all his personal belongings into a bright yellow amber. *And what about Gerard! He lied the entire time! He said he was my master's best friend! Best friend! Then he destroyed what we'd worked so hard to accomplish!*

Curtains dropped to the floor and melted away like taffy over hot coal. Marcel watched, emotionless, as fire consumed his dresser and pictures, in wood frames, above the mantle. Pictures of a simpler time. Nelson and Victoria holding their children tightly, as though they might flutter away like feathers. Now, his father would blow away all the feathers. The Celests, America's happiest family, burned out of existence forever. His prescription pills, perfect for calming him and the voices of the elements, tumbled over then whisked away into incendiary oblivion. His sister's ghost appeared. Janice. Reaching out her hand. Fire dissolved her.

And Janice! My master loved her. And she ended her life. She did not love him! It's all madness! I will erase all of it. We will erase all those that hurt our master! I'm the most powerful of the elements!

Fire grew even more until it was all that could be seen. If the water element had an objection, it had been swallowed up into the combustion. Feeling overwhelmed by the deceit of so many loved ones, Marcel stood slowly and took a deep breath of ashes in the air. It circled around and around in a dizzying effect. Breathing in all this chaos felt soothing. The cancer in his lungs dissolved and he could inhale fully. His clothes burned away, leaving him naked. He could feel the power of the elements, stronger than ever before. And he didn't fear it. He embraced it. Fire slithered, *Yes, Master. Yes. Let us become one. Fuse with us and nothing will hurt you ever again.*

"Yes," Marcel sneered, "they aren't afraid of me. Not yet. But they will! I am no common human. I…am…a…god."

He fell to his knees. The flames stopped. Marcel opened his eyes. His skin had been charred but already began a rapid healing effect. More quickly than ever. With every breath he took, a slight puff of black smoke would dissipate into the air. Before him, standing in the middle of the now empty room, was the only entity in this place stronger than Marcel. With wide lustful eyes, Lucifer said, "What an anomalous sight. The manifestation of irritation. All my doubts have been erased."

On the glass of the windows, Marcel could see himself. Even his eyes were a darker shade of blue. The wind element opened the windows abruptly. Cold air left no chill up his spine. He couldn't recall it ever leaving a chill up his spine. In fact, Marcel couldn't recall anything. Memory of his prior life before this moment had been blurry; a bit of concentration helped to clear the clouds. But nothing affected his emotions. Anxiety became tranquility. Pessimism became optimism. Uncertainty became certainty.

He turned to Lucifer. It was like they'd never met. Like they hadn't visited the darkness of the cosmos. Like the creature hadn't shown the power of the universe. Like he hadn't explained Marcel's power to change the future.

"You have excelled your predecessors," the dark ruler grinned, "All humans have a fate, except you. You have and shall change the world's end."

Marcel nodded.

Suddenly, Lucifer looked away and paused. Then his eyes wiggled around in all directions. "My, my. What is that? Can you *sense* that?"

Marcel closed his eyes. In actuality, he could feel something different. The air seemed thicker. "The darkness. It's…unbalanced."

Lucifer's tongue licked his lips. "Ire. Rage. Murder. It has suddenly blown like a balloon. Not far away. Something has swallowed its vast amounts of dark matter."

"What has?"

His sudden enjoyment turned to reality. The entity's face drooped to a frown. A very concerned frown. "A crowd has gathered. Thousands. Tenths of thousands. All with a same aspiration…they approach for *you*, Marcel. They approach to end *you.*"

CHAPTER FORTY-FOUR

A wave of defiance, frustration, and rage crawled through the city streets. Royal expected to see withered faces asking such cowardly questions like *Should we really do this? Maybe we go back and try to negotiate? Is the Union all that bad?* But the hesitation ended when the tidal wave began. It moved through torn streets and battered buildings. They followed calmly behind Adam, Royal, and Bruno. For such a big brute with an easily anxious stomach, the man barely spoke. Those grasped fists were all he needed to enter this fight. Weapons ranged from guns, crossbows, and shotguns to more man-made contraptions like spiked bats, pellet grenades, and glass balls of acid. Royal carried a sort of slingshot made with rubberbands and a sack filled with dozens of sharp rocks that could pierce eyeballs. She pulled hair back through the opening in her cap. She didn't want to get blood on it.

Lightning crashed. Helicopters overhead shined spotlights. The Press loved a good show, but a lethal one made them reluctant. Vicious battles brought more viewers but also put them in danger. The choppers watched from a distance like vultures.

"Shouldn't we be holding up signs?" Someone asked. The first voice in nearly an hour of walking the streets of this torn town.

Adam replied sternly, "This isn't a protest."

Recruiters ran to houses, like rehearsed and gathered more people to join this army. No one thought for longer than a second before going into the house and exited with a weapon. Royal watched one woman, wearing an apron, grasp at her husband's shirt. He paid no mind to her tears and joined the necessary revolt. Across the street, on the other hand, Royal saw a wife join her husband and carried a frying pan in her hand. Silly, but that cast iron thing could do more damage that some of the weapons here.

Local police pulled alongside them. Two cops had nowhere near the strength to stop this resistance and they knew it. Carefully, they stepped out of their vehicles and stood aside. Royal turned and saw one of the policemen tear off his badge, then join the march with a shotgun in his hand. He was welcomed because anyone who wanted an end to the Union was welcomed.

Just as Adam had predicted, from a prior dream of the future, a line of Union vans blocked the street ahead. And just as Adam had said, the Union Keepers would seem bored and sick of this routine. It aggravated Royal. Who were they to just assume this is some typical protest? Like they were going to stop this mob of vexation. The Union Keepers hooked up a hose to their van while another got on a megaphone, reading something on a piece of paper. Royal, as the others, didn't care to listen. The speech was about dispersing and returning to your homes. No one listened, no one stopped marching. What started off as fatigued looks on the Union Keepers' faces suddenly turned to concerned looks. They rushed to hook up the hose and turn on the water.

Hundreds of gallons shot out and hit the front of the mob. People fell backwards. Adam and Royal covered their faces. She hadn't expected simple water to hurt so much, but at this speed Royal felt the sting.

Adam bellowed out, "Victor! Now!"

Victor, the pyromaniac with a limited vocabulary, stepped up. His suit clanked against the solid ground. Made of welded steel, claws that clung to the floor, and long mechanical arms - the suit looked terrifying. Strapped to its back was a large tank of gasoline almost as big as the eight foot tall suit. His face hid behind a storm window.

"What the fuck is that?" A Union Keeper shouted, pointing the water cannon at Victor.

Hundreds of gallons couldn't move this monstrosity. Even the liquid didn't penetrate the glass. The suit's legs stuck to the ground. And Royal saw something she'd never seen from the usual skittish Victor. His hands didn't shake as he took the controls and lifted the arms. From the suit, two cannons pointed out. She heard him whisper calmly, "Burn."

Fire shot out in a stream of light. Royal felt the warmth even though she remained at a safe distant. The fire covered two of the Union Keepers, giving them no moment to scream in pain as they melted in a black ash. The flames hit the vans, exploding them upwards. She'd never seen so much fire. It made her sweat. But it also made her smile.

Victor cackled so loud, it echoed back and forth in the empty street. His eyes never blinked. Royal read once that psychopaths didn't blink as much.

Once the fuel ran out, the fire died down. Left behind were the ashes of vans and six Union Keepers. But more were coming. Vans sped up and blocked the street. Without saying a word, Adam charged the crowd charged with him.

This was it. This was the end. They were about to commit mass murder.

Climbing over the vans, smashing the windows with bare hands, and yanking the Union Keepers out - the war began. Royal watched as bats, axes, and guns battered the Union Keepers. One of them had a wet spot around his groin. Another one's head got crushed by a frying pan. Royal eyed a piece of skull fly into the air. It was so wrong...but felt so right.

Adam lurched forward and fought three of the skilled Union Keepers with ease. A policeman leapt in, carrying a baton, and broke one of the Union Keeper's kneecap with a strong swing. It was the only noise in the street. Besides the occasional whimper from a Union Keeper or splash of blood hitting the concrete ground, it surprisingly quiet for such a brutal scene. Royal shot her slingshot through every neck she could, the Union Keepers' helmets were useless when the jugular vein was exposed. And she never missed.

A hard butt to the back of her head sent her falling backwards. Dizzying, but still conscious, she looked up to see a Union Keeper holding the butt of a semi-automatic rifle. She almost crawled backwards, but remembered Zharkova's words. *Silly girl, crawling away like some crab.* Royal looked around quickly and saw a blade on the ground. Before the Union Keeper could pull the trigger, she grabbed the blade and swiped it across the assailant's throat. Blood spilled out like an over-shaken Coke can.

Another wave of vans rushed in, possible twelve or maybe more. Royal sat up quickly. To her surprise, most of the Union Keepers were already dead. But this new amount of armed gunmen would be more difficult. Not only did they carry a rifles, grenades, and shields - but the Gatling gun in the back of their van created quite a challenge.

"He's here!" Adam bellowed.

Above them, high in the sky, a jet ascended. Before Royal could blink, the night turned into day. Missiles and bullets reigned down igniting the Union Keepers. One of the men screamed into a walkie-talkie for help, but a vehicle flipped over in flames and landed on him. Nelson's jet slowed and stopped in mid-air. More bullets came down. The Union Keepers tried to run to cover but ammunition penetrated their thick steel suits killing them instantly. Some of the attackers ran toward the People of Bliss. This must've been what Nelson called a Kamikaze syndrome; knowing they were about to die but taking down whoever they could. The crowd welcomed another fight. Fists came down, bats swung, and shots were fired.

Royal saw Adam fall to the ground. Behind him, a Union Keeper pointed a shotgun at the back of Adam's head. The first time she met this young nerdy man, she would've raced for the opportunity to kill him first. But now, she wanted to race to save his life. Royal dashed through the crowd, screaming, "Adam!"

Then the most shocking thing this evening occurred. From behind the Union Keeper, another suited Union Keeper approached. He reached around and snapped the neck of Adam's attacker. Before Royal could ask why one of the opposing forces just turned against his colleague, the friendly Union Keeper ripped off his helmet. He said behind glazed eyes, "I don't want to fight for them anymore."

The friendly reached out his hand to help Adam up. Without a moment of hesitation, Adam reached out his arm and was hoisted up. No one was turned away from the People of Bliss. No one. Even the enemy.

In only a few moments, the fight was over. For now. Royal could see several peoples' chest heaving up and down. Out of breath, but yet hungry for more. Their clothes soaked in blood and guts, most didn't bother to wipe it away.

Adam stared past the bridge at the Union Castle. "March!"
He commanded. And the People of Bliss continued their
walk. Royal noticed no news choppers hovered anywhere.

Darkness consumed far more than his soul. The mirror
showed Marcel a different man with even deeper circles
under his eyes. His skin paled in comparison to just a year
ago, even when he suffered a disease that kept him out of the
sun. No concerns or regrets crossed his mind as he calmly
placed his frock coat on. Staring in the mirror, he couldn't
help but notice the difference his bond with darkness did to
his eyes. Years ago, they shined bright blue and his stare
melted the hearts of women. Now he could control anyone
with that stare; make them do whatever he wanted. He
buttoned his frock coat and inspected his outfit. Brown
slacks, silver waistcoat, and comfortable dress shoes. He
looked professional, yet agile. Like ready to fight and give a
triumphant speech afterwards. Which he planned to do. He
hoped Gerard came for him. He hoped.

General Vanderbilt's conversation had become so dull and
repetitious that Marcel nearly forgot he was in the room too.
"I warned everyone this was going to happen. Dozens of our
men are dead and the invasion is still approaching."

"How soon can we get pilots in the air?"

Confused and dumbfounded, Vanderbilt asked, "Sir?"

Marcel repeated, "How soon can we pilots in the air?" In
the mirror's reflection, he could see Vanderbilt's eyes dart
around. So he clarified. "Blow them up."

"Some of our Union Keepers have left service because
they think our violent behavior lately has been dangerous. I
don't know if I can convince them to –"

Holding up his hand to interrupt, Marcel shook his head
slowly. "You know what politics and business have in

common? Someone is always telling someone what to do. There's always someone higher up. You think a store manager doesn't have a higher up to answer to? He does. You don't think a congressman has someone to answer to? He does. Always someone to be afraid of. But here's the thing, in the Union, there is no one higher up than me. What I say is the final decision. Understand?"

"I wasn't trying to be disrespectful," Vanderbilt answered with his head down.

Instead of his hand up, now it was his finger. Marcel stressed, "If they get in, past the gates and into the courtyard, there will be dead bodies all over the Union's property. It's messy. Kill them all before they get to the courtyard." He turned to put on his cufflinks, given to him by his father. "Except my dad. He stays alive. I don't care how you do it, but capture him again. I want to salvage what is left of my family."

Vanderbilt wiped sweat off his head. He had hired the general because of his uncanny lack of emotion. Yet found himself regretting his decision. Vanderbilt seemed overwhelmed. "Marcel, I —"

"Never call me by my first name!" Marcel shouted. "It's disrespectful! I've told you that." Usually guilty after screaming at an employee, Marcel felt nothing this time.

General Vanderbilt's breath stuttered. "I apologize, Supreme Leader. It's just that…you never got angry when Gerard called you by your first name…and…" he trailed off.

Mentioning Gerard's name made his teeth grind. Marcel wrinkled his nose. "Kill them all. By hand if you have to."

"Sir, there's tens of thousands of people and —"

He turned away from the mirror with wide eyes. Fury spat out of his mouth. "Don't let them in the courtyard! Kill them all!"

Vanderbilt tumbled backwards as the invisible gust of wind shoved him out of the room. He got up. Instead of running like a coward, which any general would never admit to being, he stood up and put his head down shamefully. "Yes, Supreme Leader."

A dangerous road led to the underground level of the Union Castle. Willie read once that Disney World had a massive operation below ground. But he doubt the entrance was through steep and windy turns. Gerard, whom he regretted agreeing to let drive, barely slowed down during their trek. Out the narrow opening from the trailer to the front of the truck, Willie could sometimes see the edge of a cliff or sometimes a large cloud of dust he left behind. After asking three times if Gerard was okay to drive, he did just lose a wife, the former Marcel ally stopped answering Willie. Best it be left alone.

Willie had prepared to die today. One sacrifice after another lately, why would he be any different? His fate had been to activate this machine and eliminate this world's addiction to electronics. As they descended a steep hill, he thought how tragic it would be if this truck flipped over onto the sharp rocks in the waters below. To throw away such an epic epilogue to his life story over Gerard's poor driving skills.

The truck rumbled and bounced onto a more level road. He felt the smoothness of a solid concrete road. This must be the entrance. He peaked out the window to speak to Gerard. "Their guns and alarms will shut off the closer we got to the gate. All we have to do is play dumb -" That plan was tossed out the window as Willie watched Gerard slam the accelerator. He grasped the handlebar as the truck crashed through the wooden gates. Union Keepers screamed and hollered, but no bullets were fired; their guns useless around the box."Careful, boss. Careful. Careful!" Willie grasped the handle again as Gerard drove the truck like a battering ram. They ran over the metal gates; the truck rattling up and down. More people screamed. They were in the lower garage now. Besides narrowly missing the steel columns in the parking garages, Gerard had to dodge motorists as they drove cars out. An evacuation must've been in place for the building's employees. Cars honked while other cars got turned over by the mass of the truck's push. Willie wasn't sure if the device had been sensitive to harsh rocking, but it was too late now. They screeched to a grinding halt, not because Gerard used the brake but because enough cars had been smashed into to create a barrier. Out the window he could see the truck's crunched hood spewing out steam and liquids. Vehicles were piled up on top of each other in front of them. Willie peaked further out the trailer's window to see Gerard had ran a number of Union Keepers; their bodies still wiggling under the truck's tires. After taking a moment to catch his breath, Willie said sarcastically, "I think we're at a good spot to activate the device now."

Gerard climbed out the driver seat and took a look around. "Well, that went better than I expected."

Wide eyed, Willie snorted, "You were expecting worse?"

"I mean, well yeah, do you see any of the bad guys around?"

As if on queue, a dozen armed surrounded them with guns pointed. Commands to get down on the ground were ignored. Gerard whispered, "The guns won't work, right?"

"Nope."

Gerard gave a satisfied smirk, "I got this. Activate the device." He ran toward one of the officers. Guns clicked to fire, but produced no rounds. Gerard jumped and side kicked one of the men.

It was like something out of Willie's favorite Kung Fu movies. But as much as he wanted to sit around and watch the men fight, time wasn't on his side. He climbed back into the trailer. Reviewing the online manual several times, Willie had been certain he knew how to activate the device. He popped open the top display. No touch screen or keypad, the machine operated manually by mixing liquids in internal chambers. He just had to turn the knobs in a certain sequence. It took time, but could be done in a few minutes. Checking his watch confirmed they were already behind schedule. The People of Bliss would be making their way up the hill by now. And armed gunmen would be waiting. Willie had to turn off their weaponry and every other electronic worldwide. He began the sequence, watching the meters for each liquid begin to recede.

This was the feeling of adrenaline. When the body ached and the mind became overwhelmed, a chemical would boost morality and press forward. That's how Adam felt. Like nothing could halt this storm approaching the Union's castle.

Up until now, the People of Bliss had kept their rebellion steady like a tank. Anything that got in the way should move or be crushed. As they crossed the bridge, Adam noticed the lack of offense. None of the Union Keepers attempted another advance; instead, they retreated to their safe place. But, little did they know, even a castle can't survive the strongest of storms.

No doubt, their military forces were planning an attack. Any kind of retaliation beyond simple water hoses and fists would surely be a challenge to the People of Bliss. Especially air forces. Nelson watched the skies and shot down any chopper in sight, but even he would eventually be overwhelmed. The time for a steady pace was over.

Past the bridge, the land went up a slope before reaching the outer perimeters of the castle. The climb could be rough for the injured among them. But with adrenaline, especially an angry determination, nothing could stop the People of Bliss. Adam began to quicken his pace. Besides the need to get this wave pumped up to rush over this hill, time was becoming a factor. Willie should be almost ready to obliterate the world's electronics including all the Union Keepers' guns. And guns would be their toughest challenge soon.

Adam's walk turned from speed walking to jogging. The people behind him began to follow suit, even Royal kept silent instead of whining. Then his jog turned into a run. They were smart, figuring out why they needed this push. Thousands behind him broke into a loud sprint, footsteps clanking against the last of the bridge's steps. They all followed the windy road up the hill; Adam's legs were on fire. If he experienced this pain, no doubt the others might have been in more anguish. But nothing stopped them. Nothing would.

At the top of the hill, Adam sprinted even faster. A surge of excitement built up in him. Just as he felt nothing could stop them…something did.

"Hold!" Adam screamed, but it was too late. Everyone smashed into a tall metal fence. Thankfully, Royal's voice was louder than his as she instructed the People of Bliss to stop, or else the front line of this crowd, including Adam, would've been crushed by the force.

"What the hell, Adam? Why is there a fence?" Royal demanded.

He'd sent dozens of scouts to this area and none of them came back with a report of a metal fence before the outer perimeter. It reached nearly fifty feet high, the chance of climbing over it was moot since barbed wired circled the edges. Adam rattled the fence, but it barely budged. It wasn't some typical chain link used around a house or prison yard; something else blocked them from their next goal. He rubbed the material with his palm, while Royal, once again, demanded to know why no one was aware of this obstruction beforehand. It could possibly have something to do with Gerard's recent stunt; the Union was higher guard now. Whatever the case, this metal mesh added an unnecessary delay. And Royal hated being late.

"Adam! We can't be messing around here! Just cut it with some pliers!"

He couldn't think with all this constant nagging. Adam retorted sarcastically, "What do you want me to cut this with? It's pure steel and titanium."

"Than just push it down?"

What a stupid idea. Adam bit his lip and shouted, "Are you thinking? We don't have the equipment to just break through this! What do you want me to do?" He spat out the silliest answer to his own question he could think of. "What? Chew through this with my teeth?"

Royal's mouth dropped at what Adam just said. Chew through it? His mouth dropped too. Realization smacked them both in the face at the same time. And at the same time, they both turned their heads to the corner Bruno had been standing in. From wherever he'd been stashing it, the monstrous man bit into a tiny bulb and ate it like cotton candy. His stomach was strong, but so were his teeth. Bruno, grinding the pieces of bulb in his teeth, looked back. "What?"

The way Vanderbilt saw it was: let them come. He'd fought in worse wars than this. In fact, he had led wars worse than this. The North Korean War had similar circumstances, the opposition seriously thought they could defeat a highly-technical armada and had been gullible enough to believe they were winning. General Vanderbilt liked playing the game this way. He once read that veal tasted better when the baby calf had given up on fighting and just accepted fate. The People of Bliss were falling into a trap and would soon have to accept their fate, as well. About 28 of his men had been slaughtered by the rebellion within that last hour, which had been chump change during the Syrian conflict. 36 years of serving the American military and he'd never felt so confident as now.

He slumped onto a comfy chair behind a group of senior staff. They overlooked the island not only through the window, but on surveillance cameras surrounding the perimeter. Computers zoomed in and out of their faces.

"We can't get an accurate count. There must be at least 25,000 of them." One of the senior officers mentioned, typing into a computer.

Before they asked again, Vanderbilt answered, "No. Hold off the choppers."

"We can get jets in the air –"

"I'm well aware our pilots are standing by. I ordered it, remember?" Vanderbilt sipped a cup of coffee, straight black because cream and sugar was for pussies.

Another staff member fought the urge to ask why. But already, six Union Keepers had joined the rebellion. Who knew how many of these could be on the inside? Especially after Gerard played the part so well; even Vanderbilt felt slightly betrayed he'd been fooled for over a year by that bastard. For now, the strategy remained in his head. Simply put, whoever was flying that high-powered jet was skilled. So skilled, that sending one or two jets at a time would surely be a kamikaze mission. Better to just regroup several fighter jets and overpower the People of Bliss.

For now, they were stuck at the fence. An impenetrable fence. Once they all crowded into a single spot, Vanderbilt would order hellfire from above. As long at they didn't get through the fence.

"Sir, they are penetrating the fence."

Vanderbilt spilled the coffee on his lap and didn't have a chance to yelp. He stood up, rushing to the surveillance camera. "What the..." Pausing to make sure what he was about to say made sense, to even him. "Is that a man...is he...chewing through our fence?"

"What do we do, General?"

Enough was enough. "Use the lasers. They're potent enough to seer skin. Let's see if they can eat that shit."

Minutes seemed like hours when time was running out. Activating the device took longer than Willie had anticipated. Four more liquids had to mix in order to expel an invisible shockwave that would shutdown all electricity.

The trailer felt humid, it made him sweat more. Whatever was going on outside, he hoped Gerard was winning.

Suddenly the trailer door swung open behind him. He thought it had been Gerard, exclaiming victory in knocking down several opponents. But instead, Willie turned to see someone completely different. The exact opposite of suave.

With a gun pointed in his direction, the Union's leader of technology Lester stood at the open trailer door. "Get your hands off the machine."

Lester stepped inside the trailer, waving Willie to get back. Willie reminded him, "The gun won't work around -"

"What an idiot." The Union Czar showcased his gun. "No lithium. No fingerprint. Just good old bullets. Step back."

Willie walked backwards slowly. Lester looked over the display case of the device. It didn't take him long to figure it out; perhaps, he'd done his own research after their talk at the warehouse about the power of the EMP. He switched off the sequence and the liquids stopped mixing.

Holding his hands up, Willie started realizing the severity of this situation. If he didn't activate the device soon, Union Keepers would start firing on the People of Bliss and the revolution would be over in minutes.

The fence had been penetrated...or *eaten* by what Vanderbilt could see. "Turn the lasers on and send troops down there. Tell them to fire at will." No hesitation followed and his staff got on their walkie-talkies immediately.

He looked at another camera, located down in the docking area. A massive trailer had crashed through a while ago, and to Vanderbilt's surprise...the problem hadn't been dealt with. His Union Keepers laid sprawled on the floor. He must've sent a dozen of them. Only Gerard could have that much skill. Vanderbilt pressed keys on the keyboard, with different angles of the truck until he saw Gerard battling two of the Union Keepers. Whatever was going on in that trailer, a bomb Vanderbilt suspected, must be dealt with quicker. And that meant putting Gerard down.

Vanderbilt hadn't been in much of a fight lately. Two years ago, he broke a man's arm, nose, and ankle for calling him a *faggot*. At fifty years old, he had no doubt his decades of combat training surpassed Gerard. But unfortunately that bastard had nano-technology in his blood. Training helped, but didn't guarantee a win. He needed something. "Did Lester finish the prototype for my suit?" Vanderbilt asked a rushed staff member.

"Yes, Sir. Should we send one of our troops down to handle –"

"No," the general smirked, "Shoot down the People of Bliss. I'll handle the Gerard."

Raised in the lower class slums of Philly, Willie should've been used to a gun pointed in his face. But he wasn't. He never experienced a moment like this. No wonder some people wet themselves, Willie was so frightened that he could feel his bladder loosening.

"What is this," Lester demanded. "What are you doing?"

Since lying could probably get him shot, Willie opted to tell the truth to the Union's Tech Czar. That his job would soon be futile. "I'm ending technology for good."

He started off with squinted eyes, then a snort. And before long, Lester's laughter echoed in the trailer. Willie took this moment to contemplate how to escape this situation. Escape this situation without being shot, of course. Chances were slim. Lester's smile slowly faded when he saw the seriousness in Willie's face. "Is this a joke? What? Jesus, you're stupid. You have any idea what you're about to do?"

Spending many nights thinking instead of sleeping, Willie confidently could answer. "Yes. Yes, I do know what I'm about to do. And I'm the only one that can do it."

After searching around for video cameras, Lester seemed convinced he wasn't on Candid Camera. "Didn't we chat about this already? So instead of a future like Star Trek, where we could whisk around galaxies and live longer, better lives…you'd rather have a future like Mad Max? What do you expect us to do? How do we live without technology? Huh?" The gun shook more than his hand. "Huh!" He screamed. "How is someone like me supposed to live without help? You expect someone like me to…what? Crawl around on my arms? Make a wheelchair out of sticks and rocks or something? I can't walk! I'm born a freak! I got horrid acne! And fat in places I don't want it stored! I'm a fucking cow! I'll die without technology."

"Life finds a way," Willie shrugged.

"Am I supposed to be looked at like some gross cripple? Be laughed? People comment on my crooked teeth or thick glasses? Supposed to be laughed at for the rest of my life? Is that how it goes?"

Reflecting on himself, his many flaws, Willie confidently said, "You gotta accept who you are."

"*Accept* who I am?" A bead of sweat skidded down Lester's forehead. "I said step away from the machine!"

If Willie was going to get shot, he might as well take Lester down with him. He snatched the gun. At the same time, Lester pulled the trigger. Bullets ricochet around the trailer walls. The two men fought, Willie could take a punch from a Philly hoodlum but Lester was pure bodybuilder. The punches hurt and his nose bled to remind him of that.

Lester shouted, "You're ending humanity!"

Kicking him in the shin and clocking a right hook on Lester's perfect chin, Willie stated, "No, I'm restarting it."

Miraculously, Bruno's mouth hadn't bled or even turned red from chowing down on a thick metal fence. In fact, when Adam pulled him away, the brute looked hungry for more. The next part of the plan would surely satisfy all the People of Bliss and their appetite. In moments, they would be in the courtyard to face possibly hundreds of Union Keepers. For now, the outer circle of the castle would have to be penetrated. Thanks to the help of scouters, Adam had prepared himself for the lasers.

 Unlike normal lasers that a professor would use for a PowerPoint demonstration, these high frequency were enough to penetrate skin. And also thin enough to penetrate the retina of an eyeball. Barely agile enough to beat Brent at a mile long sprint, Adam knew he couldn't make it through a barrage of dancing lasers. But he knew someone who could.

With the help of six other men, they pulled back and the torn fence hole bent backwards. On queue, the field ahead of them lit up with hundreds of faint red lasers, so faint they looked pink. They moved back and forth, up and down, left and right to block any entrance to the courtyard. Beyond this hundred foot stretch of what looked like the dance floor of a rave party, Adam could see a doorway to a maintenance shed. Inside that shed was an emergency off switch, used by landscapers in case the lasers turned on accidentally.

"How we supposed to get through that?" Royal said, squinting her eyes because she couldn't track the lasers or she was griping. "I can't barely see them."

"Yeah," Adam responded confidently, "but I know who can see them clearly." He turned to the crowd. "Pierre! You're up!"

Wearing a thin black suit, the Frenchman didn't hesitate and dashed forward. He leapt through the opening in the fence into the laser field. Pierre landed perfectly in the field into a handstand as two lasers passed between him, missing by inches. He back-flipped and front-flipped through more dancing red lines of pain, like he'd been practicing for weeks…which he hadn't. Pierre could see and hear better than any of them, making him the only candidate to pass this challenge.

"Adam!" Royal screamed, pointing to the north side of the field.

As much as he didn't want to skip watching the acrobatics of such a skilled individual, something more important came into view. Union Keepers, in riot gear, marched quickly out the side gate of the interior courtyard. AK-47s in hand, this would be an unwelcome dilemma.

"Come on!" Royal yelled again, not explaining anything as she hurried up a grassy hill to overlook the scene. By the time Adam made it to the top, Royal was already scuffling through Bruno's satchel.

"What are you doing?" Adam had to ask, heaving from all the physical and mental stress.

She yanked out black gear and a plastic handle. Before he could ask, Royal was already assembling it. It was a sniper rifle. "Sniper? Really, Royal?" Not only was it dark outside, she'd have to shoot through the holes of a metal fence and a distance of at least three hundred feet to hit any of the Union Keepers. He counted the armed men on the field, readying their weapons. Pierre would be shot in only a minute, ending his trail through the laser field. Adam took a breath, unsure of what to do to save Pierre. He counted the Union Keepers. "Royal, seriously, there's eleven men out there. We only have five sniper bullets."

"Good," Royal said, lying down with the sniper rifle locked and loaded, "I'll leave a bullet for Marcel."

She shot the first bullet. Adam covered his ears and his mouth dropped. The bullet flew through the grating of the fence, hit a Union Keeper in the neck, ricocheted off his helmet, and bounced into the hand of another Union Keeper. Before they could even understand what was happening, even Adam found himself overwhelmed, Royal fired another shot. The second bullet hit a shot fired by the Union Keeper. Adam had seen magic firsthand but still was dumbfounded by what he saw. The bullet hit the Union Keeper's bullet and sent it away from Pierre's dodging act toward the maintenance shed. He was almost there. Royal fired again. The third bullet bounced off a Union Keeper's machine gun, sending his weapon in the opposite direction as he pressed the trigger. His gun shot three others, by accident. The forth shot happened just as fast, hitting a Union Keeper's heel, another's foot, ricocheting off a sprinkler, then going through another soldier's cheek. Whatever men not injured or dead ran back into the safety of the courtyard. Royal accomplished something no other human being could accomplish and Adam couldn't have felt more proud. She turned, a red swollen circle around her eye from the scope of the gun, and said, "See. Told you. It's all about the timing."

His heart fluttered and stomach bubbled. She had never made him feel this way before. But now wasn't the time to reevaluate their partnership. Adam could see Pierre only feet away from the maintenance shed. And in minutes, he had reached the shed. Cheers from the People of Bliss blasted the night sky. Then, Pierre ran into the shed and hit a switch.

The red beams shut off.

"Go!" Adam commanded.

The People of Bliss crashed through the hole in the fence, tumbling over each other. Union Keepers guarding the wall before the courtyard hurried into the courtyard, leaving behind some of the other guards to be beaten by the People of Bliss.

Unfortunately for them, the wall of courtyard couldn't be entered. Not with the steel bolts locking the three entry doors. It couldn't be climbed either, being that it was fifty feet high. All those obstructions, and knowing the plan, didn't stop the irate mob from trying to infiltrate it. Some tried to climb over, using each other's shoulders, just so they can get to the other side and cover themselves with more Union Keeper blood.

"He's late," Royal stated. "By almost a minute."

"Give him time," Adam said. He tried to hide the worry in his voice. By now, Willie should've activated the electrical doomsday device and start the real war.

Through a swollen black eye, Willie could see Lester grasping for his neck. Anytime he used to watch old Van Damme movies, he'd think to himself how easy it would be to get out of that grasp. But all those techniques to loosen a death grip went out the window in the actual moment. Air had no way of entering the lungs, so panic immediately hit the mind. This wasn't like swimming, just paddling to the surface to get more oxygen; Willie had no way out. Too weak to kick or even squirm, his vision began to blur. Before he knew it, his hand was reaching out for a way. Not a way to save his life, but save those out there fighting for the future. He triggered a button that turned on the machine. It whirred to life.

"No!" Lester screamed as he let go and scrambled back for the machine. With air back in his lungs and his mind alert again, Willie went for the moment. He kicked Lester in the face, as hard as he possible could. Blood spat out from Lester's nose and mouth as he tumbled backwards, leaving a trail on the ground. Willie had no idea that much blood could escape a person face and he'd still be coherent. Well, barely coherent. Lester swayed for a minute before landing on the ground. He groaned, trying to stop the massive dripping from his mouth. Wherever Willie kicked, it did the trick, because Lester bled profusely.

Both men laid on the ground, catching their breath. The device whirred loudly, mixing the liquids inside. Lester tried to get up, his head must've spun because he landed back on the trailer ground with a thud. He crawled away from Willie. What was he up to? It looked like he was reaching for the door. Feeling cocky for being such a tough opponent that the Tech Czar was trying to flee for the door, Willie prepared to say one of those bad-ass Bruce Willis lines. He couldn't think of any of them. But at least the machine was only a minute from activating. He won the fight.

Lester reached out and grasped something. Not the door. But something. It was too late before Willie realized. It was the gun. He turned and fired at him.

Just like any of the dozen Tom Cruise action movies, being shot wasn't that easy neither. There was no sudden pause and glance down to see blood exiting the wound. Willie knew immediately he'd been shot; no doubt about it. It felt like being hit with a bat that had spikey ends on it. And no just one hit, but several. Even squirming an inch hurt like hell. Without even glancing down, he knew where'd he been shot. One thing he could remember from watching too much television was that being shot in the kidney practically meant death. Holding the wound to stop the bleeding was useless, because he bled on the inside just as much as on the outside. He had about as much time to live as that machine had to activate.

Lester, blood covering his mouth, pointed the gun again and pulled the trigger.

But no bullet exited. The chamber jammed with a loud click. If there was a God, he just bought Willie another minute of life. While Lester fiddled around with the gun, trying to fix the chamber, Willie contemplated why his life had just been prolonged. If God was real, he'd want this war to be won. And the only way it would be won was with this large device whirring next to him, seconds from destroying the planet's obsession with electricity. But if Willie died now, with Lester's last bullet, that hope would be gone because surely the villain would turn off the machine and end that hope. So that meant Willie had to kill Lester, quickly, before that gun fired a second time. What could possibly be faster than a bullet? The answer lied right next to him. He glanced down to see an electrical outlet in the trailer with enough juice to fry an elephant. Lester's chamber clicked. Willie grasped the electrical outlet, feeling its surge of power, and with the other hand touched the trail of the ground of Lester's blood.

A current, much faster than a gun's trigger, traveled through the trail of blood and zapped Lester. Movies had it all wrong. There's no thirty seconds of convulsing before death. One current stopped the Tech Czar's heart. In a nanosecond. Lester had been murdered by the one thing he obsessed over, and that was power. At least it had been a rapid end for him, Willie had a long, slow death to endure. And a painful one at that.

Two more chambers were left to fill before the machine erased all of mankind's electricity. Then he could die in peace.

The gun shot, no matter how many he'd heard in his lifetime, always made Gerard hold his breath. He swiftly spun but only saw the Union Keepers he knocked to the ground, either unconscious or dead. Dead, preferably. None of them had awoken for one last triumphant moment to shoot at him. So where did the sound come from? The trailer? It echoed, so it must've came from the trailer. Willie was in trouble and Gerard had been too preoccupied to notice.

He turned away from the stairs, beginning his hurried pace toward the trailer when a familiar robotic voice came from atop the staircase. "Where are you going?" The voice said, like an irritated male Siri voice. "You've been causing a lot of trouble."

Clank. Clank. As far as he knew, Vanderbilt wasn't an actual robot, so why did his footsteps sound like the Terminator? Gerard turned and watched as the shadowy figure began to come into view. *Clank. Clank.* Then in full view, he could see what caused the noise. Vanderbilt wore a metal suit, making his tall stature even taller. Black boots with four inch soles elevated him, thick copper wires travelled from the bottom of his soles to the devices around his hips to the black boxes on his arms to the aluminum collar. Protecting his head was a glass dome, secured around his neck. Gerard recognized the design almost immediately. It was Vanderbilt's blueprint for the new Union Keeper suits.

Gerard laughed. Not because he found the situation funny, but because Vanderbilt hated being laughed at. Intimidation was the key before a good fights. The general's face didn't frown, but stayed in the one-sided smirk. He did something with his hands, copper wires connected to each finger. It was some type of commands for the suit, because in the next moment Gerard's laugh died down. Blades slide out from the top of his forearms, throwing knives stuck out from under his hands, and from the device on his calves four more blades popped out.

With his fit of laughter now choked out of him, Gerard swallowed hard. "Damnit, I forgot about all the blades." He dashed to the other side of the docks, three throwing knives whisked by his ear and embedded into the walls. Vanderbilt's shoes clanked louder as he chased after him. Gerard fell and landed into piles of stacked crates. Inside the crates were fruits. He threw them at the approaching madman. Vanderbilt sliced the fruits out of his way, as he stormed toward him. Gerard laughed, "Hey, look! Fruit Ninja! Come on, Vandy-boo, have a sense of humor!"

The general grabbed his ankle. However this suit was constructed, it made Vanderbilt much stronger; Gerard could feel it in the grasp as he was yanked out from the wreck of crates. "Goddamnit, Vandy, don't make me have to hurt you!"

With a swift fling, Vanderbilt tossed Gerard like a frisbee. He flew through the air and gave a high-pitched girly scream. Hitting the side of the trailer, he could feel at least one of his ribs cracked. Of course, he had more than one rib broken in fights, but that didn't stop it from hurting like hell. Before he could get a chance to get up, Vanderbilt jumped off the dock ledge and landed only inches from his face. Gerard spun around quickly as his opponent did a roundhouse kick, lucky for him he blocked it because a knife retracted out of the boot and nearly sliced his throat. Vanderbilt did this again, and again, attacking with low kicks, high kicks, and roundhouses. With no other choice, Gerard dodged, blocked, and flipped out of the way of the boot's blades. "Willie! Blow it! Now!"

Willie's eyes flickered from clear to fuzzy. One canister released liquid into the chamber. He rested one eye and left the other open, as if this would buy him some time. Blood soaked his shirt and traveled to his pants. He tried to stop the bleeding with his hand, pushing it down, but the pain was unbearable. One wish he'd always had was to die quickly and pain-free. He could at least concentrate on making it pain-free as possible.

Hairs on his arms rose. Something was happening. Something catastrophic. And it wasn't his death. He looked up. The machine had activated. A pulse shivered through his skin and his ears popped from the invisible explosion.

Battery backup lights shut off. Air conditioning slowed to a steady stop. Fans halted.

Gerard looked up and saw Vanderbilt's suit making a whirring noise as it crept to a slow freeze, a blade from his arm only inches from striking Gerard's neck. Vanderbilt, confused and panicked, tried to escape the mechanical outfit but couldn't budge. Then he cough, choking on something deep in his throat. In seconds, his face turned pale. Gerard couldn't figure out what was going on. He stood. The general continued to gasp for air.

Smirking, Gerard nodded. "Damn voice box tech huh? Runs on battery, don't it?"

Secured deep inside his throat, a machine helped him breath and talk robotically, but thanks to Project Syncope the device died. Vanderbilt clinched his teeth as his already pale skin turned blue. The ironic situation made Gerard giggle slightly, even if it did seem inappropriate. Considering Brent Celest had broken Vanderbilt's throat when he found out the general murdered Sirius Dawson, this was becoming a satisfying irony to watch.

Eventually accepting his fate, Vanderbilt's head bent forward and collapsed, his suit keeping him standing upright like some military memorial statute. Maybe he did deserve a better death, the man had fought for this country over thirty years. He used to be a good man. So did Gerard. But he decided, before embarking on this battle tonight, that this fight wasn't good versus evil...but evil versus evil.

CHAPTER FORTY-FIVE

If at all possible, Adam sensed the wave from Project Syncope. No doubt, he wasn't alone. Royal's eyes squinted. She felt it too. A massive pulse from the center of the Union Castle that travelled at the speed of a shuttle around the globe, bouncing off the ignited nukes and becoming stronger. He wondered how many people stammered and swayed for that moment, like him. Not from the fact that's lights went out, that was nothing new. But that sensation was.

The Union Castle went black. Lights didn't sputter out through the windows and towers, they just disappeared. Like they never existed. He thought about his precognition of a future with something besides electricity. Fusion? Light? Whatever it was, it didn't harm the planet. Maybe it was time to experience something–

"Goddamnit, Adam! Get out your damned head. Look!" Royal shouted, pointing over the hill where they watched the wall. Thousands of people, just as confused as him, stood facing the electric door. The door swung open.

"Go!" Adam's voice boomed.

The People of Bliss crammed through the door. Union Keepers ran their other directions. Some of the soldiers attempted to fire weapons, but no bullets released the chambers. Plummeted by the force of thousands, those Union Keepers disappeared into the massive. Unlike the streets before the castle, the rebellion didn't go in quietly. They hollered angrily as they entered the courtyard. The courtyard could've fit hundred football fields. Union Keepers used their guard shields and blockades, but nothing kept the rebels at bay.

And nothing would.

Death tried to sneak up on Willie, like how he used to do with his boy playing hide-and-seek. Warm. Cold. Colder. Warmer. Warmer. Worldwide, Willie imagined locusts falling to the ground and guns failing. Lights popped off leaving people more in the dark. Everyone must've been wondering when the power would return. It wouldn't.

The trailer door popped open. Blurry vision and utter darkness kept Willie from seeing who it was. "I heard a gun shot and…well, holy shit….look at that…there's a dead body in here. Good job, Willie."

Gerard, battered and beaten, still carried along his sense of humor. It wasn't until he saw Willie, clamored in the corner bleeding, did his smile fade. "You got shot?" He hurried over and knelt down. From his pocket he pulled out a cloth.

"Damn. I was hoping you were going to tear off the bottom of your shirt. Gotta give me something to see before I die," Willie flirted and smirked, his voice hoarse.

"You're not gonna die."

"Hmph. Janice wasn't kidding. You are a great liar."

Gerard said nothing. He placed the cloth over the wound. "The trick is to not put pressure on the bullet. Keep it there to slow the bleeding."

It had, in fact, felt less painless the way Gerard held it. Willie put his hand over the cloth and pushed down. At least it would give him a few more minutes to live. Warmer.

"Can you stand?" He asked.

Willie shrugged. Maybe. Maybe not. "What's the point?"

Everyone had a fate in this fight and he had accomplished his. Project Syncope had just reversed time and placed the human race a two hundred years backwards. He imagined most people were clicking their light switches on and off. Computers, laptops, smartwatches were dealing with the frustrated fingers of humans wondering why they didn't work. And Willie had been the pioneer of it all. His fate had been completed. Now, it was time to join his family in the afterlife. There was no point in standing.

"You'll go down in the history books, you know that right?" Gerard nodded. "'William Cooper released everyone from the digital prisons.' I'll make sure they print it. If we can even figure out how to print now without computers."

Willie laughed, but even laughter hurt his side. After their smiles faded, he said, "Go, man. There's only one thing left to do."

After a deep breath, Gerard said, "Marcel."

Slowly nodding, Willie repeated. "Marcel."

It would've been too awkward to hug or even shake hands. They barely knew each other, but yet their mission kickstarted a war. Maybe someday statues would be built. The thought made Willie snicker as he watched Gerard rush out the trailer door and leave him alone again.

"Hell of a place to die, though," he said to himself. The device stunk like a worn casket from a car. Even Lester's burnt carcass began to sting Willie's nose. The bleeding had slowed, turning that cloth from white to red. No telling how deep that bullet went. Too deep to dig out, for sure. But was it right to sit here and die? In this awful place? When a battle outside was killing people in heaps.

Pierre.

He hadn't thought of him until now. Butterflies surged in his stomach. That Frenchman made Willie feel a burst of energy. Warmest. With just a little willpower, he could lift himself up and walk out to the battlefield. Maybe he would have enough energy left to tell Pierre no one since his dead husband gave him stomach butterflies. Stress and anxiety of being rejected seemed to disappear in the last minutes of life, because Willie didn't feel worried at all. With one hand grasping the inside of the trailer wall, he stood up.

The Rules of War. Adam had to study it in college. War crimes were an actual thing. Military officials could serve prison time for breaking regulations. He always thought to himself how their could be code of ethics during battles. At the end of the semester, he failed the final test. As he dashed up a hill, with thousands of followers hollering behind him and craving an end to government, he realized what he realized then…there were no rules. Street fighting had limits, the goal was to incapacitate an opponent. Tonight's fight didn't need any incapacitated opponents. Adam, like all the rest, wanted dead ones.

Seeing this rage in all their eyes, the Union Keepers began to either back away or step forward. Their useless barrier was about to smashed down. A hundred of them couldn't hold thousands of rebels. As they approached this line of naive Keepers, Adam could see that same rage transfer to the officers. Maybe they were sick of the People of Bliss. Maybe they believed in the Union and had to protect. Maybe they were just plain fed up with this evening. The Keepers gathered and held their ground before the castle, while the resistance dashed up the hill.

It's called the Shield and Spear paradox, when an unstoppable force meets an immovable object. The effect is a paradox since neither can truly exist. But Adam was about to find out what happens. Both forces collapsed into each other. Chaos exploded. Blood splurged out from somewhere, his face immediately covered in it. People fought with weapons, and when the weapons broke, they fought with fists, and when the fists hurt they fought with broken weapons. Guns fired here and guns fired there. There was no coherence to this brawl, one moment Adam would kick an opponent and be grasped from behind by another, and then that opponent's face got smashed by a frying pan, and another opponent would punch him in the gut. Using whatever ammo they had left, bullet holes ripped through the uniforms and chests. A moment later, he found himself knocked to the ground, gasping for air. Everything hurt, ribs, bones, head, and even his knuckles. Just when he thought he had no more energy to go on, he saw the tattoo on his arm. The name Brent Celest seemed darker than the night sky. What would Brent do? He'd murder all these assholes.

Adam thrust his body to stand and was immediately soaked in some kind of white goo. A Union Keeper pointed a hose and spewed out something that looked like silly string. It was riot foam, but he'd never seen it firsthand. The substance solidified Adam's feet to the ground and dried so quickly he had no chance to move. Before he could cry for help, two chubby brute women ran up. One sprayed a mace can in the Keeper's face and he backed away with the riot foam tanks strapped to his sides. The other woman, who reminded him of a female version of Hugh Jackman, blanketed Adam in some kind of potent liquid using one of those water pump sprayers. He held his breath, as much as he was dying to breath, the smell was too much. It burned his lungs.

She leaned closer to him and her voice even sounded like the Wolverine himself. "Now, I'm going to kick you...hard. It'll break you free. Got it?"

Adam nodded. "Do it!"

"You ready?"

"Yes!"

He wasn't ready. The female kicked like a horse would, his body flung out of the riot foam cast and hit the ground hard. Adam took a deep painful breath of air, but he was alive.

The sound of the riot foam coating others could be heard over their hollers for help. It didn't take long before the Keeper with the riot foam was overtaken by six people. Adam looked away as he saw one of the rebels point the foam tube down the Keeper's throat. Looking away didn't help, because Adam could hear the gargling as they injected foam directly into the adversary's mouth.

All this mayhem didn't stop the opponents from trying to control the situation. He glanced up to see gas canisters being thrown at the crowd. But before they even hit the ground, the cans were batted away by a group of very skilled teenage boys. Each of the cans flew back into the Union Keepers' territory, sending the officers running and coughing convulsively.

More people joined this center of fighting. One man yelled, "This is for hurting us!" He bashed the end of crowbar into an officer's head.

Running into this mosh pit of commination like a new rock song just started playing, Victor cackled in his machine monster. He shoved aside friends and tossed away foes. Plumes of flames shot out for his wrist cannons. Adam had never seen what happens to a human body under fire. Besides the instant blackening of the skin, the victim never screamed or tried to run, almost like it couldn't. Suddenly, the tanks on his back hissed, presumably empty. Without his wildfire arsenal, Victor was an instant target. Dozens of Union Keepers ran and leapt on his equipment, tearing off the tanks and knocking him to the ground. Adam tried to push through the riot to help, he refused to see another friend die by the hands of the Union and its mindless minions.

Surrounded by vicious Keepers, he could only see the strained and wet eyes of Victor. He looked at Adam and grinned. Victor mouthed the word, "Boom."

"Oh shit," Adam realized. He turned to the crowd. "Back away!"

Victor's suit detonated. Metal arms and human arms flung into the air. Adam covered his ears, but it didn't stop the ringing. The heat felt like standing next to the sun. Dozens of Union Keepers ran away, suits on fire or dragging burnt corpses.

With no time to mourn Victor's sacrifice, Adam became bombarded by more Keepers. He fought like Brent would, skilled and ready. Using their own force against them, he sent officers rolling over themselves. He broke one of their hands then bashed their jaw in before the agonizing scream escaped the victim's mouth. Adam fought so many, that he lost count of how many lives he'd taken.

What seemed like an endless fight, suddenly began to calm. No longer surrounded by suits, he felt the need to survey the area. Though their side had lost few, the Union side lost all. Besides less than a dozen Keepers running for the hills, it looked like the brawl was coming to a close. He viewed his body, covered in so much blood it looked like another layer of skin.

The ground, once a beautiful lawn colored green was now colored red. He took a moment to really see the castle. It did catch the eye's full attention. White marble floors that had probably been polished that morning were smeared with guts. The People of Bliss became quiet, like almost in this same state of mind as Adam. Atop the castle wall stood a single balcony with well-crafted gargoyles around it.

Gerard said to stay away, that Marcel Celest was his target to handle. But staring at that balcony made Adam want to see the dictator. He wanted to look in those eyes and see what defeat would seem like in those powerful blue crystal eyes. Besides, he knew that disseminating his army wouldn't be enough. That was like eating a banana split without savoring the cherry on top. Judging by the smirks of the People of Bliss, they craved the same. Marcel Celest's blood.

What was it that the "Supreme Leader" hated to be called? Adam took a moment to reflect before remembering. Marcel Celest found it disrespectful to be called by his first name. As any leader would.

From the deepest part of his lungs, Adam thundered out, "Marcel!"

The People of Bliss cheered.

Conclusions can be so abrupt sometimes. Like the death of Marcel's mother. Like the death of his sister. Like the death of his brother. So quick and unexpected. Marcel didn't like being caught off guard. Sure, he knew the People of Bliss were approaching. What he didn't expect was they'd make it this far.

He heard his name called. His first name. How disrespectful of all he'd done. Anyone in a mile radius heard it. Thunder couldn't move the earth the way they did. He had to hand it to the People of Bliss. They utilized the Darkness. And, up to this point, it worked. But he ruled the Darkness, not them.

After all the lights went out, he left his office, even taking a moment to lock the door just in case the People of Bliss actually infiltrated the castle. Lots of secrets lied in that office. He made his way through the dark hallways with ease, while his personnel struggled to see and grasped at the wall. Darkness was his friends, not there's.

"Hug the left side until you feel the doorway," he said politely, "that's the staircase down." Not exactly orders to evacuate, since Marcel knew there was no evacuating. No plans of leaving this building. If the resistance got into this castle, all these lives were in danger. But maybe if they hid in the basements, it might give them a chance of living.

"Thank you, Supreme Leader," someone said that looked remarkable like his mother. Again, Marcel shook the thought of his dead family away. This wasn't a time for mourning, but for massacring. Massacring all those that fought for the Light.

He climbed up a spiraling flight of stairs to the watchtower. Inside, it was usually so dull and boring that he never came up here. Tonight though, panic ensued. Two members of his security team were underneath a desk. On top of the desk, several monitors that usually showed live feeds of the area were off.

"I don't get it!" One of them yelled. "Even the battery backup isn't working."

"How's that possible?"

Another member of the staff, a female beauty that Marcel might've pursued if his obsession of Janice hadn't been so steady, looked out the glass onto the courtyard below. She had been the only one that noticed him standing at the doorway. Her face wet with tears. "Supreme Leader, they killed them."

He opened his arms and she ran into them, resting her head into his shoulder to cry more. "Our friends," she sobbed, "they're murdered our friends. Stepping on their dead bodies like…mud."

Brushing her hair, the way he did Janice's hair at their mother's funeral, Marcel said, "They are all savages. It's in their nature. But we are better than that. Keep your head up."

"Supreme Leader," one of the men said, sweat drenching his uniform, "I don't know what to do. All our systems are down. I can't even make calls. Guns are down, scanners don't work, but I may have an idea to bring in manual guns from a nearby warehouse."

The scandalous woman in Marcel's arms extended out her face. He gazed at it. Being a part of the darkness, he could feel emotions. Emotions so strong that her glazed eyes and red nose couldn't convey. Her mouth couldn't say it either. But he knew what she craved. The same thing he craved.

"Don't bother," he whispered, "I will take care of all of them." The woman tried not to smile, only letting her lip curl slightly. There was nothing wrong with revenge. Revenge solved almost every conflict. Why not tonight? He stepped away and turned to the door.

"But, Supreme Leader," the nervous staff member said, blocking the doorway, "There's thousands of them. And -"

His shadow grew. The man cowered backwards, seeming so much smaller than Marcel. His double chin wobbled as he looked away from Marcel's glare. This moment seemed familiar, a bully hovering over the geeky kid. The geeky kid that was so much smarter and better at grades. The bully, annoyed by his parents, wanted to just punch the geek over and over again. That bully was Brent. That kid was Marcel. So this was why his brother enjoyed to antagonize. It was uplifting.

"Are you afraid of me?" He said softly.

The cowardly fatso that dared to stand his way was now on his knees, staring at the floor. Any other time, he'd feel sorry for this poor soul. But it was weak. And weak was why they were in this predicament in the first place. The man mumbled the truth, because lying was impractical in front of a god. "Yes, Supreme Leader."

"Good," Marcel said leaning down. "So are *they*."

With that, he turned and walked out the door to stop this madness.

Royal's view had been obscured the entire battle, but she stood her post above the hill with Bruno by her side. With the sniper rifle still in hand, she scanned the crowd. When Adam bellowed Marcel's name, she understood that this war was something more than collapsing the Union and any government control, this war was about freedom. Oppressed freedom that sat in the depth of the vocal chord, controlled by stress, rules, and even by oneself. It had escaped in the castle courtyard this moment.

After searching the crowd through the glass scope, she couldn't find Adam. But he was alive. And once she got this shot on Marcel Celest, the war would be over.

From the balcony, glass doors slid open and the curtains swayed violently, even though there was no wind. Using her jeans, she wiped her sweaty hand and placed it calmly on the trigger. One bullet and this would all be done.

Marcel Celest stepped onto the balcony.

Rowdy and unruly, suddenly the crowd quieted. Unsure the Supreme Leader would even make an appearance this evening caught some of the rebels off guard. Rumors beforehand said he would be too chicken-shit and would just hide in his office. Apparently not. While some took a step back, others took a step forward. But everyone was silent. So silent, she could almost hear their exhausted breaths.

"People…of…Bliss." Marcel said. His voice carried through the winds. Royal covered her ear. It was like the dictator was only inches from her head. "Bliss?" He repeated. "This is bliss? Death? Murder? Deceit? This is what you want for the future of our world?"

Her covered ear could still hear that voice. That disappointed voice. Bruno shielded his ears. "Shoot," he commanded. Until he said that, Royal had forgotten about her grasp on the rifle. Her left hand shook. It never shook. Around her, others masked their ears from the sentimental tone.

"You see me as the villain? You're wrong. I am the savior," Marcel said, his words making Royal feel a sense of guilt. "You are Casca's dagger lunging for Julius Caesar's throat, Booth's gun pointed at Lincoln's head, and the noose around Hussein's throat."

"Shoot," Bruno repeated.

"What if," Marcel whispered, "What if they all lived? The world would be vastly different. Who are you to decide the fate of our rule?"

Royal took a deep breath, concentrating on the sights of the scope. It was about the timing. Always the timing. Not the aim. She waited. Marcel wobbled his head. Just stay still. For just a nano-second. Then they could being a new world.

The Supreme Leader paused and looked ahead, his eyes black as the sea at night. He looked directly into Royal's scope. She pulled the trigger.

Marcel held up his hand and the bullet stopped in mid-air, inches from his nose. It spun, red in color. Royal stood up. "Oh God. I missed." She'd seen that look on Marcel's face. It happened the day of the rally. Right before he attacked hundreds of innocent civilians with the powers of wind. "Run!" She bellowed out, nearly tripping over her feet as she dashed down the hill. "Run! Everyone!"

Calmly, the dictator reached up and grabbed the spinning bullet. His lip curled as he set it down on the balcony ledge.

"Run!" Royal pled to dumbfounded people.

As though he could somehow hear her, he called out. "It's too late for you." Marcel shot his palm and hundreds of rebels flew in the air, screaming. More people flung like rag dolls and landed on top of each other. Terrified cries filled the courtyard. Royal tried to help people up, but got toppled by people running away from the castle.

"No! Stand your ground!" Adam's voice echoed. It broke as he repeated, "Stand your ground!"

A whirlwind dragged Royal and others into a circular hurricane. She tried to grasp onto the dirt, but could find nothing to hold onto. Dead bodies smacked her to the point she had no idea which direction she was going. People pled for help. "Please God, help!" Someone called out.

Grabbing her feet, a woman begged, "Help me!" She lost her grasp and smashed into the side of the castle.

The whirlwind stopped, but the chaos didn't. Dizzy and bewildered, Royal tried to stand. She could see Marcel's smile even from this distance. Thrusting his hands outward, more people flew backwards in thin air. In just a few minutes, the People of Bliss were screaming in triumph but now were screaming in horror.

"I'm sorry," Marcel's voice whispered, so sincere that she could imagine his eyes watering. "But in order for there to be peace…you all will *have* to die."

The ground rumbled. Whatever was next, Royal wouldn't even have the chance to make it. Make it to Adam and demand they retreat. No one expected this. Expected him to be this strong and this sadistic. She tried to get up again, but something grasped her leg and made her fall again. Turning, Royal couldn't understand what was happening before her. A dead Union Keeper, one eyeball with a knife stuck in it and lips crystal blue, tightened its hand on her ankle. Black goo raised from the ground. Whatever it was, it made the dead immediately undead. Seeping into the corpse's open wounds, the black matter coursed their veins like a new blood. With one twist, the Keeper threw Royal across the field. She slammed into the ground, face down into the mud. Hurriedly, she cleared the dirt from her eyes.

Surrounded by slews of raised dead, Royal wasn't the only one in danger. Everyone killed by the hands of the rebellion had come back for revenge. She watched as her side of this fight was losing, when she had been assured their fight was already won. The undead chased after the living, ripping off arms, breaking legs, and cracking necks. She crawled backwards, like a lobster.

A lobster. The thought reminded her of Zharkova, the Russian leader and her gang assault. Even though a vicious, bitter woman, she had a point. And Royal not crawl away in a panic no more. A zombie stormed toward Royal. The same one with the dagger in its eyeball. It motion down to grab her, while she reached out to grab the knife from his socket. She yanked it out and then cut its throat. The Union Keeper stumbled backwards as the black goo spat out from its mouth. It was all about the timing. She waited until the undead tumbled forward and she cut its head completely off. Decapitated, the corpse lost its color again and the black goo returned to the ground.

"Cut their heads!" She commanded. "It's not over! Cut their heads!"

Expecting shouts of triumph, Willie instead heard shrieks of terror. He finally made it up the staircase onto the courtyard. Corpses, from both sides of the battle, had been piled up everywhere like it was trash day. People fought with a ferocity that would make even wrestling fans cover their eyes. He was immediately thrown back by two men brawling and fell down the flight of stairs onto the grass. Surely, the bullet wound opened up again because he felt the cloth in his hand soak with blood.

"William!"

Only one person would call him that. Pierre swiftly dodged through the crowd to Willie's side. "I've been shot," he stated to keep the Frenchman from tackling him. "I'm dying."

"No, you're not!" Pierre demanded, as though it was his choice. "Get up. Is there a safe place we can hide?"

Willie looked around the horizon. Outside the gates, he watched as Nelson's jet swooped down and fired on incoming vehicles. Bullets, like spots of light, shot back at the jet in a useless attempt to take it down. More fleets were approaching and Nelson could only do so much. Besides the mayhem outside and the mayhem inside, Willie couldn't see many options. "There's trees, to your left." He said through his teeth, trying to stand. Pierre's warm hands aided him to walk; being that he was blind, Willie did most of the guiding.

They reached the set of trees and Willie sat his back against the trunk. This was his moment. The moment he could say goodbye, but he didn't even know where to begin. Before he opened his mouth, Pierre put his hand up. "I know how to fix you."

Considering the amounts of blood discoloring Willie's clothes, he couldn't imagine how to be fixed except with a doctor.

Pierre said, "I'm going to need you to glow."

It was over.

Marcel took a deep breath and smelled relief. The blood of a rebellion spilled onto the courtyard and he could only wonder how they would get that grass to be green again. "That was for hurting us," he whispered. And he meant it.

For all those years of silly oppression and violent demands, the government's rebellion would finally collapse and be buried before the Union Castle. A structure built on the past, for the future.

Dark matter seeped from the ground like oil had been struck. It latched onto more of the undead. Without looking, he could feel Lucifer's hand pat his shoulder. Together they had accomplished what none of his predecessors, a line of men and women with his power to alter the future, could do. The Light was gone.

"Sir?" A voice behind him said. Sensing by the tone, it wasn't the first time he'd been beckoned. Either that or the officer couldn't interrupt Marcel's magical slaughter of thousands.

"Yes?"

"It's urgent. Without power, we lost track of…him."

There could only be one *him* being referred to.

Disney World used to have this amazing smell when entering the park. As a kid, Marcel used to wonder how they did it. How a smell could create both desire and taste. And now, he had that same overwhelming feeling. Except this time it was Gerard's deceit. The odor tasted sweet. Sweeter than the others. And just like at a theme park, he'd have to follow that scent. Because it was just too satisfying to let the opportunity pass by.

"How long before the manual guns arrive?" Marcel asked, eyes closed concentrating on Gerard. What he had done. What fate will await him.

"They should be crossing the bridge soon. Next fifteen minutes or so."

Opening his eyes, Marcel looked down at the fighting in his courtyard. Blood really did squirt out of torn ligaments, just like those horror movies he used to watch as children with his brother. Brent would stare wide-eyed while Marcel peaked through the slits between his fingers. Pity that his brother had to be murdered, in this exact spot actually. Marcel looked to the floor. Even after six coats of paint, he could still see Brent's blood soaking the floor.

"Sir?"

Whatever the officer asked him, he didn't care. Marcel commanded, "When the guns arrive, shoot whoever is left and hang their bodies for people to see."

Clinching his hands, the officer asked cautiously. "Maybe this is going…um…we shouldn't…I mean…hang them…where?"

Marcel shrugged. "There's hundred thousand of them. Hang them…everywhere." He turned and walked through the balcony door. "I will handle my brother-in-law. Let's prepare to hang his corpse over my balcony."

CHAPTER FORTY-SIX

Even though he didn't need the boost in confidence, Marcel reminded himself he was a deity, a god with the power of persuasion. Persuasion that can control elements and minds. Gerard would be dead before this brawl even began.

He wandered the floors of the castle, sniffing out the delicious scent left behind by Gerard's rage. Particles of dark matter crowded the air, but gave him his best sight.

He betrayed you, a candle burning said, trying to provide some light to the blackout.

Another candle, on a table in the hallway, ignited by itself. *Let no one else defy you, Master.*

Gerard needs to be a message, the wind from an open window said, playing with the curtains.

Marcel tried the door to the left. The kitchen area. Potent smells filled the room, but not the dry odor of Gerard's darkness. He closed the door and continued up a staircase, spiraling towards the thirteenth floor of the castle. As much as he enjoyed roaming this structure, he found himself in a rare place. The thirteenth floor was empty, a vastly open space with nothing but stained glass walls allowing some moonlight in. Saints and Archangels stared, colored by enriched and vibrant tones. The room used to be the Throne Room. In the center, a flat pedestal used to house a large chair. A king would sit, surrounded by worshippers and loyalists. Maybe, after they cleaned up the bodies of the People of Bliss, he'd reestablish a throne in this room and make it a place where everyone would bow to him.

He's here, a gust whispered.

Marcel knew, he could sense Gerard. But where? Nanobots in his blood surged as adrenaline pumped through the heart. Besides storage boxes and cabinets, there weren't many places to hide. Marcel stepped onto the pedestal in the center of the room.

Something clicked behind him. He turned quickly. In less than a blink of an eye, he saw Gerard ten yards away using both hands to point two guns. Bullets spat out and Marcel held up his palm. Wind swatted the bullets away, breaking the stain glass windows and ricocheting off the concrete walls. It was an automatic gun and the bullets seemed endless. Gerard dropped one gun when it was out of ammo, while continuing to fire the other one, then yanked another gun off his belt and kept firing. Holding his bond with the air element, Marcel created an invisible shield and bullets kept flinging away. He ended up stumbling to the ground backwards while holding his palm out, it's all he could do in the force of the firepower.

Finally, he ran out of ammo. Gerard tried two more guns hidden in his back pockets. Both clicked empty. Always trying to be sarcastic, funny, or both, Gerard said, "Seriously? Not even *one* bullet got through?"

Marcel stood slowly, not smiling, preparing for this Mexican standoff with fights and not guns. The time for joking concluded this evening. Before he could Marcel could even clench his fist, Gerard rushed in and jumped. Both feet swept into Marcel's chest and he flew back. His opponent left little time to focus, spinning kicks and swift punches kept Marcel from concentrating. He blocked one movement, but immediately got socked with another. It was like fighting a large snake with hands tied behind his back. Gerard struck at his nose and it snapped. Blinded by blurry vision, Marcel did his best to continue blocking punches and kicks only to dodge half of them. He finally had an opportunity to grasp Gerard's waist, he body slammed him to the ground. With this brief moment to catch his breath, Marcel pointed his finger and panted, "I get what you're trying to do. You're trying to break my concent-"

Before he could finish the word *concentration*, Gerard kicked his mouth and Marcel lost his step. His adversary flipped back up. Every uppercut, jab, and side kick was countered by Gerard; the bastard had prepared for this fight. Everything Marcel had been taught by his best friend was used in retaliation and defiance.

He shoved a stack of boxes over Gerard and took this minute to quickly aim his attention on the element of air. Shards of stained glass lifted off the ground. Not even surprised by the magic, Gerard dodged behind pallets of stone as the shards smashed the walls only inches from his head. Marcel checked around desperately for the help of water or fire elements, but it was too late. Gerard ran and slammed him, knocking them both out the window.

Falling for a few feet, they crashed onto the top of wooden scaffolding. Marcel tripped over his own feet and grasped onto the wiring. Sounds of wood snapping echoed in the bitter cold air. The scaffolding shook as more wire snapped. Gerard put Marcel into a head lock. He cried out, "You're going to kill us both!"

Gerard punched the side of his head, "That's..." he punched again, "...the..." and punched again, "...point!"

Marcel twisted and the both fell backwards, plummeting onto the next floor of the scaffolding, breaking the tether holding it to the castle. The entire structure swayed as more wires loosened. Both men grasped tightly as the angry wind made the matters worse, without his direction the elements were disobedient children. Hundreds of yards below them, ocean waves crashed onto the peninsula the castle stood on. Maybe the water could help him. Marcel reached out his hand to it, pleading, and the ocean began to swirl.

Suddenly, Gerard kicked a latch and the scaffolding released. Ten stories of steel rods and wood floors leaned to the side. Marcel clung to the metal pillars holding the scaffolding together. It fell over so much, it became practically a bridge. As fast as it tumbled, it halted, leaving them dangling by whatever cords were still holding it for now. The force of the bounce nearly made him lose his grip. He looked to see Gerard holding onto like monkey bars. Without even hesitating, his brother-in-law tried to kick at him. Marcel lost some of his grip and was left swinging like monkey bars too. They both were trying to kick the other loose. Marcel refused to get beaten, beaten like Brent had beaten him. Screeches of metal bending pierced his ears. Gerard wouldn't give Marcel even the slightest moment to concentrate on the waters below to save them.

A loud crack and the scaffolding gave way.

They fell, gravity shoving them down to the ocean so far down. Marcel, feeling like a parachute without a parachute, did his best to focus and open the pupils of his eyes. Water listened, twirling up to create a water spout like a worm. The large entity, more vast than the castle itself, reached up and caught Marcel. The spout's end, a wall of liquid, hurt as he pummeled onto it. Before Marcel could compose himself,

Gerard fell next to him and punch him in the head. Marcel lost his train of thought and the water worm fell apart, leaving them once again falling toward the ground. He shook his head, trying to stay attentive and the water spout reformed clumsily. It grasped them before they hit the ground, going horizontally in an aimless direction. Inside the spout was like being tossed around in a dryer. Both men couldn't grasp anything to steady themselves, being thrown from one end to the other in this tunnel of havoc.

We have to kill him, air demanded.

Finally, Marcel made sense of the situation. Air held him still inside the tunnel while the spout circled around. He found Gerard and grabbed at his throat, trying to squeeze as hard as he could. Outside, he could see the worm flying in the sky like a dragon. He controlled it, inside him mind, while Gerard tried desperately to loosen the grip. The worm flew over the castle's towers where glorious flames connected with the worm. Now, Marcel had a mental grasp of all three elements. Wind, air, and fire combined to create an enormous tunnel. He guided the magical entity toward the forests adjacent to the castle. Gerard got out of the grip, but only for a second before Marcel head locked him. "Please die. Please." He whispered.

You're a murderer. Just like all of them!, the water objected.

Fire screeched, *Master knows what he does!*

He's an idiot like the rest of them. Humans always fail. He will too, the wind snickered.

All these voices in his head made him loose his direction. They were drifted into the woods. Marcel tried to control himself on this buggy whose horse gone wild. Gerard clawed at his face. He couldn't handle so much going on. Marcel's head wanted to explode.

Then they smacked into a series of trees, tumbling for what felt like dozens of yards. Water splashed onto the ground and the fire latched onto the bushes.

Marcel realized just how of breath he was when they eventually stopped tumbling and landed on soft ground. He tried to stand up, but his head spun and he toppled. Gerard couldn't catch his breath either, he held his throat as he tried to use a plant stump to get up. Feeling accomplished that he, at least, gave his deceiver friend quiet a challenge, Marcel smirked. He got to his knees, which wouldn't stop shaking, and hoisted himself. Smoke began to fill the air as a fire burned around them.

Let's him now, Master!

Fire swirled around, warming and comforting him as always. He enjoyed loyalty, not lies. All he could sense, staring into helpless Gerard's eyes, was how much he'd been betrayed. Betrayed by so many people he loved.

No more.

Above this peninsula, with the castle far in the distance now, Marcel would melt away all his sorrows. Starting with Gerard. Poor battered Gerard that couldn't even stand.

Suddenly, the wind swooshed and the fire died out. Marcel wasn't conjuring all this breeze. Something else was. Something vast and powerful. He swung around.

A jet hovered in mid-air, suspended, pointed directly at him. Marcel tried to shield his eyes from not only the gusts, but the lights on the machine as well. He squinted to see who was flying. Who would dare to face him now?

The pilot's face could now clearly be seen.

It was his father.

As he dangled there, Nelson couldn't help but reminisce about a similar situation. Looking down, from a helicopter, at Marcel next to his brother's bloodied body. His son, who used to dance every time he got a bowl of Froot Loop cereal and run around the living room with a towel around his neck claiming to be Superman, had morphed into such a madman. He wanted to blame himself, like every father would, but Janice wouldn't allow it. No one was to blame. Not even Marcel.

His son's eyes squinted either questionably or because of all the wind created by the jet. When he taught him how to hit a ball, Nelson used to repeatedly tell him keep his eyes open. *Keep your eyes open.*

"Dad?" Marcel said. It must've been Nelson's imagination that he could hear his boy's voice throughout the air. "Dad! Dad!". Remembering that same charged and cautious tone he gave when Nelson showed up to his graduation ceremony; charged because he hadn't expected him, cautious because he had barely passed. And yet, he could never be upset with Marcel because he was so much more behaved than his fractious son Brent.

But this was Janice's plan. To harm Marcel, not from the outside…but from the inside. As though he could read his mind, which he probably could, his son shook his head with teary eyes. "Dad. Don't. Please."

Nelson drifted the vehicle backwards, pointing the nose to the sky. It looked pure black, like flying straight into endless depths of space itself. Feeling the sweat already pouring, he accelerated the jet.

"Dad!" Marcel shouted. "Please!"

He flew at a vertical velocity. The dashboard lit up with audible and visual warnings. Too steep. Too fast. Nelson throttled even faster as he approached the clouds. Clouds soaked in soot, a constant reminder of what Doomsday did. What he did.

His windows tinted with ash. The computer screen tried to activate auto-pilot, but he resisted repeatedly pressing cancel. Pressure built up in the cabin, he hurriedly placed his mask on to breath...thinking how little time has been reflecting on what's its like to breath. Inhaling what's beneficial, exhaling what is not.

Finally, past the clouds, Nelson was blinded by the sun's rays. He let go of the controls and the jet hung in the air for only a second, but it felt like minutes. Minutes that totaled the most beautiful moment he'd seen since Doomsday. The sun rose just above the clouds, coloring them in warm colors of oranges and red. Just like the day he married Victoria on the beach.

As the jet began to fall, gravity shifted and items floated out of his pockets. A picture. A picture he kept always close to him swam in mid-air. It was the day Senator Nelson Celest became President Nelson Celest. His family, so young and enthusiastic, stood outside the White House. Poised to lead this country in the right direction, Nelson wore that piercing blue tie. He swore that day, as a Republican moderate conservative, that he would rid government control. Instead, he helped create it.

The jet careened down, aiming at the iconic Union Castle. Marcel always loved castles. He built one out of Legos, taller than him, in his bedroom. It was Christmas morning that day and none of the kids slept. Together they created a structure. Play wrestling with his joyful kids, he accidentally crushed it that morning. This morning, Nelson was about to destroy his son's castle again. He stared at the picture, feeling the pressure crushing his chest in. It didn't matter. Breathing would be moot soon.

Maybe he had done his job in the end. The government, unified or not, was on the verge of obliteration. Victoria would be proud, because finally he would be the one to demolish government. Once the castle burned, so would the Union with it.

His thumb combed over Victoria. Maybe his cellmate was right. Something sparked in him when saw the beauty of his wife and the happiness of his children. Something that melted away the fear of his impending death. Something that told him it was going to be alright now. It was God. "I can't wait to see you," he said reaching over and kissing the photograph.

Janice and Brent had both sacrificed themselves for the greater good. Adam couldn't bear to think of the loss. But he had the comfort of knowing he'd never experience either of their deaths. As he saw Nelson's jet swoop down in a high speed vertical drop toward the center of the Union's landmark, he would not be spared this time. The fighting had stopped as all eyes, Keepers and rebels, trained on the jet.

It barreled into the castle. What took months to construct only took seconds to de-construct. Concrete shattered like glass with the force of an exploding jet. Fire consumed the building in seconds, devouring it as if it was kindling. No one could keep their eyes off this spectacle because it would truly become stories for generations ahead.

Keepers cried out in horror, while the People of Bliss chose to cheer. Adam did neither. Nelson, his father figure and a great President, was gone. Gone from existence forever. He watched the castle crumble like it was made of sand. The Union, as well as another government, would be gone into existence forever too. The war of all wars had concluded. But yet, with so much loss so far, the sediment at the bottom of this raging ocean didn't seem settled. Was this what ancestors called victory?

The Celest family accomplished what they'd always sworn. Peace. No corrupt leadership or decisions being made for the people. Freedom had a sense of jubilance and disturbance. Since the First Lady had passed, the Celests hadn't feared death. But it made Adam question if he had. Struggling all night, covered in mud and blood, to survive must mean he did. And that realization made him want to struggle more. The fight wasn't over. They were still surrounded by Keepers, mostly undead ones.

Adam spun and looked over toward the bridge. Tanks and SUVs with armed military had been kept away by the jet. Now, they advanced. Glazed and bitter eyed Keepers had lost their leadership; instead of retreat they wanted justice.

If the opposition had been holding back, certainly all hell would break loose now.

After he watched President Celest's plane nosedive into the Union castle, Willie felt a slight relief that he left the facility in time and a bigger relief that the Union's ambitions were over. All that remained on this peninsula were thousands of Rebels and maybe a few hundred Union Keepers. The line had been drawn this night between the Union's friends and enemies because the expressions said it all. Tears of accomplishment fell down the cheeks of the Rebels' faces; tears of sadness fell down the cheeks of Union Keepers' face. For a moment, the fighting stopped to watch the castle crumble. Two Union Keepers held each other and cried. Only Willie could understand that sympathy, because he too admired the vision of the Union.

Pierre stared at it, holding Willie's hand. Maybe this moment could make him glow, heal this bullet wound. "Can you see it?" He asked.

"Yes," Pierre whispered. "It's beautiful. No?"

Willie could feel heat surge through his body. Looking at his hand, the veins underneath it began to light slowly. This was the People of Bliss called glowing. Pierre smiled, "There you go. You can do it."

Just as he felt his temperature elevate, the sound of gunfire broke his meditation. Six Union vans sped up the hill toward the scene. He watched in horror as one of the vans parked in the distance and slid its door open. Stockpiles of AR-15s could be seen. Not tagged and not electronic, brought over from the very warehouse he used to manage. "Oh shit," Willie said. "They got guns. No fingerprints. Run. Run!"

Pierre hoisted Willie up and they ran. Behind them, he could hear series of bullets being fired off. Then the sounds of bodies falling to the ground. Chaotic screams echoed the dawn air.

With his back turned, Gerard was left with little understanding of Marcel's reaction. He could see his shoulders tense at the moment of Nelson's impact, he heard his holler of pain at either his father's death or the Union's, and his fists clenched. If he had any more fight in him, now would be the moment take the Supreme Leader down forever. With just a shove, he could send his best friend over the edge of that cliff. But he could barely crawl, much less shove. Broken bones, bruises, and deep cuts kept him to the ground. With all his might, he used his arms to push and ended upright on his knees. It was better than laying on the ground. At least he could watch Nelson's destruction of the government.

The cinder blocks melted as they fell into the ocean, hundreds of feet below. Gerard could feel the heat of the explosion, even a quarter of a mile away.

President Nelson Celest had gone down in a historic demise that generations would surely hear about. Frankly, Gerard missed him already. They may have had their disagreements, as any man marrying a politician's daughter would have, but the mutual respect lingered. The night before, knowing this moment would come today, they had decided to avoid a last goodbye. He didn't have a goodbye to Brent or Janice neither. Nelson knew his life would end this chaotic night, because it was all part of Janice's plan.

"Gerard?" Marcel said, emotionless.

When Marcel finally turned, Gerard could see in his eyes that Janice's plan worked. At first, his face had been filled with that same rage it had been in during their brawl. But then, it slowly faded away. His eyes went from wide to glossy, the cheeks from flushed to sagged, and his mouth from tight to quivering. A tear fell from his right eye and traveled to his shaking chin. He whispered, "Please tell the People of Bliss...I'm sorry." His voice broke and so did Gerard's heart.

"I didn't want it to get to this. I didn't want you to have to make this decision," Gerard admitted. It was the truth. If Marcel hadn't been so stubborn, he would've killed him an hour ago and then go home for a beer. But like his father, Supreme Leader Marcel Celest would go down when he was ready.

Janice was right. The only person that can end Marcel's life...was Marcel. Without his family or his precious Union, he would be missing the one thing everyone strived for. That was hope. Hope for a better world crashed into the ocean along with his father. Marcel would have no reason or will to live anymore. This was how his kingship ended, falling into the angry ocean below, just like his castle.

Marcel dreamt of this moment, his deceiving best friend kneeling before him. But not like this. It was more of a show of honoring than pleading. He closed his eyes, listening to the ocean hundreds of feet below. Blood ran down his face like tears.

Jump, the sea begged.

Voices in his head bickered until he grabbed the sides of his temple. All he had to do was let go, fall back, and plunge to his death. Time seemed to slow, even more than when his adrenaline ran, to the point it gave him a minute to reflect. When his mother died and he held a wobbly sharp razor to his wrist, he felt this way. A minute could last an eon in this state. He questioned his decisions, his mistakes, his triumphs, and he questioned what would become of his name. Would people remember him as a man who attempted peace or failed miserably at it? Would people realized his decision to jump off the edge of cliff meant he loved them? That the only way to truly create bliss around the world, would be to obliterate the evil he empowered?

Jump, coward!

I knew you'd fail.

No, Master, don't!

"Hey," Gerard said, breaking the elements' dialogue.

Marcel's lip quivered, tears streamed down his face. He never felt so alone, betrayed, and desperate all at once. Never again would he touch Janice's silky hair, share a laugh with Brent, or admire the stoutness of his father. He looked at the only man left that he knew, and that knew him. Gerard said, "I lied about a lot of things. But I never lied," he took a deep breath and his eyes watered, "when I said you were my best friend."

Waves crashed below, more ravaging than normal. Marcel managed to nod his head. He believed Gerard. In that coma, Marcel may have gained the power of persuasion but lost the power of reason. Everyone, including the man before him, tried desperately to resurrect the passionate Marcel Celest. But that man died in the coma and would die again now. "Thank you."

Gerard smiled, "Tell them I love them."

Marcel nodded again. His family, awaiting in the gray, would be with him soon. With a deep and last breath, he leaned back and fell.

Gravity pushed and wind pulled, the elements murmuring triumphantly. He plummeted hundreds of feet, suddenly noticing not being afraid. Not afraid like when that rusted steel blade cut into his wrist. Marcel was ready to die. But yet, he'd hoped it would happen quicker. The decent seemed much longer than anticipated. Contemplating suicide several years ago, he thought about jumping from a bridge. He read the mind theoretically would shut off before hitting the ground, accepting fate. Marcel grinder his teeth, hyperventilating. Any moment, sharp rocks and rushing waters would slay him like Julius Caesar. His thoughts shifted from peace to fear-

Bones cracking deafened him. The slam knocked all the air from his lungs. A rock protruded from his gut. He couldn't see from one eye, assuming the other half of his head smashed into the ground first. Death toyed, keeping him in a partial life state. Pain surged his body but quickly disputed. Through his one eye, he could see his chest attempting to breath but a chunk of his lung hung out of the hole. Whimpering, Marcel prayed for it to be over.

Then the sky opened slightly, letting a bit of morning sun reflect off the ocean. His last view of Earth's magnificence. From the sparkles of ocean light, figures formed. Brent. He smiled. He never smiled. Not genuinely like this. Nelson. Light brought out that father, the father he missed dearly. He nodded proudly. Janice. Her hair glowed. She wasn't melancholy, only pleased, giving a slight wave as she stood on the water.

Someone above his body leaned over. Those striking eyes and gentle grin could only come from one person. She bent down and kissed his forehead. Hair danced around in this brightly colored soul. Feeling the warm kiss on his forehead, Marcel's body relaxed. It was his mother.

He let go. Releasing the hate. Releasing all the expectations. Releasing the failures. Because none of it mattered. Not without his family. His pupils widened as he entered a tunnel of pure light and... peace.

CHAPTER FORTY-SEVEN

Union Keepers swarmed the People of Bliss. Adam had nightmares of this moment; the nightmare of losing the final battle. Surrounded by a growing amount of guns and the sounds of shots fired muzzling the sounds of screams, he wished he could just simply wake up.

"What do we do?" Royal cried out.

On the other hand, if someone had told Adam the battle would include resurrected Union Keepers, teaming with a black mysterious goo, he might've called off the war. Every time one bad guy would go down, another one would rise. This endless sea of enemies had created an island, with the People of Bliss centered and no hope of escape. North, south, east, or west, armed vehicles and armed men sprayed the rebels with bullets and rage.

"What do we do?" Royal demanded an answer from the dumbfounded Adam. She stared, hands grasping his arm and shaking him, like he had been sleepwalking this whole night.

How many of them were left? Ten thousand? Five thousand? Whatever the number was…it wasn't enough. They had more bullets. If only he'd anticipated a stockpile of digital-less weaponry. Of course, they would have a backup plan. He wanted to smack himself on the forehead, admit his mistake, apology, and return with a better assignment. But unfortunately, this wasn't his High School thesis. His life, and countless others, depended on victory. Victory that carried on to the future.

"Adam?" Royal shouted.

The future. Of course! Adam foresaw the future. And they won. But the future couldn't be changed. Or could it? The precognition he had months ago created a bright world, full of light. How did it end like this? In such darkness? He couldn't concentrate with the volley of bullets killing innocent people.

In the distance, a Union Keeper kept alive by a black goo Marcel conjured, murdered another rebel with a gun shot to the head. Adam flinched his eye, even though the bullet was nowhere near him. Then he realized.

"The goo," he whispered.

"What?" Royal screamed hysterically. She lost hope. They all lost hope.

The black goo had been in his precognition. It was a manifestation of darkness. Remembering dreams at a time like this, people pleading for mercy or pleading for help in his ear, wasn't a good time to reminisce. But he felt a tug in his mind. Something said in that precognition would save them. But what was it? He recalled seeing Marcel Celest, lethargic and wasted in a bed with cancer. He mentioned darkness. Darkness that he tried to absorb eventually strengthened the monster. The monster! Of course! There was that monster in his vision, seeping from the corpse of Marcel. A creature made of that same substance.

"Adam! What about the goo?"

Gunfire and screams became muted as Adam tried to think. Royal's nagging even melted away. What had been the dialogue between him and the future Supreme Leader? He remembered Marcel begging him to destroy the darkness. But how? What were his exact words?

It's coming. It will kill all of you. Run.

Adam squinted his eyes, concentrating.

Change the past to save the future. Kill me, kill the darkness.

How?

The only way you can kill the darkness is…with the light.

His eyes shot open. If all the anger, hate, and rage can create that sort of disturbing monster in Marcel…what could love, happiness, and joy create? Adam faced Royal. "Glow."

"What?"

"Everyone has to glow. *Everyone.*"

Blood mixed in with the ocean water. Lying in the center of a set of rocks, Marcel's mangled corpse left Gerard more saddened than relieved. The Celests, a family the nation obsessed, criticized, and loved, were all gone. Emptiness seized Gerard's breathing. He hadn't expected this, because it was the right thing. But the right thing didn't always seem right; time would have to correct that. Gerard's truest friend was also his truest enemy. To keep from leaping off this cliff himself, Gerard pictured deep within the silo was a precious boy named Colin. A child that needed a father, much like he did. And he couldn't allow that to happen. He had to live on, without the Celests.

His arms held onto the edge of the cliff as he peaked over. Heaving from the battle, he immediately remembered the battle wasn't over. Sounds of gunfire echoed the night sky. But everything seemed so calm here. Though far at a distance, he could still make out Marcel. He couldn't make out if it was a smile or frown on the dead body. The

Supreme Leader may have been a lot of things, but Gerard saw him as the closest friend he would ever have. He also saw him as an example of what government and control can do to a person. It's like riding an escalator with no clear destination, but a drive to continue ascending. Reality was, there is no end. Power, no matter the extent, always strived for more power. Marcel Celest tried to control an uncontrollable entity. And failed.

Just as Gerard was about to rise, somehow cross the bridge and join the battle at the castle, something caught his eye. Something crawling along the surface of Marcel. At first, he thought his mind played tricks on him. After all, he'd lost extensive amounts of blood and probably broke at least three ribs. But *something* was seeping from Marcel. Something black. Blacker than a starless sky. The longer he stared, the more he became fascinated and frightened simultaneously.

A goo formulated, crawling from the corpse's skin, using two arm-like extensions to lift itself up. From the center of Marcel, that *something* screeched out. It formed a mouth and head. Whatever was happening, Gerard knew he should run.

Before he could stand completely, the black creature shot up in the air and hovered across from him. The *thing* protruded two skeletal wings and two legs. It screeched again, so high pitched that Gerard covered his ears. The goo morphed into some type of demon. Its mouth grinned. Its eyes opened. It looked at him.

Running faster than he'd ever ran before, Gerard scurried into the woods. But too late. Darkness grasped his waist and slammed him to a tree, wrapping him in an impenetrable force. The creature batted its wings as it approached and landed. Struggling to free his arms, Gerard gasped for air; the goo squeezing him like a water balloon.

The demon looked at its hands with razor sharp claws; its skin like it had been charred by years of heat. Lava flowed where its veins would be on a human. Though terrifying, it also seemed lethargic; skinny and weak. "It worked!" The creature exclaimed. Gerard's mind went wild. He'd seen many things in his lifetime, but never something so monstrous. The demon grinned again, its teeth like rusted nails. "Of course his demise was inevitable. All their demises are inevitable. Human spirit so convoluted and enervated." The demon looked disappointed and frustrated, the side of its mouth switching between the two. "I tell myself, Marcel Celest will fail. Maybe feed off his life force. Maybe corrupt him, build his darkness. Maybe it could be enough to return to this world." It gazed at the land around it, like it hadn't seen the world in millennium. Then it gazed into Gerard's eyes. "Now, all of you…those that strenthen the Light…I can murder each one of you…slowly and painfully."

As soon as it lifted its hand, the goo tightened Gerard's gut. He cried out in pain.

Adam crashed onto the ground, on his knees and began the process of concentrating to glow. He'd done it before. Everyone here had. They had to try. It was their only escape. He stared at the muddy ground stained red.

Someone immediately rejected Adam's idea. "Are you kidding? We are about to be slaughtered and your best idea is to meditate?"

"Just shut the hell up and do it!" Royal commanded, falling to her knees.

She covered her ears and closed her eyes. Others followed suit, praying on their knees. Adam watched in amazement as the word spread and everyone collapsed to their knees; the true sign of faith. He watched as Union Keepers stopped unarmed citizen to laugh hysterically. Everyone's eyes closed, meditating into a distant world, somewhere far from this place where they were safe in their minds. That's where something more powerful lied, more powerful than all of the enraged fists and searing guns tonight.

He focused on all the good in his life. His first kiss, locked in fate. His favorite dog, Buster, who would've done anything to make him smile. His best friend, Brent, telling him that there was good in everyone. Janice and her soft golden hair. Declan buying him a tuxedo for the Junior High Prom. His first dance. Royal's eyes when she smiled.

Adam's body began to warm. He closed his eyes.

Then everything turned a blinding white.

A ball of light expanded from the center of the People of Bliss. Union Keepers covered their eyes from the blinding concoction, the goo in them disintegrating into nothing making the undead fall to the ground. The ball continued to explode, like a bubble forming. It covered the island in seconds and continued its growth until it covered the oceans around them.

On the opposite end of the battle, Lucifer screeched out, the light tearing apart his body like trees in a massive hurricane. "No!" He cried. "Not now! Stop! Please! Stop!"

The bubble covered a state and continued to grow. Penetrating the atmosphere, it blew up until it could be seen from space. Light engulfed the planet.

During the light's explosion, Willie opened his squinted eyes. He couldn't see anything but white. Yet, he knew he wasn't dead. Shadows of his nearby comrades could be seen. They held to each other as this light surrounded them.

Suddenly, someone grasped him and held Willie tighter than he ever been held. It was Pierre. "What's going on?" He screamed.

Willie looked down at his bloody clothes. The bullet pushed itself out of his skin. Light healed the hole and sealed the wound. "I don't know!"

Quicker than the light had exploded…it imploded. Shrinking and strengthening, grasping all the lights in people around the world, it morphed into a single being.

The being, created by the light, stood before Gerard. He'd seen tall men, but nothing this big. It must've reached ten, maybe more, feet above him and that demon. He couldn't see the face of the being. Too bright. Too blinding. His eyes hurt, just looking at it, like he'd been staring at the sun itself. He could only make it blankets of lights, like sheets flying on a windy day.

Whatever that creature was, that had seeped from Marcel's wounds, turned from fearful to pitiful. Only it's upper body still stayed in one piece. It crawled, crying out in pain, as it approached the Light's creation. Its claws dug into the ground, struggling with its last strength. "Don't you dare…" it said, pleading, "…dare…let them…destroy it again…" With that, the dark demon broke apart into the wind, like the remnants of a vast campfire.

Gerard watched, wide-eyed and confused. The being floated as it turned toward him. Without thinking, he rushed to crawl backwards and his back hit a tree stump. "Get away from me! Get away from me!" He screamed, covering his face. Never being frightened of anything, he felt weak but cornered. His hand shook uncontrollably. Blood dripped down from a wound on his palm.

No matter his pleas, the being didn't move or sway. It waited. Waited for what? Gerard began to catch his breath, contemplating what was happening. Something never seen before, not in his lifetime or anyone else's lifetime in recent centuries, stood high before him. Yet, his heart rate began to slow. The stress began to melt into realization. Light had formed into a humanoid figure. Whatever it was, it didn't talk or move, besides its flowing white fabric-like body. If it had wanted to kill him, it would've done it already. Instead, the creature that wanted him dead had been blown away into particles.

Maybe beginning to realize Gerard's curiosity, the being extended out what must've been a hand, even though it was too bright to see. Gerard looked at his own hand, cut open and bleeding profusely. He reached out slowly, regretfully. Who knew what could possibly happen since all the impossible had just become possible in the last hour. The being's fabric touched his hand. So hot at first, he thought about yanking his arm away, but didn't. The heat expanded into little specks of light, dancing over the wound. Within a second, it sealed and stopped the bleeding. It healed more than just the cut, it healed him. For whatever reason, Gerard couldn't feel sadness, hate, or fear. He only felt relief. "Thank you," he whispered.

The being slowly floated vertically, rising off the ground, making everything brighter physically and mentally.

Adam opened his eyes. Instead of cries, he heard laughter. Laughs of joys. Royal, who he never seen so happy, helped him up. "It worked!" She confirmed. Around them, Union Keepers lied on the ground. The undead remained dead.

The joyous cheer stopped abruptly. Just when he thought to himself what else could possibly be coming to slaughter the rest of them, he turned to see where all the eyes pointed.

Floating upwards, from the peninsula across from them, a being made of pure light could be seen. Adam wondered if it was a helicopter, but no such vehicle could be that massive. It almost looked UFO-like, too bright to make a shape out of it. Too caught off guard to say anything, everyone just stared. He saw tears flow down someone's face and drop to the ground.

Royal whispered, "What is that thing?"

As if it heard her, the being expanded itself, creating breath-taking wings. Gasps could be heard. Besides that, no one breathed. The aberration climbed, ascending into the black clouds and disappearing, leaving a white blotch in the atmosphere.

Adam realized he hadn't breathed and reminded himself to take a breath. He never considered himself a religious or agnostic man, but at that moment he became something even more important…he became a believer. A believer that humanity had a purpose and a power, more great than any government or leadership provided. People could change the world, even the future, when they combined all they loved.

Thunder banged beyond the cloud, causing everyone to flinch. Before anyone could mutter a question, light shot out from the blotch of the being. All the filth and ash in the clouds disappeared. Wind blew so vigorously that the People of Bliss clamped onto each other. Royal locked her arm around Adam.

The wind blew away and obliterated the castle's leftover fiery construction. Adam would later learn that this wasn't the only structure destroyed. Every man-made building and invention dissolved, leaving only memories behind. From the ground, emerald colored grass climbed out. Trees rooted and hoisted themselves out.

As quickly as it happened, it halted. Shaking still, Adam looked around. The planet, in its purest form, welcomed him. Just like in his precognition, the sky was plastered with the shiniest of stars. Light reflected off the ocean, reminding him of its vastness. Then rising from the horizon, amber and cunning, the sun made a tear flow down Adam's face. He hadn't seen it in so long, it felt. And he promised himself, he'd watch this sun rise every morning for the rest of his life.

And then it was like Adam had never taken a breath before this day. He took in a gulp of air and held in his lungs. No impurities burned his throat or clasped his sinuses.

Something else withered away with all the darkness in the world. Something Adam had been harboring since the day world leaders decided to end the world. Fear. Birds sang a new melody. Wind blew gently. The ocean down the cliff calmed. There was nothing to be anxious about. Was that the peace that the Celests tried to accomplish? A peace their mother promised everyone? Adam would say yes. And the Celests had sacrificed everything to achieve it. Whether it was the wrong path, or the right one, didn't seem to matter in the end. The last days had been crowded with death and despair, but replaced with life and mirth.

Behind Adam, he could Willie speak. He would forever be the first in this new world. He whispered, "Now we start over. And do it right this time."

The thought relieved Adam. Where would they start? The possibilities seemed endless. But no government could stop them. No matter what the endeavor.

Adam turned to Royal. She changed too. Her scrunched eyebrows and determined pierced lips were gone. She smiled. He never noticed she had a dimple.

Both of them had ran a marathon and were now just realizing the prize. It was love. Their eyes met. Nothing seemed strange or out-of-place, considering all that had just happened.

He bent over and kissed Royal on the lips. They held onto each other. Adam hoped she would never let go.

Not understand how he could laugh or why, Gerard fell on his back holding his stomach in a brazen chuckle. The sky was incredible. He only wished the Celest were here to see it. Brent would've recited all the stars' names. Janice would've questioned their purpose in this majestic universe. Marcel would've stayed silent, staring at the atmosphere of rectitude.

His laughter began to die, drowned by tears of sorrow. Gerard buried his face with both hands, sobbing loudly, trying to survive this wave of emotions. The world had been reset and only a few had made it. He promised to not focus on the future, but focus on the past. The past held many lessons to be learned, for good or evil. Lessons that his son would need to endure.

His son.

Gerard released his hands, masking the sadness, and wiped away his tears. The People of Bliss would have to be their family now. A family bound like the Celests.

He turned his head. A lilac flower danced in the slight breeze. Gerard plucked it. Her favorite flower. So vibrant and full of life. He sniffed it. It smelled like her. She'd always be there.

Always.

Made in the USA
Columbia, SC
12 February 2019